THE GREEN TRAP

Tor Books by Ben Bova

THE
GREEN TRAP

BEN BOVA

A TOM DOHERTY ASSOCIATES BOOK
NEW YORK

THE GREEN TRAP

This book is printed on acid-free paper.

Book design by Mary A. Wirth

A Forge Book
Published by Tom Doherty Associates, LLC
175 Fifth Avenue
New York, NY 10010

www.tor.com

Forge® is a registered trademark of Tom Doherty Associates, LLC.

Library of Congress Cataloging-in-Publication Data

Bova, Ben, 1932–
    The green trap / Ben Bova.
        p.   cm.
    "A Tom Doherty Associates Book."
    ISBN-13: 978-0-765-30924-2
    ISBN-10: 0-765-30924-6
    1. Microbiologists—Crimes against—Fiction.   2. Cyanobacteria—Fiction.   3. Hydrogen as
fuel—Research—Fiction.   I. Title.

    PS3552.O84G74 2006
    813'.54—dc22

                                                                                            2006004876

First Edition: November 2006

Printed in the United States of America

0 9 8 7 6 5 4 3 2 1

Still and always to Barbara,
to D. H. (again),
and
to the memory of Melvin Calvin

ACKNOWLEDGMENTS

My thanks to Eric Von Leue, who provided crucial technical advice and support. The section titled "Novel Reaction Produces Hydrogen" is reprinted with permission from *Science News,* the weekly newsmagazine of science, copyright 2005.

Science knows no country, because knowledge belongs to humanity, and is the torch which illuminates the world.

LOUIS PASTEUR (1822–1895)

THE GREEN TRAP

Gasoline Prices
Expected to Climb Higher

WASHINGTON—There's pump shock at every corner gas station, with prices well over $7 a gallon—and the government says you'd better get used to it.

The Energy Department projects high gasoline prices at least through next year as producers struggle to keep up with demand, which has not slackened appreciably despite rising prices.

Crude oil prices climbed to an all-time high of $112 per barrel yesterday, triggering a 634-point drop in the Dow-Jones Industrial average on the New York Stock Exchange.

"We can expect to see gasoline prices soar as high as nine or ten dollars a gallon this summer," said James Dykes, chairman of the Federal Reserve Board. "Gas prices have nowhere to go but up."

Energy Department officials blamed the climbing oil prices on the growing demand for petroleum by China and India, two of the fastest-growing economies in the world, coupled with the fact that global oil production has peaked and is unlikely to increase.

"There hasn't been a major new oil field discovered in well over a decade," said Roberta Groves, head of Gould Energy Corporation's explorations division. "With global oil production flat and global demand increasing steadily, oil prices will continue to climb for the foreseeable future."

—*FINANCIAL NEWS*

T U C S O N :
T H E   M I R R O R   L A B

Paul Cochrane dreaded leaving the Mirror Lab. Set beneath the massive slanting concrete of the University of Arizona's football stadium, the lab was only a three-minute walk from Cochrane's office, but it was three minutes in the blazing wrath of Tucson's afternoon sun. It was only the first week of May, yet Cochrane—who had come from Massachusetts less than a year ago—had learned to fear the merciless heat outside.

As he limped down the steel stairway toward the lab's lobby, he mentally plotted his course back to his office at the Steward Observatory building, planning a route that kept him in the shade as much as possible.

He was a slim, quiet man in his mid-thirties, wearing rimless glasses that made him look bookish. Dressed in the requisite denim jeans and short-sleeved shirt of Arizona academia, he still wore his Massachusetts running shoes rather than cowboy boots. And still walked with a slight limp from the auto crash that had utterly devastated his life. His hair was sandy brown, cut short, his face lean and almost always gravely serious, his body trim from weekly workouts with the local fencing group. Although his Ph.D. was in thermodynamics, he had accepted a junior position with the Arizona astronomy department, as far from Massachusetts and his earlier life as he could get.

He reached the lobby, nodded to the undergrads working the reception desk, and took a breath before plunging into the desert heat outside the glass double doors. He saw that even though the window blinds behind the students had been pulled shut, the hot sunlight outside glowed like molten metal.

His cell phone started playing the opening bars of Mozart's overture to *The Marriage of Figaro*.

Grateful for an excuse to stay inside the air-conditioned lobby for a moment longer, Cochrane pulled the phone from his shirt pocket and flipped it open.

His brother's round, freckled, red-haired face filled the phone's tiny screen.

Surprised that his brother was calling, Cochrane plopped onto the faux leather couch next to the lobby doors. "Hello, Mike," he said softly as he put the phone to his ear. "It's been a helluva long time."

"Hi, there, little brother. How's your suntan?"

Michael Cochrane was a microbiologist working for a private biotech company in the Bay Area of California.

"I don't tan, you know that."

Mike laughed. "Yeah. I remember when we'd go out to Lynn Beach. You'd get red as a lobster, and the next day you were white as Wonder Bread again."

Cochrane grimaced, remembering how painful sunburn was. And other hurts. His marriage. The auto wreck. Jennifer's funeral. Jen's mother screaming at him for letting her drive after drinking. He hadn't even been out of the wheelchair yet. Everybody in the church had stared at him. Just the sound of Mike's voice, still twanging with the old Massachusetts inflection, brought it all back in a sickening rush.

"I try to stay out of the sun," he said tightly.

"So you switched to Arizona," said Michael. "Smart move."

Keeping his voice steady, Cochrane asked, "How long has it been, Mike? Six months?" He knew it had been longer than that. Mike hadn't called since Cochrane had asked his brother to repay the thirty thousand dollars he'd loaned him.

"Don't be an asshole, Paulie."

"Come on, Mike. What's going on? The only time you call is when you want—"

"Stuff it," Michael snapped. "I've got news for you. Big news. I'm gonna pay you back every penny I owe. With interest."

"Sure you will." Cochrane couldn't keep the sarcasm out of his voice.

"I damned well will, wise-ass. In another few days. Your big brother's going to be a rich man, Paulie. I've come up with something that's gonna make me a multimillionaire."

Cochrane raised his eyes heavenward. Ever since they'd been teenagers Mike had touted one get-rich-quick scheme after another. His bright, flip-talking big brother. Quick with ideas but slow to do the work that might make the ideas succeed. The latest one had cost Cochrane a chunk of his insurance settlement from the accident.

"Mikey, if you want to get rich you shouldn't have gone into research," he said into the phone.

"Like hell," his brother replied tartly. "What I've come up with is worth millions."

"Really?"

"You bet your ass, little brother. Hundreds of millions."

Cochrane started to say *Really?* again, but caught himself. Mike had a short fuse.

"Well, that's great," he said instead. "Just what is it?"

"Come on over here and see for yourself."

"To San Francisco?"

"Palo Alto."

"Near the big NASA facility."

"That's in Mountain View," Michael corrected.

"Oh."

"So when are you coming? This weekend?"

"Why can't you just tell me about it? What's so—"

"Too big to talk on the phone about it, Paulie. C'mon, I know you. You've got nothing cooking for the weekend, you dumb hermit."

Cochrane thought about it bleakly. Mike was right. His social life was practically nonexistent. He wouldn't have a class to teach until Tuesday morning. And there were all those frequent flier miles he'd piled up in the past eighteen months attending astronomy conferences.

"Okay," he heard himself say halfheartedly. "This weekend." He never could oppose Mike for very long.

"Good! E-mail me your flight number and arrival time and I'll meet you at the airport. See ya, squirt."

PALO ALTO:
CALVIN RESEARCH CENTER

Mike wasn't at the airport to meet him.

Cochrane's Southwest Airlines flight from Tucson arrived at San Francisco International twelve minutes early, but the plane had to wait out on the concrete taxiway for twenty minutes before a terminal gate was freed up. Once inside the terminal Cochrane searched for his brother at the gate, then walked down the long corridor pulling his wheeled travel bag after him. Mike wasn't at the security checkpoint, either.

"Just like him," Cochrane muttered to himself. He went down to the baggage claim area even though he only had the one piece of luggage, on the off chance that Mike might be waiting for him there.

Nettled, Cochrane yanked out his cell phone and called his brother. The answering message replied brightly, "Hey, I can't take your call right now. Leave your name and number and I'll get back to you pronto."

Anger seething inside him, Cochrane took the bus to the Budget car rental site, phoned Mike again while he stood in line, and again got the cheerful recorded message. He started to call Mike's home number, but by then he was at the counter, where a tired-looking overweight Asian-American woman asked for his driver's license and credit card.

It was late afternoon, with the sun still a good distance above the low hills that ran along the coast. Speeding down U.S. 101, Cochrane decided to pass his hotel and go straight to Mike's office. He's probably working in his lab, Cochrane told himself. He never did have any sense of time.

The Calvin Research Center was nothing more than a single window-less boxlike building off the highway in Palo Alto. Not even much of a sign on it: merely a polished copper plaque by the front entrance. Cochrane parked his rented Corolla in a visitor's slot and walked through the pleasant late-afternoon breeze to the smoked-glass double doors. The young woman behind the receptionist's desk smiled up at him.

"Michael Cochrane, please. He's expecting me."

"And you are?" she asked. She was a pert redhead, her hair full of curls, her smile seemingly genuine.

"Paul Cochrane. His brother."

Her brows arched. "You don't look like brothers."

"I know," he said, almost ruefully. All his life he'd heard that.

She turned slightly to tap at her keyboard and Cochrane saw that she had a miniaturized microphone next to her lips on that side of her face. A wire-thin arm extended up into her bountiful curls, which hid her earplug.

She frowned slightly. "He's not answering, Mr. Cochrane."

"He's probably busy. Maybe I could go back and knock on his door?"

"I'm afraid that's not possible," she said, shaking her head. "Security, you know. He has to come out here and escort you in."

"But he *asked* me to come out here and see him," Cochrane insisted. "He's *expecting* me."

She shook her head. "You're not on the expected list, Mr. Cochrane. I'm afraid there's nothing—Oh! That's funny."

"What?"

"His voice mail just went into its 'out of office' message. He's left the building."

"What? Just now?"

"I guess. Maybe you can catch him in the parking lot."

"What's he drive?"

The receptionist grinned knowingly. "A Fiat Spider convertible. Fire-engine red. Great car." Tapping at her computer keyboard, she added, "Slot number fourteen. That's around back."

"Thanks."

Cochrane hurried out of the lobby and sprinted around the square building, limping slightly on his bad leg. Mike probably just remembered he's supposed to pick me up at the airport, he grumbled to himself. Several cars were leaving the parking area, but he didn't see a red convertible among them and slot fourteen was empty. No Fiat Spider in sight.

"Sonofabitch," Cochrane muttered. "He's gone to the frigging airport. Or he forgot all about my coming here today and went home."

Walking slowly back to his rental car, Cochrane phoned his brother's home number. This time the answering machine's message was in Mike's wife's voice. Nobody was home, Irene pronounced slowly and distinctly, like the kindergarten teacher that she was. Please leave your name and number. Christ, Cochrane said to himself, I hope they haven't taken off for the weekend. That'd be just like him, the irresponsible pain in the ass.

With the GPS tracker mounted on the rental car's dashboard, Cochrane left the highway and headed for Mike's house, maneuvering through residential streets until he found the place. It was an unpretentious clapboard two-story house, painted white with Kelly-green trim and a neat little lawn in front bordered by pretty flowers. A hefty silver SUV sat in the driveway: a Chrysler gas-guzzler, Cochrane saw. No Fiat Spider, though.

Cochrane pulled up on the driveway beside the SUV and got out of his Corolla. He rang the doorbell once, twice. No answer. He tried the doorknob; locked. Feeling angrier by the microsecond, he went to the garage and stood on tiptoe to peer through the dusty windows of the garage door. It was empty.

Shit! He's at the goddamned airport looking for me and getting mad, Cochrane said to himself. I was an idiot to come out here. Maybe this is Mike's idea of a practical joke, get me out here on the promise of paying what he owes me and then leaving me hanging here like a stupid fool. My big brother, the wise-ass. He's got the laugh on me on this one, all right.

He thought about leaving a blistering message on Mike's cell phone but decided against it. Not with Mike's unforgiving temper. Never say something you'll regret later, he told himself. Dad's wisdom. All those years of letting Mom nag and complain without ever yelling back at her. People thought Dad was pussywhipped. Cochrane knew better. He just didn't care what Mom said. It wasn't important to him.

Instead, Cochrane told his brother's cell phone which hotel he'd be at, waiting for him. It was hard to keep the irritation out of his voice.

The university travel office had reserved a room for him at the Days

Inn in Redwood City, the lowest hotel rate they could find in the Palo Alto area. Friday going-home traffic was jamming the highway now and as Cochrane inched along, fuming over his brother's thoughtlessness, he decided he'd check out the next morning and get the hell home and let his brother laugh at him all he wanted to.

Damn! He *asked* me to come out here. And then he just leaves me here stuck in traffic like a goddamned idiot. No wonder he and Irene never had kids. Mike'd forget where the hell he left them. He's so goddamned completely self-centered.

Cochrane was feeling sweaty and thoroughly aggravated by the time the little map on the GPS dashboard display told him to take the next off-ramp. It took nearly ten minutes to inch through the crawling traffic and finally get off the highway. He passed a sign warning that minimum speed was forty. He'd been unable to get up to fifteen for the past half hour.

At the hotel's front desk he informed the room clerk that he'd be checking out in the morning instead of staying the weekend. The clerk didn't bat an eye. He rolled his travel bag to his room and didn't bother to unpack it; he merely pulled his laptop computer and toiletries kit from the bag and went into the bathroom for a long, steamy shower. Mike didn't call.

After a mediocre, solitary dinner, Cochrane went to his room and tried the home phone again. Again Irene's voice-mail message. Fuming, he watched television for a while, then turned in. He tossed uncomfortably on the hotel bed: the pillows were too thin, the air conditioner too loud. The room smelled funny, like disinfectant. At last he fell asleep and dreamed of being a little boy lost in an airport.

A pounding on the door awakened him. Startled, he sat up in the bed, blinking sleep from his eyes. Squinting, he saw that the digital clock on the bed table's green glowing display read 1:38 A.M.

The door thundered again. "Police! Open up!"

Cochrane hadn't packed a robe. Still slightly fuddled with sleep, he clicked on the bedside lamp, then grabbed for his jeans, thrown over the room's only chair.

"What do you want?" he called as he pulled the jeans on.

"We want to talk to Paul Cochrane."

Cochrane pulled on his glasses, then grabbed his shirt and wormed his arms into it. Without bothering to button it, he went to the door and peered through the peephole. Two men in dark suits stood out in the hall: one white, one black. They sure looked like cops, he thought.

"Can I see some identification?"

The black man pulled a slim wallet from his back pocket and let it fall open in front of the peephole. Cochrane saw a silver badge.

He unlatched the security chain and opened the door. The two police detectives pushed in, forcing Cochrane backward toward the bed.

"What's this about?" he asked, trying to sound resolute.

The detectives' eyes shifted, taking in the whole room, the meager furnishings, Cochrane's opened bag on the stand next to the television.

"You're Paul Cochrane," the black man said, more of a statement than a question.

"Yes."

"You have a brother, Michael?" asked the white detective. He was burly, sour-faced, his eyes sagging, his mouth curved downward.

"Yeah. What's happened?"

"Sorry to break the news, sir," said the black man. "I'm afraid your brother is dead."

"Dead?" Cochrane's knees went wobbly.

"Murdered," said the white cop.

Cochrane sank down onto the rumpled bed.

REDWOOD CITY: DAYS INN

Murdered?" Cochrane heard his voice squeak.

"A blow to the head with a blunt object," said the sad-eyed white detective. "In his office at the ..." He hesitated a moment.

"The Calvin Research Center," the black detective finished for him.

"Mike? Murdered?" Cochrane couldn't get his mind around the idea. "Are you certain it's him?"

The white cop pulled a three-by-five oblong of photographic paper from his inside jacket pocket. "This your brother?"

Cochrane took the photo in a trembling hand. And almost retched. Mike's face was distorted, his mouth twisted, his eyes open and staring blankly, his hair matted with blood that pooled beneath his battered head.

"Well?"

Fighting back the bile burning up his throat, Cochrane handed the photo back to the detective. "That ... that's my brother," he managed to say.

"Several people at the research lab identified the body," said the black man.

Cochrane sat on the bed, breathing hard, staring at the floor. He realized that he was barefoot; it made him feel stupid, exposed.

"I'm Sergeant McLain," the white cop said. "He's Sergeant Purvis. We need to ask you a few questions."

"Yeah, sure," Cochrane murmured, barely hearing him. "Go right ahead."

McLain pulled a slim notepad from his jacket pocket and flicked it open. The only light in the room was from the bedside lamp. He squinted and read, "You arrived at San Francisco International at three-eighteen this afternoon, right?"

Cochrane nodded as Purvis pulled the chair from the corner, turned it around, and sat on it backward, facing Cochrane, his arms folded on the chair's back.

Still standing, McLain said, "You drove past this motel and went straight to the Calvin lab, didn't you? The receptionist remembers you coming in around four, four-fifteen."

"That's right. My brother wasn't there."

"Yes, he was," said Purvis softly.

Before Cochrane could react to that, McLain said, "You had time to meet your brother out back in the parking lot first. He'd bring you into the building through the rear entrance. You could have doubled back to the parking lot and then come in the front way, so the receptionist would see you."

Realizing what the detective was saying, Cochrane protested, "That's not true! I didn't—"

McLain went on, "Then you drove here to the motel, checked in, and made sure plenty of people saw you having dinner in the restaurant. And you told the room clerk you were checking out tomorrow instead of staying the whole weekend."

"I didn't kill my brother!"

McLain's hard expression didn't alter by a millimeter. "I didn't say you did. I'm just talking theoretical."

"I didn't kill Mike. I didn't even see him."

Purvis said, "He was murdered just about the time you were at the lab."

"I didn't do it," Cochrane repeated.

"You were at his house, too," McLain added. "Fingerprints on the front door, the garage door. What were you looking for?"

"My brother!"

For a long moment McLain stood in sour-faced silence in the middle of the motel room, his shadow against the wall huge and menacing in the light from the bedside lamp. Purvis sat straddling the chair, his eyes boring into Cochrane.

Cochrane remembered, "Wait a minute. At first the receptionist said his phone didn't answer. Then it went into the voice-mail mode. While I was there in the lobby! You can ask her."

Purvis looked up at his partner. "That means that his brother was murdered while he was in the lobby."

"If he's telling the truth," McLain said, as if Cochrane weren't there.

"It's the truth!" Cochrane insisted.

"We can check it out easy enough," said Purvis.

McLain seemed to think it over, his baggy eyes studying Cochrane all the while. At last he nodded to Purvis. "Okay, that's it. For now. Let's go, Ty."

Purvis got to his feet, then fetched a card from his shirt pocket. "You think of anything, anything at all, give me a call."

Struggling to his feet, Cochrane accepted the card, his hand still trembling. "I've got to get back to Tucson. My job...."

"We can't keep you here," McLain said, sounding disappointed about it. "Just don't try to leave the country."

Cochrane shook his head. The two policemen left, closing the door softly behind them. Cochrane went back to the bed and sat on it. He sank his head in his hands.

Mike's dead. Murdered. Somebody killed him while I was in the fucking lobby of the building asking for him. Who in the name of Jesus H. Christ would kill Mike? Why?

He fell back on the bed, his unbuttoned shirt crumpled against his back.

Irene! he thought. Mike's wife. Where is she? Where was she when Mike was killed?

Sitting up again, he reached for the phone on the bed table, then realized he hadn't memorized Mike's number. He opened the drawer and fumbled for his cell phone, pressed buttons until his brother's home number came up in the tiny screen.

Irene's patient schoolteacher's voice said mechanically, "We're not home at the moment. Please—"

Cochrane snapped his cell phone shut.

Mike. Cochrane saw in his mind the redheaded kid he'd played baseball with. The older brother who'd lorded it over him all his life. The grown man with the wise-guy grin and the endless enthusiasm for everything he did. And the hair-trigger temper. He's dead. Somebody bashed his skull in while I was standing a couple of hundred feet away like a stupid idiot.

On an impulse he tried Mike's cell number again. He can't be dead. This is all some kind of mistake. He'll answer the phone and—

"Hey, I can't take your call right now. Leave your name and number and I'll get back to you pronto."

Cochrane shook his head. No, Mikey, you won't get back to me. Not ever.

He clicked the phone shut and wondered why he couldn't cry. He wanted to. But the tears would not come.

Melvin Calvin

A member of the faculty of the University of California at Berkeley from 1937 until his death in 1997, Calvin received the Nobel Prize in chemistry for identifying the path of carbon in photosynthesis, which led him to a lifelong interest in adapting photosynthetic techniques for energy production. In his final years of research, Calvin studied the use of oil-producing plants as renewable sources of energy. He also spent many years testing the chemical evolution of life and wrote a book on the subject that was published in 1969.

TUCSON:
STEWARD OBSERVATORY

ochrane sat behind his desk wondering if he was sinking into paranoia. His office had only one window; it looked out on the campus, mostly concrete with a few trees offering scant shade to the students who walked or bicycled along the paved paths between buildings.

He'd gotten back to Tucson late Saturday afternoon, after spending most of the day in the San Francisco airport waiting for an available flight. By the time he'd reached his apartment building just off the campus, he was exhausted. But there was something subtly wrong about his living room, something that sent a chill of anxiety up his spine.

It wasn't that the place had been ransacked; the apartment seemed as neat and orderly as when he'd left it. But he didn't remember leaving the newspapers on the sofa like that, and he *never* stacked his journals in the bookcase flat on their covers, he always stood them up, spines facing out.

Somebody's been in here, he thought. Cochrane searched through the apartment. Nothing much seemed out of place, really. Nothing stolen. Not that there was anything much to steal. Living room, bedroom, everything as he'd left it, pretty much. Maybe I did leave the newspapers on the sofa, he said to himself, scratching his head as he stood in the middle of the living room.

He went to the kitchen and opened the dishwasher. It was empty. He distinctly remembered it held a week's worth of dirty dishes; he'd turned it on just before he'd left.

The dishes and glasses were back in their cabinets now. The forks and spoons were in their drawer.

A burglar who doesn't take anything and leaves the place neat and tidy? Cochrane shook his head. What was he looking for? How could he get in? The front door was still locked when I got here.

Puzzled and more than a little worried about his own mental state, Cochrane went to bed. Mike's murder is making you paranoid, he told himself. Sleep it off.

He awoke early Sunday morning, the vague memory of unpleasant dreams troubling him as he showered, shaved, and then phoned Irene again. Still nothing but the damned answering machine message.

He made up his mind to go to his office. Nothing better to do, and the silent apartment gave him the creeps. The campus was quiet as he parked in his assigned slot in the cavernous parking garage. He walked slowly to the observatory building, paying no attention to the scent of orange blossoms that wafted on the cool morning breeze or the bees that hummed tirelessly from flower to flower. His leg throbbed sullenly, but exercise was good for it, according to the doctors. A pair of National Guard jets growled through the cloudless blue sky as he pushed open the building's front door.

Once in his office, Cochrane couldn't work up the interest to boot up his computer. He simply slouched in his desk chair and swiveled around to stare out the window. He tried to phone Irene again and got the damned answering machine message once more.

I should've stayed in Palo Alto, he said to himself. I should've gone to the house. She must be home. Maybe I could've gotten those cops to find her for me. Absently, he dipped a finger into his shirt pocket, then realized he'd left the card Sergeant Purvis had given him at his apartment.

Then a new thought hit him. Maybe they killed her, too! Maybe she's lying dead in their house. The SUV was parked out on the driveway. Jesus!

He picked up the phone on his desk and punched out Mike's home number again. The phone rang once, twice . . .

"Dr. Cochrane?"

He looked up. A young woman was standing in his office doorway. No student, he immediately realized. Too well dressed. She was wearing a tailored white blouse and a midthigh skirt of deep green. Her face was oval, with lustrous dark hair pulled back tightly. Green eyes, almond-shaped, almost Oriental. Good figure. Nice legs.

She took a step into the tiny office and smiled at him. "You are Dr. Cochrane? Paul Cochrane?"

He put the phone back into its cradle. "Yes."

She took in the office with a single sweeping glance: the bookcase filled with journals and reports, the cluttered desk, the full-color poster of the Eagle Nebula's breathtaking clouds where new stars are born. With a single little nod, as if confirming her expectations, she came fully into the office and sat pertly on one of the two plastic chairs in front of Cochrane's desk.

"I'm Elena Sandoval," she said, her voice a throaty mezzo. "I'm with the Department of Justice."

Cochrane blinked. "This has something to do with my brother?"

Sandoval smiled slightly. It made both cheeks dimple.

"I've been trying to reach his wife," Cochrane said. "His widow, I mean." It sounded stupid to him and he thought he'd made a fool of himself.

"Mrs. Cochrane's at home, but she's not taking calls. This has been something of a shock to her."

Cochrane nodded. "Me, too."

"I suppose so. Of course."

"What's Washington doing in this? Why are you involved?"

"Actually, it's the Department of Homeland Security who's interested in your brother's murder. I'm just a local field agent."

"Homeland Security?"

"Your brother's office was ransacked, either just before or just after he was killed."

"Ransacked?" Cochrane knew he was making an ass of himself, but he couldn't think of anything else to say.

"Did your brother confide in you? Did he tell you anything about the work he was doing?"

"Mike's a biologist, for chrissake! He wasn't involved in anything dangerous."

"Are you certain of that?"

"He worked with algae and cyanobacteria—"

"Cyano...?"

"Cyanobacteria," Cochrane repeated.

"That sounds ominous."

He didn't know whether to laugh or scowl at her ignorance. "They're harmless bacteria that produce oxygen."

"They're not dangerous, then?"

Cochrane shook his head. "They're on our side."

Sandoval tilted her head slightly to one side, as if trying to determine if he was telling the truth. Cochrane realized she was very pretty, beautiful even.

"Someone murdered your brother for a reason. I think it has something to do with his research."

"Mike said he'd hit on something that would make him rich, but—"

"Something? What?"

"He wouldn't tell me. Made me go out to Palo Alto to see for myself."

"And?" she asked eagerly.

Cochrane felt his insides go hollow. "I never saw him. The receptionist wouldn't let me in. He was murdered while I was in the building's lobby."

She pursed her lips, disappointed. "So you didn't get to see what he was working on."

"No. But you should be able to check it out on his computer."

"The laptop computer he worked on is missing. Stolen, we presume. His office was thoroughly looted of any paperwork that might have held his notes, his references, anything pertaining to his work."

"What the hell were they after?"

"I was hoping you would know," said Sandoval.

Cochrane didn't know what to say. Then his cell phone began playing Mozart. He pulled it out of his shirt pocket, flicked it open, and put it to his ear.

"Hello."

"Paul, it's me." He instantly recognized the voice of his brother's widow.

"Irene! Are you okay?"

"He's dead, Paul. Somebody killed Mike."

Glancing at Sandoval, who turned away slightly and pointedly stared out the window, Cochrane said, "I know. I was there when it happened. I went to your house."

"The police told me. I should have phoned you earlier, Paul, but I couldn't. I just couldn't."

He could hear the tears in her voice. "It's okay, Irene. I was starting to worry about you, though."

"I'm fine. Well, not really, but I'm all right. I got home from the school and there were a pair of police detectives on the front steps. That's how I found out."

"I must have just missed you," Cochrane said. Sandoval turned in her chair and studied the spines of the *Astrophysical Journals* on the top shelf of his bookcase.

"My carpool dropped me off around five-thirty. We had a teachers' meeting after classes."

You don't need to give me an alibi, Cochrane thought. Aloud, he said, "Lousy thing to come home to."

Irene sighed heavily and Cochrane realized she must be struggling to hold herself together.

"I'll come out there tomorrow," he said. "I'll help with the funeral arrangements and all that."

"Oh, Paul, I'd appreciate that so much! I just can't seem to think straight for two minutes in a row. I'm such a mess."

"I'll be there, Irene. Tomorrow. Soon's I can make it."

"Thank you, Paul. Thank you."

"See you tomorrow, then."

"Tomorrow. Yes. Goodbye, Paul."

"Goodbye."

He clicked the phone shut. Sandoval focused her green eyes on him. "Would you mind if I went with you? Perhaps your brother kept some records or files at home."

"Go with me?"

"It's important that we discover what he was working on. Whatever it was, it got him killed."

"I can't believe that—"

"Please, Dr. Cochrane," she said, her green eyes pleading. "Let me go with you. Please. I'd be so grateful."

Cochrane shrugged. "Okay, I guess." He found himself thinking, Fly out there with this good-looking woman? Sure, why the hell not?

PALO ALTO:
COCHRANE RESIDENCE

Cochrane noticed that Sandoval got attentive glances from men at the airport. And from women, too. Striding through the corridors with her, sitting next to her on the plane, Cochrane caught a definite whiff of admiration from the men. For a nerd you're doing okay, they seemed to be saying. She's a keeper.

Sandoval had made the flight arrangements for the two of them, to San Jose. "It's closer than San Francisco," she had explained. "Smaller airport, easier to get in and out." She'd made the rental car reservation, as well. No Corolla for her; she drove a four-door sandy gold Infiniti north on Highway 101, tooling past the massive old dirigible hangar at Moffett Field well above the legal speed limit.

"It might be best if you introduce me as a friend," she said, her eyes on the massive eighteen-wheelers whooshing past. "The family might get nervous if they realize I'm a federal agent."

Cochrane nodded easily. He pictured the looks on their faces when he told Irene and the others that Sandoval was his girlfriend. It made him smile.

"You think that's funny?" she asked.

"I think it's cool," he replied.

She smiled back at him.

He phoned Irene as they neared Palo Alto, and she was at the front door of the house when they pulled onto the driveway: a slightly fleshy woman with frizzy dark hair hanging loosely and tiny, squinting eyes magnified by a pair of square heavy-rimmed glasses. Irene was wearing a bulky sweater and shapeless jeans, with flat sandals. She looked tired, spiritless. For the first time Cochrane noticed that her hair was flecked with gray.

As they got out of the car, he saw that Irene was surprised by Sandoval. Surprised and immediately tense, from the way her jaw set. Suspicion? he wondered. Or guilt? Or maybe just the automatic competitive instinct of a woman.

He went to his sister-in-law and embraced her, then turned to Sandoval.

"Irene, this is Elena Sandoval," he began.

Sandoval smiled and extended her hand. "I thought it would be best if Paul didn't make this trip by himself. I'm so sorry about your husband."

"You knew him?" Irene asked, her voice sharp.

"No, but if he's anything like Paul he must have been a very special kind of man."

Cochrane felt his cheeks redden.

Irene looked from her to Cochrane. "I thought you'd be staying here at the house," she muttered.

"We have reservations at the Marriott," said Sandoval. It was news to Cochrane.

Almost grudgingly Irene took them inside and offered them sandwiches and beer. From the way she talked directly to him and almost totally ignored Sandoval, Cochrane saw that his sister-in-law didn't trust this woman. Maybe I shouldn't, either, he thought briefly. Then he dismissed the idea. She's a federal agent, for god's sake. Don't get paranoid.

They stayed with Irene all afternoon. She had already contacted the local funeral parlor and Cochrane phoned the director to talk about the arrangements. Mike's body had just been released from the police morgue, the man explained in sibilant whispers: they had performed an autopsy, standard practice in homicides. The funeral was scheduled for tomorrow, Tuesday.

"Tomorrow?" Cochrane asked, surprised. "What about the wake?"

"Mrs. Cochrane said she didn't desire to have a viewing."

"Wait a minute," Cochrane said. Then, placing his palm over the phone, he called to his sister-in-law across the living room. "No wake?"

Irene shook her head. "The sooner this is over with, the better."

"But won't his friends—"

"His friends are mostly from the lab. They're not the type to spend an evening pretending to be sad."

Cochrane almost flinched from the acid in her tone, the unforgiving expression on her face. He told the funeral director to go ahead with his plans for tomorrow, then hung up the phone.

When they had finished the sandwiches Irene had made and she was carrying their lunch trays back to the kitchen, Sandoval leaned close and whispered, "Can you get her to let you look at his computer?"

Irene came back into the living room, wiping her hands on a dish towel, and sat on the sofa beside him.

Feeling awkward, Cochrane asked, "Could I go up to his office, Irene? There might be something to give us a lead on who killed Mike."

"The police went through the whole house," Irene replied. "I barely got things back in order before you arrived."

"Did they find anything?" Sandoval asked.

Irene stared at her coldly. "If they did, they didn't tell me." She turned back to Cochrane. "Come on, Paul, I'll take you up there."

Sandoval caught the definite emphasis on *you*. "I can wait down here," she said compliantly.

Following Irene up the stairs, Cochrane could feel the hostility radiating from his sister-in-law. Why? he asked himself.

Irene led him down the hall and opened the door to Mike's study. It was a small room that would have been a nursery or a child's bedroom in another home. Two walls were lined with bookshelves and there was a handsome dark walnut desk placed at an angle, with the room's two windows behind it and a pair of bottle-green leather armchairs in front of it. Except for a telephone, the desk was bare. A flat-screen TV was mounted on the fourth wall, opposite the desk.

A movie set, Cochrane immediately thought. Just like Mike. He created a make-believe office for himself. He didn't do any work here. He couldn't. This is where he got away from everything, everybody— including his wife.

"Didn't he have a computer here?" he asked.

"He used a laptop. Took it to work with him," said Irene.

Cochrane nodded, thinking, Maybe I should phone that detective and ask him about the laptop.

Irene closed the door softly, then leaned against it, partially obscuring a poster that Mike had tacked up on the back of the door: a photograph of a balding, smiling man sitting by a window. Across the top of the poster, in handwriting, was scrawled, *Melvin Calvin, 1911–1997.*

"Why'd you bring her?" Irene hissed, her voice low, venomous.

Cochrane blinked at her. "She's . . . we're friends."

"Friends."

"It's not really serious," Cochrane said, almost like an apology.

Irene softened. She put both her hands on Cochrane's shoulders, leaned her head against his chest.

"Oh, Paul. I shouldn't . . . I mean . . . she just took me by surprise. I never expected you to . . ." Her voice trailed off.

"You never expected me to have a good-looking girlfriend?"

She looked up at him. Cochrane saw tears in her eyes. "Mike was fooling around."

"Mike?"

"He was seeing somebody, I know he was."

"Mike wouldn't do that."

"The hell he wouldn't!" Irene's face went hard, bitter. "He'd screwed around before. One-night stands. When he was out of town, on a trip to some conference or on company business. It went on for years."

Cochrane wondered why he felt shocked. Mike was outgoing, always had an eye for women. But cheating on his wife?

"There wasn't anything I could do about it. He always came home to me. If I said anything about it he'd slap me around."

"Mike hit you?"

"Never on the face," Irene replied. "He was too smart for that. He knew my brothers would beat the crap out of him if they found out he'd touched me."

"I can't . . ." Cochrane stopped himself. You know Mike's temper, he told himself. He socked you often enough.

"I thought he'd broke my ribs once," Irene went on. "Hurt me to breathe for a couple weeks."

"You should have called me," Cochrane said. It sounded lame, he knew.

"There was nothing you could do about it. I just worried he'd bring home AIDS or chlamydia or something."

I don't want to know about this! Cochrane screamed silently. But Irene went on.

"The past few months, though, he started seeing some bitch here locally. Maybe she worked at the lab with him, I don't know."

"Are you certain?" Cochrane heard himself ask.

Irene nodded. "They must've had a fight and she killed him. Or maybe she was married and her husband found out about them."

"Did you tell the police about it?"

"No! That's none of their damned business."

"But if it led to Mike's murder—"

"So what? He's dead and that's that. There's nothing I can do about it."

Cochrane stared at her, not knowing what to say, what to do. But in his mind he heard a sardonic voice reminding him that Mike's company insurance would probably take care of Irene for a long time.

She won't miss him, he told himself. She won't miss him at all. Nobody will.

PALO ALTO: MARRIOTT RESIDENCE INN

reserved two rooms for us," Sandoval said as they drove away from Irene's house.

Cochrane felt a pang of disappointment, but the rational part of his mind told him that he'd been foolish to expect anything more. *She's gorgeous, but she's a federal agent. Her only interest in me is about Mike's murder.*

"Did you get a chance to get into his computer?" she asked, driving slowly through urban streets lined with neat little houses and green lawns.

"His laptop wasn't there. Irene said he took it to his office. The police must have taken it."

Sandoval shook her head without taking her attention from her driving. "There wasn't any laptop in his office. Whoever killed him must have taken it."

"Irene thinks Mike was murdered by a jealous husband," Cochrane blurted.

She smiled. "So that's the reason for the bad vibes. One look at me and she thought about her husband's screwing around."

"That's kind of cold-blooded, don't you think?"

"No, I don't. Your sister-in-law's a hot-blooded woman. Watch yourself with her."

"What?"

"It's a good thing I came with you. You need federal protection."

Cochrane felt his jaw drop open. Sandoval laughed.

The Marriott Residence Inn was a trio of imitation Spanish Colonial–style three-story buildings, sandy tan with red tile roofing, set back from El Camino Real, where Palo Alto, Mountain View, and Los Altos adjoined. As they drove up to the hotel's entrance, he found himself wondering again why a federal agent should be interested in Mike.

Before he could ask her, though, she had parked in the driveway and popped the car's trunk. Cochrane got out and went to the back of the car. By the time he had pulled out his roll-on suitcase and slung his laptop over his shoulder, Sandoval was already through the lobby's glass doors, a single shapeless tote bag in one hand. He slammed the trunk shut.

As he came up to the registration desk, Sandoval said smilingly, "I know a neat little sushi place not far from here. Interested?"

"Sure," he replied automatically.

"Okay. Give me half an hour to unpack and shower. I'll meet you right here."

Cochrane was impressed with his mini-suite. It included a kitchen, a sofa, high-speed Internet access, and even a gas-fed fireplace. The government must be paying for this, he thought. Nobody had asked to see his credit card. He set up his laptop on the coffee table, checked his sparse e-mail, and still was back down in the lobby before Sandoval.

She came out of the elevator dressed in a comfortable pair of off-white slacks and a loose rose-pink blouse with a modest collared neckline. Still she looked elegantly attractive. Cochrane couldn't help smiling as they walked together out to the parking lot.

The sushi bar was noisy with customers' laughter and conversation and the Japanese chefs yelling back and forth to one another. A busy place, Cochrane saw. Country music, of all things, wailing out of the ceiling speakers. The spicy tang of ginger and other aromas in the air. Three TV sets, all muted and tuned to sports shows. Locals crowded the bar, so he and Sandoval took a small table off in the shadows. Cloth napkins, he noticed. He began to polish his eyeglasses as a waitress took their order for hot sake.

"So what exactly was your brother working on?" she asked, after a first sip from the tiny ceramic cup.

"Damned if I know," he said, raising his voice enough to be heard over the noise. "He was going to show me but I got there too late."

Sandoval sipped at her sake, then said, "No, I mean in general. You said he was some sort of biologist."

"Microbiology. He dealt with algae and bacteria."

"Cyanobacteria."

"You remembered."

"What's so special about them?"

The kimono-clad blond waitress brought their trays. Cochrane realized he was hungry and picked up his chopsticks.

"Cyanobacteria?" Sandoval prompted.

"I'm not a biologist," Cochrane muttered as he fumbled his first try at snaring a piece of eel roll.

She gave him that dimpled smile again. "You're a scientist. You know more about this kind of thing than I do."

Finally stuffing the rice-wrapped piece of eel into his mouth, Cochrane chewed fast, swallowed hard, then answered, "Cyanobacteria are very ancient forms of life. Billions of years old. If I remember correctly, they were one of the first organisms to use chlorophyll."

"Like green plants."

"Right. But cyanobacteria are one-celled creatures. Bacteria."

"Your brother was working with them?"

"Far's I know. Yes."

She picked up a piece of sushi expertly, then took another sip of sake.

"You said that these bugs produce oxygen?" she asked.

Cochrane pushed his glasses back up his nose. "They changed the earth's atmosphere. Several billion years ago this planet's atmosphere was mostly carbon dioxide. Unbreathable. But cyanobacteria and other chlorophyll-bearing organisms put out so much oxygen that our atmosphere eventually changed to what we have now: oxygen and nitrogen."

"There's still carbon dioxide in the atmosphere, isn't there? Isn't that what causes the greenhouse effect?"

Cochrane started talking about carbon dioxide and greenhouse warming and global air pollution. But in the back of his mind he remembered the poster tacked up on Mike's office door. Melvin Calvin, he thought. Who the hell is Melvin Calvin? The name was faintly familiar, but he couldn't place it. Then it hit him. Calvin Research Center. Of course.

By the time they'd finished dinner, Cochrane had told her every bit of information he knew about cyanobacteria and the earth's atmosphere. She insisted on paying the check and then drove the Infiniti back to their hotel. Cochrane felt slightly uncomfortable, as if he were a kept man. He wasn't accustomed to having a fine-looking woman pay for his dinner.

They got into the elevator together. Cochrane punched the button for the second floor; she hit three. When the elevator doors slid open, she gave him a peck on the cheek and whispered, "See you tomorrow, Paul."

He found himself standing in the empty hotel hallway, wondering what would happen if he went up to the next floor and tapped on her door. Nothing, he told himself. Nothing but disappointment. Shrugging, he went instead to his own room.

The lights were on and a stranger was sitting on the sofa, hunched over Cochrane's open laptop. He looked up as Cochrane entered, then swiftly got to his feet.

"Ah, Mr. Cochrane." He bowed slightly.

"Who the hell are you? What are you doing with my computer?"

The man was Asian, youthful-looking, with broad cheekbones, hooded dark eyes, and a wisp of a mustache. He was barely as tall as Cochrane's chin, but chunky, solidly built. He wore a thin royal blue windbreaker over a T-shirt and faded jeans. There was a motto of some sort on the T-shirt, but Cochrane couldn't make out the words.

"My name's Arashi," he said, with a cocky grin. "Sorry to intrude on your privacy—"

"Get the hell out of here before I call security," Cochrane snapped.

Arashi raised both hands. "Whoa, hold on. Let me explain myself."

Pushing past him to where his laptop lay open on the coffee table, Cochrane saw that the display screen listed his incoming e-mail messages.

Arashi said, "I represent some people who have a vital interest in your late brother's work. My condolences, by the way, on your loss."

Cochrane felt like punching the guy's lights out.

"I didn't know your brother personally, but I hear he was a top-flight research scientist."

"Who's interested in my brother's work?"

"The people I represent are willing to pay some heavy bread for any information you might give me about his research."

"I just went over that with Sandoval."

"Sandoval?" Arashi's brows rose. "Elena Sandoval?"

"You know her?"

"We've . . . eh, met."

"She's here in this hotel. I could call her. She's a federal agent and you're a goddamned burglar."

Arashi broke into a soft chuckle. "Hey, man, I'm no burglar. And Elena Sandoval is sure not a federal agent."

Cochrane heard himself gasp. "She's not?"

"No way. I suppose she's been asking you about the research your brother was doing."

Sagging into the sofa, Cochrane murmured, "Yeah, that's right."

Arashi perched himself on the arm of the easy chair at the end of the coffee table. "Like I said, I'm authorized to pay you for the information my people are looking for."

"I don't know anything about my brother's research."

"But you could find out, couldn't you? You're a scientist. You understand this stuff."

Impulsively, Cochrane reached for the phone on the end table. He asked the operator for Elena Sandoval's room. Arashi sat on the front two inches of the chair's arm, watching him with slightly amused eyes.

As soon as she picked up he said, "Elena, it's me."

"Hello, Paul." Sandoval's voice sounded throaty, sexy.

"I've got a visitor down here. A guy named Arashi."

"Arashi?" For the first time he heard anxiety in her voice. "I'll be right down. Don't tell him anything!"

The phone clicked dead.

Cochrane put the phone down and looked at Arashi, who was smiling faintly.

"She's coming down here," he said.

"Yeah, I'll bet she is," said Arashi. "Before she gets here, listen to this: I can offer you fifty thousand dollars for pertinent information about your brother's work. Maybe even a little more."

Cochrane shook his head, grumbling to himself, How many times do I have to tell these people I don't have any more notion of what Mike was working on than they do? But then a new thought struck him: Maybe I can find out about it. Mike must have left some information with the people he worked with. Maybe I can learn about his research from them.

A light tap on the door. Cochrane got to his feet and went to it. He opened the door and Sandoval stepped into the room, still wearing the slacks and blouse she'd worn at dinner.

Arashi stood up. "Hello, Elena."

"Mitsuo," she said. "What brings you here?"

Arashi smiled. "Don't play games. You know damned well why I'm here."

Closing the door, Cochrane said sharply, "He claims you're not a federal agent."

"She's not."

"I'm not," Sandoval admitted, going to the sofa. "I didn't like to mislead you, Paul, but I needed your trust and that seemed the easiest way to get it."

"And all this is about my brother's work?"

Arashi perched on the armchair again as Sandoval sat on the end of the sofa as far away from him as possible.

"The information must be in his computer," Arashi said to her.

"It's gone missing," she replied.

"The police...?"

"They don't have it. I asked that Sergeant Purvis about it. There wasn't any laptop at the murder scene."

"His home?"

She shook her head. "Paul checked. It wasn't there, either."

"Then whoever killed him must have it."

"Most likely."

"That's not good," Arashi muttered. "Not good at all."

They both turned toward Cochrane.

He looked at each of them in turn, then said, "I guess I can ask his colleagues at the Calvin Center. Maybe they can tell us something about it."

PALO ALTO:
CALVIN RESEARCH CENTER

Arashi breezed out of Cochrane's mini-suite as soon as Cochrane agreed to try to find out what his brother had been working on.

As the door closed behind Arashi, Sandoval got up from the sofa, too.

"Wait a minute," Cochrane said, reaching for her arm. "If you're not a federal agent, just who in hell are you?"

She looked distressed, her lips pressed into a thin worried line. "Paul, I can't tell you. Not yet. Please believe me, it's much too urgent. I wouldn't have lied to you if it hadn't been so urgent."

Before he could reply, she hurried to the door and left him standing alone in the mini-suite, feeling confused, puzzled, and more than a little annoyed at her elusiveness.

If they don't know what Mike was doing, why are they so damned spooled up about it?

Cochrane slept poorly, haunted by nightmares of his brother's battered, bloody face. He woke up depressed, worn out. Mike's funeral, he knew. This is going to be a truly shitty day. He showered and shaved and then phoned Sandoval. She'd already checked out, the desk clerk told him, and paid for his room as well. Surprised, irritated, he called his sister-in-law to lamely ask her if she could send somebody over to the hotel to pick him up.

"What's the matter," Irene asked, with a hint of acid in her voice, "did your romance break up?"

"I don't really know," he had to admit.

Where's she gone? he kept asking himself. What in hell is this all about?

Within a half hour Cochrane was picked up by Irene's two brothers: bulky, swarthy men in dark suits that seemed about to split at the seams. Aside from a brief hello, they said nothing to Cochrane; they drove him in brooding silence to the church where Mike's funeral was being held. There were pitifully few mourners at the church. The service was mercifully brief; the minister stumbled over Mike's name twice. Obviously Michael had been no more of a churchgoer than Cochrane himself—or their parents, for that matter.

At the cemetery he saw Sandoval standing alone on the fringes of the tiny gathering, dressed in a black sheath. Cochrane had brought his only dark suit, which he hadn't worn since he'd left Massachusetts. It felt uncomfortably heavy, stifling. Irene was with her plump, black-dressed mother and her two beefy-looking brothers, both hefty enough to fell teams of oxen. He hadn't seen them since Mike's wedding; they'd grown even bulkier over the years. Both the brothers had their wives with them, and a half dozen small children, all of them fidgeting but quiet, looking solemn and almost frightened. They're the only family Mike had, Cochrane realized. Except for me. The rest of the small group were strangers, mostly men, somber, almost embarrassed; they introduced themselves as co-workers from Mike's lab. No sign of Arashi, but there was another stranger hovering on the grass about a hundred yards away, a big-shouldered man wearing dark sunglasses and looking like a cop. Not Purvis or McLain, though, Cochrane was certain of that.

The sunshine was warm and there wasn't any kind of a breeze at all. Cochrane began to perspire in his wool suit. The minister went through his ritual and then Cochrane followed his sister-in-law to the closed coffin, took a red rose from the hand of the somber funeral director, and laid it tenderly on the burnished mahogany.

He turned away, the photo of his brother's battered face filling his mind. Christ, what a way to die. Then Sandoval appeared before him, her face a perfect picture of sadness and sympathy. She's an actress, Cochrane found himself thinking. A goddamned actress.

He said goodbye to Irene and her family, then followed Sandoval to her Infiniti. As she drove toward the Calvin Research Center, he asked, "So just who the hell is this Arashi? What's he after?"

Her eyes flicked from the road to his face and back again. "He's a... facilitator, of sorts."

"What the hell does that mean?"

"He works out business deals, smoothes the way for big corporations, international corporations. Sometimes government agencies, as well."

"Why's he interested in Mike's work? Why are *you* interested, for that matter?"

"I'm interested because Arashi is. He doesn't show up on the scene unless there's a lot of money involved."

Cochrane thought that over for a few minutes, decided that the information content of what she'd told him was pretty close to zero.

Sandoval pulled the gold Infiniti into the Calvin Center's driveway and parked it in a visitor's slot. She turned off the engine, took the key out of the ignition, and opened the door on her side. Cochrane didn't move.

"Aren't you getting out?" she asked.

"No."

"No?"

"Not until you tell me what this is all about."

"Paul, I can't. Not now. Not yet."

"Arashi offered me fifty thousand bucks."

Her eyes widened slightly. "And what did you say?"

"Are you working with him or against him?"

"Not with him."

"So who are you working with? Who are you, anyway? What's your interest in this?"

She let the driver's-side door click shut again, fiddled with the car key, still in her hand.

"I'm not budging until I get some answers," Cochrane said, folding his arms across his chest.

"Paul, you've got to trust me."

"Why? Who the hell are you? What's so fucking important about my brother's work?"

"That's just it! I don't know! I'm trying to find out. Very powerful people are after that information. That's why Arashi's involved."

"Who are you working for?"

She hesitated a moment. "Myself."

"Bullshit."

"I'm a freelancer. I sell information to people who pay for it. You'd call it industrial espionage, I suppose."

"Elena, I don't think there's a goddamned single word of truth in what you're telling me."

Strangely, she smiled at that. "More than one word, Paul. But you're right: not all of it's true."

With that, she opened the car door and got out. Cochrane sat there for all of ten seconds, then got out of the car and trotted after her to the smoked-glass double doors of the Calvin Research Center's entrance. She's like a snake charmer, he said to himself. And I'm the goddamned snake.

The center's director was Jason Tulius, a burly, barrel-chested man with thick white hair and a full white beard fringing his face. His light gray eyes seemed guarded, almost suspicious. Give him an eye patch and he'd look just like an old-time pirate, Cochrane thought. Then he corrected himself: No, he looks more like a tired-out, unhappy Santa Claus.

"It's a terrible tragedy," he said after shaking hands with Sandoval and Cochrane. "A terrible tragedy."

Tulius wore a brown tweed jacket over an open-collared pale green shirt. His top-floor office was spacious and airy, with broad windows giving a sweeping view of the hills on the far side of the highway. Instead of sitting at his desk, Tulius directed his visitors to the round table in the far corner of the office. His executive assistant carried in a tray bearing a stainless steel coffee urn, three mugs decorated with the CRC logo, and a plate of muffins.

"My one vice," Tulius said, reaching for the mug as the young man who'd brought it in silently left the room. Then he eyed Sandoval and smiled. "Well, one of my two vices."

She smiled back at him as he poured steaming coffee into one of the mugs. He offered coffee to her and Cochrane; both shook their heads.

Cochrane got them down to business. "Ms. Sandoval thinks that Mike was murdered because of the research he was undertaking. Others apparently do, as well."

Tulius's shaggy brows hiked up. "His research? He was working on photosynthesis, just like most of my staff."

"He called me a couple of days before he died," Cochrane said. "He told me that what he was doing will bring him millions. Tens of millions."

With a patient sigh, Tulius replied, "Michael was always a . . . an enthusiast. He was always overly optimistic about his work. Two years ago he started tinkering with genetic engineering, trying to modify certain strains of bacteria to produce a form of oil that could be used as fuel."

"Didn't Calvin himself work in that area?" Sandoval asked, surprising Cochrane.

"Yes, he did." Tulius nodded vigorously. "But he never succeeded. Neither did Michael, despite his enthusiasm. After eighteen months with no positive results, I had to order him to give it up."

"What could he have been doing that might be worth tens of millions?" Sandoval asked.

Tulius took a long sip of coffee from his steaming mug. "I can't imagine," he said. "I simply cannot imagine."

"There must be something," she insisted.

"*If* Mike's death is really connected with his work," Cochrane muttered, thinking of Irene and her two buffalo-sized brothers.

"It is," Sandoval said flatly.

"His widow thinks he was having an affair, possibly with someone working here."

"No!" Tulius snapped, looking almost angry at the very idea.

"How can you be sure?" asked Cochrane.

Shaking his head, Tulius said, "This is a small organization, Mr. Cochrane. Slightly less than two hundred people. We're a pretty tight-knit group, almost like a family. When a couple of my people start fooling around, I hear about it."

"Do you? Every time?"

"They can't keep that kind of thing a secret for very long," Tulius replied.

"And you didn't hear anything about Mike?"

"Never. Oh, he might have had a fling or two, but not with anyone here at the lab. I'm certain of that."

Cochrane tried to see from Tulius's bearded face whether he was telling the truth or not, but gave it up. He didn't know the man well enough to read his expression.

Sandoval said, "So you think that his murder was connected with the research he was doing."

Spreading his hands in a gesture of helplessness, Tulius answered, "I suppose that must be it, although I can't for the life of me see what Michael was doing that would lead someone to kill him."

"Could he have been working on something on his own, without your knowing it?"

"Moonlighting?" Tulius thought about it for all of a second. "I doubt that, doubt it very much."

"So just what was he working on?" Cochrane asked.

Tulius took another sip of his coffee, then asked, "Would you like to see what he was doing?"

"Yes!" Sandoval answered before Cochrane could get a word out of his mouth.

Tulius went to his desk and picked up the phone. In a few minutes a rangy, bearded, wary-eyed man showed up at the office door. Do they all wear beards? Cochrane asked himself. No, he answered silently. Mike didn't. None of the Calvin people who showed up at the funeral did. Neither Tulius nor this new guy had been among the mourners.

"This is Dr. Kurtzman," said Tulius.

"Ray Kurtzman," he said, extending his hand to Cochrane. "Sorry about your brother."

Cochrane expected him to take them back to one of the laboratories, or perhaps to Mike's office. Instead, Kurtzman led Sandoval and himself up a flight of uncarpeted steel stairs toward the building's roof.

"Most of us work with laboratory specimens," he said as they climbed the stairs. "Me, I'm a theoretician. I work with computer models and statistics."

"And Mike?"

Kurtzman opened the door that led out onto the roof. "Your brother was an experimentalist. A tinkerer."

Cochrane had to squint in the sunlight. He started to take off his suit jacket, but realized that a cooling breeze was whipping in from the ocean, on the other side of the hills. The sky was bright blue, dotted with puffy white clumps of cumulus. A band of pearl-gray cloud was edging over the range of seaside hills, like a huge shapeless amoeba slithering over their crests.

"A tinkerer?" Sandoval asked, raising her voice above the gusting breeze.

Kurtzman led them to a flimsy-looking structure of slim metal slats and glass windows. A greenhouse, Cochrane saw.

"Mike called this his Archaean Gardens," Kurtzman said, as he opened the glass door. It wasn't locked, Cochrane noticed.

The greenhouse was filled with long straight rows of tables bearing shallow pans of water. Cochrane saw small rocks and pebbles strewn in the pans, seemingly haphazardly. Most of them were covered with some sort of slime. The water gurgled cheerfully through the pans and out to a drainpipe.

"Archaean Gardens?" he asked.

Kurtzman came close to smiling. "He, uh...borrowed the idea from some work the NASA people over at Ames were doing." Pointing at the slime-covered stones, he explained, "These are stromatolites. Very ancient form of life. Probably first came into existence three or four billion years ago."

Sandoval asked, "How did he make them if they've been dead for so long?"

"They're not extinct," Kurtzman replied. "They still exist, off in places like Australia and east Africa. Mike got some samples and decided to try breeding them here under controlled conditions."

Cochrane pointed at the thin mats of living creatures. "Are they single-celled?"

"Algae and cyanobacteria," Kurtzman said, nodding. "Mike wangled a NASA contract from Ames, up the road; they're interested in the origins of life on earth. Helps them focus their explorations of Mars and other worlds, looking for life there."

"But what did he *do* with these creatures?" Sandoval asked.

Kurtzman grinned at her. "Good question. Mike was altering the amount of water that flowed over them, varying the nutrients in the water, trying to learn how changes in their environment affected them."

"What was he measuring?" Cochrane asked.

"Oxygen output. These little critters take in water and carbon dioxide and give off oxygen. That's how the oxygen we breathe got into the atmosphere."

Sandoval seemed fascinated. "How do they do that?"

"They crack water molecules, split 'em into hydrogen and oxygen. Not an easy thing to do, but they've been doing it for more than three billion years."

"They use the hydrogen and carbon to make carbohydrate food for themselves," Cochrane said, remembering his high school biology class, "and release the oxygen into the air. Oxygen is waste matter for them."

"Yeah," said Kurtzman. "They changed the whole world. Oxygen's pretty deadly stuff for the life-forms that existed way back then. These little blue-green buggers wiped them out, mostly. Oxygen killed them off."

Cochrane stared at the stromatolites, going about their business of life as they had been for almost four billion years. The only sound in the greenhouse was the gurgling of the water washing over the rounded pebbles and slightly larger rocks. It was hot inside the glass walls. Cochrane took off his jacket, pulled his tie loose.

And asked himself, Mike got himself killed over these microbes? There's got to be more to it than this.

Greenhouse Gases Cause Rising Global Temperature

Global temperatures are rising. Measurements around the world show that the thermometer's going up. There was some doubt about this because thermometer readings at the surface showed consistently rising temperatures while satellite measurements of the upper atmosphere showed a slight cooling trend.

Research published recently has resolved the question. The satellite measurements were in error. The atmosphere is getting warmer. No doubt of it.

This has happened before. Global climate has shifted many times in the past, often within a matter of a few decades or less. We've had ice ages and climates that were tropical from pole to pole.

Today global climate is definitely warming. Spring is arriving in northern latitudes earlier than ever. Permafrost in Canada is melting. Ice shelves in Antarctica are collapsing. Migratory animals are moving northward earlier in the year. Certain plant species are moving northward, too, because it's warm enough for them to thrive where they would have frozen before.

Are human actions causing this warming? That can't be pinned down definitely. Global climate shifts involve enormous energies, and can be caused by many factors, even including slight shifts in the earth's orbit around the sun.

But the amount of greenhouse gases that human industries and motorized transport pours into the atmosphere is at least a part of the problem. Perhaps a major part. Carbon dioxide and methane from human smokestacks, chimneys and exhaust pipes certainly aren't making the climate cooler!

Trouble is, some people are convinced that they know the truth about global warming, and they won't listen to anything that counters their firmly held belief.

There are those who insist that global warming is a myth, a Big Lie invented by environmentalists and nefarious foreigners who want to blame it all on us rich Americans. On the other hand, there are those who believe that we're all going to drown in rising sea levels unless we stop burning fossil fuels and somehow instantaneously invent a pollution-free economy.

Global climate is warming. Human actions are part of the problem. Bigger and more frequent hurricanes are one of the more obvious results of this climate shift.

It seems prudent to do whatever we can to alleviate the problem. Shift away from fossil fuels. Use nuclear energy, hydrogen fuels, solar and wind power as much as feasible.

And move to higher ground.

—*NAPLES* [FL] *DAILY NEWS*
October 23, 2005

MANHATTAN:
WALDORF-ASTORIA HOTEL

This special meeting of the board of directors was held in the Beekman Suite, quietly and discreetly, where neither the news media nor pesty protestors could interfere. The long conference table was filled, except for one empty chair at its very end. On the table set up along the back wall of the conference room were arrayed trays of finger foods and an assortment of refreshments that ranged from triply distilled water to the finest Polish potato vodka.

Lionel Gould sat at the head of the conference table, of course, the third generation of Goulds to hold such power. As chairman of the board of directors and principal stockholder in the corporation, Gould could break the careers of CEOs with a snap of his fingers. He was a benign-looking man of fifty-eight, portly, his graying hair thinning, his slightly porcine face set in a kindly little smile. His light brown eyes were flecked with gold, and as cold as ice. The jacket of his impeccably tailored three-piece suit hung crookedly on the back of his chair; his maroon silk tie was pulled loose beneath his double chin. Even though the conference room was thoroughly air-conditioned, Gould was obviously perspiring.

In the past decade Gould had survived a massive heart attack, a triple cardiac bypass operation, and a hip replacement procedure. He had divorced two wives during that time and fired two CEOs. Currently unmarried, he was careless of his appearance and his physical condition. He had learned early in his teens that enormous wealth meant more to women than mere good looks or a trim athletic body.

Now he tapped the polished conference tabletop with a single manicured finger. The murmured conversations among the directors stopped like an electric light being clicked off. Each of them—eleven men and eight women—turned their faces toward him.

"Let's get started," Gould said. His voice was a deep rumbling basso. Once he had toyed with the idea of becoming an opera star, but although he had the physique and the talent (so he was told) he found that the daily grinding work of practicing was not for him.

He nodded to the board secretary, seated at his left, who read a three-paragraph summary of the previous meeting's minutes. Up and down the table, directors opened laptops or PDAs or leather-bound notebooks.

The treasurer assured the assembled directors that Gould Energy Corporation had exceeded its goals in sales, pretax earnings, and net profits over the past quarter. The directors smiled and nodded.

Gould himself interrupted the treasurer's little rhapsody. "Demand for oil in China and India is pushing prices constantly higher. Which is good. Our exploration division, however, has had no success in finding new oil reserves."

"Which is bad," piped one of the younger directors.

Gould glared at the dark-haired man, then resumed. "Increased demand without increasing supply means that the price for petroleum will continue to climb. So will our profits."

"The indications are that gasoline will go well beyond seven dollars a gallon," said the treasurer.

"Which is good," said the young man, trying to redeem himself.

The oldest woman on the board, a flinty, hard-eyed heiress, added, "Until the government puts in price controls."

"That will not happen," said Gould.

"There's talk in Congress—"

"Talk," Gould spat. "There's always talk in Washington. Washington is full of talk. A year's worth of their talk isn't worth a single barrel of oil."

"Still…"

Gould smiled tolerantly at her. "I understand. You are looking at problems that may arise in the future. Which is good. We are already taking steps to avoid price controls. Which is better."

"Steps?" several board members murmured.

Looking very pleased with himself, Gould told them, "Our research division is working with automotive engineers to produce a car that will not require any gasoline whatsoever."

"Doesn't need gas?"

"How the hell can we make money out of that?" grumbled one of the older men.

"By controlling the new source of fuel," Gould replied amiably. "We will control the market for transportation fuel lock, stock, and barrel. We will realize Rockefeller's old dream of having a monopoly on the market. Which is not merely good. It's wonderful."

TUCSON:
STUDENT RECREATION CENTER

Cochrane flew back to Tucson alone, spent a restless night of confused, frightening dreams about his brother and Sandoval and shadowy menacing figures coming after him as he struggled to get away from them.

He woke up early, his tangled bedsheets soaked with perspiration, his eyes gummy and bloodshot. Feeling exhausted, he dragged himself through a shower, skipped shaving, and phoned his department head to beg off teaching his class later in the morning. As he sat at his kitchen counter, munching on a bowlful of Grape-Nuts, she called back, sounding genuinely sympathetic, and told him to take the rest of the week off.

"Thanks, Grace. I can use some time to get my head straight."

"Of course," she murmured. "That's what TAs are for."

Sitting around his one-bedroom apartment was no help. It took less than half an hour to dust the furniture, straighten up the newspapers and magazines, place his breakfast dishes in the washer.

Why was Mike murdered? What was he working on that was so fricking important? Sandoval. Arashi. Mike's rooftop garden of stromatolites. How does it all add up?

Sandoval. The best-looking woman I've seen in—Christ, how long has it been since I've been in bed with a woman?

But she had bade Cochrane a curt goodbye at the San Jose airport after their fruitless visit to the Calvin labs.

"Forget about me," she had said, while dozens of travelers shuffled slowly through the line at the airport's security checkpoint. "You're too nice a person to get involved with the kinds of things that I do."

Just like that. Forget about me. Sure, yeah, forget about her. Easy. Who is she, really? he wondered. Whatever she's after, it sure isn't me. Hello and goodbye. I can't tell you anything. It's too urgent. You don't want to get involved.

Stuffing his dirty laundry into the mesh bag he always used, Cochrane muttered to himself, "She's right. I don't want to get involved. Mike's dead and nothing I do is going to bring him back. The hell with it. The hell with all of them!"

His eyeglasses darkened automatically as he walked out into the blistering midmorning sun, carried his dirty clothes to the laundry down on Speedway, then made his way back onto the campus and the Student Recreation Center. Walking is good for the leg, the doctors had told him. Yeah, but it makes the leg ache. Funny, fencing doesn't. When I've got a saber in my hand the leg doesn't hurt at all. Or maybe it does but I just don't pay any attention to it. Not with another guy trying to stick me with his blade.

Cochrane had been disappointed to find that the university didn't have a fencing team, not even a fencing club; the sport had been his one diversion, his only exercise, his physical therapy after the accident. He'd found a few kindred souls, though, who usually worked out at the north gym in the Rec Center. A couple of them had talked about organizing a regular club, and even gone so far as to borrow a coach who gave lessons once a week; they all chipped in to cover the man's fee.

The fencers usually practiced in the afternoons, but maybe a few of the guys would be at the gym now, Cochrane reasoned. Fencing was great therapy. It exercised every muscle of his body, and so fully occupied his mind that he could forget everything else. The fastest sport in the world. You're only an arm's length from your opponent, the flick of a wrist can be the difference between scoring a point or getting beaten.

The gym was busy with a basketball practice: tall guys running and sweating, their sneakers squeaking on the polished floorboards, shouting and puffing as they raced back and forth, cut, feinted, jumped, and shot. Cochrane watched for a few moments, noticing wryly that most of their shots missed or bounced off the rim of the basket. Not like the TV high-lights, where every shot went in.

Disappointed, he went to his locker and changed into his sweats, then climbed up to the second level and started jogging along the track that cir-cled the gym below. *Ignore the pain in your leg; it's not as bad as it used to be.* Jogging didn't help him. It was so boring that his mind kept returning to Mike and Irene and her moose-sized brothers and that grinning Arashi and green-eyed Elena Sandoval. *Especially Sandoval. I don't know how to contact her!* Cochrane realized with a pang. *She didn't leave me a phone number, e-mail address, nothing. Even if I had something to tell her, I wouldn't know how to reach her.*

He thumped around the track half a dozen times, then went to the showers to let the hot water soothe his aching leg, dressed, and walked back to his empty, silent apartment.

The message light on his phone machine was blinking.

"Paul, it's Elena." *As if he didn't recognize her voice.* "I'm in Tucson, at the Arizona Inn. Could you call me, please? Maybe we could have din-ner tonight."

He plopped down into his desk chair, his mind racing. *First she tells me not to get involved with her and now she's come to Tucson and wants to have dinner. Don't do it! You're better off without her. Let the cops find out who killed Mike. Let her and Arashi and whoever else is involved in this go chase their tails until they screw themselves into the ground. Leave me out of this. Leave me alone.*

Then he looked around his spare, silent living room. Everything neat and clean. Everything in its place. The blinds drawn against the sun, cool and quiet and orderly. *It's like a cave in here, a mausoleum. Christ,* he thought, *you're just as dead as Mike but you haven't admitted it to your-self. What the hell do you have to live for? You're alone, practically a fuck-ing hermit. Ever since the car crash, since Jennifer . . .*

He tried to picture his late wife's face. And saw Sandoval instead.

That's not right, he told himself. *Jen's mother was right, I'm a heart-less sonofabitch.*

But he didn't feel heartless. He felt hurt, and sad, and above all else he felt lonely.

He picked up the phone, pushed the "return call" button, and eventu-ally got Sandoval's voice mail.

"Elena," he said as brightly as he could manage, "I know a cool little

Mexican joint on the other side of town. Great food and the margaritas are terrific. I'll pick you up at the inn at six-thirty unless I hear otherwise from you."

Then he headed for the bathroom to shave, thought better of it, went to the refrigerator instead, and started pulling out cold cuts and a stale loaf of seven-grain bread.

After lunch he returned to the gym. Half a dozen men and women were there in fencing uniforms, lunging and parrying. The gym rang to the click of blades clashing and shouts of "Eh-*lah*!"

Cochrane started to work out with the fencers and found a fury boiling out of him that he hadn't known was there. Rage. Murderous rage. *There!* he thought as he slashed at his surprised partner. They killed my brother. *There*, you bastards. Damn cops. Damn Tulius, what's he hiding? Arashi, smug little sonofabitch. Sandoval. Elena.

"Hey, Paul." The assistant professor he was fencing against backed away from him and pulled off his mesh mask, a pained frown on his lean face. "Take it easy. You're gonna whack my arm off."

Cochrane muttered, "Sorry," but once they faced off again he couldn't control his wild, hacking attack. Despite the guy's attempts at ripostes Cochrane forced him completely off the fencing strip and still flailed away at him.

"Stop!" The wild-haired Latvian fencing coach stuck his saber between Cochrane and his frantic opponent. Cochrane dropped his arm, puffing and sweating, and yanked off his mesh helmet.

"Who you theenk you are, Conan de Barbarian?" the Latvian demanded in his heavily accented English. "Thees ees fencing, not brawl in alley."

"I'm sorry, maestro," Cochrane said mechanically. He didn't feel sorry. He wanted to kill somebody.

"Don't apologize to me," said the coach, gesturing to the sullen-faced opponent, who was rubbing his arm.

"Sorry, pal," Cochrane muttered, trying to make it sound real.

"Jeez, I can hardly lift my fuckin' arm," the young man said. "It's numb."

"Sorry," Cochrane repeated. "Too much adrenaline, I guess."

"Too much testosterone," the coach said, unsmiling.

TUCSON:
LAS CASITA DE MOLINA

Cochrane whistled happily to himself as he dressed for his dinner date, but his buoyant mood vanished the instant he saw Sandoval walk down the steps of the Arizona Inn's front entrance. Arashi was with her.

She ducked into the front seat of his dusty blue Volvo S60 beside Cochrane, while Arashi slid into the rear.

"Neat wheels, for a four-door," he said as he clicked his seat belt.

"So where's this great restaurant?" Sandoval asked, all smiles.

"On the other side of town," Cochrane said tightly, pulling the sedan away from the curb.

He drove in sullen silence along Speedway to the I-10 entrance, then down the freeway to the Valencia Road exit. Sandoval made several attempts at conversation, but Cochrane cut her off each time with a brusque word. Arashi remained quiet in the back seat, but Cochrane could see him in the rearview mirror, grinning as if he understood exactly what was going through Cochrane's mind.

"Is this restaurant in Arizona?" Sandoval asked facetiously as they drove along Valencia.

"Not far now," Cochrane muttered.

The sun had set by the time he pulled up into the unpaved parking lot beside Las Casita de Molina, but the twilight was still bright. The restaurant was an unimposing single-story building with twinkling Christmas-type lights strung along its roof edge and neon beer company logos in its windows.

Inside, it was filled with workingmen and their families, Hispanics and Native Americans mostly, sitting at sturdy polished wooden tables heavily laden with dishes of tacos, tamales, enchiladas, and bowls of salsa and guacamole. The bar displayed a long row of beer bottles, most of the brands from Mexico. The children sat in their places quietly, no crying or whining. Very little conversation. Everybody was busy eating. Country music bleated from the speakers set up in the ceiling.

Cochrane spotted an empty table near the bar and weaved through the busy diners to it, Sandoval and Arashi trailing behind him.

"Order me a beer, will you?" Arashi said as Cochrane pulled out a heavy, carved chair. "I've gotta wash my hands."

Sandoval sat opposite Cochrane, her back to the bar. He stared into her green eyes and heard himself ask, "Are you sleeping with him?"

Her eyes went wide. Then she broke into a girlish laughter. "Is that why you've been so grouchy all the way here?"

"Are you?"

"Mitsuo? Of course not! Don't be absurd."

"What's he doing here, then?"

Her face went serious. "Business. About your brother."

"Still on that."

"Yes."

Arashi returned and sat beside her. Sandoval suggested that Cochrane order for all of them. Arashi put on a pout, but glumly nodded his agreement.

Each of them had a beer: Negra Modelo for Cochrane, Corona for the other two. The waitress brought lime wedges for each of them.

"So what are you doing in Tucson?" Cochrane asked her after his first sip. He kept his voice down, just loud enough to be heard over the buzz from the other tables.

"We've come to see you," Sandoval replied.

"What about?"

Arashi was holding his wedge of lime in two fingers, as though trying to decide whether to squeeze it into his glass or drop it in whole.

"I told you," said Sandoval. "About your brother."

Arashi suddenly let the lime wedge drop to the table. His grin disappeared and he quickly looked down at his empty glass.

"Did you see him?" he hissed to Sandoval.

She looked past Cochrane's shoulder and scanned the crowded dining room. "Who?"

"Kensington!" Arashi answered in a frightened whisper. "He was there, at the door. He went back outside to the parking lot. He's waiting out there for us!"

"Are you certain?"

"It was him! He must have followed you from the San Jose airport!"

"I didn't see him. . . ."

Cochrane asked, "Who's Kensington?"

"Hired muscle," said Sandoval.

From the terrified look on Arashi's face, Cochrane guessed that Kensington must be really bad trouble.

"We've gotta get out of here!" Arashi said.

"While he's waiting for us in the parking lot?" Sandoval replied coolly.

"But—"

The waitress brought their tray, loaded with three different dinners.

"Let's enjoy our food," Sandoval said, "and worry about Kensington later."

"Is this guy some sort of goon?" Cochrane asked.

Arashi didn't answer; he kept staring at the front door.

"He can be dangerous," said Sandoval.

Pointing to the police cruiser parked outside the window, Cochrane said, "This restaurant is a favorite hangout for the local cops. State highway patrol, too. I wouldn't be surprised if there aren't a couple of them in here having dinner."

He turned in his chair and spotted two uniformed police officers a few tables away, guns on their hips, radios clipped to their epaulets. They looked Hispanic, brown skin and straight dark hair.

Sandoval smiled at him. "That's why Kensington didn't come into the restaurant."

Cochrane said, "He probably doesn't want to tangle with the local law."

Arashi looked unconvinced, but Sandoval said, "We should be all right—as long as we finish our dinner before the policemen do."

They ate hurriedly, Arashi hardly touching his enchiladas. His eyes kept flicking from the policemen at the nearby table to the front door, where he had seen Kensington. Hardly a word of conversation. Despite her cool demeanor, it seemed to Cochrane that Sandoval was just as worried about the goon as Arashi was.

"They're finishing their coffee," he whispered urgently.

Cochrane got up and went to the cashier's counter, off to one side of the busy kitchen. He saw the two cops get up from their table; Arashi and Sandoval got up, too, and followed them to the front door. Cochrane signed his credit card tab and hurried after them.

It was cool outside, now that the sun had set. Clouds of insects flittered in the lights around the parking lot like miniature blizzards. As the two police officers got into their car, a highway patrol cruiser pulled up and parked next to Cochrane's Volvo.

"Safe as in church," he muttered to his companions.

Driving back north on the freeway, Cochrane asked, "Are you both staying at the inn?"

"I've got a room at the Hyatt," Arashi said from the shadows of the back seat, "but I think I'll check out and find another hotel."

"This Kensington must be a scary dude," Cochrane said, glancing at Arashi in his rearview mirror.

"He's probably the guy who killed your brother," Arashi replied.

Cochrane felt a jolt of anger flash through him. "Then why don't we turn him over to the police?"

Sandoval said, "We don't have any proof. It's better to avoid him."

"We never got to whatever it is you wanted to talk to me about," Cochrane said. "There's a nice little bar at the inn. We can talk there."

She shook her head. "Not the inn. We shouldn't be seen together."

"We already have."

"Not the inn," she repeated.

Shrugging behind the wheel, Cochrane said, "The only other place is my apartment."

"Fine," said Arashi, turning to peer out the rear window.

TUCSON:
SUNRISE APARTMENTS

It was still early evening, but most of the parking spaces at the Sunrise Apartments building were occupied. Six stories tall, square and stolid as the cinder blocks beneath its fake adobe exterior, the Sunrise Apartments were rented mainly by elderly couples or students—the very young whose idea of a night on the town was take-home from the local pizza parlor, and the very old who couldn't afford to go out for dinner on their Social Security incomes.

Cochrane parked in his assigned space and guided them to the building's lobby, Arashi swiveling his head constantly, searching for danger.

Once inside the brightly lit lobby, Cochrane went to the dual elevators. But Sandoval stopped him.

"What floor do you live on?"

"Third."

"It's better if we walk up."

She *is* scared, he realized. She just handles it better than Arashi. With another shrug, he went to the steel door that opened onto the bare-walled staircase.

Cochrane found himself slightly nervous as he unlocked his apartment door and turned on the lights. He half expected to see some menacing thug waiting inside with a gun in his hand. No one was there, though.

"Welcome to my humble abode," he said, with as much irony as he could muster.

It was lost on them. Sandoval clicked the door's lock and hooked the safety chain into place. Arashi went to the window and peered down into the almost-full parking lot.

"I don't think he followed us," he said, staring out the window.

"That's good," Sandoval said, going across to the sofa.

Cochrane thought about offering them something to drink, but put that aside. Instead, he said, "All right, we're here and we weren't followed. Now what the hell's going on? What did you want to see me about?"

"Dr. Tulius's computer files," said Sandoval as she sat on one end of the sofa.

"Tulius? What about his computer files?"

Arashi pulled three slim CD jewel cases from his jacket pocket. "We need you to look at them."

"How the hell did you get his files?"

Arashi's sly grin returned and he waved his hand vaguely. "Oh, I have ways of my own."

"You hacked into his computer?" Cochrane asked.

"It's one of my many talents," said Arashi, his grin growing even wider.

Sandoval said, "He's good at it."

"This is illegal, you know," Cochrane said.

"So is murder," said Sandoval.

Suppressing a grimace, Cochrane took the jewel cases from Arashi's hand and went to his desk, in the corner of the living room. As he clicked the desktop computer into life he told them, "There's beer in the fridge and a couple of bottles of hard stuff in the cabinet over the stove."

"Can I make a fresh pot of coffee?" Sandoval asked.

Cochrane didn't like having people mess with his coffee-brewing machine. "I'll do it," he said, getting up from the desk chair. "It'll take a couple minutes for my old clunker to boot up, anyway."

Ten minutes later the living room was filled with the aroma of freshly brewed coffee and Cochrane was staring at a long, scrolling list of Tulius's electronic correspondence.

"Anything interesting?" Sandoval asked, leaning over his shoulder with a mug of hot coffee in her hands.

"E-mail," said Cochrane.

"Look for reports from your brother," Arashi called from the sofa.

"Thanks for the advice," Cochrane shot back.

He went through Tulius's main menu, searching for Mike's name. Tulius was a neatness freak, he saw. And a worrier. Everything filed in perfect order, but everything protected by access codes. Everything, even his personal correspondence. Reports from his scientific staffers, of course, were blocked from view.

Swiveling in his creaking typist's chair, Cochrane asked Arashi, "You wouldn't know his access codes, would you?"

"Try his birth date," said Arashi, barely looking up from the newsmagazine he was leafing through.

Cochrane nodded and opened the Google search engine, then pulled up Tulius's biography. It was impressive enough, but didn't include his birth date. He went into the biographical files of the American Association for the Advancement of Science. There it was: December 7, 1941. Huh, thought Cochrane. Helluva day to be born: a date that will live in infamy, he remembered from his history lessons.

But it wasn't Tulius's access code. Cochrane tried 120741 and got nothing. He tried 071241; still nothing. Not even writing out all four numbers of the year helped. With a frustrated huff he leaned back in the stiff little chair and stared at the stubborn screen.

"Anything yet?" Sandoval asked from across the room.

Cochrane shook his head. It's got to be something simple, he told himself. Something that Tulius could easily remember. On a hunch he went back into Google and searched out the birth date for Melvin Calvin.

"Got it!" he shouted.

Sandoval and Arashi hurried to him as Cochrane scrolled through a long list of reports from the staff scientists to their chief. He highlighted the reports from his brother and began to pore over them.

"Hey, I've gotta go," Arashi announced, looking at the clock on the kitchen wall. "Gotta find a new hotel room."

Cochrane glanced at the digital clock running in the bottom corner of his screen, surprised to see it was nearly midnight.

"No sign of Kensington out there?" Sandoval asked.

Arashi shook his head. "When he doesn't want to be seen, you don't see him."

Cochrane realized that Arashi's car must be parked at his hotel. He started to get out of his chair.

"No, no, you stay put," Arashi said, yanking a cell phone from his shirt pocket. "I'll get a taxi."

It took more than half an hour, but finally Cochrane's front door buzzer sounded. Sandoval, peering through the window, said, "It's a cab, all right."

With a grin that Cochrane thought was slightly forced, Arashi bade them good night. "I'll phone you tomorrow morning," he said. Looking squarely at Sandoval, he added, "Don't try to hold anything out on me. I want a full report on those files."

She nodded. "That's what we agreed on, Mitsuo."

The door shut softly behind him; Cochrane clicked the lock in place and hooked the security chain.

"You're pretty scared of this Kensington, both of you," he said.

She tilted her head slightly to one side. "An ounce of prevention..."

Cochrane said, "You want me to drive you back to the inn?"

"Not yet," she said. "There's still half a pot of coffee left. Why don't you see what you can find out about your brother's work?"

"You made a deal with Arashi?"

Nodding, "He got Tulius's files. I share whatever you find with him."

"Whatever I find."

"That's right."

Cochrane stared at her for a long moment, then heard himself ask, "Suppose I don't find anything?"

"Do you mean you want to cut Arashi out?"

"He offered me fifty thousand."

Now she focused her green eyes on him. "And you want more?"

"I want to find out who killed my brother. And why."

"It must have been Kensington. It's his sort of thing," she said.

"But why?"

"That's what I'm hoping you can find in Tulius's files." She pointed a lacquered finger at his computer screen.

"Hmm." Cochrane returned to his typist's chair and began sorting through his brother's reports. Sandoval went to the window, inched the blinds apart, and scanned the parking lot below.

More than an hour later, Cochrane pushed himself away from the computer and took off his glasses. "I'm going cross-eyed," he mumbled.

She came to him, put a hand on his shoulder, leaned down to look at the screen. He could smell the flowery scent of her perfume.

"Anything?" she asked.

"Nothing that makes sense. He was measuring the oxygen output of his stromatolites. Some put out more oh-two than others."

"There *must* be something in those reports."

"If there is, I'm too punch-drunk to see it." He got up from the little chair and stretched his arms toward the ceiling, vertebrae popping. "Come on, I'll drive you back to the inn."

"Are you all right to drive?"

"Yeah. Sure."

"You're certain?"

She was standing before him, close enough to touch. Cochrane studied her face. She didn't look frightened, but maybe...

"You worried about Kensington?" he asked.

Her breath caught. Then she nodded. "He's out there. He doesn't give up."

Cochrane thought it over for all of three seconds. "You could stay here tonight."

"Could I?"

"The sofa pulls out. You can have my bed."

A slow smile materialized on her face, like the moon rising in a beautiful sky. "Paul, I couldn't put you out of your bed."

He took a breath and slipped his hands around her slim waist. "We could share it, then."

"Yes, we could," she said, wrapping her arms around his neck.

TUCSON: BMAA

The instant he touched her bare flesh Cochrane thrust himself at her with a fierce urgency that blotted out everything else from his mind. Nothing existed in the universe except this warm, beautiful, willing woman who matched his burning drive with a wild passion of her own.

"Come on, come on," she panted, and after he finally exploded inside her and lay beside her sweaty and breathless, she breathed a long, sighing, "Yeah."

Then slowly she began to arouse him again with tongue and touch, but this time their lovemaking was unhurried, better, more languid, more sensitive. She locked her legs around the small of his back as she came and whispered, "Oh, Paul. Paul. Paul."

In the morning they shared passion again, and by the time Cochrane stumbled into the lavatory he was bleary, weary, and grinning like a chimpanzee.

He showered, shaved, brushed his teeth. Opening the bathroom door, he saw that Sandoval was still sound asleep. Resisting the urge to climb back into bed with her, he quietly slipped on a pair of jeans and a T-shirt. As he headed for the kitchen he noticed that the computer was still on; he had forgotten to turn it off.

"Back to work," he muttered softly to himself. No coffee; grinding the beans might awaken her. He poured himself a glass of grapefruit juice and then sat at the computer once more.

The first hint that she had woken up was the click of the bathroom door closing. Then he heard the shower turn on. Smiling, he plowed on through the reports his brother had sent to Dr. Tulius. Cryptic, he thought. It's almost like Mike was writing in code. Both Mike and Tulius knew so much about what the reports dealt with that they could communicate in a sort of shorthand jargon that was fairly baffling to an outsider.

He heard the coffee machine grinding away briefly and soon smelled the aroma of brewing coffee. The juice glass at his elbow had been empty for some time when Sandoval, wearing only one of his shirts, placed a steaming cup of coffee beside it. He looked up at her and she smiled down at him.

"Anything?" she asked.

Cochrane noticed that it was 9:49 A.M. He shook his head unhappily and pushed the little wheeled chair away from the desk.

"Far's I can make out, Mike was measuring the oxygen output of his cyanobacteria. Some emitted a lot more oxygen than others, but there doesn't seem to be any pattern to it that I can find."

She went to the sofa, sat down, pulling his shirt around her. "There must be something more. There's got to be."

"Something called BMAA," Cochrane said. "Several of Mike's memos talked about BMAA."

"What's that?"

"Damned if I know."

"Can you find out?"

He reached for the coffee, blew on it, then took a scalding sip. "I can try."

Almost an hour later, Cochrane looked up from his computer screen again, feeling grim and frustrated. Sandoval stepped out of the bedroom, dressed in her own slacks and blouse once again; she looked fresh, glowing.

"So?" she asked. "What is BMAA?"

He made a wry grin. "That depends. It could be the British Microlight Aircraft Association. They deal with ultralight airplanes; you know, like those powered hang gliders you see puttering around the sky."

Sandoval shook her head. "That wouldn't be it."

"Or some agency for refinancing home loans."

She frowned.

"Or the Bucks-Mont Astronomical Society, in Pennsylvania."

"That doesn't seem likely, does it?"

"Or it could be something called b-N-methylamino-L-alanine." Cochrane stumbled over the pronounciation.

"What on earth...?"

"It's a rare neurotoxin some biologists discovered in a plant species in Guam and New Guinea."

Her brows shot up. "A neurotoxin? You mean, like a nerve poison?"

Cochrane said, "I think so."

"Was your brother working on a nerve poison?"

"The last few memos he sent to Tulius talked about BMAA being excreted by some of his cyanobacteria. It looks to me like Mike thought the stuff was a by-product, a waste product, not what he was looking for."

"Tulius might have felt differently."

"Maybe," Cochrane conceded.

"I'll have to talk with him again," she said, more to herself than to Cochrane.

"What about Arashi? And this Kensington guy?"

"I promised Mitsuo that I'd cut him in on anything we found from Tulius's files." She went to her purse, pulled out her cell phone.

"And Kensington?"

"The best thing to do about Kensington is to avoid him," she said, pecking at her phone's tiny keyboard.

Cochrane got to his feet, stretched, then bent over and touched his toes—almost. He felt mentally drained and physically weary. He smiled to himself as he remembered an old line from his high school days: Too much bed, not enough sleep. Yeah, well, it was worth it. She's something else.

Watching her as she held the miniature phone to her ear, Cochrane saw all over again how truly beautiful she was. And she hopped into bed with me. With me! But a cautioning voice warned him, It was too easy. It didn't mean anything to her; she's using you. Yeah, he replied, and damned well, too. Don't let it go to your head, the voice insisted. He almost giggled. It isn't my head that it's going to.

Sandoval clicked her phone shut with a disappointed little frown. "Mitsuo's not answering."

"Maybe he's in the shower."

"At eleven in the morning? That's not like him."

"Is his phone off?"

"No. It's ringing. He's just not answering. No voice-mail message, either."

Cochrane shrugged.

"Well," she said, "I can't tell him anything if he doesn't have his voice mail turned on."

He took another sip of coffee. "So what's our next move?"

"I've got to see Tulius and ask him about this... what is it again?"

"BMAA."

"BMAA. If it's a nerve poison it might be what's behind your brother's murder."

"But Mike—"

"Can you drive me back to the inn? I'll call Tulius from there."

"And Arashi?"

"Him, too," she said lightly, as if it weren't important.

"Okay," Cochrane said. "My car's down in the garage."

As they went to the apartment's front door, Sandoval mused, "I'll probably have to go to Palo Alto again. Tulius won't want to talk about this on the phone, I imagine."

"I'll go with you," Cochrane said as they stepped out into the hallway. He turned to lock the deadbolt.

"It would be better if I went alone, Paul," she said.

"What do you mean?"

"I need you to collect all the information you can on this BMAA stuff: where it comes from, who's involved in producing it. Everything you can find."

The elevator doors slid open.

"But I thought we were in this together," Cochrane said.

"We are, Paul. But we can accomplish a lot more working separately right now."

"You want to go to Palo Alto without me?"

"Please believe me, Paul. You can do more here," she said, looking slightly distressed.

He fell silent as the elevator descended to the garage. One night in bed and then it's *You stay here, Paul*, he thought, fuming. She's an actress, he realized all over again. An actress. She was probably acting in bed.

And she wants to see Tulius alone. Without me. Cochrane remembered the expression on Tulius's face when he'd first seen her: like a pirate looking at a chest full of treasure.

The elevator doors opened and a tall, broad-shouldered man in a dark suit stood in front of them.

"Ms. Sandoval, Dr. Cochrane," he said in a deep, rumbling voice.

"Kensington," Sandoval whispered.

Brain-Destroying Algae

Blue-green algae (also known as cyanobacteria) are probably the most widespread and ancient life-forms on earth. They can produce a toxin called BMAA, which is biochemists' shorthand for b-N-methylamino-L-alanine. BMAA is linked with nerve-wasting diseases such as Alzheimer's and an illness similar to Lou Gehrig's and Parkinson's diseases.

Ninety percent of the more than forty cyanobacteria species studied by an international team of microbiologists produce BMAA. The researchers believe that under the proper conditions all cyanobacteria might produce the nerve toxin. The neurotoxin has been found in blooms of cyanobacteria in the Baltic Sea and in ocean waters, which means that the microbes could be releasing deadly quantities of BMAA.

Water pollution and rising global temperatures trigger such algal blooms (such as red tide) that can cover thousands of square kilometers. Scientists believe the health consequences for aquatic life such as fish and sea mammals, as well as humans, could be significant.

—*Science Monthly*

ORACLE, ARIZONA:
BIOSPHERE 2

M r. Gould wants to see you," Kensington said to Sandoval. Turning his slate-gray eyes to Cochrane, he added, "You come along, too."

"And what if we don't want to see Mr. Gould," Cochrane said, "whoever the hell he is?"

"That doesn't matter."

"Doesn't it?"

Neither Cochrane nor Sandoval had stepped out of the elevator cab. She seemed frozen, like a small animal caught in the glare of a speeding car's headlights.

"Look, Doc, I don't want to play games."

Kensington was a couple of inches taller than Cochrane, and he appeared to be solidly built. His face was hard, humorless, a stubble of beard darkening his heavy jaw. His hair was thick, jet-black, combed straight back off his broad forehead. He probably has a gun, Cochrane thought.

"Do what he says, Paul," whispered Sandoval. But she made no move to leave the elevator cab, as if she could not willingly take a step toward this dark, menacing man.

On an impulse, Cochrane tried to punch the "close door" button, but Kensington's reflexes were faster. He grabbed Cochrane's wrist in an iron grip that shot a hot streak of pain all the way up his arm.

"No games, Doc," Kensington said, his lips pulled apart in a grim rictus that might have been a smile.

"Mitsuo Arashi knows we're here," Sandoval said. "We were on our way to see him. If we don't show up—"

"Arashi's not going to worry about it," Kensington said. "He's past all his worries now."

"He's dead?"

"Very."

Cochrane stood there, seeing the terror in Sandoval's eyes as he tried to rub the pain out of his arm.

"Let's go," Kensington said. "And remember: no games."

Cochrane followed Sandoval and Kensington to a blocky black Lexus SUV that was parked in a space marked DELIVERIES ONLY. He pulled the sliding rear door open and Sandoval climbed in. Cochrane followed and sat beside her. Kensington slid the door shut, then walked calmly around the truck and climbed into the driver's seat.

"Fasten your seat belts," he said, looking up into the rearview mirror. "Lotta crazy drivers out there."

They rode in silence up Campbell Avenue, then across to Highway 77 and northward.

"Where are you taking us?" Sandoval asked.

"You'll see."

"What happened to Mitsuo?"

"He thought he was a kung fu master. I had to teach him otherwise. Guess the lesson went too far."

"Who's this Mr. Gould?" Cochrane asked.

"You'll see," Kensington repeated.

They headed toward the town of Oracle, but turned off at a sign that pointed to Biosphere 2. Both sides of the turnoff road were filled with housing developments so new that much of the land was still raw, not yet landscaped, an open wound in the desert where still more houses would be planted. They looked like expensive homes to Cochrane, all neatly laid out like brand-new chess pieces on a board. Scrawny young trees planted precisely the same distance apart from each other lined the road on both sides. They're putting in grass lawns, in the desert, Cochrane saw. Their water bills will be astronomical, he thought.

Biosphere 2 was a collection of weird-looking white and glass buildings, including a big dome-topped tower and a stepped-back pyramid, with more conventional wooden barracks-type buildings running up a flanking hillside. Cochrane remembered that the place had been built to simulate various ecological regions of earth: tropical rain forest, desert, they even had a miniature ocean inside one of the buildings. All completely sealed from the outside world. A group of volunteers had tried to live for a year inside this artificial world; they lasted only a few months. Or was it weeks? Cochrane couldn't remember.

Kensington parked the SUV in front of a brick two-story building just inside the compound's gates. Cochrane slid the door on his side open before Kensington could get out of the driver's seat. Looking out at the bleak expanse of brown hills baking in the morning sunshine, he realized there was no sense trying to run, nowhere to run to. So he climbed down onto the gravel of the parking lot and helped Sandoval get out of the Lexus. The heat of the desert sun felt like an iron weight on his shoulders.

Wordlessly, Kensington led them into the building. The lobby was empty; the entire building seemed deserted.

"No one here?" Sandoval asked.

"We're here," said Kensington. Then he nodded toward a closed door at the end of the corridor. "And Mr. Gould is in there, waiting for you."

Feeling a little like a kid who'd been sent to the school principal's office, Cochrane led Sandoval down the corridor. He rapped once on the unmarked door, then opened it.

Inside was a small office, air-conditioned so heavily it sent an instant shiver up Cochrane's spine. Sitting behind the desk was a heavyset man with thinning gray hair. His jacket had been thrown carelessly on the couch by the window, his vest unbuttoned, his shirt collar open and florid tie pulled loose. Still the man's fleshy face was sheened with perspiration. He was staring intently into the screen of a laptop, opened on the desk. He didn't bother to look up when Cochrane pushed the door shut behind Sandoval and himself.

Despite the air-conditioning, the room smelled stale, dusty, as if it had been sealed shut for a long time. Cochrane saw a parade of dust motes dancing in the sunshine slanting in through the window at one side of the desk.

They stood there uncertainly in the bitingly chill office for several long seconds. Finally the man behind the desk nodded hard enough to make his cheeks waddle, then snapped the laptop shut. He looked up at them and smiled without showing his teeth.

"Ms. Sandoval," he said, in a slightly rasping voice. "And you must be Dr. Cochrane. My condolences on your brother's untimely demise."

"Did you have something to do with it?" Cochrane snapped before he could stop himself.

"Me?" The man's thin gray brows shot toward his scalp. "Heavens, no! Why should I want him dead? We were partners—or we would have been if he hadn't been killed."

"You are Lionel Gould?" Sandoval asked.

"Yes, yes, I am indeed Lionel Gould." He spread his arms and indicated the wooden chairs in front of the desk. "Please sit down. Make yourselves comfortable. I regret that I can't offer you refreshments; this facility has been closed for some time now. I intend to reopen it, perhaps as early as next year."

Sandoval went to one of the heavy oak chairs and sat in it. From her rigid posture, though, Cochrane could see she was far from comfortable. He sat next to her.

"What's this all about?" he asked.

Gould pulled a florid handkerchief from his back pocket and mopped his face. "Desert heat. Can't say I like it."

"What's this all about?" Cochrane repeated, a trifle louder. "Why have you kidnapped us and brought—"

"Kidnapped?" Gould looked genuinely alarmed. "Heavens, no. I merely told Mr. Kensington that I wanted to talk with you. In person. In private. You're free to leave whenever you wish."

"He killed Mitsuo Arashi," Sandoval said flatly.

"In self-defense, I'm sure."

"And he killed my brother, too, didn't he?"

"That he did *not* do," Gould replied sternly. "I assure you. As I said, your brother was about to enter into a partnership with me. Many millions of dollars were involved."

"I don't understand any of this," Cochrane said. "What was Mike doing with you? What was worth millions of dollars?"

Gould's brows squeezed together. He stared at Cochrane, hard, as if trying to penetrate to his soul.

"Are you telling me that you don't know what your brother was working on?"

"All I know is that a helluva lot of people seem to be interested in it, whatever it was."

"I don't like the sound of that," Gould muttered.

"It's something to do with BMAA, I'm pretty sure," said Cochrane. Sandoval glared at him.

Gould considered this for a moment. "What on earth is BMAA?"

"A nerve toxin. Certain species of cyanobacteria produce it."

"Cyanobacteria," Gould mused. Cochrane realized that the man had heard the term before; it wasn't new to him.

"Mike was doing research on cyanobacteria," Cochrane said.

"What was the basis of your partnership deal?" Sandoval asked.

Gould smiled coldly at her. "If you don't know, why should I tell you? I brought you here because I need to know what you know. Not vice versa."

Cochrane looked at Sandoval, who had frozen her face into an impassive mask. Then he turned to Gould, who was frowning.

"We appear to be at an impasse," Gould said. "Which is not good."

"Who murdered my brother?" Cochrane demanded.

"How should I know?"

"What was he doing that was worth millions to you?"

Gould shook his head. "No, it doesn't work that way, Dr. Cochrane. I'm perfectly willing to exchange information with you, but you seem to have nothing to exchange with me."

"Look," Cochrane said, feeling exasperated, "all I'm interested in is finding Mike's murderer. I don't give a damn about whatever it was that he was researching."

"I'm afraid you don't make much of a detective, then," said Gould. "If you can uncover the details of his latest work, you will undoubtedly find his murderer. The two are inextricably linked, I'm convinced of that."

Sandoval said softly, "So we get back to the question of why you were willing to offer Michael Cochrane millions of dollars for a partnership deal."

Gould leaned back in his desk chair and thought about that for a few moments. "Yes, that's exactly where we get to."

"Was it about BMAA?" Cochrane asked. "Was Mike working on some new biological weapon?"

"Hardly that," Gould replied. "Although, I must admit, if one of the spin-offs from this research is a useful bioweapon, that in itself could be of considerable value."

"Suppose," Sandoval said slowly, "Paul and I agree to work for you and find his brother's research results—the material you were going to pay him for? What would that be worth to you?"

"What would I pay you, you mean?"

"You were willing to pay Paul's brother millions, you said."

"For the results of his research, yes," said Gould. "An exclusive partnership. Exclusive."

"And if we could dig out the results of his research?" she asked. "How much would that be worth to you?"

"A considerable sum."

"Millions?"

"Millions."

"Ten million?"

Gould pursed his lips. Then he nodded. "Ten million dollars. For the data I want. Payment on receipt of the information."

She glanced at Cochrane, then said, "I think we can get the information for you—on those terms."

Gould slowly rose to his feet and extracted a stiff white calling card from the pocket of his unbuttoned vest. He handed the card to Sandoval. "That will be good. That will be excellent!"

CESSNA CITATION VII:
38,000 FEET ABOVE NEBRASKA

Kensington sipped on a Diet Coke and stared out at the endless expanse of gray cloud far below. He didn't like flying; he much preferred
to keep his feet solidly on the ground. But he had to admit, if you've got to
fly, Gould's personal executive jet was the way to do it. Beats standing in
airport lines and jamming your butt into an overcrowded airliner.

The Citation VII could accommodate eight passengers, but Kensington and Gould were the only two aboard. Up front in the cockpit were the
pilot and copilot. No flight attendant. Kensington thought that a cute and
willing stewardess would be a fine addition to the luxuries of this flight.
These seats are big enough for two, he thought. Especially when you
crank them back. Almost as big as a bed.

Gould was sitting in the facing chair, on the telephone, as usual: a
plug in one of his tiny pink ears and a pinmike practically touching his
whispering lips. He's either on the phone or on the computer, Kensington

said to himself. I could be screwing two stewardesses right in front of him and he wouldn't even notice.

So he was surprised when Gould plucked the plug out of his ear and said to him, "You look unhappy."

"Me?" Kensington shrugged his broad shoulders. "I got no complaints."

"None whatsoever?" Neither man had to raise his voice. The cabin's acoustic insulation was so good that the noise of the plane's twin jet engines was little more than a background purr.

"None whatsoever," said Kensington.

"What do you think of this man Cochrane?"

"The one with Sandoval?"

Gould leaned forward in his seat, his cold brown eyes focused intently on Kensington's face. "Yes, him."

"He looks like a wimp, but I think maybe he's got some guts. He's smart enough to know when he's overmatched."

"And Sandoval?"

"She'd make a good hooker."

Gould made a sound that might have been a grunt, or perhaps a stifled laugh.

"You really offered her ten mil to find what you're looking for?" Kensington asked.

"If the deceased Dr. Cochrane actually found what he claimed to have found, the results could be worth hundreds of millions," Gould said fervently. "Thousands of millions. The results could change the entire world!"

"If the guy really found it—whatever it is."

Gould smiled slyly. "Yes. Whatever it is."

"You know what it is, don't you?"

"I know what the late Dr. Cochrane promised to deliver to me. A breathtaking breakthrough. Absolutely breathtaking."

"If it's real."

"Yes." Gould nodded. "If it's real."

"You think they already know what it is? Sandoval and the stiff's brother?"

"No, they appear to be totally ignorant about the man's research work."

Kensington considered that for a moment. "I could find out how much they know. Wouldn't take more'n a half hour or so."

"The way you found out how much Arashi knew?" Gould shook his head hard enough to make his wattle quiver.

Kensington sank deeper into his seat. "You're the boss," he muttered. But he thought about what it would be like to interrogate Sandoval. Could be fun. All sorts of fun.

TUCSON:
SUNRISE APARTMENTS

Sandoval had been absolutely silent while Kensington had driven her and Cochrane back to the apartment block. Nor had Cochrane much to say.

Now, though, as they stepped through the front door of his apartment, Cochrane asked, "Ten million dollars? On a handshake?"

She dug her cell phone out of her handbag, then dropped the bag on the slim table by the door. "It must be worth enormously more to Gould," she said, tapping on the phone's tiny keyboard.

"Who're you calling?"

"Airline. I've got to see Tulius again. He knows more than he's told us. A lot more."

"We're going back to Palo Alto?"

"I am. I can get more out of Tulius alone than I can with you along."

Cochrane froze in the middle of the living room. Yeah, he said to himself, and I know just how you'd do it.

He reached out and yanked the phone out of her hand, then tossed it across the room, onto the sofa.

"What are you doing?" she asked, her eyes going wide.

"We've got to get a few things straight," he said.

"Oh, for—"

"Last night was great. But did it mean anything to you, or was it just your way of keeping me in line?"

Her mouth clenched into a bitter line. "Don't go macho on me, Paul."

"It's not machismo. I just need to know where I stand."

Shaking her head, "How should I know? We just met a couple of days ago. With all this going on—"

"With all this going on you went to bed with me last night."

"Yes," she said, smiling slightly. "That's right."

"And now you're going off to see Tulius."

"Paul, don't be possessive."

"I'm not being possessive," he said, realizing the truth of it as he spoke. "I'm just trying to figure out if there might come a time when you and I could be serious."

"I'm not a whore, if that's what you mean."

"But you'll go to bed with Tulius if that's what it takes."

"For ten million dollars? Damned right I will!"

Cochrane turned and walked slowly to the sofa, picked up the cell phone and held it out to her at arm's length. She stood there by the front door, motionless, her face unreadable.

"You know Gould's not going to part with ten million," he said. "He'll take whatever we can dig up for him and then let Kensington or some other hired goon kill us. Just like he did to my brother."

"I don't think he killed your brother."

"Somebody did. And Gould thinks whatever Mike was doing is worth a lot of money."

She seemed to soften, her face relaxing into an uncertain, almost vulnerable expression. Moving to him, Sandoval said, "Paul, I want to find out who killed your brother, too. Whether we like it or not, though, we're involved in something big. Very big."

She took the phone from his hand.

"Last night was a beginning for us, Paul. But only a beginning. We can't build any kind of relationship while all this is going on. You can see that, can't you?"

He nodded wordlessly. But he thought, You're an actress, Elena Sandoval. A damned good one, but an actress nevertheless. I was a damned fool to think otherwise, even for a microsecond.

"I'll talk to Tulius," she said, clutching the phone in one hand. "Talk. That's all. I promise."

"And I'll stay here?"

"You've got to go through those computer files that Mitsuo brought us and pull out every shred of information about your brother's work. That's vital, Paul!"

"Uh-huh. Vital."

"I'll come back here. I'll move my things from the inn."

Cochrane told himself, That's the deal. She'll sleep with you as long as you're useful to her.

"Okay," he said reluctantly. "You go talk with Tulius. I'll wait here for you."

She smiled and twined her arms around his neck. "I promise you, Paul. I'll be back as quickly as I can. If I have to stay overnight I'll phone you from my hotel."

"Yeah."

He went to his desk and booted up the computer while she phoned for an airline reservation. He even plugged into the Internet to print her boarding pass and hotel confirmation. Then he drove her to the Arizona Inn, where she checked out and moved her luggage to his apartment.

They went to a nearby restaurant, Le Bistro, for dinner. Cochrane hardly tasted the food. She was tense, too, knowing that he was on the edge of anger. They finished a bottle of Chablis, but that didn't help. They drove back to his apartment and went to bed. That did help.

In the morning, Cochrane drove her to the airport. By the time he got back to his apartment, two uniformed police—a man and a woman—were waiting for him out on the parking lot.

"You're Paul Cochrane?" the female officer asked as he got out of his car.

"Yes."

"You're wanted for questioning in the homicide of some guy named Mitsuo Arashi."

White House Calls for New Technology as Solution to Energy Problems

WASHINGTON—Saying that "this problem did not develop overnight and it's not going to be solved overnight," presidential science adviser Maxwell Bishop issued a call for new technological developments to help solve national and global energy problems.

The president's science adviser said that nuclear power generation, hybrid automobiles and new types of fuels to replace gasoline must all be pursued to ease the nation's dependence on oil imported from overseas. He suggested a combination of federal grants, tax breaks and other incentives to stimulate "innovation and invention."

"Technology is the ticket," he said. "It's time to turn the genius of American scientists and engineers to solving our energy problems."

—*ARIZONA DAILY STAR*
May 14, 2005

TUCSON:
POLICE HEADQUARTERS

All that Cochrane had ever seen of police stations had been in movies and television shows, where they always looked grungy, hard-used. He imagined they smelled of sweat and fear and urine.

Tucson police headquarters, though, was clean and modern and new-looking. Even the slats of the window blinds pulled down against the morning sun looked as if they'd recently been thoroughly sponged down. Cochrane smelled coffee perking somewhere. The squad room buzzed quietly with men and women in street clothes talking intently on telephones or leaning across their desks to ask questions of suspects and witnesses.

The two officers showed Cochrane to what looked more like a small conference room than an interrogation cell: blinds on the windows, an oblong table with molded plastic chairs, a TV screen built into the back wall.

"Lieutenant Danvers will be with you in a minute, sir," said the female officer.

Cochrane looked around as the officers left and closed the door. No one-way mirror, as far as he could tell. No surveillance camera up in the ceiling or anywhere else in view. He pulled up a chair and sat where he could see the door, thinking, Lieutenant Danvers. In Palo Alto it was two sergeants. I'm coming up in the world.

The door opened and Lieutenant Danvers stepped in. She was a small African-American woman, almost petite except for being obviously over-weight. Too many doughnuts, Cochrane found himself thinking. Her skin was the color of dark chocolate. She wore a starched white blouse and a knee-length navy blue skirt. Her hair was iron-gray, but her face looked more like a kindly aunt or youngish grandmother than a police officer.

"I'm sorry to keep you waiting, Dr. Cochrane," she began, walking past him and taking the chair at the head of the table. She placed a black notebook and a television remote control wand on the tabletop. Cochrane noted that she carried a pistol in a holster tucked into the waistband of her skirt. "We had to set up a videophone connection with the Palo Alto police."

Before Cochrane could say anything, the TV screen came to life and Sergeant McLain's puffy-eyed face stared out at him.

"Sergeant McLain," Cochrane said.

"You've got another dead body on your hands," McLain said, smiling sardonically.

Lieutenant Danvers said, "We're here to determine if there's a connection between the murder of Mitsuo Arashi and"—she glanced down at her notebook—"Dr. Michael Cochrane."

She looked up at Cochrane. "Your brother?"

He nodded.

"What can you tell us about Mr. Arashi?" Danvers asked.

"Not much. I didn't really know him."

"We have information that says otherwise."

"Information? From who?"

"You had dinner two nights ago with him and a third person, a woman."

McLain jumped in. "Was that the same woman you were with when you talked to Dr. Tulius at the Calvin labs?"

Cochrane started to answer, then hesitated.

"You're not under arrest, Dr. Cochrane," said Danvers gently. "We would appreciate any help you can give us."

"I only met Arashi a few nights ago," he said. "I had dinner with him."

"We already know that," McLain said.

"And that's it." Cochrane spread his hands, palms up. "That's all I know about him. He was interested in the research my brother was doing. He asked me what I knew about it and I told him I didn't know a damned thing. Which is the truth."

"Is it?" McLain snapped.

"Dr. Cochrane," Danvers asked more reasonably, "do you think there's a connection between your brother's murder and Mr. Arashi's?"

"They were both beaten to death," McLain said.

The picture of Mike's battered face flashed into Cochrane's mind again. He shook his head. "I don't know if there's a connection," he said to Danvers.

"But you said Mr. Arashi asked you about your brother's work."

"Yes, that's right."

McLain said, "So the chances are that whoever killed your brother offed Arashi, too."

"I suppose so."

Danvers glanced down at her notebook again. "Now, about this woman who was with you and Mr. Arashi—"

"I'm sorry," said Cochrane, "but I don't want to talk about her."

"Why not?"

"It's personal."

"But you can tell us her name, at least."

"I'd rather not," Cochrane said, wondering as he spoke why he was protecting Sandoval. Because she slept with me? That meant as much to her as brushing her teeth, he thought. Still, he balked at bringing her name into the police investigation.

"We could place you under arrest," McLain threatened.

"Then I'd have to get myself a lawyer," Cochrane countered.

Danvers sighed. "Dr. Cochrane, we don't want this to get messy. But there have been two murders and they appear to be connected. We need your help."

"I've told you what I know."

"Not the name of the woman involved in this," said McLain.

Cochrane decided that if he wanted to keep Sandoval's name from them, he'd better stop talking to them altogether. He pushed his plastic chair away from the table; it made a nerve-grating screech on the tile floor.

"I want to leave now," he said, getting to his feet.

Danvers looked disappointed. "Dr. Cochrane, do you think you're following the wisest course of action here?"

"They've already killed two men." McLain practically snarled from the TV screen. "You might be next."

Cochrane slowly shook his head. "I doubt it. I don't know anything that they'd be interested in—whoever they are."

"Maybe they think otherwise."

He could feel Danvers's eyes on him as he went to the door and opened it, thinking, If she's going to arrest me, she'll do it now. But Danvers said nothing and Cochrane walked through the subdued intensity of the squad room and out into the hot, glaring sunlight.

It wasn't until then that he realized he didn't have his car here. The police had driven him to the headquarters building. Squinting in the heat, he saw a pair of taxicabs parked at the corner. He thought for a moment about going back inside and demanding that Danvers provide him transportation back to his apartment. But only for a moment. Fuck that, he told himself. Take a taxi.

During the ride across town he sat in the back of the poorly air-conditioned taxi, wondering why he refused to name Sandoval to the police. They're trying to find out who murdered Mike, he said to himself. You ought to be helping them, not holding back information.

But there's something going on here, he argued within his mind, something deeper than finding out who killed Mike. Or Arashi, for that matter. *Why* were they killed? What was so important about Mike's work that it cost him his life? Sandoval knows. She knows a part of it, at least. And she can't tell me what she knows if she's locked up in jail.

The taxi pulled up in front of the Sunrise Apartments. Cochrane got out, paid the driver, and gave him a small tip, then limped through the broiling sun to the building's lobby.

It was blessedly cool inside the lobby. As he headed for the elevators, Cochrane saw out of the corner of his eye that several magazines and journals lay strewn haphazardly on the shelf by the mailboxes. Christ, I haven't even looked at my mail in almost a week.

Sure enough, the journals were for him. They shouldn't be out here, where anybody could pick them up, he thought irritably. Then he almost laughed at himself. Who the hell in this building would pick up the latest *Astrophysical Journal?* Well, you never know, he thought; I might have an astronomy student for a neighbor. He fished his mailbox key from the pocket of his jeans and opened his mailbox. Sure enough, it was stuffed full.

Cochrane tugged the bent and folded mail out of the little box, went to the wastebasket at the end of the row, and started discarding the junk mail. Credit card offers. Discounts from local retailers. Catalogs.

And a letter bearing the return address of the Calvin Research Center, with a scrawled *MSC* beneath. Mike's initials.

TUCSON:
SUNRISE APARTMENTS

Cochrane dropped his other mail on the table by his front door, neither noticing nor caring that most of it slid to the floor. He nudged the door shut with his foot, then tore open Mike's letter. It had been typed on a computer: Mike's laptop, Cochrane thought.

> PAUL: I'm playing with the big guys now. And I've had it with Irene. So I'm going away for a while. Please take care of the papers in my safe-deposit box. They're worth a lot. MIKE.

A small flat key was Scotch-taped to the bottom of the letter. He didn't even sign it, Cochrane realized. And he didn't tell me where his goddamned safe-deposit box is!

He went to his desk and phoned Irene. No answer, just that damned voice-mail message of hers. He booted up his computer and started looking

up the locations of banks near Mike's home and near the Calvin lab. Six of
them. He started phoning.

"Hello, I'm trying to determine if my brother kept a safe-deposit box
in your bank."

"I'm sorry, sir, we can't divulge that information on the phone."

"Look, I'm in Tucson. My brother died last week and he left me the
key to a safe-deposit box but he forgot to tell me which bank it's from."

"That's very unusual, sir."

"His name is . . . was Michael Cochrane."

"We can't confirm—"

"Can you at least tell me if Michael Cochrane was a customer of
yours? Did he have an account with you? Please, it's important."

"Just a moment, sir. I'll connect you with the bank manager."

And Cochrane repeated the same routine with the bank manager. Six
times, each with a different bank. The best he could get was:

"We have no accounts with a Michael Cochrane."

"None? No checking account? Nothing?"

"Nothing."

"How about his widow, Irene Cochrane?"

"Sir, the information you're asking for is private. We can't divulge
such information over the telephone."

"I see. I understand. Thank you."

Cochrane thought about phoning Purvis and asking him to find out
which bank Mike used. Not McLain. He realized the two detectives were
using a good-cop, bad-cop routine on him, but he still didn't like McLain.
He found the card Purvis had given him, picked up the phone again, and
hesitated.

Do I want to tell the police about this? They'll be all over me, worse
than ever. Can't I find which bank Mike used by myself?

He put the phone down, leaned back in his desk chair, and tried to
think. Okay, all those banks claim Mike didn't have an account with
them. No reason to think they're lying. It's one thing to say they won't tell
me, but if they say Mike wasn't a customer of theirs, I guess they're
telling the truth.

Cochrane closed his eyes, tried to picture his brother alive, that wise-
ass grin of his. If Mike wanted to hide his papers, Cochrane told himself,
he wouldn't have gone to a bank in his own neighborhood. Great. That
leaves about six zillion other banks in the region.

Why didn't he tell me which bank the damned key is from? And the
answer rose in Cochrane's mind: Because he thought I'm smart enough to

figure it out for myself. Another one of his little practical jokes. *Here you are, Paulie. You're so frigging smart, find the answer to this one.*

Not a bank in his neighborhood, Cochrane mused to himself. Then where?

Trip reports! Buried in Tulius's files were reports that Mike sent to his boss after every trip he took for the company.

He inserted the first of the CDs that Arashi had given him and started searching for Mike's trip reports. The sun was setting when he finally pushed himself from the desk, bleary-eyed, and shambled to the refrigerator for a glass of fruit juice. Mike had traveled a lot: scientific conferences, consulting meetings, visits to other laboratories around the nation. Sipping at the grapefruit juice he'd poured for himself, Cochrane went back to the computer and listed Mike's trips in chronological order.

Almost all Mike's trips had been to different places: Denver, New Haven, Ann Arbor, Albuquerque, he'd even visited Tucson three months earlier. *And he never told me. Never looked me up or let me know he was in town,* Cochrane grumbled to himself.

There were only two destinations that Mike had visited more than once: NASA's Johnson Space Center near Houston three times, and MIT in Massachusetts six times. Cochrane remembered that Mike was working under a contract from NASA Ames; he must have gone there plenty of times. But Ames was only a short drive from the Calvin Center; traveling there wouldn't be considered a trip, necessitating a report that detailed expenses and told what results had been accomplished.

Maybe I should find out who he was working with at Ames, Cochrane said to himself. Then he realized that the police would already have covered that base. McLain and Purvis must have been there.

MIT. Near Boston, where we grew up. A rush of memories flooded through Cochrane's mind. *Massachusetts. Playing in the snowbanks after a blizzard. Sailing Sunfishes on the pond down at the end of our street. The leaves in autumn. Going down to Fenway to see the Red Sox.*

His door buzzer jarred Cochrane out of his reverie. With something of a jolt he saw that it was fully night. And his stomach was growling with hunger. He hadn't eaten since breakfast with Sandoval.

The thought of her soured him. *She's in Palo Alto, probably climbing into bed with Tulius right about now.* Cochrane remembered the way Tulius had looked at her, his smiling comment about his two vices.

The buzzer sounded again. *Probably the cops,* Cochrane thought. *Or some pizza delivery kid who's got the apartment number wrong.* Reluctantly he went to the intercom by his front door.

"Yes?"

"Paul, it's me."

Sandoval's voice!

"Where are you?" he asked, and immediately realized it was a stupid question.

"Down here in the lobby. Would you let me in?"

"Sure!" He leaned on the button that unlocked the building's entrance door, then rushed out into the corridor toward the elevators, impatient as a kid at Christmas.

The elevator pinged, the doors slid open, and there she stood, wearing the same sleeveless frock she'd worn when he'd driven her to the airport.

For an instant he didn't know what to say, what to do. And then she was in his arms and he was kissing her and holding her body pressed tightly against his own. A door opened down the hallway and an elderly woman walked hesitantly toward them, smiled as she pressed the elevator button. Cochrane took Sandoval's shoulder bag and walked her back to his apartment, his arm around her slender waist.

As soon as he shut the front door he kissed her again, longer, deeper.

"I thought—" he started to say.

"I know," she said, her green eyes locked on his. "I couldn't do it, Paul. I just couldn't. I had to come back to you."

He was breathless with the wonder of it.

"Tulius was very slick," she said, taking her bag back from him. "He told me a little about your brother's work, but it didn't amount to much. He hinted pretty strongly that he knew more, but it was tied up in the company's proprietary rights and he couldn't talk about it. Then he invited me to dinner. He knew what I was after, and I knew what he was after. It might have worked out. But I left him at his office and took the next plane back here."

"To me."

"To you."

Cochrane felt like baying at the moon.

TUCSON:
SUNRISE APARTMENTS

In the morning Cochrane told Sandoval about Mike's note and the key to the safe-deposit box.

"But he didn't say which bank it's from?" she asked, sitting across the kitchen's tiny fold-down table from him.

Cochrane spooned up a mound of bran flakes, dripping milk. With a shake of his head, "That's just like Mike. Typical."

"He forgot to tell you."

"Either that or he's playing head games with me. I can just hear him: *You're so smart, Paulie, let's see you figure this one out.*"

Sandoval looked thoughtful. "Or maybe he thinks you already know."

"How the hell should I know? There must be a thousand banks within a five-minute drive of his house."

"His wife?"

Cochrane shook his head even harder. "He didn't want Irene to know

about it. He was going to leave her. Whatever's in the bank box was supposed to be his insurance, his stash."

"But you don't know which bank it could be in." She looks disappointed, Cochrane thought. Disappointed in me.

"I even went through his trip reports, to see where he'd been traveling. Figured he might have opened an account in one of those cities."

"And?"

"Nothing popped out at me. He didn't seem to go to any particular
city on a regular basis, except maybe Cambridge, MIT."

"Massachusetts," she said, lifting a white Steward Observatory mug to
her lips. She had brewed tea for herself; Cochrane was drinking coffee out
of a maroon and gold Boston College mug.

"Massachusetts," he confirmed. "Land of the bean and the cod. Where
Mike and I were born and grew...." Cochrane's voice faded into thoughtful silence.

"What is it?" Sandoval asked.

Slamming his mug down on the flimsy table hard enough to slosh coffee out of it, Cochrane said, "I bet I know which bank he used! I'm sure of
it!"

By midafternoon they were on a Delta jetliner, heading for Boston's
Logan Airport.

Lionel Gould interrupted a meeting with a group of bankers from
Lebanon to take Kensington's call. He excused himself from the conference room and went to his office next door. Sitting heavily in his high-
backed swivel chair, he fiddled with the keyboard on his desk until
Kensington's dark-jowled face appeared on the plasma screen mounted on
the walnut wall paneling.

"Boston, you say?" Gould said, making no effort to hide his surprise.

"Two tickets to Boston. First class," said Kensington, nodding tightly.

"Boston," Gould mused.

A grudging smile crept across Kensington's face. "That Sandoval is
something else. She got Delta to bump two confirmed first-class fares back
to coach."

Gould rubbed a stubby-fingered hand across his fleshy chin. "She can
be very persuasive, true enough."

"So you want me to go to Boston, track 'em?"

"I suppose so," Gould said uncertainly. "How quickly can you get
there?"

"Can I use the Citation? I could land at Logan before their flight comes in."

"Very well," said Gould. "I'll phone the airport."

It was sunset by the time their flight landed at Logan Airport. Sandoval rented a Subaru Outback Sport wagon, a glittering metallic aqua blue, the only car available at Dollar Rent A Car.

"Couldn't you at least get a different color?" Cochrane complained as he slid in behind the wheel. "This thing looks like it ought to be at a baby shower."

"Beggars can't be choosers," Sandoval replied. "I got a good rate for this. And it's got four-wheel drive."

"Just what we need for driving in Boston," Cochrane muttered as he put the car in gear. But he smiled at her as he said it.

He didn't go into Boston proper, of course. Cochrane remembered the route over the Tobin Bridge (which he still remembered from childhood as the Mystic River Bridge) and out the back way through Chelsea and Everett to Route 60 and finally Arlington, where he'd grown up. But it was all changed. In the gathering darkness he hardly recognized any of the old familiar landmarks, and the bridge was clogged with trucks and semis, all bleating their horns as they snarled through the unforgiving traffic.

Then it started to rain.

Cochrane was sweating by the time they reached the familiar intersection of Massachusetts Avenue and Pleasant Street. Squinting through the sloshing windshield wipers, he saw the bank, just as he remembered it from the days when his family lived a few blocks away, down Pleasant Street. But the sign on its front said Cambridge Savings Bank. Cochrane remembered it as something else, Shawmut maybe. It was a long time ago, he told himself. You've been over at Amherst for years. A lot has changed in the old neighborhood. Little local banks get bought out by the big guys.

"There it is," he said as they waited for the Mass Av traffic light to change. "That's where Mike and I started our first savings accounts, when we were kids."

"It's closed," said Sandoval.

"Well, yeah, this time of the evening."

The light turned green and he nosed the car across the avenue, down Pleasant Street, past Lakeview and the house he'd grown up in. He felt a brief tug of curiosity, or maybe nostalgia for his childhood. It was never that wonderful, he told himself. It's nothing to feel sappy over. He drove past the street without slowing down.

While he turned onto Route 2 and headed toward Cambridge, Sandoval phoned for a hotel room.

"Is the Radisson decent?" she asked, one hand covering the phone.

"Used to be," said Cochrane. "It's right on the Charles River. Nice view."

It was too dark and rainy a night to enjoy the view. Cochrane closed the heavy drapes across their window and climbed into bed beside Sandoval. She turned out the light.

"Tell me something," he said in the darkness.

"What?"

"Where do you get the money for all this—airlines, hotels, car rentals?"

She was silent for a moment. "You don't really want to know."

"Yes, I do," he said earnestly, turning toward her. "I have to know if we're going to have any kind of a future together."

Again she hesitated. At last, "I found out in high school that I could get boys to jump through hoops if I wanted them to. But I was more interested in getting someplace, learning, making something of myself. I didn't want to end up a druggie, or a whore."

"Where'd you grow up?"

"Right here in Boston. Not the best part of town, though. Brighton."

"Brighton?"

She pulled in a sighing breath. "Crappy old Brighton. I got a scholarship. I was going to be an anthropologist. The new Margaret Mead."

"Really?"

"Except I got married and quit school. Then the bastard dumped me for a bigger bustline."

"You've got a terrific bustline."

"He didn't think so. Or maybe he was intimidated because I was brighter than he was. Anyway, there I was, broke and alone in goddamned Denver, Colorado."

"Denver?"

"He was a petroleum geologist."

"Oh."

"And... well, one thing led to another and I wound up doing industrial espionage. I found out that I was good at it."

Cochrane thought she had jumped across a lot of territory. Just as well, he told himself. I don't need to know all the shitty details.

He turned over onto his back and tried to fall asleep. But all the shitty details filled his mind with images he wished he could erase.

Is It Time to Shoot for the Sun?

Ask most Americans about their energy concerns, and you're likely to get an earful about gasoline prices. Ask Nate Lewis, and you'll hear about terawatts. Lewis, a chemist at the California Institute of Technology, is on a mission to get policy makers to face the need for sources of clean energy. He points out that humans today collectively consume the equivalent of a steady 13 terawatts (TW)—that's 13 trillion watts—of power. Eighty-five percent of that comes from fossil fuels that belch carbon dioxide, the primary greenhouse gas, into the atmosphere. Now, with CO_2 levels at their highest point in 125,000 years, our planet is in the middle of a global experiment.

To slow the buildup of those gases, people will have to replace most, if not all, of those 13 TW with carbon-free energy sources. And that's the easy part. Thanks to global population growth and economic development, most energy experts predict we will need somewhere around an additional 30 TW by 2050. Coming up with that power in a way that doesn't trigger catastrophic changes in earth's climate, Lewis says, "is unarguably the greatest technological challenge this country will face in the next fifty years."

Clearly, there are no easy answers. But one question Lewis and plenty of other high-profile scientists are asking is whether it's time to launch a major research initiative on solar energy. In April, Lewis and physicist George Crabtree of Argonne National Laboratory in Illinois cochaired a U.S. Department of Energy (DOE) workshop designed to explore the emerging potential for basic research in solar energy, from novel photovoltaics to systems for using sunlight to generate chemical fuels. Last week, the pair released their report.

The report outlines research priorities for improving solar power. It doesn't say how much money is needed to reach those goals, but DOE officials have floated funding numbers of about $50 million a year. That's up from the $10 million to $15 million a year now being spent on basic solar energy research. But given the scale of the challenge in transforming the energy landscape, other researchers and politicians are calling for more money.

It's too early to say whether the money or the political support will fall in line. But it is clear that support for a renewed push for solar energy research is building among scientists. Last month, Lewis previewed his upcoming report for members of DOE's Basic Energy Sciences Advisory Committee (BESAC). Despite a painfully lean budget outlook at DOE, support for a solar research program "is nearly unanimous," says Samuel Stupp, BESAC member and chemist at Northwestern University in Evanston, Illinois.

Why? Terawatts. Even if a cheap, abundant, carbon-free energy source were to appear overnight, Lewis and others point out, it would still be a Herculean task to install the new systems fast enough just to keep up with rising energy demand—let alone to replace oil, natural gas and coal. Generating 10 TW of energy—about one-third of the projected new demand by 2050—would require 10,000 nuclear power plants, each capable of churning out a gigawatt of power, enough to light a small city. "That means opening one nuclear reactor every other day for the next fifty years," Lewis says. Mind you, there hasn't been a new nuclear plant built in the United States since 1973, and concerns about high up-front capital costs, waste disposal, corporate liability, nuclear proliferation and terrorism make it unlikely that will change in any meaningful way soon.

So what is the world to do? Right now the solution

is clear. The United States is currently opening natural gas plants at the rate of one every 3.5 days. A stroll through Beijing makes it clear that China is pursuing coal just as fast. Fossil fuel use shows no signs of slowing.

Hand-wringing geologists have been warning for years that worldwide oil production is likely to peak sometime between now and 2040, driving oil prices through the roof. The critical issue for climate, however, is not when production of fossil fuel peaks, but its global capacity. At the 1998 level of energy use, there is still at least an estimated half century's worth of oil available, two centuries of natural gas, and a whopping two millennia worth of coal. The upshot is that we will run into serious climate problems long before we run out of fossil fuels.

What's left? Solar. Photovoltaic panels currently turn sunlight into three gigawatts of electricity. The business is growing at 40 percent a year and is already a $7.5 billion industry. But impressive as that is, that's still a drop in the bucket of humanity's total energy use. "You have to use a logarithmic scale to see it" graphed next to fossil fuels, Lewis says.

What solar does have going for it is, well, the sun. Our star puts out 3.8×10^{23} kilowatt-hours of energy every hour. Of that, 170,000 TW strike earth every moment, nearly one-third of which are reflected back into space. The bottom line is that every hour, earth's surface receives more energy from the sun than humans use in a year.

Collecting even a tiny fraction of that energy won't be easy. To harvest 20 TW with solar panels that are 10 percent efficient at turning sunlight into electricity—a number well within the range of current technology—would require covering about 0.16% of earth's land surface with solar panels. Covering all 70 million detached homes in the U.S. with solar panels would produce only 0.25 TW of electricity, just one-tenth of the electricity consumed in the country in the year 2000. This means land will need to be dedicated for solar farms, setting up land use battles that will likely raise environmental concerns, such as destroying habitat for species where the farms are sited.

Solar energy advocates acknowledge that a global

solar energy grid would face plenty of other challenges as well. Chief among them: transporting and storing the energy. If massive solar farms are plunked down in the middle of deserts and other sparsely populated areas, governments will have to build an electrical infrastructure to transport the power to urban centers. This is certainly doable, but expensive.

A tougher knot is storing energy from the sun. Because electricity cannot be stored directly, it must be converted into some other form of potential energy for storage, such as the electrochemical energy of a battery, or the kinetic energy of a flywheel. The massive scale of global electric use makes both of these forms of energy storage very unlikely. Another possibility is using electricity to pump water uphill to reservoirs, where it can later be released to regenerate electricity. Electricity can also be used to generate hydrogen gas or other chemical fuels, which can then be delivered via pipelines to where they are needed or used directly as transportation fuels. But that, too, requires building a new expensive infrastructure that isn't incorporated in solar energy's already high cost.

If all this has a familiar ring to it, that's because many of the same arguments have been used before. In the wake of the oil shocks of the 1970s, the Carter Administration directed billions of dollars to alternative energy research. The big differences now are the threat of climate change and the current huge budget deficits of the U.S. Some of the cost numbers have changed, but the gap between solar energy's potential and what is needed for it to be practical on a massive scale remains wide. The April DOE meeting explored many ideas to bridge that gap, including creating plastic solar cells and making use of advances in nanotechnology.

But Richard Smalley, a chemist at Rice University in Houston, Texas, who advocates renewed support for alternative-energy research, notes that unless research progresses far more rapidly to solve the current energy conundrum by 2020, there is essentially no way to have large amounts of clean energy technology in place by 2050. "That means the basic enabling breakthroughs have to be made now," Smalley says.

Of course, a major sticking point is money. At the

April meeting, DOE officials started talking about funding a new solar energy research initiative at about $50 million per year, according to Mary Gress, who manages DOE's photochemistry and radiation research. Lewis is reluctant to say how much money is needed, but asks rhetorically whether $50 million a year is enough to transform the biggest industry in the world. Clearly, others don't think so. "I don't see an answer that will change it short of an Apollo-level program," Smalley says.

With Congress close to passing an energy bill that focuses on tax breaks for oil exploration and hybrid cars, it doesn't look as if a big push on solar energy will be one of those "new things" anytime soon.

At least compared with DOE's earlier push for progress in hydrogen technology, many researchers expect that a push on solar energy research will be a far easier sell. "With hydrogen it was a lot more controversial," Stupp says. "There are scientific issues that are really serious [in getting hydrogen technology to work]. With solar, it's an idea that makes sense in a practical way and is a great source of discovery." If that research and discovery doesn't happen, Lewis says he's worried about what the alternative will bring. "Is this something at which we can afford to fail?"

—Robert F. Service
Science
July 22, 2005

ARLINGTON: CAMBRIDGE SAVINGS BANK

Harold Wilcox looked exactly the way Cochrane expected a bank manager to look: gray-haired, gray-suited, a little overweight, plastic-rimmed eyeglasses, a strained smile on his doughy-white face.

"This is a little unusual," Wilcox said, looking at the key Cochrane had laid on his desk. "The box is registered in *Michael* Cochrane's name."

"Mike died last week," Cochrane said evenly. "I'm his brother."

"Do you have a death certificate or any other evidence of Mr. Cochrane's demise?"

"No, I'm afraid I don't."

"A power of attorney? A last will and testament?"

"No, nothing like that."

Wilcox looked pained. "I'm sorry, but without proper documentation—"

"But Mike gave me the key."

"Yes, I can see."

Sandoval spoke up. "Perhaps Mr. Cochrane put his brother's name on the list of those approved to open the box."

Wilcox focused his gaze on her. Sandoval was wearing a pastel green pantsuit over a pale yellow blouse. He smiled at her.

"Let me check." The bank manager turned to his desktop computer screen and flicked his fingers across the keyboard. He squinted, leaned toward the screen, jabbed at the keys again.

"Why, yes," he said, smiling at Sandoval. "There is a Paul Cochrane on the approved list. No one else, though."

"I'm Paul Cochrane."

Wilcox asked for identification. Cochrane pulled out his wallet and showed his Arizona driver's license, his university ID, and a Costco credit card, all bearing his photo.

The banker peered at the cards, then nodded, satisfied. "You understand the reason to be cautious about these things," he said apologetically. "It's for your own protection."

"Yeah, sure," said Cochrane.

Wilcox led Cochrane and Sandoval out of his office in the nearly empty bank, past an open massive steel vault hatch, and into a metal-walled chamber lined with rows of safe-deposit boxes. Using the key that Cochrane had given him, plus a second he had attached to a keychain from his pocket, the bank manager opened one of the little oblong doors and slid out a long metal box.

"You can open the box in the privacy of one of our booths," he said as he handed the box to Cochrane. It felt lighter than Cochrane had expected it to be.

The booth was tiny and felt crowded with Sandoval in with him. Wilcox closed the slatted door so quietly that Cochrane tried the knob to make certain it was shut. There was only one chair, and Sandoval sat in it. But she looked up at Cochrane expectantly, waiting for him to open the box.

He lifted the hinged lid and swung it back. Inside the steel box were a half dozen CDs.

"Probably like the ones Arashi hacked out of Tulius's files," said Cochrane.

"But there are twice as many," Sandoval replied.

"These must be Mike's files."

"Copies of what was missing in his laptop."

Cochrane started to stuff the slim jewel cases into his jacket pockets. "Let's get back to Tucson, where I can dig into these."

"We could rent a computer here," she suggested.

Cochrane shook his head as he closed the safe-deposit box. "No. My own machine is better. I know what's in it, how to run it. No learning curve."

She was silent as he carried the box back to Wilcox, in his office, and put it down on his desk. Cochrane thanked the bank manager and they left.

It was a sunny morning, cool, with an east wind blowing soft white cumulus clouds across a deeply blue sky. Cochrane took a deep, invigorating breath of Massachusetts air and started for their wagon, in the parking lot behind the bank.

But Sandoval grabbed for his arm. "Is there a post office near here?" she asked.

"Yeah, down on Mass Av."

"Let's mail the CDs to your apartment. I don't want to have them on us."

He looked at her sharply. "You worried about Kensington?"

"Or someone else. There could be other players involved in this."

"Involved in what? What's this all about, Elena?"

She gave him a little smile. "That's what we're trying to find out, isn't it?"

"Yeah, but—"

"If Gould is willing to toss out numbers like ten million, whatever this is all about must be worth an incredible fortune."

He stood there on the sidewalk in front of the bank, his mind trying to work it all out. She's right, he thought. She must be right.

"Okay," he said. "The post office is down this way."

They walked to the post office, where Cochrane mailed the CDs first class to his apartment in Tucson while Sandoval used her cell phone to make a flight reservation.

"The earliest I could get is tomorrow morning," she told him as they headed back for the bank.

"Then we've got all day with nothing to do."

Nodding, she said, "This is where you grew up, isn't it? Is your house near here?"

"Five minutes' walk."

"Let's go see it."

He hung back. "It's not much to see."

"But I'd like to see it. Can't we? Please?"

With a shrug, he headed for Pleasant Street again.

Lakeview was a narrow street that sloped down to Spy Pond. A pair of yellow-brick condominiums flanked the intersection with Pleasant Street. The old Cochrane residence was a Dutch Colonial on the other side of one of the condo parking lots.

"Used to be a big old maple tree here," Cochrane said, pointing to the wire mesh fence that bounded the parking lot.

The house hadn't changed much, he saw. Paint flaking off here and there. The roof looked like it needed patching. Just like the old days, he thought. Dad was always working on the house, trying to hold it together while Mom yapped at him about the leaking cellar and the browning lawn and the busted steps on the front porch.

"It's a beautiful location," Sandoval murmured as she looked over the house.

Pointing down toward where the street dead-ended on the water, Cochrane said, "I guess it is. Mike and I used to sail Sunfishes on the pond."

"Isn't that a big body of water to be called a pond?"

He laughed. "Around here, any body of water that doesn't have a stream feeding into it or coming out of it is called a pond. Doesn't matter how big it is."

"But it must be several miles across."

"Yep, it is. They found tusks from an Ice Age mammoth buried on the shoreline. Dad used to tell us stories about mammoths marching down the street for a drink of water."

"You must have had a lovely childhood."

"Not really. My parents fought a lot. Or rather, my mother yelled at my dad and he ignored her. The other kids on the street were okay, I guess." He started laughing, remembering.

"What is it?" Sandoval asked.

Walking slowly down to the end of the street, by the shore of Spy Pond, Cochrane recalled, "One day a Japanese family that lived in the condos across the street left and went back to Japan. They left a ten-year supply of condoms in the trash at the curb."

Sandoval smiled appreciatively.

"Mike and I didn't know what the damned things were. They looked like balloons to us."

"You went through their trash?"

"Oh, sure. Everybody did in those days. Nosy neighbors, kids, everybody poked through peoples' trash."

"And you found hundreds of balloons."

He laughed again. "We toted the boxes down to the pond and sailed the balloons across the water. A regular armada."

Sandoval laughed, too.

"The cranky old widow who lived in there"—he pointed to a study brick house at the water's edge—"got really sore at us. Phoned my mother and called us perverts. She whacked me with a wooden cooking spoon when I got home."

"Your brother, too?"

Cochrane's laughter faded. "Naw. I was the first one through the door, so she whacked me. Pretty damned hard, too. Mike was smart enough to wait until she got winded. He always got away with murder."

He could see from the sudden change of her expression that he'd picked the wrong word.

REVERE:
FOUR POINTS SHERATON HOTEL

Kensington was furious enough to break somebody's back.

He'd flown to Boston on Gould's executive jet and actually landed a good fifteen minutes *before* the Delta flight that Cochrane and Sandoval were on was scheduled to arrive. And the Delta flight was late, at that. But by the time the limo that Gould had laid on for him got him through the airport's weaving roads to the Delta terminal, the goddamned flight had landed, its passengers disembarked, and neither Cochrane nor that hot-looking Sandoval were anywhere in sight.

Using his private investigator's credentials and a good deal of physical intimidation, he'd finally found that they'd rented a goddamned Subaru wagon from Dollar. But where the hell they'd gone to from there was a complete blank.

Gould's people had reserved him a room at a Sheraton near the airport, but that turned out to be another fiasco. "Near the airport," according to Gould's travel office, turned out to be all the way the hell out in some town called Revere, miles of jampacked, confusing roads from Logan. It had taken Kensington almost an hour to find the goddamned dump, even with a GPS system in the car he had to rent.

He'd phoned Gould to report the bad news, got an assistant that he wouldn't talk to. His deal with Gould was that he worked for him and nobody else; he reported to Gould and nobody else. Gould wanted it that way.

So he stayed up half the night in this threadbare little hotel room waiting for Gould to phone him back. Nothing. He ordered a bottle of scotch from room service and was told that they served single drinks only.

"Okay, bring me six Johnnie blacks on the rocks."

When Gould finally phoned him, early the next morning, Kensington felt gummy-eyed and headachy. He was glad the hotel didn't have videophone service.

"It's not your fault," Gould said, once he'd heard the unhappy news. But his voice sounded less than pleased.

"You oughtta tell your travel people to try staying at some of the hotels they make me stay in," Kensington groused.

Gould ignored that. "Cochrane grew up in the Boston area, according to our information. Why would he go back there?"

"With Sandoval."

"You don't know which hotel they went to?"

"I got a friend in Washington could check her credit cards."

Gould said, "Useless. By the time you find which hotel they used, they'd be long gone."

Kensington thought it over for a few seconds. "Only thing to do is go back to Tucson and stake out Cochrane's place."

"Yes, I've come to the same conclusion. But you'll have to use a commercial airline, I'm afraid. I need the Citation today."

Kensington nodded, but he didn't like the idea.

AMERICA WEST FLIGHT 64: BOSTON TO TUCSON

Cochrane and Sandoval recognized Kensington as he came aboard the plane and made his way down the aisle with the other embarking passengers. The man was taller than everyone else, except for a pair of buzz-cut Marines in olive-green uniforms and a gangling black teenager wearing a Boston University varsity basketball T-shirt.

Sandoval, in the window seat, turned her head abruptly once she saw him. Cochrane looked down at his shoes.

"Do you think he saw us?" Sandoval whispered to him.

"Maybe."

They sat in tense apprehension as the passengers stuffed their carry-ons into the overhead bins and the flight attendants tried to get everyone seated and buckled up. The pilot came on the intercom with his usual chatter about the flight and then, at last, the plane backed away from the terminal.

One of the flight attendants came up and bent over the woman sitting in the aisle seat beside Cochrane. She grumbled a little, but got up and headed aft. Kensington sat down in her place, all smiles.

"Well, well, well," he said jovially. "Look who's here."

Sandoval half whispered, "How long have you been staking out the airport?"

Kensington chuckled, low and ominous. "No stakeout. Just dumb luck. It happens sometimes."

Seated between Kensington and Sandoval, Cochrane felt trapped and scared. But as the Boeing jet taxied to the end of the runway and took off, engines roaring, a different emotion began to take hold of him. Anger. This sonofabitch has been following us, he thought. He's working for Gould, trying to steal whatever we learn about Mike's work so that Gould won't have to pay us for the information. He's probably the guy who killed Mike in the first place.

Kensington seemed perfectly relaxed. He cranked his chair back as far as it would go, leaned his head against the headrest, and stuck his long legs out into the aisle. He closed his eyes. Sandoval, on Cochrane's other side, seemed to be trying to make herself as small and invisible as possible, like a rabbit facing a grinning wolf.

"I been thinking about that ten mil Gould offered you," Kensington said, without opening his eyes. Cochrane barely heard his low voice over the thunder of the plane's engines.

"You hear me?" he demanded, louder.

"I heard you," Cochrane said.

"Maybe I could get you more, from a different buyer."

Cochrane stared at the man, surprised. Kensington's eyes were open now, he was looking up at the plane's ceiling.

"Yeah, I'd cross Gould—for enough of a payoff."

Sandoval leaned across Cochrane slightly. "How much could you get for us?"

"More than ten," Kensington said, still staring at the ceiling. "Maybe a lot more."

"And how much would you want?"

"Half."

She shook her head. "A third. There's three of us."

Kensington turned his head to look at her. "You're counting *him* in?"

"He's part of this," she said.

Cochrane said, "Hey, I'm right here. And I'm in this as much as you are."

Kensington made a sour face. "Listen, geek boy, I can find a hundred guys to run a computer for me. You're dispensable."

"You think so?"

"I know so."

"Like my brother was dispensable?"

"I never saw your brother."

"Yeah, sure. But I wonder if the cops would believe you."

Kensington slowly lifted his head from the seat's back and pushed his face so close to Cochrane's that their noses almost touched. "You call the police, four eyes," he whispered venomously, "and it'll be that last phone call you ever make."

Before Cochrane could think of a reply, Sandoval reached out and placed a placating hand on Kensington's arm. "No one's going to call the police. There's too much at stake now."

"Damned right," Kensington muttered.

They flew the rest of the way in cold silence.

Kensington used the plane's in-flight telephone to reserve a rental car at the Tucson airport. Once there, he drove Cochran and Sandoval to Cochrane's apartment.

Wordlessly he went up in the elevator with them. As they stepped out into the third-floor hallway, Cochrane asked:

"Where are you staying tonight?"

"With you, pal. I'm not letting you out of my sight until you tell me what you were doing in Boston. We're going to be a cozy little family."

Cochrane unlocked his apartment door and the three of them entered his living room.

"You two can have the bedroom. I'll sleep on the couch," Kensington said.

"It pulls out," Cochran told him grudgingly.

"Big enough for two, huh?" Kensington grinned at Sandoval. "Maybe you'd rather sleep with me, Elena? Leave geek boy to get his beauty sleep by himself."

She didn't reply, simply turned sharply away from him and walked into the bedroom.

Cochrane followed her, seething inside. He can't be carrying a gun, he thought. They would have stopped him at the airport. He didn't check any baggage; he only had a carry-on and that went through the X-ray machine. So he's unarmed. He's a lot bigger than I am, but I can even the difference.

"What are you doing?" Sandoval asked as he opened the bedroom closet.

Cochrane didn't answer. He dragged out his bag of spare fencing equipment, unzipped it, and pulled out a saber. Its steel guard was dull with age, dented, but the blade was new and clean.

"Paul! Don't! You have no idea—"

But Cochrane hefted the slim blade and went back to the bedroom door. Kensington was in the kitchen, at the refrigerator, bending down as he searched for something to eat.

"Get out of my home," Cochrane said, his voice trembling with rage.

Kensington straightened up and looked at the saber. "What the fuck's that, a toy sword?"

"Get out," Cochrane repeated. "Now."

"Hey, four eyes, you think that thing scares me? I'll stuff it up your ass."

"Try it and I'll take your eyes out," Cochrane said, moving another step into the living room. Out of the corner of his eye he saw Sandoval at the bedroom door, wide-eyed with fear.

Kensington slammed the refrigerator door shut and scowled at Cochrane.

"So you're gonna be a big hero for her, huh? Dumb schmuck." He pulled a thick-bladed carving knife from the butcher's block stand next to the stove.

"Now, this knife really cuts, doesn't it, geek boy?" Kensington crouched slightly as he came around the kitchen counter and into the living room to face Cochrane.

Cochrane stood his ground as Kensington approached him, grinning toothily, waving the knife back and forth.

"I'll give you a chance to drop that toy sword of yours," Kensington said. "If you don't, I'm gonna carve your balls off."

"Try it," Cochrane muttered, dropping into an en garde crouch.

"Your funeral, geek."

Kensington stepped toward Cochrane, feinted once, then lunged with the knife, point first. Cochrane twitched at the feint, recovered fast enough to jump back out of Kensington's reach. The coffee table's behind me, Cochrane realized. He edged sideways until he could see it in his peripheral vision.

Kensington lunged again, faster. This time Cochrane parried the thrust, then snapped a flashing riposte to Kensington's wrist. Kensington yelped with sudden pain and lurched backward.

Cochrane advanced on him, smacked the knife blade sharply out of the way, and then slashed a backhand cut to Kensington's cheek. Blood spurted.

"It's not sharp," Cochrane said, holding the blunted point of his saber before Kensington's eyes, "but it's as thin and flexible as a whip."

Kensington wiped sullenly at the blood trickling from his cheek. Then he made a sudden lunge toward Cochrane. With a blur of speed Cochrane slashed at the knife hand. Kensington howled with pain as the knife flew out of his hand and landed on the carpet at Sandoval's feet.

Slack-jawed, Kensington looked up at Cochrane with newfound respect in his eyes.

"Get out," Cochrane said. "That's all I want. Get out of my home and stay out."

"Okay," Kensington said, rubbing his hand. "Okay. You win."

He started for the door, but as Cochrane moved back away from him Kensington suddenly dove at his knees, knocking him over the coffee table. They thudded into the sofa, the air blasted out of Cochrane's lungs, the saber still clutched in his right hand but useless now as Kensington raised a fist the size of a basketball and slammed it into Cochrane's face. Cochrane's right arm was pinned to the sofa, his legs flailing helplessly as Kensington, grinning now like a demon, raised that big fist again.

And squealed in sudden pain, his body arching backward as Sandoval drove the heel of her shoe into his kidney again, then chopped viciously at the back of his neck. Kensington slumped to the floor. Cochrane pulled himself out from under him and got shakily to his feet.

"You…" He couldn't say more. He had to gulp for breath.

"He would've beaten you to death," Sandoval said, looking suddenly frail and frightened.

"Just like he beat Mike."

She nodded.

Kensington moaned and rolled over onto his back. Sandoval went to the bedroom door and picked up the carving knife. Cochrane pulled in a deep breath and realized he still gripped the saber in his right hand.

"What do we do with him?" he asked her.

She shook her head. "I'd say push him out the window, but you're only three floors up."

Cochrane stared at her. She was serious.

Kensington slowly sat up, looked up at Sandoval with the knife and Cochrane with the saber.

"Get out of here," Cochrane said. "That's all I want. Just go away and leave us alone."

Slowly Kensington raised himself to his feet, leaning heavily on the coffee table to do so. Without another word he stumbled to the front door and opened it.

"You haven't seen the last of me," he said, his voice wickedly low. Then he left and pulled the door shut behind him.

TUCSON:
SUNRISE APARTMENTS

"You were... fierce," Sandoval said, looking at Cochrane with new wonder in her eyes.

"You were damned good yourself. Where'd you learn that kung fu business?"

"A woman has to be able to protect herself," she replied. "But you! I never realized how strong you can be."

He rubbed his throbbing cheek. "Yeah, I almost got myself beaten to death."

She went to him and kissed his cheek tenderly. He winced, despite himself.

"No, Paul, you were great. Wonderful...." Her voice trailed off, and he saw tears in her eyes. She was trembling.

"Hey," he said, taking her in his arms. "It's all right. He's gone."

"Do you think he'll come back?" she asked, in a tiny, whispery voice.

As he went to the door and hooked the security chain in place, Cochrane replied, "I guess we shouldn't be here if he does."

"Where can we go?"

"As far from here as we can."

"Maybe…" She pulled away from him, sank down on the sofa. "Maybe that's what he's expecting. Maybe he's out there waiting for us."

Cochrane sat down beside her. "Do you have Gould's phone number?"

"He gave me his card," Sandoval said. "It's in my purse."

"Phone him. Tell him to call off his dog."

Sandoval seemed to think it over for a moment, then she nodded tightly and went back into the bedroom. She came out holding Gould's card in her hand, sat at Cochrane's desk, and picked up the telephone.

Cochrane went to the refrigerator and packed a half dozen ice cubes into a dish towel, then pressed it gently to his swelling cheek. It burned.

"Mr. Gould, please," Sandoval was saying into the telephone. "No, it's personal. Tell him Ms. Sandoval is calling, with important news."

Holding the makeshift ice pack to his face, Cochrane went to the desk and clicked the button that turned on the phone's speaker. Sandoval replaced the handset with a brief piercing screech of feedback.

"Mr. Gould will be with you in a moment," a man's voice scratched through the phone speaker.

"Thank you," Sandoval replied.

They waited. She looked up at him. He pressed the ice to his aching cheek, and noticed that his saber was lying on the floor between the coffee table and the sofa.

"Hello, Ms. Sandoval." Gould's growling voice sounded even raspier in the phone's speaker.

"Mr. Gould," she said.

"You have news for me. That is good."

"We've just had a brawl with your man Kensington," she said, her eyes on Cochrane. "We'd like you to tell him to leave us alone."

"Kensington? A brawl?" Gould sounded surprised.

"He made advances on me." Sandoval stretched the truth slightly. "Dr. Cochrane threw him out of his apartment."

"I'm stunned," said Gould. "Cochrane actually got the better of Kensington?"

"He did."

"And this is the news you're calling about?"

"You obviously know that we went to Boston, Dr. Cochrane and I."

"Yes. I told Kensington to keep an eye on you, not to engage in mayhem."

Cochrane jumped in. "We found my brother's computer files. If he set down the results of his work anywhere, it's on those discs."

"That is good," Gould said. "Very good indeed."

"Does your offer of ten million still hold?" Sandoval asked.

"Of course."

Cochrane said, "We should be able to tell you what my brother was working on within a few days."

"A few days? But you said—"

"A few days," Cochrane said firmly. "In the meantime, I don't want Kensington anywhere near us."

"I see."

"You can trust us," said Cochrane.

They heard Gould make a noise that sounded like a grunt. "I will have to trust you, obviously."

"We'll call you in a few days with the results of what we find."

"I shall await your call eagerly."

"By the way," Sandoval added, a hint of venom in her voice, "Kensington told us there are other prospective buyers for this information."

"He *what?*"

"We know that you're not the only possible market for our information," she went on. "And we thought you should know that Kensington might not be as reliable as you think."

"That is bad," Gould growled. "I'll have to speak to him."

"Do that," said Sandoval. And she pecked at the button that cut the phone link.

Cochrane looked at her. "You're going to get Kensington in deep shit with his boss."

"He deserves it," she said, with a malevolent smile.

For two days Cochrane pored over his brother's CDs. The first disc he examined was little more than a duplicate of what he had gleaned from Tulius's pirated files: cryptic results of experiments with the stromatolites, trip reports, expense vouchers.

The second disc, however, went into more detail about his experiments. Mike was measuring the oxygen output of different strains of the cyanobacteria he had cultured in his Archaean Gardens.

"For the life of me," he said to Sandoval over dinner, "I can't see anything that Mike was doing that's worth his getting killed over."

"It must be there," she said, sitting across the tiny kitchen table from him. "Gould doesn't make offers of ten million dollars on a whim."

He rubbed his bleary eyes. "If it's there, I haven't found it yet."

"You will, Paul. I know you will."

He shook his head, then picked at the frozen dinner she had pulled out and microwaved.

"Have a drink," Sandoval suggested. "Relax a little. Then we'll go to bed and get a good night's rest."

That brought out a grin. "When we get into bed together I don't feel like resting."

She smiled back at him. "Neither do I, if the truth be told."

It was after they'd made love and Cochrane lay sweaty and sticky with her body warm and musky beside him that he suddenly thought to ask, "What's this guy Gould do, anyway? Where's he get his money from?"

"He owns Gould Energy Corporation."

"Never heard of it," Cochrane said into the shadows of the darkened bedroom.

"It's a holding company. They own electric power utilities, oil refineries, some research facilities. I think he tried to buy Calvin Research Center last year."

Cochrane thought that over. Then, "Guess he found it cheaper to buy Mike."

"I suppose that's how he saw it."

"And now he wants to buy us."

"If you can deliver what he's looking for."

"We'll see." But as he lay there waiting to fall asleep, Cochrane started building a chain of logic: Elena told Gould that there are other buyers looking for Mike's results. If we don't deliver to Gould he might think we're dickering with the competition, looking for more money. He won't like that. He won't like that at all.

DALLAS: GOULD ENERGY CORPORATION HEADQUARTERS

Of all the gaudy office towers erected during the oil boom of the 1970s, the forty-five-story skyscraper that housed the headquarters of Gould Energy Corporation was among the more modest. No neon lights outlining its silhouette at night. No glittering metal spire at its top. A simple glass-and-steel structure from the outside, with the finest climate control and electronic security surveillance on the inside.

Lionel Gould's office was opulent without being extravagant. It was large, but furnished elegantly. Persian carpets on the floor and Renaissance masters on the walls. Gould sat behind his modernistic curving desk of teak and stainless steel, impatiently drumming his stubby fingers. He never enjoyed meetings with his chief financial officer. The woman was a climber, and she had climbed the slippery corporate ladder so high that her next move had to be against Gould himself. She was clearly unhappy about being summoned to the office on a Saturday morning, and even more clearly determined to show Gould that she had the determination to do whatever was necessary to further her career.

"If you wanted the results of Cochrane's research," she was saying in an *I told you so* manner, "you should have let us buy out the Calvin labs."

She was a youngish-looking fifty, thanks to exquisitely skillful cosmetic surgery. Her hair was a rich chestnut brown, her face sculpted beautifully without looking taut or waxy, her figure trim. She wore a dark business pantsuit, with a tailored white blouse under the severely cut jacket.

Gould looked at her with a jaundiced eye. "Tulius caught on to what we were seeking. He raised the price to the sky."

"Still, it might have been worth it."

"May I point out," Gould said, "that it was your own office's analysis that recommended against the buy?"

The CFO allowed a wintry smile to crook her thin lips. "Since when did you allow anybody's analysis to shape your judgment?"

He smiled back at her, with equal warmth. "I determined that it would be far cheaper to buy the man instead of the entire company."

"But he's dead now, and you have nothing."

Gould heaved a sigh. "I have my hopes. This thing is far too big to allow minor setbacks to stop us."

The CFO started to reply, hesitated, then finally asked, "Do you actually believe you can pull it off? Change the entire automotive industry—"

"Someone will," Gould said firmly. "It is inevitable. The world demand for oil is constantly increasing, the world supply of oil is constantly decreasing. Sooner or later the price will go so high that the market will collapse."

"But until that happens our profits will be astronomical."

Gould leaned back in his padded desk chair. "My dear lady, the reason I sit *here* and you sit *there* is that I can see beyond the p-and-l statement for the next quarter."

Her face flushed but she said nothing.

"I look further into the future than you—or any of the board members, for that matter. And what I see is a disaster of monumental proportions. Which is bad. Bad for us, bad for the industry, bad for the nation and the world."

"I've seen disaster scenarios, too," said the CFO.

"But you don't believe them."

"You do?"

"I certainly do. There is a point, up in the future somewhere, when there simply isn't enough oil left on earth to sustain the world's industrial needs. Not to mention the needs for transportation: automobiles, trucks, airliners."

The CFO shook her head. "That's so far in the future...."

"How far?" Gould snapped. "Twenty years? Ten? Five?"

She did not answer.

"We must be ready for that time. We must be!" He slammed the flat of his hand against his desktop. "And I'm thinking that the time will come sooner rather than later. The world is heading at breakneck speed toward a global disaster! *Why sit we here idle?*"

"You haven't been exactly idle," the CFO pointed out. "We've bought half a dozen nuclear power plants in the past two years, six overseas refineries, and if this deal with Chrysler-Daimler goes through—"

"Piffle!" Gould spat. "Fingers in the dike. We've got to develop a fuel to replace petroleum. The oil's running out, and if there's nothing to replace it, the world's economy will collapse."

"The government won't allow that to happen."

"The government!" Gould fairly shouted. "Don't look to those politicians in Washington for an answer. They're part of the problem!"

She was silent for several moments. At last she asked, "You really think it could happen in five or ten years?"

"An economic collapse that will make the Great Depression of the 1930s look like a church picnic. Factories shut down for lack of fuel. Cars without gasoline. The airlines, freight lines, trucks, ships—all stopped dead."

"My god," the CFO half whispered. "We've already gone to war over oil."

"More than once."

"But this..."

"War and terrorism and god knows what else. That's why we must act! Act now! Act decisively."

"You should have bought Calvin Research while you had the chance. It still may not be too late."

"No," Gould said firmly. "Tulius and his people don't have what we want. But I'm on the verge of getting it from another source. And when I do..." He smiled contentedly and laced his fingers across his vest.

"You'll save the world from this disaster," said the CFO, with un-feigned admiration in her voice, her expression.

"And make unholy profits for this corporation," added Gould. "Which is good. Which is very good indeed."

TUCSON:
SUNRISE APARTMENTS

Cochrane peered at the digital clock display on his desktop's screen: 11:42 A.M. Close enough for a lunch break, he said to himself. He got up from his chair and stretched his arms over his head; the ceiling was almost low enough for him to scrape his fingertips. His spine popped satisfactorily and he grunted with the effort.

"Anything?" Sandoval asked. She was sitting on the sofa dressed in denim shorts and a tan T-shirt, bare feet tucked under her, reading a novel from his bookshelf: *The Sun Also Rises*, he saw.

Heading for the kitchenette, Cochrane replied, "I can see what Mike was doing, but I still don't understand what makes it so goddamned important."

He opened the refrigerator, pulled out the drawer where he kept the lunchmeats. "There's nothing there that's worth ten million bucks."

She laid the opened book face down on the coffee table and stepped to the bar that separated the kitchenette from the living room. "There must be something, Paul," she said as she perched on one of the stools. "There's got to be."

Cochrane pulled dishes from the overhead cabinet, a loaf of sliced whole wheat bread from the breadbox. "How's the Hemingway?"

She hiked her eyebrows. "The novel? It's about a nymphomaniac and a man who was castrated in the war. Very romantic."

He couldn't decide if she was being sarcastic or not.

Halfway through their sandwiches and fruit juice Cochrane asked, "What do we do if I can't find anything?"

She chewed thoughtfully for a moment, then swallowed. "We'll have to tell Gould."

"He won't like that."

"Neither will I. No ten million."

"He might think we're holding out on him. Holding him up for more money or going to another bidder."

Sandoval's eyes shifted away from him for a moment, then back again. "Yes, he might at that."

"What then?"

She shrugged. "We disappear. One way or the other."

"Are there really other bidders?"

"Kensington thought so."

"Who could they be?"

She gave him a sad smile. "We won't know until we find out what they'd be bidding on."

Cochrane put down his half-eaten sandwich. "Okay. I'll get back to work."

"I'll do the dishes."

"Woman's work," he joked.

"Watch yourself."

Chuckling, he went back to his desk. Doggedly he plowed through Mike's notes: his experiment design, the different strains of cyanobacteria he was working with, the variables of water flow, temperature, hours of sunlight, nutrients in the water.

"Same old shit," Cochrane muttered under his breath. The BMAA stuff had been a sideline, a red herring, he knew now. Mike wasn't after a way to produce neurotoxin.

Then Mike's reports started dealing with something quite different. Gene splicing. Genetic engineering. Altering the genetic structure of several lines of cyanobacteria. Checking their output of oxygen against the changes made in their DNA.

Three hours later he pushed his wheeled chair back and got to his feet again.

Sandoval looked up from her book hopefully.

"It makes sense," Cochrane said, "but it doesn't make sense."

"You'll have to explain that," she said.

He came over to the sofa and sat beside her. "From what I can see, Mike was engineering some strains of cyanobacteria. Making deliberate changes in their DNA."

"What for?"

"That's what doesn't make sense," Cochrane said. "It looks like he was trying to see how he could make them put out more oxygen. At least, that's what he was measuring: oxygen output."

"Oxygen," she murmured.

"That isn't worth ten million dollars. You can buy all the oxygen you want from commercial producers like Linde."

"Why would he want to make oxygen more efficiently?" Sandoval wondered aloud.

Cochrane looked into her sea-green eyes: they were troubled, questioning, searching for an answer.

"Wait a minute," he said, unconsciously rubbing his chin. "Just because oxygen is what Mike was measuring doesn't mean that oxygen is what he was after."

"I don't follow you."

"He was measuring oxygen output, yes. But maybe he was looking for something else, and measuring the oxygen his bugs gave off was just the easiest way to see—"

His whole body stiffened. "Holy shit!"

"Paul, what is it?"

Cochrane grinned like the only kid in class who knew the answer. "How do those bacteria produce oxygen?"

"How should I know?"

"They split it out of the water molecules!" Cochrane was so excited he started bouncing up and down on the sofa. "Water is haitch-two-oh! Two hydrogen atoms for every oxygen atom!"

Sandoval was staring at him, her eyes wide now.

"Two hydrogens for every oxygen! Don't you get it? Don't you see?"

She shook her head.

"Mike was making the cyanobacteria produce hydrogen for him. Hydrogen! For fuel!"

"Hydrogen for fuel?" she echoed.

"Look," he said, grasping her arms intently. "Lots of people have been talking about using hydrogen to replace gasoline, diesel fuel, jet fuel for planes—"

"Fuel cells for cars," Sandoval interrupted. "Don't they use hydrogen in the fuel cells?"

"Right. And the waste product is water."

She nodded.

"You can use hydrogen in your car, just burn it instead of gasoline. What comes out the exhaust pipe is water vapor."

"No greenhouse gas," she said, starting to share his enthusiasm.

"No imported oil. No OPEC. No more crap from the Middle East."

"And your brother found out how to do this?"

Calming down a bit, Cochrane replied, "The big problem with hydrogen is producing the stuff."

"You get it from water, don't you? You just said so."

"Yeah, but the water molecule isn't easy to crack. Takes a lot of energy. In fact, it takes more energy to pry the damned water molecules apart than the hydrogen gives you back when you burn it as fuel."

Sandoval sank back into the sofa's cushions, looking disappointed.

"You can electrolyze water," Cochrane went on. "High school kids do it in chemistry class. But it takes too much energy to do it on a practical scale. You'd have to build hundreds of new power stations and run them day and night at top capacity to turn out enough hydrogen to replace all the gasoline we burn. The price would be too damned high."

Sandoval said nothing. She waited.

"But green plants break the water molecule all the time. Split it apart into hydrogen and oxygen, use the hydrogen and carbon from carbon dioxide in the air to make carbohydrates for themselves and release the oxygen into the air."

"And cyanobacteria?"

"They've been splitting water molecules for damned near four billion years." He snapped his fingers. "Just like that. No sweat."

"So what did your brother accomplish, then?"

Cochrane shook his head admiringly. "Mike tinkered with some strains of cyanobacteria to get them to split more water molecules than they need to live on. They release not only oxygen into the air, they release the excess hydrogen, too."

"They give off hydrogen?"

"They sure do. Mike turned those little blue-green bugs of his into tiny hydrogen factories. They make hydrogen just as naturally as God makes little green apples. They're going to make hydrogen fuels cheap enough to replace gasoline and all the other petroleum-based fuels we use! They're going to transform the world!"

"No wonder Gould is after it."

Cochrane leaned back on the sofa and grinned happily at the ceiling. "I'd say that's worth ten million bucks, wouldn't you?"

Hydrogen Fuel Storage for Automobiles

Modern gasoline-fueled automobiles can go approximately 300 miles on a tank of gasoline. While environmentalists have praised the idea of fueling autos with nonpolluting hydrogen, cramming enough hydrogen into a car's fuel tank to provide a 300-mile range before needing a fill-up is a daunting problem.

Despite all efforts to date, engineers have not yet come up with a way to get enough hydrogen—the lowest-density element of them all—into an automobile.

The most common method for storing hydrogen on board a car is to compress the hydrogen gas to as much as 10,000 pounds per square inch (psi) or cooling the stuff down to a cryogenic temperature of -252 degrees Celsius, at which point hydrogen turns from a gas into a liquid. Rocket boosters such as NASA's space shuttle burn liquefied hydrogen. But compression or cooling can only produce about half the density needed to stuff enough hydrogen into a normal automobile's fuel tank and produce a 300-mile cruising range.

More recently, research efforts under way at several automotive laboratories have turned to cryoadsorption and destabilized metal hydrides.

In the cryoadsorption technique, the hydrogen gas is first cooled to the temperature of liquid nitrogen (-196 degrees C) and then compressed to about 1,000 psi. Both these conditions can be achieved rather inexpensively. The cooled and squeezed gas can then be adsorbed by materials with high surface area, such as powdered carbon.

However, synthetic substances such as high-porosity polymers or organo-metallic hydrocarbons offer promise of adsorbing considerably more hydrogen, perhaps enough to provide a 300-mile driving range with an ordinary-sized fuel tank.

—*SCIENCE MONTHLY*

TUCSON:
ARIZONA INN

Let's celebrate," Sandoval said happily.

"We've got something to celebrate about," said Cochrane, "that's for sure."

She got up from the sofa and tugged at his hand to get him to his feet. "Pack a bag and we'll go to the inn. We can spend the rest of the week there, right through the weekend."

"The Arizona Inn?"

"You'll love it," she said, leading him to the bedroom. "I'll get us a beautiful suite."

Cochrane hesitated. Looking around his living room, he had to admit to himself that they'd been cooped up in this little cave for days now. A break would be great. And with ten million coming to them, he could afford a comfortable suite at the inn or anywhere else. But...

"Aren't you going to call Gould?" he asked.

"Yes, sure. I'll set up a meeting for early next week."

"Okay," he agreed. "I'll pack my toothbrush."

"Bring a swimsuit," she said as they entered the bedroom.

"I don't have one," he realized.

She laughed brightly. "We'll get one at the inn. Or go shopping some-where. There's plenty of malls in town."

Cochrane had never seen her so cheerful, so delighted. It was infec-tious. He started whistling happily as he pulled his battered travel bag from the closet and began tossing in socks and underwear.

"Don't forget your laptop," Sandoval said. Her capacious tote bag was on the bed and she was rummaging through the dresser drawer that she had appropriated for her underclothes.

Suddenly Cochrane stopped packing, lifted her bag off the bed, and let it drop to the floor. She gave him a puzzled look, then understanding lit her face and she melted into his arms.

"If we're going to celebrate," he murmured into her ear, "let's do it right."

The Arizona Inn was a walled-off oasis of beauty and ease set in the middle of a residential neighborhood only a few blocks from Cochrane's office on the University of Arizona campus.

It's another world here, he thought as he sat back in a wrought-iron chair on the patio outside the inn's lounge. The inner square of the hotel was blooming with colorful flowers, birds flitted among the tall palm trees, and stately, slender cypresses swayed in the warm breeze.

Sandoval seemed in her element, completely relaxed, smiling at him as they sat side by side and sipped at tall, cool glasses of Pernod and water. Sandoval had ordered the drink and Cochrane followed her lead. The pale pastel-green liquor tasted of licorice.

She was wearing a light sleeveless short-skirted dress of pale green, almost matching their drinks. Expensive-looking gold jewelry glittered with gemstones at her wrists, throat, and earlobes. Her contented smile tightened a bit as she asked softly, "You brought the discs, didn't you?"

He tapped the pocket of his short-sleeved shirt. "Right here, next to my heart."

She laughed. "We ought to make a copy of them and put them in a safe place, Paul."

"I already did," he replied. "Soon as I booted up the laptop when we got into our room."

"Good." She sipped at the Pernod. Then, "Are you sure the copy is safe?"

"Copies," he said. "I made three copies and sent them to three different places."

"Good," she repeated, although she seemed a little less certain than before.

"Did you talk to Gould?" he asked.

"I left a message for him. He's out of the country until Monday. We'll hear from him before then, trust me."

Noticing that Sandoval's purse, lying on the table, was hardly bigger than her hand, he asked, "Did you bring your cell phone with you?"

"It's back in the room, recharging."

Cochrane nodded and looked over the greenery and the low pink buildings of the inn. She's really relaxed if she didn't bring the phone with her. He felt totally content. The sky was a perfect cloudless blue, with a thin white contrail so high above that he could neither see nor hear the plane that was making it.

He pulled in a deep, satisfied breath. "You know, a guy could get accustomed to living like this."

Sandoval gave him her brightest smile.

The message light on their telephone was blinking when they returned to their spacious room.

"Gould," she said, going to the night table beside the king-sized bed.

Cochrane watched her face as she sat on the bed and listened to the message. She nodded as she put the phone down.

"He'll send his own plane to the airport here in Tucson Monday morning. He's invited us to have dinner with him that evening."

"Where?" Cochrane asked.

"New York. Manhattan."

"His own plane, huh? I've never flown in a private jet."

Sandoval pointed to the open laptop. "You're certain that you've got the copies in a safe place?"

"You don't trust Gould?"

"Why should I? Ten million is a lot of money, even for him. If he can get the information for free, why pay us?"

Why not kill us? Cochrane thought. Aloud he said, "I sent the data on the discs to three different friends of mine in zip files, with instructions not to unzip the files unless they find out I'm dead or disappeared."

"You trust them?"

He smiled at her. "We all went to high school together. We were pretty tight."

She nodded, seemingly satisfied. Cochrane waited for her to ask for more details, and found that he was glad when she didn't. Three high school buddies. He tried to picture their faces. Haven't seen them in years. But they're all I've got. If I can't trust them, I can't trust anybody.

MANHATTAN:
GOULD TOWER

Lionel Gould was in rare form as he sat at the head of the dining table in his penthouse atop the Gould Tower on Park Avenue West. Through the sweeping windows on one side of the spacious dining room, Cochrane could see the row of hotel and condominium towers across the open space of Central Park silhouetted against the purple glow of the twilight sky. Lights were beginning to twinkle in the windows like a galaxy of stars coming to life. Far, far below the noise and dirt and stress of everyday life on Manhattan's streets were nothing more than a faint background buzz.

Gould was playing host to Sandoval and Cochrane, telling ponderous jokes, graciously approving of the wines that his servants brought for him to taste, explaining the origins of the mussels and scallops of their first course, the baby lamb chops of the entrée.

"Irish lamb," he said grandly, tucking a starched white linen napkin under his chin. "The Irish don't do many things well, but lamb is their gift to the world."

Sandoval dabbed lightly at her lips. Seated across the table from Cochrane, she was wearing a glittering green sequined dress that she'd bought that afternoon in Saks Fifth Avenue. On Gould's credit. They were staying at a town house on Sixty-eighth Street that Gould owned; he had insisted on that.

She smiled at Gould and said, "I thought that the Irish have given the world most of the great poetry and prose of the English language: Shaw, Yeats, Wilde—all the great British writers are actually Irish, aren't they?"

"Shakespeare?" Gould countered, his face alight with the joy of intelligent conversation with a beautiful woman. "Churchill?"

"Christopher Marlowe," Cochrane heard himself say, surprised that he remembered anything from his English Lit classes. "If he hadn't died so young—"

"You can't count Churchill," Sandoval said, still looking at Gould. "He was a politician."

"And a journalist," Gould countered. "As well as a historian."

"Like Theodore Roosevelt," she said, dipping her fork into the vegetable ratatouille on her dish alongside the lamb.

That started them onto a discussion of American presidents. To Cochrane's surprise, Gould favored liberals such as Wilson, Franklin Roosevelt and Kennedy. Sandoval was harder to read; she kept her approvals to old-timers such as Lincoln and Jefferson.

"Chester Arthur," Gould said, his voice booming with enthusiasm.

"A nonentity," said Sandoval.

"Yes, a political hack. Became president by the accident of Garfield's assassination. But once in the White House he pushed through the civil service reform. Ended the spoils system for federal jobs. Which was good."

"And ended his own political career," Sandoval pointed out.

They were still at it as dessert was served: a delicate sorbet with fresh tropical fruits.

"Can I ask a question?" Cochrane butted in.

They both turned toward him.

"Now that you know what my brother accomplished, where do we go from here?"

Still beaming cheerfully, Gould pulled the napkin from his open shirt collar. "You go anywhere you please. Ten million dollars gives you plenty of options."

"I mean, about the hydrogen process Mike invented."

"Ah. That."

"You'll be able to produce hydrogen so cheaply that it can sell for less than the price of gasoline—"

"Eventually," said Gould.

"Eventually? Why not right away? Why not now?"

Gould puffed his cheeks and sighed heavily. "Infrastructure, for one thing. Distribution."

"I don't understand," Cochrane said. Across the table, Sandoval's face had settled into a puzzled, almost worried expression.

"Distribution," Gould repeated. "What good is this process for producing hydrogen unless we can distribute the hydrogen to the one hundred and thirty-seven million owners of automobiles in this country?"

"You can convert gas stations into hydrogen stations, can't you?"

"In time, yes. It can't be done overnight."

Cochrane nodded, accepting that fact. But then he thought aloud, "You know, it ought to be possible to produce membranes that consist of colonies of Mike's cyanobacteria. Put them into the cars. Then all they'd need for fuel is water!"

Gould leaned back in his chair and stared at Cochrane appreciatively. "That…that is little short of brilliant, Dr. Cochrane."

"You could start converting from gasoline to hydrogen right away."

Sandoval made a forced smile. "There's more to it that that, I should think."

"Indeed there is," Gould said. "Indeed there is. For one thing, we must get this hydrogen process patented. We'll need patent protection. We don't want someone else to steal the process out from under our noses, do we?"

"Obtaining a patent takes time," Sandoval said.

Nodding, Gould said, "My legal department can push the patent application through, but still, the patent office is something of a law unto itself. They can only be pushed so far."

Cochrane looked from Sandoval to Gould and back again. "But in the meantime—"

"Then there's the delicate matter of international trade. Petroleum imports are a major part of the U.S. trade balance."

"That's why our trade deficits are so big," Cochrane said. "Now we can cut them back."

"That will require some rather delicate political negotiations with the OPEC nations, my boy. You can't simply tell Saudi Arabia and the rest of them that we won't be buying their oil anymore. That could cause enormous repercussions all over the Middle East. All over the world."

"Well, we can phase it in, I suppose," Cochrane agreed reluctantly.

"Yes," said Gould. "Slow but steady wins the race."

Cochrane felt an uncomfortable wave of misgiving.

"The first step is for you to deliver your brother's data to my scientific staff. Then my legal people will apply for a patent."

"When do your engineers start developing the system for automobiles?" Cochrane asked.

"For that, we must get together with the leaders in the automotive industry. They will be delighted with this new development, I'm sure. Absolutely delighted."

Again Cochrane looked across the table at Sandoval. She would not meet his eyes.

Gould laid on a limousine to take them to his town house. Cochrane rode the few blocks in a gloomy silence.

A butler admitted them to the house and showed them to the elevator that brought them to the third floor, where their scanty luggage had already been delivered to their bedroom.

Cochrane closed the bedroom door firmly, then leaned his back against it.

"Do you think he's got the place bugged?" he asked.

Sandoval's eyes flicked to the ceiling light fixture. "Probably," she said.

"Let's take a walk, then."

"At this time of night? Out on the street?"

"Just around the block. There's plenty of streetlights, people on the street. We'll be okay."

She looked dubious.

He forced a grin. "I'll protect you."

Smiling back at him. "You don't have your saber with you."

"True enough," he admitted.

Sandoval glanced at her wristwatch. "Lincoln Center ought to be letting out about now. There should be a decent crowd on the streets if we walk in that direction."

"Okay," Cochrane said. "Let's do it."

"Just give me a minute to change into something less noticeable."

They walked toward Lincoln Center, Sandoval in a pair of slacks and a loose blouse, Cochrane still in his one and only business suit. There were plenty of pedestrians on the street, restaurants were open, windows blazing light.

"It's bothering you," she said as they reached the corner of the block.

Cochrane nodded. "He doesn't want to put Mike's invention to use. He wants to suppress it."

"I don't think—"

"He's in the oil business, isn't he?" Cochrane said with some heat. "He's not part of the solution, he's part of the problem."

"Paul, ten million dollars."

"Hush money."

"*Our* money!"

A block away, Lincoln Center stood bathed in brilliant lights, a sea of limousines and taxis lapping around its colonnaded façade.

He stopped walking, turned to face her. "Do you really think he's going to give us that money? Wouldn't it be easier for him to get rid of us once we've given him Mike's data?"

"Paul, I don't think you understand," she said, her face grim. "He'll get rid of us if we *don't* give him your brother's data."

MANHATTAN:
GOULD TRUST HEADQUARTERS

Thirty floors below Lionel Gould's penthouse living quarters were the offices of the Gould Trust. Established by Gould's grandfather, the trust donated funds and expertise to a variety of educational and charitable institutions. Gould money built libraries and research laboratories at poorly endowed universities, bought scholarships and medical care for the underprivileged, supported struggling symphony orchestras and opera companies in small and midsized cities all across the United States. It made for wonderful publicity for the Gould family. And it was all tax-deductible.

Gould himself much preferred New York City to Dallas, where his corporate headquarters were located. Dallas was the heart of the international petroleum industry, although Gould and most of his peers assiduously maintained the illusion that Arab oil sheikhs and Middle Eastern dictators controlled the price of petroleum worldwide.

Gould went along with the convenient fiction, but Manhattan was where he had been born and where he preferred to live. His private office in the trust's headquarters suite was small but sumptuous. Gould often quoted Polonius's advice: "rich, not gaudy." Dark paneling of Philippine mahogany lined the walls, hundred-year-old Persian carpets covered the floor, the furnishings and Old Masters on the walls reeked of old money.

His desk had once been the centerpiece of the Oval Office. Now its gleaming dark surface was uncluttered by anything except a compact white telephone console. On the wall beside the desk a plasma screen that usually showed a sequence of Turner and Constable landscapes now was filled with the harried, balding face of Gould Energy Corporation's chief of security.

"I'm waiting for an explanation," Gould rumbled, drumming his stubby fingers on the desktop.

The security chief was in Dallas. Behind his balding head Gould could see the gaudy skyline against a bright Texas morning sky. Gould could see beads of perspiration on the man's high forehead.

"According to the limo driver," he said, "he dropped them off at your building at nine-thirty. Right on schedule."

"But they never showed up for their meeting with my science people," Gould said.

"Yessir. So I understand. We're looking into that."

"What happened to them?"

"Er...we don't know yet, sir."

Gould took in a deep, exasperated breath, then let it out again in an annoyed sigh. "Did the chauffeur actually see them enter the building?"

"Apparently not, sir."

"Apparently?"

"We...we don't know for certain. Not yet."

Gould closed his eyes briefly, then with murderous calm he said, "You had better find out, then. I want to know where they've gone. I want to know *now*, this morning. Without fail."

"I'm already on it, sir."

"Call me the instant you find anything."

"Yessir!"

Gould jabbed a thumb on his phone console, cutting the connection.

Gone. They just got out of the limo and disappeared. I should have expected something like this from that man Cochrane. An idealist. Ivory tower dreamer. I should have known, I should have seen this coming from the way he talked to me last night. Damned fool. Damned stupid idealistic fool!

He sucked in another deep breath, trying to calm himself. Sandoval's with him, of course. She'll stick with him wherever he goes. He's her ticket to ten million dollars. She'll find a way to contact me. All I have to do is wait. Be patient.

But what if he ditches her? What if he runs off somewhere on his own?

Gould frowned as he contemplated the consequences. No, he assured himself, he won't go anywhere without her. She's got him well and truly hooked. He won't let go of her. He can't, the simpleminded fool. Wherever he goes, he'll take her along with him.

She might try to go to another source, Gould realized. Then he smiled to himself. But there is no other source. Whoever she might go to is in this with me. At this level of threat there is no competition in the industry, we're all in this together.

No, she'll let him run for a while and then contact me. She wants that ten million. Dr. Cochrane is a means for her to that end.

Satisfied that he had analyzed the situation correctly, Gould tapped a speed-dial number on his phone console.

Kensington's gaunt, humorless face filled the screen on the wall.

"Yes, sir, what can I do for you today?"

"Where are you?"

There was a noticeable delay before he answered, "Anchorage, finishing up that business with the wildcatters."

"Ah, yes," said Gould. "I want you back here as soon as you can get to New York. This man Cochrane is becoming troublesome."

Kensington fingered the thin cut under his right eye. It was still red, sore.

"Cochrane, huh? I'd like to meet up with him again."

Is Hydrogen Clean?

Although hydrogen has been touted as a clean, non-polluting fuel for the future, can hydrogen itself be produced cleanly?

Currently, the two most common methods of producing hydrogen are electrolysis and gasification of fossil fuels such as coal and natural gas.

In electrolysis, electricity is used to split the water molecule (H_2O) into hydrogen and oxygen. But to provide the massive amounts of hydrogen that would be necessary to replace gasoline and other fossil fuels, unprecedented amounts of electrical power would be necessary.

Hydrogen enthusiasts have suggested building hundreds of new nuclear generating stations, which could run 24/7, providing the electricity needed to produce hydrogen from water. Nuclear power stations, of course, have their own environmental and political problems, to say nothing of the huge costs and long time-spans of their construction.

In gasification, fossil fuels such as coal or natural gas are put through a steam process that releases hydrogen gas. But the process leaves carbon dioxide, a major factor in the greenhouse warming of the atmosphere, and other pollutants as waste products. In producing "clean" hydrogen to replace polluting fossil fuels, enormous amounts of CO_2 pollution would be created.

Moreover, burning hydrogen for energy produces water vapor, which is itself a potent greenhouse gas.

Hydrogen enthusiasts claim that since the fuel comes originally from water, there is no net gain in greenhouse effects. However, if hydrogen is generated from fossil fuels, the greenhouse factor is very real. And troublesome.

—*FUTURES*
August 2005

INTERSTATE 95:
BRIDGEPORT, CONNECTICUT

Rain spattered the windows of the lurching Bonanza bus. Cochrane stared bleakly out the streaked window at an unbroken stream of trucks, semi trailers, cars, vans, and other buses splashing along the highway at seventy-five miles per hour and more, regardless of the downpour.

All burning petroleum, he said to himself. All spewing carbon dioxide into the air. Greenhouse gas. Global warming. Well, once we switch to hydrogen we'll put an end to that.

Sandoval sat beside him, in the aisle seat, looking unhappy.

Cochrane had made up his mind the night before to skip out on their meeting with Gould's research scientists. Sandoval objected, tried to persuade him to go through with it, but he told her he wasn't going to the meeting. Take it or leave it.

She had fallen silent for several long moments, while his heart thudded against his ribs. At last she had said, "All right, Paul. If you don't want to do it, we won't. I'll go with you wherever you want to go."

So they had allowed the liveried chauffeur to drive them from the town house to the Gould Tower, taken their meager travel bags from the limo's trunk, and watched on the sidewalk as the limo edged back into the growling, honking stream of West Park Avenue traffic. Then Cochrane had hailed a taxi and gone to La Guardia. At the airport they had switched cabs and ridden back into Manhattan, to the Port Authority bus terminal.

"Boston?" she had asked as he purchased two one-way tickets.

"Boston," he had said, glad that she didn't ask him where in Boston he wanted to go. He didn't know.

But now, as they jounced past Bridgeport on I-95 in the driving rain, Sandoval leaned close to him and said, "Gould will find us if we register at a hotel."

"We could use phony names," he muttered.

She almost smiled. "And what will we do for money? If we try to use our credit cards we'll be giving ourselves away. Besides, all of mine are just about maxed out. We need cash, Paul."

"I could get cash from an ATM."

"You'd have to use your credit card," she reminded him.

"So what? Gould doesn't have the FBI working for him."

"Doesn't he?"

He stared at her. "Well," he temporized, "I could get us a dorm room or something at BU."

Sandoval shook her head slowly. "That would be what he'd expect. He'll have Kensington on our trail by now. You won't be able to surprise him the way you did in Tucson. He'll be wary of you. And that makes him more dangerous."

Cochrane had to admit to himself that she was right. He turned and looked glumly out the bus window. Interstate 95 wound along the shoreline now. He could see yacht harbors and clustered buildings, gray and dreary in the rain.

"I just thought," he mumbled, "that we'd be able to hide from him in Boston long enough."

"Long enough for what, Paul?"

"Long enough for me to figure out what to do."

"You don't want to give your brother's data to Gould?"

"So he can bury it? No way."

"Then what?"

"You said there were others interested."

"Do you think they'd want to go ahead with your brother's work any more than Gould does? None of the major players is going to upset the industry. My god, Paul, you're talking about the global oil industry, the automotive industry—they're not going to allow *anyone* to upset their business."

"Maybe."

"Maybe? Paul, they control governments! They run the world's business! You can't stop them. They'll grind you to bits!"

He felt his jaw clenching. "You think Gould really can get the FBI working for him?"

"One way or another, yes."

The bus hit a pothole and bounced hard. "Sorry folks!" the driver called cheerfully. But he didn't slow down at all.

"Grind me to bits, eh?"

Sandoval didn't answer for a moment. Then she said softly, "And me, too."

He pulled in a deep breath. "Christ, Elena, I don't know what to do."

"Give Gould what he wants," she urged. "While you still can."

"And then?"

"And then we take ten million dollars and live wherever we want to."

"No," he said. "We'll never see that money. He'll kill us. Just like he killed Mike."

The rain ended as they crossed the Massachusetts border and by the time they were speeding past Springfield on the Mass Turnpike the clouds broke up and the sun shone through.

As the towers of Boston's skyline came into view, Sandoval said, "I know where we can stay. At least for a few days."

"A safe place?"

"Completely safe. Kensington would never think of looking for us there, and we won't need to use our credit cards to pay for anything."

Cochrane leaned back in the stiff plastic-covered chair and closed his eyes. "Okay," he said. "Good. We need a place where nobody'll find us."

But in the back of his mind he wondered how far he could trust her. She wants me to give Mike's data to Gould. She wants that ten mil. He turned his head slowly to look at her. Sandoval seemed tense, uptight. Yet still beautiful. Gorgeous, he thought. Am I being fair to her? She's gone along with me; even though she doesn't agree with what I'm doing, she's sticking right here beside me. Could she really be interested in me? A sardonic voice in his head answered, Yeah, as long as you have something in your pocket worth ten million dollars.

. . .

South Station looked seedy in Cochrane's eyes. This town's so old, he thought as they shuffled down the bus's aisle and down the steps to the sidewalk. Not like Tucson; not like the West. Boston's been around a long time and the town looks it.

They retrieved their bags at the side of the bus and pushed through the crowd milling around the terminal to the taxi stand. No cabs in sight. Sandoval looked perplexed, but Cochrane grinned tightly at her and headed up the street, travel bag in hand.

Less than two blocks from the terminal he hailed a taxi cruising along the street. The driver popped the lid of the cab's trunk but didn't get out to help them. Cochrane tossed his bag and then Sandoval's into the greasy-looking trunk, slammed the lid as hard as he could, then ushered her into the taxi's tattered back seat.

As he got in and closed the door, the driver asked over his shoulder, "Where to?"

"The Isabella Stewart Gardner Museum," said Sandoval.

Cochrane felt his jaw drop open in surprise.

The driver asked, "Ya know how to get theyeh?"

BOSTON:
ISABELLA STEWART GARDNER
MUSEUM

Cochrane laughed to himself as Sandoval began to give directions to the museum on the Fenway. Boston cabdrivers asked for directions for two reasons:

One, they truly did not know how to navigate the area's bewildering patchwork of independent towns and cities, all overlaid on a mad anarchy of twisting streets whose names changed arbitrarily, seemingly for no better reason than to confuse drivers. It had been said, Cochrane recalled, that the region's street scheme was designed to puzzle the Redcoats, should George III ever send troops once again to Massachusetts.

The second reason was that if the passenger displayed the slightest lack of knowledge, the driver would gleefully undertake a scenic tour of eastern Massachusetts while the cab's meter clicked away merrily.

Cochrane was impressed all over again with Sandoval. She was giving inch-by-inch directions, telling the glumly nodding driver exactly where to turn and which streets to avoid.

"You know Boston," Cochrane said admiringly.

She turned toward him and smiled. "I told you I was born and raised here. I went to school here, too."

"Which one?"

"Harvard."

Now Cochrane was truly impressed. How the hell did she afford Harvard? he wondered. She must come from money. The best he'd been able to do was Boston College, and he had to work nights and summers to get through. It meant he'd had no social life at all: he attended classes and then rode the T to work. It was a rare night when he could have a beer at one of the local bars with his classmates.

Despite being a native of the area, Cochrane had never been to the Isabella Stewart Gardner Museum. He knew it was on the Fenway, within walking distance of the Boston Museum of Fine Arts. Not all that far from the Red Sox' home at Fenway Park, either. When the cab pulled up and they got out, Cochrane saw a little gem of a Venetian palazzo, a stone façade so intricately designed it looked almost like lacework.

He paid the driver and added a minimal tip. Then he pulled their bags from the grimy trunk of the cab. Cash is running low, he realized, not knowing yet what to do about the problem. The afternoon was warm and bright, with a breeze starting to blow in from the sea. They toted their bags to the museum's front entrance.

Inside the lobby sat a middle-aged receptionist and an overweight uniformed rent-a-cop security guard. Cochrane felt grimy, travel-weary, as he and Sandoval deposited their bags on the black-and-white squares of the marble floor.

"We'll be closing in less than an hour," the gray-haired woman said, in a near-whisper.

Sandoval gave her an understanding smile and said, in an equally hushed voice, "Actually, we're here to see the director."

"Mrs. Neal? I'm not sure she's in at this time."

"Could you call her, please? Tell her Elena Sandoval is here."

Looking doubtful, the woman picked up her phone and punched in a number. She spoke briefly, nodded once, then put the phone down.

"Mrs. Neal will be down directly," she said, as if she didn't believe it.

Cochrane saw that there were no chairs in the lobby, except the receptionist's and a spare beside her desk on which the security guard was firmly planted. The walls had a couple of small pictures on them, nothing that looked all that artistic to him.

"Ellie?" a woman's voice boomed loud enough to echo off the walls. "By god, it really is you!"

Turning, Cochrane saw a large swirl of voluminous multihued fabric sweep through the lobby and clasp Sandoval so vigorously she was nearly lifted off her feet.

"Fee!" Sandoval managed to say, her voice muffled by the embrace, as she hugged the older woman with both arms.

Once released from the clinch, Sandoval turned back to Cochrane. He'd never seen her grinning with such complete joy.

"Paul, please meet Fiona Neal, my surrogate mother. Fee, this is Paul Cochrane."

Fiona Neal was just about six feet tall, Cochrane estimated; despite the colorful floor-length muumuu, he could see that she was large in every dimension. Her face was long, seamed with age, her hair wispy thin yet still dark. Her eyes beamed with intelligence and goodwill. She was obviously overjoyed to see Sandoval again.

"How do you do?" Fiona Neal said solemnly, extending her hand. Fiona's grip was solid, her skin leathery. She works with her hands, Cochrane realized.

"Come on back to the residence," she said, wrapping one arm around Sandoval's shoulders. "Golly, it's good to see you again."

Cochrane picked up both their bags and started to follow them. Out of the corner of his eye he saw the receptionist, looking completely flabbergasted by the warmth of her boss's greeting for these two strangers.

Fiona led them out into an exquisite little courtyard dotted with sculptures. None of the modern lumps of unidentifiable shapes, Cochrane saw. These statues were of men and women, graceful, human, the real thing.

The two women were both chattering away at the same time; Cochrane wondered how they could understand one another, but they seemed to be getting along just fine. They went through a door set into the far end of the courtyard without even a glance back at Cochrane. He shrugged inwardly. Obviously they had a lot of catching up to do.

"The residence" turned out to be a two-story apartment with a spare bedroom and its own bathroom, with even a Jacuzzi tub. Twin beds, he saw, but what the hell. Beggars can't be choosers. The apartment was comfortable and beautifully appointed. Cochrane was impressed; the museum might be dedicated to past glories of art, but Fiona Neal lived with all the modern conveniences.

Fiona sat them in her living room and brought out a bottle of Chardonnay.

"Can you do the cork, Paul? My wrists aren't as strong as they used to be."

Cochrane got the feeling that she was stretching the truth just to give him something to do. He nodded and took the corkscrew from her hand.

"Fee, I need a favor from you," Sandoval said as she sat in one of the plush armchairs.

Fiona took the wooden rocker, her bulk filling it almost to overflowing.

"Name it," she said.

"Paul and I need a place to stay for a few days, a place where no one will bother us."

Fiona cocked an eyebrow. "Honeymoon?"

"Not really."

With a grin, Fiona said, "I guess living in sin is more exciting."

"It's important that nobody knows we're here," Sandoval said.

Fiona's grin disappeared. "You're in trouble?"

"Not with the law," Cochrane blurted. "There's nothing illegal involved."

"Except living in sin." The older woman's smile returned.

Hybrid Sales Lag

With the price of gasoline topping $7 a gallon you would think that hybrid cars, which get double the gas mileage of ordinary cars, would be the hottest sellers on the automobile market.

Alas, sales of hybrid autos are in the doldrums, lagging far behind sales of conventional gas-powered autos.

"They're just not moving," complained William French, owner of one of the nation's largest automobile sales companies. "Sales were pretty brisk when they were first introduced, but now the hybrids are just sitting there. Nobody's even kicking their tires anymore."

Industry analysts have proposed several explanations for the poor sales of hybrid cars, which run on a combination of a gasoline-powered engine and a hydrogen-powered fuel cell that generates power for an electrical engine.

Hydrogen fuel is not easily available, for one thing. Most service stations do not provide hydrogen, making it difficult for owners of hybrids to get the hydrogen their cars' fuel cells require. "Hydrogen is difficult to transport through ordinary pipelines," explains Gordon Shaftoe, an engineer with Gould Energy Corporation. "The stuff leaks through ordinary gaskets and seals. You need very special equipment to pipe hydrogen cross-country. That makes it very expensive."

Many drivers and gas station owners are fearful of

hydrogen, as well. "That's the stuff that blew up the *Hindenburg,* isn't it?" asked Maria Esposito, of Carmel, California, recalling the tragic explosion that destroyed the German dirigible in 1937, killing 33 passengers and crew.

But Derek Copella, of Newark, New Jersey, voiced another complaint about hybrid cars: "They got no pep, no juice. Sure, they get fifty miles to the gallon, but they got no vroom-vroom."

—*FINANCE DAILY*

BOSTON:
TOP OF THE PRU RESTAURANT

Fifty-two stories above the street, Cochrane could look through the restaurant's big windows and all the way out to the hills of New Hampshire. The sun was setting, casting long fingers of shadows from the rows of stately brick houses lining the city's narrow streets. To the south, across the Charles River, was MIT and, farther on, the domes and red brick buildings of Harvard's sprawling campus. Looking north past Charlestown and the masts of Old Ironsides, the urban landscape gave way to countryside rich with trees and dotted by occasional slim white steeples. The sky was a flaming red in the west, slowly melting into deeper and deeper violet.

They had walked to the Prudential Center complex along Boston's busy streets, noisy with honking snarled traffic. Despite Cochrane's misgivings, Sandoval had insisted on having dinner in the restaurant at the top of the skyscraper. Cochrane had argued that it would be too expensive for them.

"There's lots of cheaper places down here at ground level," he'd said, waving an arm at the fast-food joints lining the street.

Sandoval shook her head dismissively. "Fee gave me one of the museum's credit cards. Dinner's on her."

He frowned. "You mean dinner's on the people who contribute to the museum."

"Paul, Fee *is* the museum. She's Isabella Gardner's second incarnation, really."

So Cochrane went with her up the whooshing elevator to the top of the tower and now they sat lingering over their cocktails: a vodka martini for Sandoval, a rum and Coke for him.

"She actually handed you a credit card from the museum?" he asked.

Nodding, Sandoval said, "I told you, Fee's like my foster mother. I've known her since I was a teenager."

"And she's willing to take us in, no questions asked."

"We ought to be safe for a few days, at least. Until you figure out what you want to do."

Cochrane picked up his drink and took a long pull. It was sticky-sweet. Not much rum in it, he thought.

"Paul, we ought to go over our options."

"Yeah. But let's order dinner first."

She smiled. "Good thinking."

The service was slow, but Cochrane found his prime rib satisfying, although a trifle underdone. Sandoval said that her Dover sole was delicious.

They talked over their options, which hadn't improved since Cochrane had skipped out of his meeting with Gould's scientists. Sandoval ticked them off on her slim fingers: her nails were lacquered Chinese red, Cochrane noticed.

"We can go back to Gould, apologize, and collect the money he's promised us," she said.

"And hope that we live to spend it," Cochrane added.

"Or we can go to one of Gould's competitors. Tricontinental Energy, for example."

"Who's just as bad as Gould, I bet."

She cocked her head slightly to one side. "Paul, all the energy companies are going to have the same attitude. They don't want a practical hydrogen fuel system to compete with petroleum. Not yet."

"Not until they've squeezed the last nickel in profits out of the oil."

"There's something more involved," Sandoval pointed out. "Oil is a major factor in international politics. Especially Middle Eastern politics."

"So that means," he said slowly, "that if we went to the feds with this . . ."

"They might want to suppress it just as much as Gould and the others."

"But the president says we have to develop new energy technology," Cochrane replied, his voice almost pleading. "We've got exactly what the White House wants!"

Sandoval's face took on an expression like a patient schoolteacher disappointed with a student's answer.

"Paul," she said softly, "what politicians tell the public and what they really want are two different things."

"I know," he admitted. "It's just that, well, I thought maybe if we could get to the president or somebody high up in the West Wing . . ."

She looked directly into his eyes. "How do you think Gould tracked us down? How do you think he knew where to send Kensington to find us?"

"You mean he's got access to police data?"

"Local, state, and federal," Sandoval said. "Right up to the FBI. Count on it."

"Jesus Christ," Cochrane muttered.

Their waiter coasted to tableside, smiling brightly. "And what can I bring you for dessert?"

Despite the anxieties gnawing at him, Cochrane slept soundly in the museum residence's guest bedroom. When he awoke, though, the other bed was empty.

Quickly he showered, shaved, and dressed. When he opened the bedroom door the aroma of sizzling bacon hit him. He went down a narrow corridor and found the kitchen.

Fiona Neal had wedged her bulk into the little booth tucked into an alcove, a half-finished plate of bacon and eggs before her. The windows were bright with morning sunshine. Cochrane saw the courtyard outside with its sculptures.

"Good morning, sleepyhead," Fiona said, with a smile. "Coffee's in the urn. Can you make your own breakfast or shall I?"

"Morning," Cochrane replied. "Coffee and juice is fine for me."

"Juice in the fridge," she said, pointing.

"Where's Elena?" he asked as he picked a carton of orange juice out of the refrigerator.

"She was up early. Said she had to run a few errands."

Errands? Cochrane wondered. What errands?

He poured steaming coffee into the mug that was waiting beside the urn, then took it and his juice to the booth. Sliding in, he saw that Fiona in her colorful caftan filled the other bench almost completely.

"I want to thank you for taking us in like this," he said.

Fiona shrugged. "Ellie told me all about it this morning. I'm sorry about your brother."

"Thanks."

"You two are in something of a pickle, aren't you?"

"That's one way to put it."

She picked up her coffee mug in both hands and raised it to her lips. She didn't drink, though, just held it there while she studied Cochrane with her deep brown eyes.

Feeling uneasy under her scrutiny, Cochrane said, "You must be very close to Elena."

"*Very* close," she replied.

"You've known her a long time."

"How long have you known her?"

Cochrane thought a moment. Christ, it's only been a week. No, more. He counted mentally.

"Ten days," he muttered.

"You don't know much about her, then."

"Not much," he admitted as he asked himself, Where is she? Where did she go? What's she up to?

Fiona took a sip of her coffee. Then, "Is there anything I can tell you?"

Cochrane didn't reply, but in his head he asked, Can I trust her?

She must have read the troubled expression on his face. "Well, whether you want to hear it or not, I'm going to tell a tale out of school," she said.

"What?"

"Something that Ellie probably couldn't tell you about herself. Maybe she doesn't want you to know, but I think you should."

Cochrane asked, "About herself?"

Fiona nodded solemnly. "She was twelve years old when I first met her, at a foster care home. Her father had been sexually abusing her for a couple of years and finally beat her up so badly she had to be hospitalized."

"You took her in?"

"Somebody had to. I thought it'd just be a temporary thing, till she recovered physically and emotionally. The broken bones healed soon enough." Fiona's eyes shifted away from Cochrane, as though looking into the past.

"What about her mother?" Cochrane asked.

"A tramp. She took off when Ellie was a baby. Father drank, more and more as time went by. A couple of years after Ellie moved in with me the police found him dead of a heart attack in an alley behind some bar."

"Swell childhood," Cochrane said.

"It left its scars. Ellie worked for me here at the museum, became a docent. She was good at it, too: people liked her and she really got interested in the art we displayed."

"That's good."

"But not good enough. You know how good-looking she is. After the way her father battered her she swore to me that she'd never let a man get the better of her again."

Puzzled, Cochrane said, "But...I mean, we..."

Tight-lipped, grim, Fiona explained, "She found that she could use men to get what she wanted. I tried to set her straight but she told me she was just evening the score, letting men think they were taking advantage of her while she was taking advantage of them."

Cochrane's throat went dry.

"She got pretty wild for a time. She told me once, 'They think they're screwing me, but I'm really screwing them.'"

"Shit," he mumbled.

"We went 'round and 'round on it. Fought like two cats in a cage. I know it sounds corny, but I was battling to save her soul."

"Were you able to?"

"Sort of. Ellie was smart enough to figure it out for herself, eventually," Fiona said, tapping the tabletop with her finger. "She realized she was on her way to becoming a whore and she stopped. Almost."

"She's more selective, you mean."

"Let me tell you about it. We had a robbery here at the museum back when she was living here. Six paintings taken off the walls, including a Rembrandt and two Degas watercolors. The Boston PD, the state police, the FBI—none of them could find where the artworks had been taken. Ellie did."

"She did?"

"One of the museum guards was under suspicion, but the police didn't have enough evidence to arrest him. Ellie sweet-talked him all the way to the North Shore millionaire who bankrolled the theft. He wanted to hang our Rembrandt, *Christ in the Storm,* in the fallout shelter he'd built for himself in his mansion up in Swampscott. Said he was going to convert the shelter into a chapel and hang the Rembrandt over its altar. Can you imagine?"

"Elena found it for you?"

Fiona nodded happily. "I got the pictures back and the religious millionaire got a *nol-pros* from the state supreme court."

"They didn't prosecute him?"

"Money talks. The guard got fired and the two guys who actually took the paintings off our walls are still in prison, but the man who caused it all walked."

Cochrane leaned back against the booth's cushioned wall, his mind trying to process all this information.

"Ellie got the reward money that our insurance company had offered, and she figured right then and there that she could support herself pretty damned handsomely as a sort of unlicensed private investigator."

"She told me she was doing industrial espionage."

"I suppose there's a good deal of money in that," Fiona said.

Bitterly, Cochrane said, "Well, she's good at what she does."

"Oh, no," Fiona blurted. "You're taking it the wrong way. She told me this morning that you're different. She's not interested in the money. She's interested in you."

Cochrane felt a thrill of exhilaration. But then his common sense took control. "Yeah. Nice story. But how can I believe that—"

"She's never lied to me," Fiona Neal said firmly. "In all the years I've known Ellie, she's never told me a lie."

PALO ALTO:
CALVIN RESEARCH CENTER

With a surprising pang of sorrow Dr. Jason Tulius looked over the twelve men and women who comprised his senior scientific staff. Most of them had been graduate students of his when he'd founded the Calvin Research Center, young, enthusiastic, cocky. Now there was more gray in their hair than he had ever expected to see; they were quieter, more careful, fatter.

I should talk, he said to himself. I've gained thirty pounds over the past ten years, and it's not all in my beard.

He had called his senior scientists together at the end of the nominal working day. Not that they punched out at five o'clock, like the administrators and support people. Most of the scientists stayed on long beyond the official quitting time. They enjoyed their work. They were driven, self-motivated men and women. Tulius often thought that they would pay him to let them do the research that they wanted to pursue.

The twelve of them were seated casually in Tulius's office. They had pulled chairs from his little conference table and his assistant's office out-side to form a rough semicircle facing their director, who had wheeled his high-backed swivel chair from behind his desk to face them. Tulius unbuttoned his tan corduroy jacket and leaned back in the comfortably yielding chair.

"You're probably wondering why I asked you here," he began, grin-ning.

They chuckled politely.

"To listen to old jokes?" asked Rose Peterson, his second-in-command. She was a tiny, elflike woman with a granite jaw and piercing ice-blue eyes.

"No," Tulius answered, his grin fading. "We need to discuss what Mike Cochrane was doing."

"Mike was a flake," said Ray Kurtzman. "We let him get away with murder."

"That's a clever choice of words," Dave Lincowitz cracked. Like Kurtzman, he was bearded and wore a short-sleeved, open-necked shirt.

"You know what I mean," Kurtzman retorted. "Mike went off and did his own thing. He wasn't a team player."

"He reported to me," Tulius said. "He didn't have an entirely free hand."

"Who the hell does?" someone mumbled.

"But I've got to admit that his reports weren't exactly monuments of clarity and disclosure."

Olivia Vernon, the youngest of the twelve, and in Tulius's eyes by far the prettiest woman in the center, cleared her throat and said, "Mike told me he was coming into a lot of money soon. I got the impression he was going to quit and go off on his own."

Tulius said, "That may be true. As Ray said, Mike wasn't a team player."

"He had something cooking," Lincowitz agreed. "He was working nights."

"Working on some chick he picked up in Mountain View," said Carlo Zapata, who headed the center's instrumentation engineers.

"Is that true?" Rose Peterson asked. "Did he really have an affair going on?"

"That's what he told me," Zapata replied.

"Maybe that's what got him killed," suggested Kurtzman. "A jealous husband."

"Or a jealous wife."

Tulius shook his head. "How would an outsider get into his office? Past our security?"

"It's not that tough," Lincowitz said. "Especially if Mike allowed the visitor in."

"Or brought her in with him."

"Her?"

"His wife."

"Did you see the size of her brothers at the funeral? One of them could have done it."

"Do you think Mike was stupid enough to allow one of those bozos into the building?"

Tulius raised his hands shoulder-high, palms out. "Enough of the personal chatter. I'm not interested in Mike's love life and it's the police's job to find out who killed him. I want to see what he was working on."

"You think that has some connection to his murder?" Olivia Vernon asked.

"It might. But more important, Mike expected to get a lot of money for whatever he was doing. If he made some sort of breakthrough we ought to be able to find out what it is and duplicate it."

"He was studying those stromatolites in that hothouse of his up on the roof," said Rose Peterson.

"He had some interest in genetic engineering," Tulius said.

"That was last year's hobbyhorse," replied Jake Freeman. "He was all over me for months, asking about techniques for gene splicing. Then he lost interest in it."

"I don't think Mike lost interest," Tulius said. "I think he found what he wanted to know and then went off on his own."

"Genetic engineering? Gene splicing?" Kurtzman shook his head. "He was playing with cyanobacteria, for god's sake. Not *E. coli* or some other genetic engineering subject."

"Yeah, but maybe he wanted to splice some foreign genes into the cyanobacteria."

"Why the hell would he want to do that?"

Tulius was certain that he knew the answer to that, but he kept silent.

"Maybe he wanted to make them resistant to environmental insults. Or see how they might give rise to a new species."

Within seconds all twelve of the scientists were spouting ideas and arguing with each other. Tulius sat back in his swivel chair and let them blabber. From such wild-ass debate comes new ideas, he thought. Sometimes. He folded his arms and watched their animated wrangling. This is

all my fault, he told himself. I gave Mike too much freedom, let him wander off on his own without enough control or direction.

But he definitely hit on what we were looking for. I gave him all the
freedom he wanted and then when he finds what we were after, he decides
to quit the lab and go off on his own. Christ, if the police knew about that,
they'd suspect *me* for his murder. Tulius thought about that as the argu-
ment raged among his senior scientists. Yes, he decided. Michael found
what he was looking for. But he wasn't going to tell me about it, after all
the years I supported his work.

"Wait," he called out.

The scientists stopped their arguing and turned toward him.

"Let's organize this debate. What do we know for certain about
Michael's work?"

"He was dealing with the cyanobacteria."

"Measuring their oxygen output."

Tulius added, "And he had shown an interest in genetic engineering."

"But he dropped that."

"Or went underground with it," Tulius suggested.

"Underground?"

"The chances are that Michael was going to quit the center and go out
on his own," Tulius said.

"He couldn't, not legally," said Zapata. "He signed a nondisclosure
agreement just like the rest of us."

"Some smart lawyer could crack that."

"You think so?"

"That's what lawyers are for, dammit."

Kurtzman got them back on subject. "So Mike was going off on his
own with his oxygen-producing cyanobacteria."

"And a working knowledge of genetic engineering," added Rose Peterson.

Lincowitz shook his head. "That doesn't sound like it's worth a big
jackpot of money to me."

"Maybe Mike was just bragging. Exaggerating?"

"Why?" Tulius asked.

"To impress us."

"Or whoever his girlfriend was."

"I don't believe that."

"Does anybody here know who the woman was?"

"If there was one."

"From what he told me," Zapata said, "it was somebody he'd met at a
conference in Denver. Not one of our people."

"He was romancing some girl in Denver?"

"Woman," Rose Peterson corrected.

"Hey, Rose, I could've said broad."

Zapata said, "I got the impression the, uh, woman came here. She was living here locally someplace."

Tulius raised his voice again. "Let's forget about the gossip and concentrate on Mike's research. We've got to retrace his steps and find out what he was doing."

They all nodded, with varying degrees of enthusiasm.

"I take it," Rose Peterson said, "that this scavenger hunt will be in addition to our regular work?"

"That's right."

She sighed heavily. "There are times that I wish I was on an hourly wage."

"Yeah," Kurtzman agreed. "Then we could collect overtime pay."

Tulius smiled paternally at them. Grousing was normal. He knew they were just as curious as he about the research that got Michael Cochrane murdered.

But Tulius was also curious about something else. His financial people had been handling a takeover bid from some holding company in New York with a Wall Street address. The offer had been good enough to tempt Tulius, and only his fears of being pushed out of the laboratory that he had created, the organization that was his chief joy in life, led him to turn down the Wall Streeters.

Then the offer was suddenly withdrawn. A week before Michael Cochrane was killed.

Now, squarely in the middle of his desk, was a memo from his chief financial officer. The buyout offer had been renewed. The CFO advised Tulius to phone a certain Lionel Gould, in New York City.

MANHATTAN:
GOULD TRUST HEADQUARTERS

I'm delighted that you called," said Gould to the image on his wall-mounted screen.

He saw that Jason Tulius looked slightly uncomfortable as he sat behind his desk in Palo Alto. Perhaps not uncomfortable, Gould thought, so much as uncertain, even a little fearful. Good, he said to himself. Fear is good. It stimulates the mind, encourages the imagination, leads one to make decisions that are not necessarily logical. That is good.

Warily, Tulius said, "My CFO tells me you've expressed interest in buying into Calvin Research."

"Indeed I have," said Gould, smiling his best smile.

He noted with approval that Tulius was in his shirtsleeves, as he himself was. Gould's office was heavily air-conditioned, yet he worried that he might be visibly perspiring. Gould always felt uncomfortably warm; his body's metabolism was somehow pitched at a near-fever level. He knew that many of his staff complained about the frigid temperature of his office.

Some of the women grumbled that he kept it cold so that their nipples would be stiff. There were even rumbles now and then of a sexual harassment suit. Ridiculous! Gould sniffed at the very idea. They can wear sweaters, can't they?

Tulius shifted uneasily in his desk chair. "Mr. Gould, you have to understand that Calvin Research Center is pretty much my whole life. I have no intention of retiring."

"Retiring?" Gould was genuinely surprised at the idea. "No, no, that is not what I have in mind. Not at all. You are the very heart and soul of Calvin Research; I understand that."

"You'd let me remain in charge, then?"

"I would insist on it," Gould said, with complete honesty. "We could draw up an ironclad guarantee of it in our agreement."

Tulius still looked suspicious, as wary as a bearded pirate being offered amnesty instead of hanging.

"Could you tell me, then, just why you're interested in my company?"

"Gladly," said Gould, with a cavalier wave of his hand. "The Gould Trust is dedicated to supporting the arts and sciences. We finance hundreds of scholarships each year."

"I know," said Tulius. "I've Googled you."

"That is good. However, I feel that the time has come for the trust to become more deeply involved in energy research."

"Gould Energy Corporation has a very well-funded research laboratory."

"Indeed it has. Indeed it has." Gould leaned toward the microcam on his desk and lowered his voice a notch. "But, truth to tell, the corporation's research efforts are geared toward the past, not the future."

Puzzlement clouded over Tulius's face. "I don't understand...."

Folding his hands over his belly, Gould said, "Just between you and I, Dr. Tulius, the corporate research labs are focused on improvements in fossil fuel technology. They're trying to find better ways to locate new oil fields, cleaner methods of burning coal, new techniques for handling liquefied natural gas."

"They're working on magnetohydrodynamics, too, aren't they?"

Gould frowned for a moment. Magnetowhatever?

"MHD power generation," Tulius said.

"Ah, yes!" replied Gould, relieved. "Yes, indeed. MHD might allow us to burn high-sulfur coal without breaking the EPA's air quality standards."

"That sounds pretty futuristic to me," Tulius said.

"Perhaps so. But the corporation will not support research into alternative energy sources. No wind or solar power work."

"They're into nuclear energy."

"Yes, but when I suggested to the board of directors that we should be looking into the possibilities of fusion energy, they voted me down. Almost unanimously."

Unbidden, a smile crossed Tulius's face. "I didn't realize that your board dared to cross you."

Gould shrugged good-naturedly. "It happens occasionally. Not often, I grant you. In the matter of fusion research, I must admit that they were probably right. It's much too far in the future."

Still smiling, Tulius said, "The physicists say that fusion power is just over the horizon."

"Yes, and the horizon is an imaginary line that recedes as you approach it."

Tulius laughed and Gould knew that he had established his bona fides with the scientist.

"But to get back to our business," Gould said, "I feel strongly that the Gould Trust must become involved in energy research for the future: solar, wind power, hydrogen fuel, that sort of thing."

"But we're a biochemistry research center. I don't see where our kind of work could help you."

Gould leaned back in his yielding chair and pursed his lips. For a long moment neither man said anything. They simply looked at each other, each of them trying to take the measure of the other.

At last Gould said, "Dr. Tulius, let me be perfectly frank with you. One of your staff scientists, the late Dr. Cochrane, led me to believe that he was on the track of a considerable breakthrough in producing hydrogen fuel."

Despite his beard, Tulius couldn't hide the surprise in his expression. "Michael Cochrane? Hydrogen fuel?"

"That's what he led me to believe. Of course, I'm no scientist, but—"

"Photosynthesis," Tulius said, more to himself than Gould. "Splitting water molecules into oxygen and hydrogen."

"The Gould Trust is prepared to fund your center's research quite handsomely," Gould said. "All your research efforts, every project you have going."

"Including the work that Michael Cochrane was engaged in."

"Especially the work that Michael Cochrane was engaged in," Gould purred.

"I see."

"For legal and administrative reasons, the trust cannot simply hand out grant monies to your center. You are a profit-making enterprise, and the trust is set up only to fund not-for-profit endeavors."

Tulius smiled bitterly. "We try to make a profit, that's true. It doesn't always work out, though."

Gould knew better. Calvin Research Center made a modest profit on contract research, although Tulius plowed almost every penny back into more research.

"It will be necessary for the trust to buy your center outright and convert it legally into a not-for-profit organization."

Tulius scratched at his bearded chin thoughtfully. "That sounds tricky. Our existing customers—"

"We can work that out," Gould said quickly. "My legal people will take care of every detail."

Nodding, Tulius said, "I'd like to think about this, if you don't mind."

"Of course," Gould said grandly. "This is a big step for you. Naturally you should consider it quite carefully."

Tulius promised to get back to Gould before the week was over, then said a gracious goodbye and cut their phone link.

As the scientist's image winked out on his wall screen, Gould took in a deep breath of satisfaction. I've got him! He'll go for it, he told himself. The prospect of guaranteed funding for all his projects is too good for him to refuse.

Spinning his swivel chair gleefully in a complete circle, Gould thought, And once the Calvin Research Center belongs to the Gould Trust, we will be the owners of any and all patentable inventions they make. I'll have this hydrogen fuel discovery locked up tight, in my own hands. No matter how Tulius or anyone else feels about it.

BOSTON:
ISABELLA STEWART GARDNER
MUSEUM

It was late afternoon when Sandoval returned. Cochrane had spent the day wandering through the museum, looking at the Manets and Vermeers and Degas without really seeing them. His mind was on what Fiona had told him about Sandoval.

She's a high-class hooker, he told himself as he walked slowly through the sun-filled courtyard, past a life-sized statue of some Greek goddess. Industrial espionage is a fancy name for it, but what she does is screw guys to get information out of them that she sells to her customers. Nothing but a whore working wholesale instead of retail.

And yet. And yet. Fiona says she's interested in me, not the money. Yeah. Right. Ten million bucks doesn't mean anything to her. Sure.

He returned to the residence and wearily climbed the narrow stairs to the bedroom level. Then he heard the front door, downstairs, open and close. He raced down the stairs, eager as a schoolboy. Sandoval smiled to see him. She was wearing a beige trousered suit that he hadn't seen before, and had a large leather tote bag slung over one shoulder.

"Where've you been all day?" he heard himself ask, accusation sharp in his tone.

"Shopping," Sandoval replied.

She brushed past him and started up the stairs. Cochrane followed her.

"All day? Shopping?"

Over her shoulder Sandoval said, "When the going gets tough, the tough go shopping."

"On Fiona's credit card?"

She reached the top of the stairs and went to their bedroom. Tossing the tote bag onto her bed, she turned to face him, still smiling.

"Paul, I spent most of the day shopping in the best stores in town. Then I went to Filene's basement and bought this suit, on sale, fifty percent off."

"Somebody could've seen you," he said, his emotions jumbled within him. "If Kensington's looking for us..."

She put both hands on his shoulders. "Who's going to pick me out of the crowds in the department stores, Paul? I was safer there than I am here."

"Still," he mumbled.

"You were worried about me?"

He nodded, not able to tell her that he was worried she had shacked up with some guy to earn them some cash.

"You're sweet." Sandoval gave him a peck on the lips. Then she turned to the tote bag on the bed and pulled out a paper bag labeled FILENE'S; in it was a dress Cochrane recognized. She must have worn that when she went out this morning, he thought.

"Have you decided what we should do?" Sandoval asked as she hung the dress in the massive mahogany dresser that loomed in the corner of the bedroom. Cochrane had been surprised, the night before, that the piece had no TV set inside it.

"Decided?" He sat on his bed, shoulders slumping. "No. I haven't even thought much about it. I spent the day wandering through the museum."

"It's wonderful, isn't it? Did Fee tell you about the Rembrandt?"

"She told me it was stolen once. And you got it back."

Sandoval didn't bat an eye. "I was working here then. I was barely out of my teens."

He nodded glumly.

She came over and sat on the bed beside him. "Fee told you a lot more, didn't she?"

"Some," he admitted.

"So you know about me. What I do."

"Yeah."

"Does it make a difference to you?"

He tried not to say it, but he couldn't. "Of course it makes a difference! How could it not make a difference?"

Strangely Sandoval smiled again. "That's good, Paul. You'd be a really insensitive jerk if it didn't."

He stared at her, searching for words, searching his own emotions. At last he asked, "So where do we go from here, Elena?"

"Where do you want to go?"

He grasped her and pulled her to him. "I don't know, but I know that wherever it is I want you to be with me. Wherever. I want you."

She melted into his arms and murmured, "That's what I want, too, Paul. Wherever you want to go, I want to go there with you."

By the time they got out of bed it was deep twilight outside. Sandoval showered first, then Cochrane did.

"Wear your suit," she called to him through the shower's frosted glass door. "We're taking Fee to dinner."

The restaurant was down in a cellar beneath one of the posh shops on Boylston Street. Tiny, intimate, and French. The maître d' practically brushed the floor with his forehead when Fiona swept in, regal in a voluminous floor-length dress of dark blue with silver threads.

"Madame Neal!" he exclaimed. "So wonderful to have you with us again."

Fiona took it all with the good grace of a noblewoman accustomed to such deference. The maître d' led them to the biggest booth in the little restaurant. As soon as the three of them were seated, a pert waitress in a black short-skirted uniform brought a bottle of sherry and three aperitif glasses.

"Amontillado," Fiona said as the waitress poured. "I've been a sucker for it ever since I first read Edgar Allan Poe."

Cochrane sipped at the wine and felt it warming its way down his innards. The menu was mostly in French, but he followed Fiona's lead. And Sandoval's: she showed no hesitation in ordering what turned out to be frog's legs. Cochrane, like Fiona, had a small but beautifully prepared steak.

"Since I'm not the perfect hostess," Fiona began, once their entrées had been served, "I'll ask outright: how long do you two plan to stay with me?"

Sandoval glanced at Cochrane and said nothing. He mumbled, "A couple more days, if that's all right with you."

Fiona nodded. "From what Ellie tells me, you need some friends in high places."

"We've got enough enemies in high places," Sandoval said, almost lightly.

"I know Lionel Gould," Fiona said. "Charity affairs, social circles. He puts on a good front, but Gould Energy Corporation is his baby. He'll do whatever he can to suppress your brother's work, Paul."

"Who won't?" Cochrane rejoined. "The energy companies, the oil combines, the automobile corporations—it's all one big global club."

"And their reach goes right up to the top levels of government," Sandoval added.

"So what do you want to do?" Fiona asked. "Surrender to Gould and hope he'll stick to the deal he offered?"

Cochrane shook his head. "We'll have a fatal accident before his check clears the bank."

Fiona nodded, agreeing. "So, like I said, you need friends in high places."

"You know any?"

"Maybe. The senior senator from Maine is an old friend of mine. Wanted to marry me, donkey's years ago."

"Senator Bardarson?" Sandoval asked.

"Ian Bardarson," said Fiona. "He's a maverick up there on the Hill, but he's got a whale of a lot of seniority."

"He's the ranking minority member of the Senate Energy Committee," Sandoval pointed out.

"And if the elections in November go the right way," Fiona said, "he'll become the committee's chairman."

Fuel for Thought

Every few weeks, Etta Kantor goes to a Chinese restaurant and fills a couple of three-gallon pails with used cooking oil. Back in her garage, the 59-year-old philanthropist and grandmother strains it through a cloth filter and then pours it into a custom-made second fuel tank in her 2003 Volkswagen Jetta diesel station wagon. Once the car is warmed up, she flips a toggle on the dashboard to switch to the vegetable oil. Wherever she drives, she's trailed by the appetizing odor of egg rolls.

Sean Parks of Davis, California, collects his cooking oil from a fish-and-chips restaurant and a corn-dog shop. He purifies it chemically in a 40-gallon reactor that he built himself for about $800. The processed oil can be used even when his car's engine is cold, at a cost of about 70 cents a gallon. Parks, a geographer for the U.S. Forest Service, makes enough processed oil to fuel his family's two cars.

Kantor and Parks are willing to go the extra mile to reduce their dependence on petroleum and cut down on pollution. But these days environmentalists are not the only ones banking on biodiesel, as diesel-engine fuel made from vegetable oil is known. Entrepreneurs and soybean farmers are creating a new biodiesel industry, with some 300 retail biodiesel pumps nationwide so far. Commercial production of biodiesel grew 25 percent in 2004, making it the fastest-growing alternative fuel in the United States.

Even the singer Willie Nelson recently started a company to market the fuel at truck stops.

The greening of the diesel engine is a return to its roots. Rudolf Diesel, the German engineer who in 1892 invented the engine that bears his name, boasted that it ran on peanut and castor oil. "Motive power can be produced by the agricultural transformation of the heat of the Sun," he said. The inventor foresaw a future of virtually unlimited renewable energy from plants, but the idea slipped into obscurity because petroleum was so much cheaper than vegetable oil.

A century later, customers for commercial biodiesel include the U.S. Postal Service, the U.S. Army, the Forest Service, the city of Denver and numerous private truck fleets. Almost all use blends of 20 percent biodiesel mixed with standard petroleum diesel. The mixture helps federal and state agencies comply with a 2000 executive order by President Clinton mandating less petroleum consumption. Minnesota recently became the first state to require that all diesel fuel sold there be 2 percent biodiesel. Daimler-Chrysler's 2003 diesel Jeep Liberty comes off the production line with its tank filled with a 5 percent biodiesel mixture.

The major obstacle to wider use is price. Pure biodiesel sells for $2.50 to $3 a gallon, about 50 cents to $1 more than petrodiesel. To spur biodiesel's use, some European nations levy no taxes on it, and in October 2004, President Bush signed into law a 50 cent to $1 credit to fuel manufacturers for every gallon of biodiesel blended into petrodiesel.

Diesel engines differ from gasoline engines in their use of high pressure rather than a spark plug to ignite the fuel and drive the pistons. Diesel engines can run on fuel that is heavier than gasoline, making it possible to substitute filtered waste grease for petroleum. Both used and virgin vegetable oil contain glycerine—a syrupy liquid used in hand lotions. It burns well in a hot engine, as in Etta Kantor's retrofitted diesel, but clogs a cold one. Removing the glycerine yields biodiesel, which is suitable for even a cold engine.

Skeptics have questioned whether it takes more fossil fuel to produce biodiesel—to fertilize crops, transport them and process them for their oil—than the resulting biodiesel replaces. But Jim Duffield, an agricultural economist with the U.S. Department of Agriculture (USDA), says the "few lone voices" who still make the point have not kept up with improvements in agriculture and biodiesel knowledge. Indeed, a study by the U.S. Departments of Agriculture and Energy in 1998 and another in 2002 for the French government show that soybeans and canola oil yield three to four times more energy than is needed to make the fuel. (Similar skepticism has dogged ethanol, a corn-based fuel mixed with gasoline to create gasohol. But USDA and other studies show that today's ethanol provides up to 30 percent more energy than it takes to make it.)

Another benefit of burning biodiesel is cleaner air. Compared with fossil fuels, it emits less carbon monoxide and other hydrocarbons, as well as sulfur compounds related to acid rain. Pure biodiesel also substantially reduces overall emission of carbon dioxide, a major contributor to climate change, because the plants from which the oil was extracted absorbed atmospheric carbon dioxide while they were growing. A bus running on pure biodiesel would emit 32 percent less particulate matter, which has been implicated in the dramatic increase in asthma cases in cities. The only air pollution downside of pure biodiesel, according to the 1998 U.S. study, is a slight increase of smog-inducing nitrogen oxides.

The inspiration for the do-it-yourself biodiesel movement came from Joshua Tickell, 29, of Baton Rouge. While studying in Germany in 1996, he was astonished to see a farmer using canola oil to run his tractor. Back in the States, Tickell used his last student loan check to help buy a 1986 diesel Winnebago. He painted sunflowers on his "Veggie Van" and, for two years beginning in 1997, toured the country, towing a simple reactor that turned restaurant oil into biodiesel. In 2000, he coauthored what would become the biodiesel bible, *From the Fryer to the Fuel Tank*. "My goal is very simply to make OPEC obsolete," he says.

Vegetable power also appeals to 50-year-old Marty Borruso, a chemist and partner in Environmental Alternatives in New York City, who insists he's no "environmental crazy." He produces biodiesel for a generator that makes electricity and hot water for an 87-family apartment house. He also sells the fuel to a tow truck fleet and anyone who comes to a pump he operates next to his production facility in Staten Island. In a 7,000-gallon reactor, Borruso processes out-of-date virgin vegetable oils, which he buys at a steep discount, and free grease from a fried chicken emporium. But he spurns grease from a seafood restaurant. "It smells like calamari," he says. "I love calamari, but I don't know if I want to drive it."

On average, fast-food restaurants in any major U.S. city generate about 22 pounds of waste grease each year per city resident, according to a 1998 study by the National Renewable Energy Laboratory (NREL). The National Biodiesel Board, a trade group in Jefferson City, Missouri, estimates that more than 2.5 billion pounds of waste cooking grease are available annually—enough to make 100 million gallons of biodiesel.

Of course, America's appetite for petroleum is huge: 2004 consumption was nearly 315 billion gallons, including 139 billion in gasoline and 41 billion in diesel. Robert McCormack, a fuels engineer at NREL, says that biodiesel could displace 5 percent of the petrodiesel used in the United States within ten years. To replace more will require growing vegetable crops specifically for fuel—and America's soybean farmers are standing by. Some proponents envision growing aquatic algae—richer in oil than any other plant—in pools next to electric power stations. In an ecological two-for-one, the smokestack carbon dioxide would feed the algae, which would churn out biodiesel.

Grassroots fans aren't waiting. Kantor, who paid $1,400 to outfit her VW diesel with a second fuel tank, says she gets nearly 200 miles per petrodiesel gallon. "This is not about money," says Kantor, who speaks at schools about protecting the environment. "I'm doing this to set an example."

—Frances Cerra Whittelsey
SMITHSONIAN
September 2005

WASHINGTON, D.C.:
OLD EBBITT GRILL

Anderson Love looked suspicious. No, Cochrane thought, the man looks absolutely belligerent.

Cochrane and Sandoval were sitting side by side in a booth in the rear of the jam-packed Ebbitt Grill. Only a few blocks from the White House and executive office buildings, the restaurant was a popular lunch place for many of Washington's politicians, bureaucrats, and—inevitably—tourists.

Cochrane's heart had sunk when he and Sandoval had wormed their way through the entryway; the area was thick with people waiting for tables.

"We'll never find him in this crowd," he had said into her ear, almost shouting to be heard over the noise of the impatient crowd. "We don't even know what he looks like."

Sandoval had grasped his wrist and marched past the people waiting in line, straight up to the harried young woman behind the reception post.

The hostess was trying to placate a red-faced customer and talk on the phone at the same time.

"Anderson Love's table, please," Sandoval had yelled at her, louder than Cochrane had ever heard her speak before.

The woman's eyes had widened with recognition. Then she waved over to a slick-looking older man in a checkered sports jacket and jabbed a black-lacquered finger at the reservation book before her. The man smiled toothily at Sandoval and led them through the pressing crowd, past the brass and marble bar, and all the way to the plush velvet-lined booths at the rear of the restaurant, where a short, broad-shouldered, shaved-bald black man in a light gray three-piece suit sat scowling at his wristwatch.

Anderson Love half rose from the booth's bench as Cochrane extended his hand.

"Paul Cochrane," he said. "Sorry we're late."

It had been Sandoval's idea to arrive fifteen minutes late; she wanted to be certain that Senator Bardarson's aide would be there when they arrived.

Love's grip was firm, muscular. Cochrane introduced Sandoval to the unsmiling black man. As she slid into the booth, Cochrane noticed there was a scar across Love's left eyebrow. Something hit him damned hard, Cochrane said to himself. Something, or somebody.

Love already had a cup of soup in front of him. "I don't have much time," he said. His voice was a surprisingly sweet tenor.

"We appreciate your meeting us like this," said Sandoval.

"The senator said I should listen to what you have to say. But let me tell you right out, I've heard a lot of wacky stories about energy systems: everything from perpetual motion machines to a pill that turns water into gasoline."

"I suppose you get a lot of nuts coming at you," Cochrane said. He knew that Love was Senator Bardarson's aide for science and technology; the man had a BS in physics from Alabama, which made him the science expert for the senator's staff.

"So what's this all about?" Love asked, staring hard at Cochrane.

"My brother has figured out how to produce hydrogen from water inexpensively, using a bioengineered variation of cyanobacteria to split water molecules through enhanced photosynthesis." Cochrane had rehearsed that line since he and Sandoval had left Boston, knowing that once he started talking with politicians and bureaucrats he'd have to get the essence of Mike's work into a single sentence.

Love didn't blink an eye. "Produce hydrogen," he said flatly.

"Economically, efficiently," Cochrane said. "Cheaply enough to make it possible to use hydrogen to replace gasoline, diesel fuel, even heating oil."

"And I'm supposed to believe that."

Cochrane's temper swooped. But before he could reply, Sandoval said, "At least two men have been murdered over this. We're at risk ourselves."

Love studied her with his disbelieving red-rimmed eyes. "Conspiracy theory?"

Sandoval smiled. "I wish it was that simple."

Cochrane thought, No wonder he's got a scar. He felt like punching the guy's disbelieving face.

As if she knew precisely what was going through Cochrane's mind, Sandoval placed a placating hand on his thigh as she said, "We have the scientific evidence with us, if you'd like to review it."

"I suppose I'll have to," Love said reluctantly.

"Only in our presence," Cochrane said. "I'm not letting the discs out of my hands."

Love glared at him for a moment, then seemed to relent. "I suppose that's not unreasonable."

"How much biochemistry do you know?" Cochrane asked.

"Not a helluva lot."

"Me neither. My brother was a microbiologist. He—"

"Was?"

"He's one of the men who's been murdered."

Love leaned back slightly, as if trying to incorporate this new bit of information into his evaluation of the situation.

"How much biochemistry do *you* know?" he asked Cochrane.

"Not much. My degrees are in physics and thermodynamics."

"But you're with the Steward Observatory now."

Impressed that Love had looked up his credentials, Cochrane said, "We'll need somebody who can verify my brother's work."

Turning to Sandoval, Love asked, "You're not a biochemist, either?"

"No," she said, with a slight shake of her head.

"All right," Love said. "Give me a day or so to find a tame biochemist. I'll call you when I've got somebody rounded up."

"I'd rather that we called you," Sandoval said.

He looked at her suspiciously.

"Some conspiracy theories are actually true," she said, smiling.

Love smiled back, guardedly. "Even paranoids have enemies," he muttered. He reached into his vest pocket and handed her his card. Then he slid out of the booth. "I've got to get back to the office. Have a good lunch."

"He didn't even offer to pay for his damned soup," Cochrane groused.

"Rank has its privileges," said Sandoval, picking up the menu that lay on the table. "Let's order something. I'm starving!"

WASHINGTON, D.C.: DIRKSEN SENATE OFFICE BUILDING

Ichabod Crane, Cochrane thought. Senator Ian Bardarson looked like Ichabod Crane: tall and rawboned, prominent nose, knobby big-knuckled hands, long lantern jaw. But his light hazel eyes were bright with interest as Anderson Love introduced Cochrane and Sandoval to the senator. Interest and something else, Cochrane thought. Ambition.

Love's attitude had changed since their meeting the day before at Old Ebbitt Grill. He's had a chance to talk to some experts about Mike's work, Cochrane said to himself. He's become enough of a believer to get us in to see the senator on a Saturday morning.

Senator Bardarson's office was on the top floor of the Dirksen Building; through the windows Cochrane could see the wedding-cake dome of the Capitol. Just like in the movies, he thought. The senator's inner office was richly paneled in dark wood, with ceiling-high bookshelves lining two walls. Handsome leather-bound volumes filled the shelves; they looked to Cochrane as if they'd never been opened. The senator came out from behind his broad desk to shake hands with Sandoval and Cochrane, then, with a hand behind Cochrane's shoulder, showed them to plush armchairs covered in deep burgundy leather grouped around a delicate round sherry table in the corner by the windows.

Taking the third armchair in the grouping, Senator Bardarson smiled handsomely and asked what they would like to drink. Cochrane simply shook his head while Sandoval said, "Some ice water, please."

The senator nodded to Love, who went to a minifridge built into the base of one of the bookcases. "A lovely young woman like you should drink champagne," Bardarson said, smiling handsomely.

"It's a bit early in the morning," Sandoval replied demurely.

"Of course. Of course." Turning to Cochrane, the senator said, "Mr. Love is quite impressed with what you told him, Dr. Cochrane." As Love placed two tall glasses of ice water on the delicate round table, he added, "And Andy doesn't impress easily."

Pulling up one of the plush wheeled chairs from the conference table in the office's far corner, Love said pleasantly, "This could be the real thing, Senator. What they've got here could be a real breakthrough."

The senator nodded. "So it's possible to produce hydrogen fuel cheaply enough to undercut the price of gasoline, is it?"

Cochrane said, "Yes, sir. And what's more, you won't have to build a whole infrastructure of pipelines and storage facilities."

"How come?"

"You don't distribute the hydrogen; you distribute the bacteria that produce the hydrogen. Put a membrane containing the bugs into your car and then fill your fuel tank with water. The bugs split the water molecules. You pump the hydrogen to your engine and vent the oxygen out the exhaust pipe."

Love butted in. "Or you burn the hydrogen with the oxygen itself and get a more efficient use of the system."

Cochrane felt surprised. "Where'd you come up with that?"

"My connection at the National Academy suggested it. Instead of burning the hydrogen in air, which is only twenty percent oxygen, you burn it in the pure oxygen the bugs have split out of the water molecules. Higher-temperature combustion, more power to the engine."

"And more efficient," Cochrane agreed.

"Sounds fine," said Senator Bardarson.

"Senator," Love said, his dark face growing very serious, "this could be the key to an energy policy that really works. We could replace gasoline and the other petroleum-based fuels. This could be *huge*."

"If it's true," the senator cautioned.

"It's true," Cochrane said flatly.

"We have a problem, though," said Sandoval.

Senator Bardarson turned to her.

"A problem?" he asked.

"The Gould Energy Corporation is after this breakthrough," Sandoval said, a barely noticeable quaver in her low voice.

"Oh? What rights to this do they have?"

"None," Cochrane snapped. "But they've murdered two men so far to get my brother's work in their hands."

"Murdered? Do you have any proof of this?"

"One of them was my brother."

The senator glanced at Love, who shrugged in a fleeting *it's the first I've heard of this* gesture.

"Do you have any proof?" Bardarson asked again.

Cochrane shook his head.

Sandoval said, "We are personally in danger."

"I know Lionel Gould," the senator mused, almost to himself. "He can be very ... single-minded."

"There's something more," Love said, almost reluctantly.

"What now?"

"Dr. Cochrane—Michael Cochrane—was an employee of the Calvin Research Center when he made this discovery. They will probably claim proprietary rights to his work."

"Mike worked on his own," Cochrane said. "The people at Calvin Research didn't even know what he was doing. They still don't."

"Still, it could get into legal complications," Love insisted.

The senator waved a careless hand in the air. "That's what lawyers are for. We can straighten out the legal questions, one way or another. The important thing is that this breakthrough could revolutionize our energy picture."

"That's for sure," said Love.

"So"—Bardarson glanced at his wristwatch—"what can I do to help you?"

"We need protection," said Sandoval.

"Do you really believe that Lionel Gould would send thugs after you?"

"He already has," Cochrane said.

"And he won't give up easily," Sandoval added. "We are in serious personal danger."

The senator glanced at Love, then turned his eyes back to Sandoval. "I suppose I could get you some protection. Secret Service, maybe. Or a private security outfit."

"Temporarily," said Love.

"Long enough," Senator Bardarson said. "As long as necessary. That's a promise."

Sandoval reached a hand out to him. "Thank you," she breathed. "Thank you so much."

Bardarson engulfed her hand in one big, bony paw and patted it with the other. "It will be all right, I assure you."

Cochrane felt annoyed. He asked, "So where do we go from here?"

With another fleeting look at Love, the senator said, "I'm going to ask the National Academy of Sciences for a full study of your brother's work, Dr. Cochrane."

"We'll expect you to cooperate with them," said Love.

"That could take months."

"Yes, I understand. But in the meantime I'm going to bring up this matter with the full Senate Energy Committee. We've got to start the wheels rolling on this right away."

Then he turned to Sandoval, "And I'll have my people contact the Secret Service right away to arrange protection for you."

With that, he pulled himself out of the armchair like a carpenter's ruler unfolding, all lanky legs and arms. Cochrane got to his feet and extended his hand.

"Thank you, Senator."

"Just doing my job, Dr. Cochrane," the senator said, taking his hand in a firm, well-practiced grip.

He turned to Sandoval and took her hand again. "Don't you worry about a thing, young lady. I'll see to it that you're completely protected."

Cochrane thought he sounded like an insurance salesman.

Once Sandoval and Cochrane left his office, Senator Bardarson returned to his desk.

"This is really going to work?" he asked Love.

The aide nodded his shaved head vigorously. "From the little they told me, it sounds like the real thing. My pigeon over at NSF said it sounded good to him."

"We'll need to check this out thoroughly, Andy. I can't make a fool of myself over this."

Love nodded. "I'll phone the National Academy."

"Tell them I need a preliminary assessment as fast as they can get it to me."

"Right." Love hesitated, then added, "But if Gould has his fingers in the pie..."

"Yes, I know. It could get tricky."

Love stood before the senator's desk, a compact dark bundle of sinew and determination. "Senator, you know that I'm not a political adviser. But this thing could make a presidential candidate out of you. You could come out with an energy policy that *works*. Man, you could tell OPEC to go pound sand up their asses."

Bardarson grinned at the thought. But his expression sobered almost immediately. "If it's for real, Andy. If it's for real."

WASHINGTON, D.C.:
J. W. MARRIOTT HOTEL

This is still on Fiona's credit card?" Cochrane asked, once the bellman had put their bags in the room's closet and left with a minimal tip out of the last cash in Cochrane's pocket.

Nodding as she looked around the small room with its queen-sized bed and tall wardrobe of bleached pine, Sandoval said, "Fee knows I'll pay her back. It's okay."

Cochrane went to look out the room's only window. The concierge level, he thought. Not all that different from a regular room. Better than the airport flea trap we slept in last night. This high up, he could see the Mall and the phallic spire of the Washington Monument.

"I thought," he said, turning back to her, "that since we've got Secret Service protection now, we could start using our own cards again."

"Maybe," Sandoval replied. "But we haven't seen any Secret Service agents yet."

As if in response, there was a rap at the door.

Cochrane went to answer it, hesitated, then squinted through the peephole. Distorted by the fish-eye lens, he saw a stubby redheaded middle-aged woman in a navy blue jacket over a starched white blouse.

"Who is it?" he called through the door.

"Senator Bardarson's people sent me," came the reply.

Cochrane opened the door.

The redhead introduced herself as Sharon Quinn. Not from the Secret Service, she headed a private security company that the senator often used. She was small, but wiry and hard-eyed, her lean face set in a flinty expression.

"My company will be providing you protection twenty-four seven," she told Sandoval and Cochrane. "You won't see my people, but they'll be taking care of you."

She handed each of them a palm-sized black plastic paging device. "Carry these with you at all times. If you have any reason to be alarmed, any reason at all, beep us. We'll be at your side in less than a minute."

"Really?" Sandoval asked.

"You can bet your life on it," said Quinn.

"We will be, won't we?" Sandoval replied.

Quinn glared at her. "If you don't like this arrangement, lady, you can call the senator and tell him about it. In the meantime, my people will be providing your security."

She turned abruptly to Cochrane. "Any questions?"

"I guess not," Cochrane heard himself reply.

"Good. Have a pleasant day." She turned on her heel and left the room, letting the door swing shut behind her.

Cochrane looked at Sandoval. "That's our protection?"

She shrugged. "She seems professional enough."

"How many people do you think she'll have watching us?"

"One at a time, I imagine. A total of three for round-the-clock security."

With a wary shake of his head, Cochrane said, "I can't imagine her taking on Kensington."

"Maybe her other people are bigger," Sandoval said.

They spent the afternoon walking down to the Mall, taking in the Lincoln Memorial, strolling among the tourists along the Reflecting Pool. Cochrane kept looking around for Kensington's menacing figure or anyone who looked like he or she might be their bodyguard. He saw only tourists from all over the nation, all over the world. It was a warm but pleasant day, with fat puffs of cumulus clouds sailing slowly across the sky, providing shade from the late springtime sunshine.

By four o'clock they found themselves among the crowd thronging the streets of Georgetown. Wisconsin Avenue was jammed with growling, fume-spewing cars inching along from stoplight to stoplight.

"It's a wonder we're not all asphyxiated from the exhaust fumes," Sandoval said as they wormed along the crowded sidewalk.

"Once cars switch to hydrogen fuel," Cochrane said, feeling sweaty, "their exhausts will be water vapor. The humidity on the street will go through the roof."

"My hair will curl better."

"Nobody'll be able to keep a crease in his pants."

"It could start a whole new fashion trend."

They ducked into a quiet French restaurant on M Street and had a long, leisurely dinner.

"Do you think Senator Bardarson will handle everything properly?" Sandoval asked, over *canard au l'orange*.

"Did you see the light in his eyes?" Cochrane replied. "He wants to ride the hydrogen wagon all the way to the White House."

She nodded. Later, as dessert was being served, she asked, "Those three other people you sent your brother's results to, are you sure they're trustworthy?"

"I've known them since high school, Elena. We've been friends for a long time."

But inwardly a tendril of doubt began to gnaw at him. *I haven't seen any of them in years. Don Mattson, Vic Cardoza, and Sol Roseman. The Four Musketeers. It'd been a long time since high school. You drift apart. We exchange Christmas cards and an occasional e-mail. But how close am I to any of them? To anyone in the whole frigging world?*

Yet who else is there? I've been a loner all my life, except for those three. He remembered the time they cooked up a batch of chlorine gas in the high school chem lab. Mr. Miller took one look at that green cloud rising up to the ceiling and banged the fire alarm. Cleared the whole school. Vic talked them out of being suspended. Cochrane saw Cardoza's beautifully crafted look of innocence as he protested that they didn't realize the gas would escape the retort they had used to produce it.

Cochrane smiled at the memory of it. Across the table, Sandoval smiled back at him, misreading his inner thoughts.

I never made friends like them, Cochrane realized. Not really tight buddies like we were in high school. Once I got to college I had to work and study and there wasn't any time for making friends. That's when I became a loner.

Jennifer pulled me out of it, but once she died I've gone right back to being a hermit. I don't really have any friends. Not real friends, men I can count on.

He realized that Sandoval was gazing at him, her expression thoughtful, caring.

"Are you all right, Paul?"

He nodded and dipped a spoon into his *crème brûlée* to hide his embarrassment. She's the only person in the world I'm close to, he realized. She's entrusting her life to me. She could walk away from all this and be clear of me and whatever danger we're in.

Yes, said that sardonic voice inside his head. She'd also be walking away from ten million dollars.

But that's all gone now, he told himself. Once she agreed to go to Senator Bardarson with this, Gould's ten mil flew out the window. We won't get a penny for this. Mike's heirs will get whatever money the patent brings in. Irene's going to be a rich widow and Elena is sticking with me, even though there's no money in this for her anymore.

By the time they returned to their hotel room, Sandoval looked truly concerned about him.

"You've been awfully quiet all evening, Paul."

"Thinking," he said.

"Thinking about us?"

"About us. Yeah. About what's happening to us. About Mike and that Arashi guy and Kensington and Gould and the whole mess."

"It's a lot, I know."

"Yeah," he said, sitting on the bed to pull off his shoes.

She sat beside him. "You can change the world, Paul. It's in your hands."

He thought about that for a moment. "Elena, I don't want to change the world. I just want to find out who killed my brother."

"But the discovery he made..."

He looked into her sea-green eyes. "It's a laugh. Everybody wants to know the frigging secret. They all want Mike's data. But the secret really is that he did it."

She looked at him strangely, as if she didn't understand or didn't believe what he was saying.

"It's like this," Cochrane went on. "Mike figured out how to produce hydrogen cheaply from some microscopic bugs. The secret is that it works! Now any biologist with half a brain can figure out how to do it again. All this chasing around after Mike's data, it's bullshit, pure and simple. There isn't any secret, really. What one scientist can do, some other scientist can duplicate. There isn't any secret, not really."

"No, Paul, you're wrong," she said softly. "Oh, I'm sure you're right about the science part. But what Gould is after is much more than the science. He wants to *control* this new discovery. He wants to get a patent for it, so no one else can use what your brother discovered unless they pay Gould for the privilege. That's why he's dangerous. He wants a stranglehold on the entire global energy industry."

"A stranglehold...?"

"That's why he's willing to kill to get your brother's data into his own hands. That's why we're in danger."

Cochrane suddenly felt bone-weary, tired of the whole crazy business. This is too big, he said to himself. What the hell am I doing in the middle of all this crap? The global energy industry. A senator with White House ambitions. Who the hell cares about them?

"All I want," he said in a whisper, "is to find out who killed Mike. I owe my brother that much."

"You will, Paul. You're strong and determined. You'll find his murderer. I'm certain of that."

"Yeah," he said, in a long tired sigh. "But right now what I really need is a good night's sleep."

He was too exhausted, drained emotionally as well as physically, to make love with her. They lay together in the bed, the warmth of her body soothing him, making him feel safe, almost content, making him feel *wanted* and understood and no longer alone.

"Paul," she whispered in the darkness.

"Yes," he replied drowsily.

"Those three old friends of yours...the ones you sent your brother's data to."

"Hmm."

"Don't you think I should know who they are?"

"Huh?"

"I don't know who any of them are. If anything should happen..." She stopped, as if suddenly afraid of where her thoughts were leading.

"You mean if anything should happen to me."

"God forbid! Don't even speak about it." She was quiet for a few heartbeats. Then, "I suppose we have to face all the possibilities, though. I mean, it would be extra protection. Backup. If anything should happen to you, then I'd know where the information was being kept."

"Yeah, true enough," he mumbled.

"Are their names in your computer files?"

"Names, addresses, phone numbers, everything," he said, yawning.

"Don't you think I ought to know who they are?"

"The Four Musketeers," he mumbled sleepily. "Don Mattson, Vic Cardoza, Sol Roseman, and me."

"The Four Musketeers?"

"That's us. Now lemme go to sleep."

She kissed his ear lightly. "Good night darling. Sleep well."

"Night."

WASHINGTON, D.C.:
SENATOR BARDARSON'S OFFICE

While the Senate is in session, a senator's daily schedule is often turned upside down. Mornings are devoted to committee hearings, afternoons to actual sessions of the Senate—which can carry on into the late hours of the night. Then there are the luncheons, cocktail parties, dinners that form the backbone of the Washington social and political scene. A senator's meetings with his or her staff have to be squeezed into the odd hours of the day, or night.

Senator Bardarson's office manager had scheduled this strategy session four different times over the past two days, and each of the four times the senator had to cancel because other commitments got in the way. Now, close to midnight, he at last sat behind his desk with Anderson Love, his man for science and technology, and Avery Hunter, his most trusted political adviser.

Hunter was nondescript in appearance: average in height, medium in build, thinning sandy brown hair that had retreated from his forehead far enough to hang the nickname "egghead" on him. He had been a computer analyst for a struggling data management firm in Bangor when he'd volunteered to work for Ian Bardarson's first political campaign. Almost singlehandedly, Hunter had set up a computerized database that fed Bardarson up-to-the-minute information on what Maine's voters wanted, what they feared, what they would vote for—or against.

Since then, Hunter had served as the senator's strong right arm. Bardarson did not always follow his fellow down-Mainer's advice, but he always depended on Hunter when he had an important decision to make.

"Is this for real?" Hunter asked. He was seated in one of the burgundy leather-covered armchairs in front of the senator's dark cherrywood desk, swirling a glass of single-malt scotch on the rocks in his right hand.

"Seems that way," replied Anderson Love, sitting beside him in the other armchair. He, too, held a glass in his hand: Dr Pepper. "The people I've talked to at the National Academy are pretty excited about it."

Senator Bardarson asked, "How soon will the academy's report be ready?"

Love's dark face opened into a smile. "They wanted three months. I told them we needed a preliminary assessment by the end of the week."

"And Cochrane is cooperating with them?"

"Dr. Cochrane is happy as a pig in shit. He's working with National Academy scientists. He thinks it's an honor."

Bardarson grinned back at his aide. To Hunter he said, "Andy thinks I could ride this hobbyhorse to the nomination next year."

Hunter was silent for several heartbeats, then he replied slowly, "Energy is going to be a major issue next year. Already is today."

"Is it enough to get me the nomination?" Bardarson asked.

"Couldn't hurt."

With a mock frown, Senator Bardarson said, "Avery, don't go into your Delphic Oracle mode. I need concrete answers."

"Wellll," Hunter replied, stretching out the syllable, "everybody wants an answer to the energy problem. Voters aren't happy paying more than seven dollars a gallon for gasoline. If you can show that you have the answer—and nobody else does—then you'd be in first place by the time the national convention starts."

Bardarson reached for the untouched glass of cream soda on his desk.

"Of course," Hunter went on in his measured drawl, "the oil companies and the auto companies aren't going to like it. They don't want a solution to high energy prices. Right now they're happy as clams at high tide, no matter how many ads they take out on television to tell the people how hard they're workin' on solving the energy problem."

The senator sipped at his soda. "There's a lot of money we won't get."

"Ay-yup. They'll support the opposition, whoever it shapes up to be."

"Are you sure of that?" Love asked.

Hunter gave him a pitying look. "If you were head of a big oil corporation or an auto company, which would you prefer: rakin' in obscene profits from high fuel prices or sinking billions into retooling for some new technology that might not even work?"

"The car companies are hurting from high gasoline prices," Love argued. "Their sales are down across the board."

"Maybe so," countered Hunter. "But they'll shit bricks before they retool their whole industry to convert to hydrogen fuel."

"But it won't be that major a retooling," Love insisted. "It won't be like they have to redesign their engines from scratch. Most car engines could be converted to hydrogen pretty easily. At your local garage or gas station."

"Really?" Hunter seemed surprised.

"Really," said Love.

"Well, even so, you've still got the oil companies. And they're multinational. This has implications for our foreign policy: Israel and the whole Middle East."

"Let 'em all sink into the sea," Love grumbled.

"Wait a minute," Senator Bardarson said. "How would the Jewish vote go for this?"

Love replied sourly, "The damned Jews don't have enough votes to matter one way or the other."

"Don't kid yourself," Hunter objected. "The Jewish vote can swing New York."

"And they control a lot of the news media," Love admitted.

"And Hollywood."

Hunter laughed. "You two sound like a pair of anti-Zionists."

"Well, it's true, isn't it?" Bardarson said.

"The Jewish vote didn't elect Kerry," said Hunter. "Or Gore. Or anybody else. They're an important bloc to consider and you don't want to get them actively against you, but the Jews can't elect a president. Not by themselves."

Bardarson considered that for a moment. Then, "So how will they react to my hydrogen program?"

"They'll like it. Love it, in fact. Anything that reduces the influence the Arabs have over us, they'll be in favor of."

Looking nettled, Love asked, "And how much do we lose by alienating the Arabs and the rest of OPEC?"

"I'd worry more about the automobile industry," Hunter replied. "Lots of electoral votes in Michigan and the rest of the Rust Belt."

"Wait a minute," Bardarson said. "That Cochrane fellow said that Gould Energy is already involved in this."

"He said they're trying to grab control of the research breakthrough," Love added.

"That means that Lionel Gould is involved."

"Lionel Gould?" Hunter's brows shot up.

"He's been a big supporter of mine," Bardarson said. "He handed us a ton of soft money last time around."

Hunter scratched at his soft, round jaw. "I think you'd better have a quiet little chat with Lionel Gould. See where he stands on this."

Senator Bardarson nodded. In his mind he recalled the three laws of politics enunciated decades earlier by Senator Everett Dirksen:

1. Get elected.
2. Get reelected.
3. Don't get mad, get even.

Bardarson did not want Lionel Gould to get mad at him. On the other hand, he deeply wanted to be elected the next president of the United States.

WASHINGTON, D.C.:
NATIONAL ACADEMY OF SCIENCES

For the first time since he'd learned of his brother's murder Paul Cochrane felt relaxed. He was sitting on a concrete bench outside the headquarters building of the National Academy of Sciences, beneath a cloud-flecked sky of flawless blue, feeling the warmth of the springtime sunshine soaking into him. On the bench beside him sat Owen Esterbrook, a microbiologist from nearby Georgetown University.

Both men were in their shirtsleeves, munching on burgers from a fast-food joint a few blocks up Fifth Street. Cochrane squinted through the early afternoon brightness at the slightly larger-than-life statue of Albert Einstein across the lawn from where they were sitting. Like them, Einstein was seated casually on a park bench, dressed in rumpled sweater and slacks, a benign smile on his saintly face.

"I wonder what he'd think about this," Cochrane said between bites on his burger.

Esterbrook was a much older man, bald except for a fringe of white hair ringing his pate, lean and long-legged.

"Who?" he asked.

Cochrane pointed with his chin. "Old Uncle Albert."

Esterbrook laughed. "When I was a kid there was a comic strip with an alligator that they called Uncle Albert."

"I meant Einstein."

"Yes, I know. The Pope of Physics, that's what Wigner or one of those guys called him when he decided to come to America."

"I guess this microbiology business would be out of his field," Cochrane said.

With a slight shrug Esterbrook replied, "I don't think he considered anything outside his field. He was interested in the whole universe, remember."

Cochrane shrugged back at him. "I suppose so."

"It's going well, though," Esterbrook said. "Your brother's results seem quite solid. His engineered cyanobacteria produced hydrogen like good little troopers."

Esterbrook had been asked by the National Academy to examine Michael Cochrane's research results and try to validate them.

"I think we can tell Love that your brother hit the nail on the head," Esterbrook said.

"How soon?"

"Another week, I should think. The results look good, and thoroughly reproducible. We'll start writing the preliminary report in a couple of days."

Cochrane nodded happily. It was all coming together. Under Senator Bardarson's protective wing, they'd eventually be able to tell Gould and his goons to go to hell.

Cochrane spent the afternoon in Esterbrook's laboratory on the Georgetown campus, surprised at how small and almost shabby the lab looked. Then he remembered the old dictum: a neat, well-scrubbed laboratory is the sign that no creative work is being done. When you've got wires festooned from the ceiling and a crazy maze of glassware tangled over the benches and cables snaking across the floor, then you're getting some real work accomplished.

He was back at the Marriott in time to walk with Sandoval down to Water Street and a dinner of blue crab at Phillips Seafood, outside on the patio in the long, lingering sunset by the bank of the gently flowing Po-

tomac. Couples were working paddleboats along the river while the glowing twilight silhouetted the dome of the Jefferson Memorial, across the
Tidal Basin.

They strolled leisurely back to the hotel, Cochrane talking about how
well the work with Esterbrook was going, Sandoval silent for the most
part, just drawing him out, encouraging him to tell her every detail.

Back in their room, Cochrane suddenly asked, "So what did you do all
day?"

She smiled and tilted her head to one side. "Oh, this and that. I had a
long chat with Fiona, told her it's probably going to take longer than we
thought to pay her back."

"Huh. Yeah, I guess it will."

"It's all right. She doesn't mind. She knows we're good for it."

"I ought to be getting a paycheck from the university," he said.

"You're not having it sent here!"

"No, no," Cochrane reassured her. "To Senator Bardarson's office.
Andy Love will let me know when it arrives."

Sandoval nodded guardedly.

"Still worried about Kensington?"

"Aren't you?"

"Not anymore. Gould can't take on the senator."

"Paul, Gould *owns* senators."

Cochrane had no reply for that. He thought about the tough-looking
little redhead, Quinn. Haven't seen any signs of her people around, he
thought. But in another week or so we won't need any protection. Esterbrook'll hand in his report to the senator and the whole process will be out
in the open where Gould can't grab it for himself. Then it's over. Finished.

Except, he remembered, you still don't know who murdered Mike.

They watched television for a desultory hour, then got ready for bed.
When Cochrane finished brushing his teeth and came out of the bathroom, he saw that Sandoval was wearing a shapeless white T-shirt that fell
just past her hips. Usually they both slept in the nude.

He flopped on the bed and when she crawled in beside him and
clicked off the lamp on the night table, he started to run a hand up her
thigh.

"I've got my period, Paul. Sorry."

He felt surprised. "Oh! Okay."

She snuggled close to him and whispered mischievously, "I don't have
lockjaw, though."

He grinned in the darkness. "No, it's okay."

"You sure?"

He slid an arm around her shoulders and felt her head nestle in the hollow of his shoulder. Cochrane sighed contentedly.

"You're happy?" she asked.

"Yeah. I really am."

"That's good. I am, too."

"We're not going to get rich, you know. We're not going to get that ten mil from Gould."

"It doesn't matter."

"You sure?"

"Yes, Paul. I'm completely sure."

He fell silent, staring into the darkness, feeling her warmth beside him, feeling protective and safe at the same time.

"Fiona told me about your father," he said, in a whisper.

"I know. And the rest of it, too, didn't she?"

"She did."

"I was pretty wild there for a time," Sandoval admitted. "I still was, I guess. Until I met you."

It's too good to be true, Cochrane told himself. But then he remembered something from a science history class, something that Michael Faraday had said: *Nothing is too wonderful to be true.*

"Elena?"

"Hmm," she murmured.

"I love you, Elena. I really do."

"I know, Paul. And I'm glad, 'cause I love you, too, darling. Madly."

Until he spoke the words, Cochrane hadn't realized it was true. I love her, he said to himself. I really do love her. For the first time since Jennifer died he felt that there was something to live for. No, he corrected himself: some*one* to live for. He was overjoyed at her response to him, even though there was still a tendril of doubt in his mind. The hell with it, he told himself. We love each other. She's willing to throw away ten million dollars because of me. If that isn't love, then what the hell is?

He turned and kissed her gently.

"Good night," he whispered. And fell asleep with a smile on his lips.

NEW YORK:
UNITED NATIONS SECRETARIAT
BUILDING

Jason Tulius clipped the visitor's badge to the lapel of his jacket and nodded idly as the receptionist gave him directions to the offices of the United Nations Educational, Scientific and Cultural Organization. He had been there more than once in the past few years; he knew the way through the maze of corridors and offices that honeycombed the UN Secretariat Building.

He felt tense, on edge, as he entered the elevator and punched the button. The buzz of conversations in many languages was nothing more than a background hum in Tulius's ears as the elevator filled up. Shamil isn't going to like the news I'm bringing, he thought. Finally the doors slid shut and the elevator rose from the lobby level. Tulius felt crowded, almost trapped. Too many bodies pressing too close together. Most of the men in the elevator wore Western business suits, despite their national origin or skin color. The women were more individualistic and colorful, although even they were clad mainly in Western dress.

Compared to some of the ambassadors' suites Tulius had seen at the UN's headquarters the UNESCO offices were a drab, functional ants' nest of bureaucrats. Not that anyone scurried busily; the outer office was large and fully staffed with men and women at their desks, but the place was quiet, almost languid. No guards that Tulius could distinguish; not even terrorists were interested in harming UNESCO personnel. Not yet, Tulius thought. Eventually the day will come.

He was met at the long counter that blocked access to the big room's interior by an exotically good-looking young woman wearing a swirling, colorful robe.

"May I help you?" she asked in lilting English.

"Mr. Shamil, please. He's expecting me. I am Dr. Jason Tulius."

"One moment, please, sir." The woman went back to her desk, picked up a headset, and pecked at her keyboard. After a few words she looked up and smiled at Tulius, then ushered him through the maze of desks to the private office of Zelinkshah Shamil.

Shamil was a Chechen who worked as a professional administrator in UNESCO's labyrinthine bureaucracy. He was a dour, unsmiling man of sturdy build, at least two inches taller than Tulius himself, with skin that looked as if it had been stained by tobacco, a thick black mustache, muscular shoulders, but a soft, bulging middle. His dark eyes always glowered with suspicion.

"Salaam, Dr. Tulius," he said, in a rough, rasping voice. "To what do I owe the honor of this visit?"

Tulius waited while Shamil firmly closed his office door and went to his gray steel desk, gesturing to the hard plastic visitor's chair.

"I'm in New York to meet with Lionel Gould," Tulius said. "He wants to buy the center. I thought you should know."

"Gould Energy still wants to buy the Calvin Center?" Shamil grumbled.

"Not Gould Energy Corporation," Tulius corrected. "The Gould Trust."

Shamil shrugged annoyedly. "Gould Energy, Gould Trust, what difference? It's all the same man."

"He's making an offer that will be very difficult to refuse."

"I see. And our arrangement? What of that?"

For four years Shamil had quietly been diverting UNESCO funds to the Calvin Research Center, on the promise that Tulius's scientists would find a way to make cheap hydrogen fuel. A fugitive from the devastation of Chechnya, Shamil knew that a breakthrough in producing hydrogen would shatter the international oil market. OPEC would suffer, but that did not bother Shamil. Russia—the world's second largest producer and exporter of petroleum—would suffer more. And for the barbarous destruction that Russia had unleashed on his native Chechnya, for the slaughter that Russia was still wreaking on the people, the women, the babies of Chechnya, for the utter destruction of Grozny and other Chechen cities, Shamil had sworn vengeance.

Jason Tulius, grandson of a Lithuanian lawyer who had died in a Soviet gulag, had just as little love for the Russians as Shamil. He would be glad to see their main source of foreign capital dry up in a global move from petroleum to hydrogen.

Tulius squirmed uncomfortably in the squeaking plastic chair. "One of my staff apparently made the breakthrough we were looking for," he began.

"Apparently?"

"He was murdered. His data was stolen."

"By Gould," Shamil snapped.

"I don't think so. Why would Gould want to buy the laboratory if he already had what he wanted in his hands?"

"Then ... who?"

Tulius shook his head. "I wish I knew. I have my staff working balls-out to reproduce the murdered man's work. His brother is involved, too. With some woman named Sandoval. A very beautiful woman."

Shamil took a deep, sighing breath. "I have taken many risks to fund your research. I don't want your work to go to Gould."

"Does it matter?" Tulius asked. "I mean, does it matter who owns the hydrogen fuel patent? So long as the world market for petroleum collapses?"

Stroking his mustache thoughtfully, Shamil replied, "It matters if Gould wants control of the hydrogen work merely to suppress it."

"Suppress it?" Tulius felt shocked.

"The man has enormous interests in petroleum, does he not? It wouldn't be in his best interests to break the back of the oil market."

"I'd never thought of that."

"You are a scientist. To you, the beauty of the research blinds you to the realities of the world."

"Perhaps," Tulius admitted reluctantly. "But even so, I can't very well say no to Gould. His offer is too good to refuse."

Shamil went back to stroking his mustache. "But suppose you took his offer, reproduced the breakthrough the murdered man made"—he smiled—"and still give me the information."

Tulius's eyes widened. "If Gould found out ... he'd kill me."

"Not necessarily," said Shamil gently. "Of course, if you refuse to give me the information after all the millions I've siphoned to you, well ... some of my fellow Chechens are much more impulsive than I. Much more violent, as well."

WASHINGTON, D.C.: GEORGETOWN UNIVERSITY

If anything, Dr. Esterbrook's office was even smaller and shabbier than his lab. It was little more than a cubbyhole containing a heavy old-fashioned scroll desk that looked to Cochrane as though the old man had picked it up in a rummage sale, a mismatched pair of straight-backed wooden chairs, and a wall covered with ceiling-high bookshelves. The one window looked out on an alley that, this late at night, was dark with menacing shadows except for a lone street lamp half a block away that cast a forlorn pool of light that only seemed to make the darkness more sinister.

Esterbrook's computer was first-rate, though, Cochrane realized as he worked with the older man on writing their report. Cochrane was sitting on one of the stiff wooden chairs with his laptop, appropriately enough, on his lap. His computer was connected wirelessly with Esterbrook's desktop machine as they laboriously wrote the report they would send to the National Academy and Senator Bardarson.

"Writing is always such a chore," Esterbrook muttered as they struggled through a paragraph describing the genetic modifications of the cyanobacteria.

Cochrane nodded agreement. "Research would be fun if you didn't have to write the damned papers."

Esterbrook glanced up from his desktop screen. "Still, you know what Faraday said: 'Physics is to make experiments and to publish them.' It isn't science until someone else can test your results, and no one can test your work unless you write it down for them to read."

Cochrane grunted, thinking, Faraday again. For a cobbler's son the man had a lot to say.

He had been working with Esterbrook on this mother-loving report all day, and into the night, taking only a brief break at seven o'clock to grab a quick dinner with Sandoval. Then he had kissed her good night and hurried back to the Georgetown campus.

Despite the old man's grousing, Esterbrook seemed to be in his element. Cochrane was impressed by how he could take the complex bioengineering that Mike had done and express it clearly and succinctly. This report isn't just for other scientists, Cochrane knew. Or even for Andy Love. The senator's the real audience for this. It's got to be written so that a scientific illiterate can understand it.

And it was shaping up that way, he saw as he scrolled through the paragraphs they had put together. Cochrane himself was no microbiologist, so he was serving more or less as a devil's advocate for Esterbrook, pointing out phrasing that depended too much on specialized jargon, asking questions where the report brought up subjects that he didn't know about.

Cochrane glanced at the time displayed in the lower right corner of his laptop's screen: ten P.M. We've been at this for more than twelve hours now, he realized.

"I'm starting to see double," he temporized.

Esterbrook peered at him over his half-glasses. "Tired, are you?"

Trying to make it sound humorous, Cochrane asked, "Don't you have a wife to go home to?"

"No," the older man replied, completely guileless. "I've been a bachelor all my life."

"Well, I'm wasted."

With a patient little smile, Esterbook said, "But you're the one who's in such a rush to get this report out."

"I know, I know," Cochrane said, his fingers shutting down the laptop's program. "But I—"

The phone rang.

Cochrane's insides jumped. Then he thought, Nobody knows I'm here except Elena. She's probably wondering when I'm coming home.

Esterbrook stared at the phone. "Now, who would be calling at this time of night?"

"It's probably for me."

Gesturing to the phone console on his desk, Esterbrook said, "You may answer it, then."

Cochrane picked up the handset. "Hello."

"Paul, it's me." Elena's voice: high, hurried, frightened. "Kensington's here. He—" Her voice cut off.

"Elena?" Cochrane fairly screamed.

"She's all in one piece," Kensington's dark voice came through the earpiece. "If you want to keep her that way, get yourself back to your hotel right away. And I mean right away."

WASHINGTON, D.C.:
J. W. MARRIOTT HOTEL

Cochrane's insides were churning so badly he thought he'd throw up in the taxi. Traffic wasn't too heavy at this time of night, the rational part of his mind noticed, yet still the cab seemed to inch along through the streets. At last the taxi pulled up to the hotel's entryway. Cochrane stuffed his last twenty-dollar bill into the little receptacle built into the plastic partition that protected the driver, then dived out of the cab and ran through the lobby to the elevators.

His hands were shaking. It took three tries for him to get his key card into the slot. The light turned green and he pushed the door open.

Kensington was sprawled lazily on the sofa, his long legs resting on the coffee table, watching television. He grinned as Cochrane half staggered into the room.

"Took your time getting here," he said, reaching for the remote and clicking off the TV. "I was starting to think you wouldn't show up."

"I got here as fast as I could," Cochrane said, panting.

Kensington slowly got to his feet. "Too bad. I was just starting to think about how much fun I could have with her if you didn't show up."

"Were is she? What—"

"Relax, four-eyes. She's okay. So far."

"What do you want?"

"Nothing much," Kensington said, stepping around the coffee table. He brushed a fingertip against the crusty scab beneath his right eye. "Nothing much," he repeated.

He rammed a lightning-fast fist into Cochrane's midsection. Cochrane felt as if a bulldozer had slammed into him. He doubled up, his body flaring into pain, his breath knocked out of him, and collapsed to the floor.

"That's for marking me with that toy sword of yours," Kensington said.

Cochrane couldn't speak. He gasped for breath. The pain was overwhelming, thundering through him.

Kensington knelt down on one knee and leaned close to Cochrane's ear. "Now, you just do what you're told and everybody'll be happy. Understand?"

Cochrane tried to speak, couldn't.

"Understand?" Kensington repeated sternly, jabbing Cochrane's shoulder with stiff fingers.

Cochrane nodded.

"Good. The cunt's in a safe place. Nobody's going to hurt her as long as you deliver the goods."

"Deliver . . . the goods."

"All your brother's discs," Kensington said. "And the report you're supposed to be working on for the senator. Understand?"

Cochrane nodded again. The pain was dulling to a sullen agony, like being slowly roasted over a bed of hot coals.

"And we want the names of those three friends of yours that you mailed the data to. That's important. Names, addresses, phone and e-mail numbers. Got that?"

Squeezing his eyes shut against the pain, Cochrane realized that they knew everything. Everything. All the cards were in Gould's hands.

"Okay." Kensington got to his feet. "Now we understand each other."

Cochrane didn't even try to get up. He lay on the carpeting, face down, helpless with pain.

Kensington started for the door, hesitated. He turned back toward Cochrane. "Oh, yeah, one more thing."

He kicked Cochrane in the small of his back. White-hot agony flared through him. He screamed from the pain, but nothing came through his throat but a strangled groan.

"That's for telling Gould that I was willing to sell him out." Kensington studied Cochrane's prostrate form, nodded as if satisfied with his work, then said, "Have a nice day."

He left Cochrane lying there, awash in sweat and misery. He remembered the pager that Quinn had given him, started to fumble in his pocket for it. What's the use? he said to himself. Too late now. He's gone. Too late. He felt himself slipping into unconsciousness, felt grateful for the dark oblivion that swallowed him.

The insistent ringing of the telephone awakened him. Cochrane blinked gummy eyes, focused on the phone. It was on the night table beside the bed, a hundred miles away. Just lifting his head off the carpet brought on a surge of agony that made his insides heave.

The ringing stopped. Cochrane licked his brittle dry lips. Got to get up, he told himself. With infinite effort he reached for the coffee table, leaned one arm on it, and tried to lever himself up to his knees.

The damned phone started again. Stiffly, slowly, Cochrane crawled on all fours toward the night table. It seemed to take an hour to cross the few feet of distance.

Fumbling the phone off its base, he sat against the bed and mumbled, "Hello?"

"Dr. Cochrane? Paul? It's me ... Owen Esterbrook."

"Dr. Esterbrook?"

"Are you all right? You left the office in such a rush."

"How ... how'd you get this number?"

"The phone stores the numbers of incoming calls. I just pushed the 'return call' button."

Cochrane felt foggy, totally weary.

"Are you all right?" Esterbrook repeated.

"I'll live. I think."

"You sound terrible."

"Listen," Cochrane said, suddenly remembering what he had to do. "That report we're writing. Forget it. Destroy it. Erase it from your hard drive."

For a long moment Esterbrook didn't reply. Then, "What do you mean? I can't erase—"

"Erase it!" Cochrane shouted. The effort brought a fresh wave of pain. "It's my data. I want it erased. Destroyed."

"But Senator Bardarson—"

"Screw Senator Bardarson. I want that report erased. Totally. Your own life might depend on it."

"My life?"

Cochrane tried to get fresh air into his lungs. His entire body was aflame; he could only take shallow little breaths.

"I don't understand you," Esterbrook said.

"Look," Cochrane replied, more reasonably. "Things have changed. I don't want to deliver the report to Senator Bardarson. Or anyone else. I want it destroyed. In its entirety."

"This is ... well, it's very unusual, to say the least."

"I realize that."

"We don't write reports and then erase them."

"Please. I need your cooperation. Don't ask me to explain. Just do as I tell you."

Another silence, longer this time. At last Esterbrook said, "I'll stop working on the report, if that's what you wish. We'll need to talk about this face to face."

"Okay," Cochrane said, too exhausted to feel pleased. "I'll call you ... tomorrow. We'll talk then."

"Are you certain you're all right, Paul?"

"Yeah. I'm okay."

"Well ... good night, then."

"Good night. And thanks."

It took every ounce of his remaining strength to reach up and hook the phone back on its receptacle. Then he sank back to the carpeting and passed out.

Catch-22 for Lite Fuel

Ford's latest fuel-cell-powered car faces an energy conundrum

By Leonard Eames Ryan

Test-driving a car powered entirely by a hydrogen-fed fuel cell is something else. Ford's new H2X is peppier on city streets than most gasoline-powered economy cars. It feels different, too, because the fuel cell powers an electric motor instead of a normal gasoline engine. There's no growl, no roar, no lurch of shifting gears. The H2X feels more like a golf cart than an automobile.

Fuel cells generate electricity by combining hydrogen fuel with oxygen from the air. Then the electricity powers the quietly purring motor. Ford is betting that such pure electrical cars will outperform and outsell hybrids that use fuel cells as well as a normal internal combustion engine.

Hydrogen can be extracted from water, in theory, but it takes a lot of electrical power to split the H_2O molecule so that its hydrogen can be used for fuel. Hydrogen is more efficient than gasoline, however. A liter of hydrogen (roughly a quart) yields as much mileage as a gallon of gasoline: approximately 57 miles. And what comes out of a hydrogen-powered auto's exhaust pipe is nothing more than water vapor, not greenhouse-warming carbon dioxide.

But hydrogen is very bulky, requiring an oversized fuel tank that makes the H2X's trunk space minimal and its rear seat claustrophobic. Even so, the H2X's range is only about 150 miles—and there aren't many service stations around where a driver can fuel up on hydrogen.

Another problem is that hydrogen is difficult to distribute. The gas leaks out of normal pipeline seals and joints. Until there is a significant demand for hydrogen fuel, no one is going to take the investment risk to build special hydrogen distribution systems and hydrogen "gas" stations. And until such distribution infrastructure comes into being, the hydrogen car will remain nothing more than a lovely dream.

Catch-22.

—*New Times Monthly*

PHILADELPHIA:
THE FRANKLIN INSTITUTE

The larger-than-life statue of Benjamin Franklin smiled down benignly at the horde of schoolchildren pouring through the science museum's main lobby. The planetarium show had just ended, and the youngsters were streaming toward their waiting school buses, the din of their chattering, yelling, laughing echoing painfully off the lobby's high walls.

Senator Bardarson winced at the noise, thinking that it was a waste of time and money to bring these kids to a science museum. All they did was trash the exhibits and race uncontrolled through the halls. Pearls before swine. Publicly, though, the senator always voted in favor of spending federal funds to support "outreach" programs that paid to send ghetto kids to cultural institutions.

The senator had motored up to Philadelphia in one of his limousines. No paper trail of airline or train tickets. Only his chauffeur accompanied him, and the man was quiet-mouthed and completely loyal.

Lionel Gould had driven down from New York. Philadelphia was a good halfway point for their meeting. Gould was not in the noisy, crowded lobby, of course. A slim young African-American woman pushed her way through the tide of schoolchildren, frowning distastefully at them.

"Senator Bardarson?" she asked.

Bardarson nodded and smiled while he thought that she would have to be a real brain-damage case not to recognize the only adult male in the lobby, except for a trio of uniformed guards who were pointedly ignoring the scrambling flow of children.

"Mr. Gould is waiting for you," the young woman said.

She led him up a narrow winding marble staircase to a set of offices that were blissfully quiet. Extending a graceful slim arm, she gestured to a closed door.

"In there," she said.

Bardarson stepped into a fair-sized library. Its walls were stacked with bookshelves, except for a pair of windows that looked out on the greenery of the broad Parkway, where cars and buses flowed smoothly along. It was starting to get cloudy, Bardarson noticed. I'll probably go back to Washington in the rain, he thought.

Lionel Gould was seated at the head of the library's only table, intently poring over a thick book that looked to Bardarson like an atlas of some kind. Gould's suit jacket lay over the back of the chair nearest him; his necktie was pulled loose, his shirt collar unbuttoned.

When he looked up from the atlas and made a perfunctory smile, the senator could see that Gould's face was shining with perspiration. There's something wrong with the man, Bardarson thought. I wonder how long he has to live.

"Good afternoon, Ian," Gould said cheerfully. "It's good of you to come all this way to see me."

Bardarson pulled out the heavy oak chair closest to Gould and sat down. "You came just as far, Lionel."

"Indeed. Indeed. A meeting of equals, eh?"

The senator nodded and smiled. "This is an unusual place to meet, isn't it?"

"Perhaps so," Gould agreed easily. "The Gould Trust supports this museum handsomely. And it's just about halfway between your base and mine. Besides, it's not likely to be staked out by nosy reporters."

"The paparazzi don't haunt science museums, true enough."

"So," Gould said, closing the massive atlas and pushing it aside, "it seems our interests have intersected."

"Interesting choice of words, Lionel."

Gould threw his head back and laughed, a hearty, full-throated bellow that almost rattled the windows. Bardarson wondered what was so funny.

"I choose my words carefully," Gould said as he took a handkerchief from his back pocket and mopped his face. "I am interested in this hydrogen fuel process that Dr. Cochrane discovered—"

"Invented," Bardarson corrected. "Since we're choosing words carefully."

With a smile, Gould conceded, "Invented. Have it your way."

"And I," said Bardarson, "intend to use the hydrogen fuel card as the cornerstone of my proposed new energy policy."

"You intend to ride hydrogen fuel to the White House," Gould said, his smile gone.

"I hope to have your help in my campaign, Lionel."

"Indeed. Which is why we need to understand each other."

Bardarson nodded.

Clasping his hands together on the tabletop and hunching forward, Gould said, "I am perfectly prepared to support your candidacy for president. Support you generously, I might add."

The senator was silent for a moment, studying Gould's sweat-sheened face. At last he asked, "In exchange for what?"

Staring straight into the senator's eyes, Gould replied, "In exchange for your understanding. Nothing more than that."

"Understanding?"

Deadly serious, Gould said, "This hydrogen fuel thing must be handled carefully. Very carefully."

"You mean suppressed."

"No! Not suppressed. Certainly not."

"Then what?"

Gould pursed his lips, then continued, "It must be phased in carefully. We cannot simply switch from fossil fuels to hydrogen overnight."

"I understand that, Lionel."

"Do you?"

"Of course. I know Detroit can't convert its assembly lines to a new kind of engine without enormous retooling, reinvestment. The whole industry will be affected. They'll need considerable help from the Energy Department."

"And the Department of Labor," Gould added, almost mournfully.

"That's why," Bardarson said, slipping into his speech-making mode, "we need a carefully thought-out, fully integrated energy policy. One that involves our relations with OPEC and all the Middle East."

"And the Russians," Gould added. "They are major petroleum producers, don't forget."

"Of course, of course."

"But the key question," said Gould, "is who will *control* the hydrogen
process."

"Control it?"

"This man Cochrane discovered—or invented, if you will—a means
of obtaining hydrogen from water cheaply, efficiently. A process that won't
require building a whole infrastructure of piping and new service stations."

"So I understand," said Bardarson.

"Gould Energy Corporation should control it."

Bardarson had seen it coming. Of course Gould would want to control the hydrogen fuel process. Why else would he be interested in it? If I
want Gould's support in my run for the White House, the senator told
himself, I'll have to let him have control of the hydrogen fuel process.
That's politics. Give and take. I'll scratch your back if you scratch mine.

"Do you have a proprietary position on this?" he asked guardedly.

Gould made a sound halfway between a grunt and a snort. "We would
have, if the late Dr. Cochrane had lived long enough to honor the verbal
agreement he made with me."

"Oral agreement," Bardarson murmured, remembering some old
movie mogul's dictum: *An oral agreement isn't worth the paper it's written on.*

"I was prepared to give Cochrane ten million dollars for the rights to
his work. I am still prepared to give his brother and that call girl he's running around with the same amount, if and when they deliver the process
to me."

"Call girl?" Bardarson felt surprised. And intrigued. "That Sandoval
woman? Is she really a prostitute?"

"The next thing to it," Gould muttered. "She uses her body to get
what she wants."

"Really?"

With a smirk, Gould asked, "Are you interested?"

The senator suppressed a grin. "Let's get back to business, shall we?"

"By all means."

Leaning back in the hard, unforgiving chair, Bardarson asked, "Once
you get the information about this hydrogen process, what do you intend
to do with it?"

"Patent it, first of all," said Gould.

"That will take a year or more."

"Piffle!" Gould waved a chubby hand. "Once we have the patent in hand, we can begin to bring together leaders of the petroleum and automobile industry to start the process of integrating hydrogen fuel into the existing energy and transportation industries."

"In other words, delay the conversion to hydrogen as long as possible."

Gould started to reply angrily, but caught himself and forced a smile instead. "As long as oil prices keep rising, why should we upset the applecart?"

"Because you'll be bleeding the American taxpayer to death!" Bardarson snapped.

"You mean the American voter, don't you?"

"One and the same."

Gould shook his head. "Senator, do you actually believe you can capture your party's nomination without the support of the energy and automobile industries? And their unions?"

Bardarson did not reply. He realized that what Gould was threatening was not merely to refuse to support him. *He'll support whoever runs against me. He'll support whoever plays ball with him.*

"I'm not an unreasonable man," Gould said, more gently. "I understand how much an energy policy based on this new discovery will enhance your candidacy. But you've got to be reasonable, too."

Almost in a whisper, Bardarson asked, "What do you suggest?"

Gould took a deep breath, mentally choosing his words. "This hydrogen process works in the laboratory, yes. But that's a long way from being practical, a long way from being available for the average man's automobile."

"True enough," Bardarson said tightly.

"Use the discovery as the cornerstone of your proposed energy policy. Talk freely about converting to hydrogen fuels. Bring the ecologists and the greenhouse warming freaks into your tent. Tell the voters that your energy policy will bring back cheap fuel for their cars—eventually."

"Eventually."

"Yes, eventually," said Gould. "You can make the voters think that *eventually* means within a few years, within the span of your first term in the White House."

"I see."

"But it will actually take longer than that."

"Much longer."

"That depends on many factors. Global demand for oil. Political relations with the Middle East and Russia. Greenhouse warming. Many factors."

"And you'll decide how quickly we convert to hydrogen."

Gould nodded. "That decision should be made by the people who best understand the needs of the global energy and transportation markets."

"Meaning you."

With a smiling little dip of his chin, Gould agreed, "Meaning me."

"You'll support my election campaign under those terms?"

"And your reelection campaign, four years later," said Gould.

The senator fell silent again, weighing his options.

Gould enticed, "Ian, the world will move from petroleum to hydrogen fuel sooner or later. It's inevitable. All we're talking about is the timing. It's only a matter of a few years: the span of your first term in office, perhaps. Or the second, certainly."

Bardarson knew when he was being lied to, but he reluctantly extended his right hand. Gould grasped it firmly and said, "You won't regret this. Not once you're in the White House."

Bardarson said, "I suppose not."

WASHINGTON, D.C.:
J. W. MARRIOTT HOTEL

Cochrane was awakened by someone yelling at him in Spanish. He was lying on the floor beside the bed when the chambermaid let herself into his room, took one look at his prostrate form, and decided he was a drunk or a druggie.

Stiff and aching, Cochrane tried to pull himself to his feet. He grabbed the bedsheets and struggled up to a kneeling position, then crawled onto the bed, grunting with exertion. He tried to speak to the maid but his throat was too dry to get any words out. She probably doesn't understand that much English anyway, he thought. Looking thoroughly disgusted, the chambermaid walked out of the room, grumbling in her native tongue.

Where did they take Elena? His mind raced. What are they doing to her? Christ, I need help. I've got to find her, get her back from them. Who—

Two men in business suits burst into the room.

"Sir, are you all right?"

Cochrane looked at them with bleary eyes. *I'm stretched out on the bed fully clothed and they're asking if I'm all right.*

"I think so," he said, pushing himself up to a sitting position. His back throbbed sullenly but he was more stiff than injured.

"The maid..."

"I know. I must have fallen asleep on the floor last night."

"Do you need medical attention?" asked the other one of them.

"No!"

"Are you certain, sir? We could have the house doctor look you over."

The idea was tempting, but Cochrane slowly shook his head. The effort made his insides lurch. "I'm all right," he insisted.

"Are you sure?" the first one demanded.

"Yeah. I'm okay. I just need some rest."

They looked uncertain, but the first one said, "Okay. I'll put the do-not-disturb sign on your doorknob."

"If you need anything," the second one said, "call the concierge."

"Right. Thanks."

They left, reluctantly, shutting the door with a soft click. Cochrane heard something, turned his head, and saw that rain was spattering on the window. A gray day out there. Perfect. He sank back onto the bed, wanting nothing more than to sleep for a hundred hours or so.

But he couldn't. Too much to do.

Okay. First step, he told himself: see if you can make it to the bathroom.

He swung his legs off the bed and climbed stiffly, shakily to his feet. Leaning on the night table, then the wall, and finally the bathroom door, he got to the lavatory.

No blood in my urine, he saw, peering into the toilet bowl. *You're not that bad off.*

A quick hot shower softened the pain and stiffness in his back. Naked, he padded back to the bed and punched out Dr. Esterbrook's number.

"Paul, is everything all right?"

"Not really," he said. "I've got to have that report. It's urgent. Something's come up and that report could save a woman's life."

He heard Esterbrook gasp. "A woman's life?"

"I can't explain now. But please, *please,* take up the pages we've done so far and e-mail them to me. Then erase them from your hard drive."

"I can't erase it. You're talking about a report commissioned by the National Aca—"

"I'm talking about my property," Cochrane snapped. "That data doesn't belong to the academy or anyone else except me."

"But Senator Bardarson expects—"

"I'll square it with the senator. I'll take full responsibility."

"Are you sure—"

"Yes, I'm sure! Positive! Do it now!"

He could picture the confusion and uncertainty on Esterbrook's chalk-pale face.

"If that's what you really want, Paul."

"It's what I need," said Cochrane. He hung up so he wouldn't have to argue further or explain. Then he pecked out Senator Bardarson's number. After speaking to several office flunkies, he finally got Anderson Love.

"The senator's out of town," Love said.

"I've got to talk to him," Cochrane insisted. "It's vital."

"What's it about?"

"I've got to withdraw the hydrogen information. I can't give it to you."

"You've already—"

"I've got to take it back!" Cochrane shouted into the phone.

"But you've already told us about it. We got the National Academy into this, for god's sake."

"Look, Mr. Love," Cochrane said, trying to be more reasonable, "I can't go through with it. Do you understand, I *can't!*"

"The senator isn't going to like this."

"That's why I need to talk to him. To explain what's happened. I need his help."

Love went silent for a few heartbeats. Then, "Okay, I'll buzz the senator on his cell phone. Where can he reach you?"

Cochrane gave him his own cell phone number, trying to remember how recently he'd charged its battery.

"I'll ask the senator to phone you," Love said, his voice heavy with doubt and suspicion.

"Thanks," Cochrane said.

He phoned room service for a light breakfast, then dressed as quickly as he could, his back still painfully stiff. Where is Elena? What's happening to her?

He tried her cell phone, got an answering machine's robotic answer. Then he opened his laptop and sent a message to the three friends he'd entrusted with copies of Mike's work.

PLEASE ERASE THE FILE I SENT YOU. THIS IS URGENT. ERASE THE FILE
AS SOON AS YOU READ THIS. SEND ME A CONFIRMATION THAT YOU'VE
ERASED THE FILE. PLEASE DON'T ASK QUESTIONS. JUST DO IT.

He hoped that they would do what he asked.

Elena's life depends on this, he thought. Then he realized his three friends' own lives might depend on it.

With an aching sigh, he looked up their phone numbers, then began to telephone them directly.

INTERSTATE 95:
DELAWARE MEMORIAL BRIDGE

As the limousine drove through the gloomy late afternoon rain, Senator Bardarson was sipping a scotch and soda. The double span of the Delaware Memorial Bridge humped like the spine of an ancient dinosaur, gray and misty in the rain. Far below, the river looked even grayer. The senator's cell phone abruptly started playing the opening bars of "The Stars and Stripes Forever."

As he pulled the phone out of his inside pocket and flipped it open, he idly thought that perhaps in a couple of years he could change it to "Hail to the Chief."

Anderson Love's face filled the minuscule screen, looking darker than usual.

"Andy," said the senator.

"Something's gone wonky with Cochrane. He's reneging. He wants to withdraw everything he's given us."

Bardarson's first thought was that Gould had gotten to the scientist. He said guardedly, "I was afraid something like this would happen."

"I checked with Quinn's people," Love went on. "Cochrane had a visitor at his hotel room last night. And the Sandoval woman didn't spend the night there with him."

"Where is she?"

"Quinn says she took the Metroliner to New York yesterday. Quinn was kind of sore about it; complaining that she hasn't got enough people to go chasing up and down the East Coast."

"Sandoval took the Metroliner by herself? Alone?"

"Apparently."

"And Cochrane wants to pull the rug out from under us."

"I checked with Dr. Esterbrook. He was supposed to deliver the National Academy's preliminary report in a couple of days."

"And?"

"Cochrane demanded that he erase the report. Said a woman's life depends on it."

"Sandoval, obviously."

"Obviously."

Bardarson thought about it swiftly as the limousine sped off the bridge and into the state of Delaware. Traffic was sparse for a Friday afternoon, he thought with a corner of his mind.

Love added, "Cochrane wants to talk to you. Says it's urgent."

"It sounds like he's worried about Ms. Sandoval."

"I guess so."

With an exaggerated sigh, Bardarson said, "All right. Get him on the phone and patch him through to me."

"Right."

The senator put his phone on the seat beside him and reached for his half-finished drink. Gould's gotten to Sandoval, one way or another, he thought, and he's using Sandoval to twist Cochrane. Insurance on our deal, Bardarson said to himself. Gould wants absolute control of the hydrogen thing. He'll let me use the issue in the election campaign, but only if he has control of it. Smart. Very smart.

Once I'm elected, though, I can use the Justice Department to pry the hydrogen loose from Gould's hands. They can use the antitrust laws or something. There's always a way. It'll make an enemy of Gould, but once I'm in the White House, who cares?

It wasn't until they had crossed the line into Maryland that Bardarson remembered that Gould could be a very formidable adversary in his reelection campaign. Or a very helpful ally, so long as he allowed Gould to play this hydrogen business the way he wanted to.

Cochrane had spent a frustrating couple of hours trying to reach his three high school buddies by phone. He got answering machines at Don Mattson's and Sol Roseman's numbers. The telephone company reported that Vic Cardoza's number was no longer in service.

Friday afternoon, he thought. They're probably out for the evening. Maybe the weekend. He left messages for Mattson and Roseman, then fretted in his hotel room about Cardoza. He hoped his e-mail message got through as he paced the hotel room, not knowing what he could do next.

The Marriage of Figaro startled him. He rushed to the cell phone, still lying on the night table where he had left it.

It was Love, he saw. "I can patch you through to the senator," said the aide.

"I appreciate it," Cochrane replied.

The phone gave off a series of clicks and beeps. Love's image disappeared, replaced by the senator's long, lank-jawed face.

"Dr. Cochrane." The senator smiled professionally.

"I have to withdraw my brother's data," Cochrane said, with no preliminaries. "I'm sorry, but it's important. Vital."

"So Andy tells me. What's happened?"

"They've got Elena. Ms. Sandoval. Gould's thugs have her and they won't let her go until I turn everything over to them."

Bardarson's face got even longer, frowning. "Are you certain about this?"

"Yes! It's a matter of life and death!"

The senator's hand seemed to waver; his image jumped out of the phone's tiny screen. It looked to Cochrane as if he were sitting in a car of some kind.

"Sorry," Bardarson said as his face reappeared. "Pothole."

"I've got to give the data to Gould's people," Cochrane insisted.

"Of course. Of course. We can't do anything else, can we?"

Cochrane sank onto the edge of the bed. He had expected opposition from Bardarson, or at least a request to allow him to help find Elena.

"I've asked Dr. Esterbrook to destroy the report we were writing," he told the senator.

"Yes, Andy Love's already spoken with Esterbrook. Are you sure that's what you want?"

"Absolutely sure."

"Well, it's your decision. Do you want me to notify the FBI? If this is a kidnapping, they should be involved."

"No," Cochrane replied automatically. Then he added, "It wouldn't do any good."

"Are you certain Gould's people have done this?"

"Yes. Certain."

"I could talk with the man. Possibly he doesn't even know about it. You know how your staff people sometimes do things on their own."

"Sure, talk with him. All I want is to assure him that I won't give my brother's data to anybody but him. I want Elena returned to me safely."

"I can understand that," said the senator. "You give the information to Gould's people. I'll talk with Lionel himself and see if we can straighten this out."

"Thanks," Cochrane breathed.

The connection clicked off. Cochrane held the phone in his hand, staring at it as if it could tell him what he wanted, needed to know.

That was too easy, he thought. Bardarson just let me walk away with the key that could open the door to the White House for him. Too damned easy.

Unless, he realized, the senator's already in bed with Gould.

As his limousine splashed through the darkening rainy evening toward Washington, Senator Bardarson leaned back in the black leather rear seat, clicked his cell phone shut, and tucked it back into his pocket.

The poor fool, he thought. Cochrane's in this way over his head. He doesn't have a clue. Poor naïve fool.

The senator reached for his unfinished scotch and soda. After one sip, though, he thought: Or maybe he's not such a fool after all. Maybe he's negotiating with one of the other energy giants. Maybe he's realized that he could get a fortune for the information he has.

Bardarson sipped again and shook his head wearily. A man could get himself killed playing that game.

MANHATTAN:
GOULD TRUST HEADQUARTERS

I want this business finished, once and for all," said Elena Sandoval.

"So do I," said Lionel Gould. "So do I, most emphatically."

Gould looked her over appreciatively. A beautiful woman, he thought. Very attractive light blue silk blouse with a darker knee-length skirt. Sensible attire, yet on her it looks enticing. Which is good. He especially enjoyed the way her skirt fit snugly on her hips. But she's more than beautiful. She's intelligent. And determined. Which could be either good or bad, depending on how she's handled.

He rose from his high-backed swivel chair and came around the dark mahogany desk toward her. Sandoval stood her ground, although she gave away her nervousness by clasping her hands together.

"Come," Gould said, gesturing toward the delicate inlaid table by the windows and the pair of upholstered chairs on either side of it. "We might as well be comfortable while we discuss the situation."

Staying an arm's length away from him, Sandoval went to the table and sat. Through the window she could see Central Park, a misty island of green in the rain, surrounded by the cold gray towers of the city.

"I agreed to come here voluntarily," she said as Gould eased his bulk into the other chair. It creaked slightly as he made himself comfortable. As usual, Gould was in his shirtsleeves, his vest unbuttoned, his tie pulled down from his open collar. The room felt frigid to Sandoval, yet still Gould was perspiring freely.

"It's all very simple," he said, leaning slightly toward Sandoval. "I must have Dr. Cochrane's data in my hands. There must be no other copies anywhere."

"Paul can do that," she said.

"I'm sure he already is. My man Kensington told me that Cochrane agreed to cooperate fully."

"Good."

"He believes that you are in some degree of danger," said Gould, with a slight smirk.

"Am I?"

"Not in the slightest! Of course not." Gould hesitated a heartbeat, then added, "As long as Cochrane cooperates."

"I don't want him hurt," she said.

"An admirable sentiment. Apparently he feels the same about you."

"Yes," she murmured. "He would."

Gould spread his arms. "So there we are. I get the hydrogen process and no one gets hurt. A happy conclusion to our business."

Sandoval looked doubtful. "Senator Bardarson's brought the National Academy into this. Paul might not be able to stop them from issuing a report."

"Yes, so I've been told." With a shrug and a sly grin, Gould said, "I'll deal with Bardarson. I don't hold you or Cochrane responsible for what the National Academy of Sciences does."

He saw recognition instantly change her expression. "You and the senator—"

"That's politics," Gould said. "It's of no concern to you or your Dr. Cochrane."

Sandoval appeared to think it over for several moments. At last she said, "There's one more thing."

"Yes?"

"Paul wants his brother's murderer brought to justice."

Gould leaned back in the fragile chair, pursed his lips. "That, I'm afraid, is completely out of my hands. I have no idea who murdered Dr. Cochrane's brother."

"It wasn't Kensington?"

"Emphatically not. Michael Cochrane was about to conclude a deal with me. Why would I want him murdered and his data stolen?"

"Which brings up the matter of our financial arrangement," Sandoval said.

"Ah, yes."

"We were talking about ten million."

"That was when I had no inkling of where the late Dr. Cochrane's data was."

"I did my part," she said. "I've brought the data to you."

"It's not yet in my hands."

"It will be. Paul will deliver it to you."

"In exchange for your safety."

Her lips tightened into a grim line. "Yes," she admitted.

"You are worth more than ten million dollars to him."

"I've earned that money," Sandoval insisted.

Gould swung his head in an emphatic negative. "The dynamics of the situation have changed dramatically. I can get the information from Cochrane for nothing more than your freedom."

"You said I was in no danger. I went along with you just to get Paul to deliver his brother's data. I don't want him hurt."

"Yes, so you said. And he doesn't want you hurt. So why should I spend any of my hard-earned money on either of you?"

Sandoval bristled. "We had a deal!"

"Had, my lovely young lady. Had. Past tense. The situation has changed and so has our deal."

Her face set into an angry scowl, but only for a moment. She took a breath, and Gould noticed how alluringly her blouse moved.

"So what is our deal now?" she asked, her voice low, accepting defeat.

Gould smiled at her. "I think one million is fair. Generous, even. One million dollars, tax-free."

"One-tenth of your original offer."

"Yes, but this is money you'll be able to spend. Not talk. Not promises. Cash. Which is good."

"One million," Sandoval repeated.

Gould folded his hands over his belly.

"All right," she said. "One million dollars."

"When I get the data from Dr. Cochrane."

"It's probably on its way to you."

"And all copies of the data have been either destroyed or delivered to me."

She nodded, then said, "The National Academy..."

"As I said, I will deal with that aspect of the situation."

"And Paul won't be hurt," Sandoval said.

"Not in the slightest."

"Then that's it," she said, almost in a whisper.

Gould nodded, but then said, "There's one additional proviso." Leaning forward to pat her knee, he repeated, "One additional proviso."

WASHINGTON, D.C.:
J. W. MARRIOTT HOTEL

Christ, Cochrane thought, I'm pacing the floor like a caged animal. But that's exactly what I am, he realized. A caged animal, stuck in this room, trapped, in prison.

It was full night outside, still raining. The lights of the city were smeared into tears flowing down the hotel room's window. Cochrane had spent the whole day trying to reach the three men he'd sent copies of the data to, his desperation ratcheting up each time he got the same answering machine replies or the robotic voice of the telephone company's automated "out of service" message about Cardoza.

His room was a mess: bed still unmade, dishes from his room service lunch scattered over the coffee table and sofa. He forced himself to shave, although his hands trembled so badly he feared he'd slice himself.

Where is Elena? he kept asking himself. What are they doing to her? Kensington said she'd be all right if I delivered the data to Gould. Okay,

I've e-mailed him everything I've got from Mike. No reaction from Gould. No call from Elena. Maybe they killed her. Maybe that Kensington monster...

No, he warned himself. Don't go there. Don't start painting pictures in your head.

Did Esterbrook really wipe his files? Or did he just tell me he did and sneak his report to Bardarson anyway? Why haven't Don or Sol returned my calls? Jesus, I must have called them a dozen times now. Where the fuck is Vic? How can I reach him?

His phone started playing Mozart.

Cochrane swiveled his head, looking for the cell phone. On the sofa, next to the tray that lunch had come on. He scooped it up with shaking hands.

"Hello!"

"Hi, Paulie. It's me, Don."

Don Mattson. Cochrane felt a flood of relief surge through him.

"Don! Hang on a minute. Let me put you on my laptop screen."

The laptop was open on the mussed-up bed. Cochrane tapped keys until Mattson's face appeared on its screen.

"Hey, Paulie. How are you? What's going on?"

"You got my message," Cochrane said.

"All sixteen of 'em. And the e-mails, too. What's going on? You sound kind of frantic."

Cochrane hadn't seen his friend since Jennifer's funeral. Mattson had a long, bony face. He wore plastic-framed eyeglasses. For the first time, Cochrane realized that Don's hairline had receded noticeably. He remembered in high school Don wore his sandy hair down to his shoulders. Now it was cropped stylishly short, like a businessman or some executive.

"I'm in a... a situation, Don. I need you to erase that first e-mail I sent you. The one with the attachment. It's important."

"Can't do it, pal."

Cochrane flared, "Whattaya mean you can't? You've got to!"

"Wish I could, Paulie, but some sumbitch kids broke into the house last night while we were at the movies and took my damned computer."

"What?"

"Ripped it right out of my desk, printer, scanner, microphones—the works. Took the whole entertainment center out of the living room, too, the little bastards."

Cochrane felt a cold shudder run through him. "Took your computer?"

Mattson nodded unhappily. "That's where Trudy and I were all day: first talking with the cops and then shopping all goddamned afternoon—Wal-Mart, Circuit City, Best Buy, the works."

Of course, Cochrane told himself. They'd want the computer's hard drive, to make certain nobody could make any more copies off it.

"They stole your computer," Cochrane repeated.

"Sure as hell did. And this used to be a perfectly safe neighborhood. Now Trudy wants to rig the house with a goddamned burglar alarm system."

Cochrane thought, Well, they got Don out of the picture. Without hurting him.

"What about Sol and Vic?" he asked.

"Sol and Judy took their kids to Israel. Sol Junior's bar mitzvah. They won't be back for another week."

And when they get back they'll find that their home's been burglarized, too, Cochrane said to himself. His computer will be gone.

"Vic?" he repeated.

Mattson shook his head. "He's off in the Wild West someplace. Got fed up with Lillian and just headed for the hills."

"But his e-mail address is still working."

"Maybe so. But who the hell knows where he is? You know Vic, he could be anywhere."

"Yeah."

"Like the time he took that model down to Bar Harbor for a weekend. Remember that? Told her he was taking her out for a lobster dinner and—"

"Don, I've gotta run now. Good talking to you. Sorry about the break-in."

Mattson looked surprised, then puzzled, then hurt. "Where are you, anyway? What kind of trouble are you in?"

"Don't have time to explain, pal. Later, when this clears up."

"Anything I can do to help?"

"Not really," Cochrane said, thinking, Just be glad you're out of it.

"Well... if you need anything..."

"I know, Don. I appreciate it. I really do."

"Okay."

"So long."

"So long, Paulie."

Cochrane clicked his phone shut and Mattson's image winked out on the laptop screen.

Kensington's gotten to Don and Sol, he thought. And he must be hunting for Vic.

Then a new thought struck him: How did he find out about the three of them? I haven't told anyone but Elena—

Oh, my god! They got it out of Elena! Maybe they drugged her with truth serum or . . . or . . .

His cell phone started playing Mozart again. Cochrane flicked it open and Sandoval's face lit up his laptop screen.

"Elena!"

"Hello, Paul."

"Are you all right?"

All he could see of her was her face, filling the display screen. She seemed unhurt, no obvious marks on her, just as beautiful as ever. But somber, grave, her green eyes dull and cold, her lips pressed into a bitter line, her dark hair hanging loose, framing her face.

"Have they hurt you?"

"I'm fine, Paul," she said, her voice flat, low. "I'm perfectly fine."

"Where are you?"

"That's not important. Mr. Gould says he received the data from you."

"Good," Cochrane said. "How soon can you come back to me? Or do you want me to come to where you are?"

"They know about your three friends," she said.

"Yeah."

"They've gotten what they want from two of them, but they can't find the third one."

"Vic Cardoza," Cochrane said. "He's sort of disappeared."

"You've got to find him, Paul. Gould won't let me go until that third copy of the data is in his hands."

"But I don't know where he is! Nobody knows."

She fell silent for a moment. Then, "Kensington's hunting for him. It would be better, though, if you found him first."

"I'm not a detective, for chrissake," Cochrane said. "How the hell can I find him?"

She shook her head, just the slightest movement, but Cochrane felt as if a load of wet cement had just been poured over him.

"Gould won't let me go until that third computer is brought to him."

"Elena, look, I've done everything I could. I've scratched the National Academy report. I've—"

The phone connection suddenly went dead. Cochrane stared at the empty screen, then furiously began to try to return the call. It was useless. The number was unreachable, the phone company told him.

Lionel Gould sat on his oversized bed, propped on a small mountain of pillows, and watched Elena Sandoval hang up the phone at his curved teak desk across the room. She was wearing a shimmering robe of green silk, a very old Gould family heirloom, very clinging.

"An excellent performance, Elena," Gould said, smiling at her. "Excellent. He'll lead us to this Cardoza fellow now."

Sandoval stood up. The robe slipped open.

"He doesn't know where the man is," she said.

"Perhaps so. But you've given him the incentive to find out. Incentives are good. He'll move heaven and earth to find him now."

Sandoval said nothing. She simply stood by the bedroom desk, naked beneath the delicate robe.

Gould patted the bedsheet beside him. "Come back to bed, Elena. The night is young."

Stone-faced, she slipped the robe off her shoulders and let it fall to the thickly carpeted floor. Gould perspired heavily as she walked slowly toward him.

Local Man's Car Gets 250 MPG

SAN CLEMENTE, CA—Jeff Greenbaum grins when he drives past gas stations. With gasoline prices reaching for the stratosphere, Greenbaum claims his car gets 250 miles to the gallon of gas.

That's because Greenbaum modified his car, making it a "plug-in" hybrid.

Greenbaum's Toyota Prius was a hybrid when he bought it, powered by a combination of a normal gasoline engine and a hydrogen-based fuel cell. But that wasn't good enough for Greenbaum, a retired hardware executive and dedicated environmentalist.

"Electricity is the cleanest form of energy we have," Greenbaum notes. "I figured that I could use electricity to power my auto."

So the trunk and rear sear of Greenbaum's Prius are filled with batteries that provide power to the electrical engine that is normally driven by the hydrogen fuel cell. Greenbaum plugs his battery pack into the wall socket in his garage overnight, and is ready for a day's driving in the morning.

"I just use the gasoline engine to get my buggy started," he says. "From then on she runs on electricity."

Greenbaum believes that if everyone converted their automobiles to his type of "plug-in" power, the nation's need for imported petroleum would be cut by more than half.

But electric utility spokesperson Glenda Swarthout commented that a swing toward "plug-in" power for the nation's automobiles would put an enormous strain on existing electrical power plants. "You'd see brownouts and blackouts until we could build new plants to provide the needed electricity," she pointed out.

And those power plants burn fossil fuels, such as petroleum, natural gas and coal. Asked what he thought about the potential increase in pollution from an enormous increase in the number of electrical generating plants, Greenbaum replied, "I don't know. That's not my problem. Maybe they could use solar power, instead."

When the possibility of nuclear power was suggested, Greenbaum balked. "I'm antinuke. Always have been."

—*Orange County Register*

DULLES, VIRGINIA: DULLES INTERNATIONAL AIRPORT

Cochrane's cell phone broke into *The Marriage of Figaro* the instant he seated himself in the Boeing 767. It was a full flight and he was jammed into the middle seat between an obese woman in a garish flowered blouse and a gray-bearded guy who looked like a construction worker: T-shirt sleeves cut off to reveal hard, muscular, tattooed arms. Cochrane felt almost abnormal next to them, wearing his jeans and his last clean white shirt.

They both stared at Cochrane as he struggled to pull the phone from his shirt pocket. For a moment he couldn't place the image that formed in the minuscule screen, then he recognized Grace Johanson, his department head back at the university in Tucson.

"I'm sorry to bother you on a Sunday morning, Paul," she began, "but it's been more than three weeks now and you haven't answered any of my e-mails."

Cochrane put the phone to his ear and kept his voice as low as he could. "I know, Grace. I've been... it just hasn't been easy for me."

"I understand, but I can't cover for you much longer," the department head said. "The semester's nearly over and you've got to be back for the finals, you know."

"Grace, I don't think I'll be able to."

A long hesitation. Then, "After four weeks' absence the dean gets involved. And the committee."

Cochrane knew what she'd left unsaid. They'd stop his salary checks unless he either came back to work or applied for a medical leave of absence.

"I'm trying to find out who murdered my brother," he said in an urgent whisper.

"But can't you at least put in an appearance, Paul? Talk to the dean. He'll understand, I'm sure."

"I'll try to e-mail him."

"That won't be good enough. He wants you—"

"Grace, I'm on a plane and they're going to close the hatch in a few seconds. I'll have to hang up now."

"Call me when you land," she said, her voice hardening.

"Yeah. Right." And he clicked the phone shut.

Cochrane sank his head back in the seat and closed his eyes as the flight attendant went through her little safety lecture and the 767 trundled away from the gate. Next stop, he thought, will be Cabo San Lucas.

Never thought I'd be going to Mexico. Good thing I kept my passport in my travel bag. Right in there with the razor and the shaving cream.

He wondered what Elena was doing. How's Gould treating her? Where's Kensington? He'd had to use his own American Express card to buy his plane ticket. Does Gould know it? he wondered. Will he send Kensington after me?

He'd sent half a dozen e-mails to Vic Cardoza after his phone conversation with Don Mattson. All day Saturday he'd alternately paced his hotel room and then sat at his laptop to tap out another urgent message to Vic. He got no "delivery failure" notices from America On Line, so he assumed that the messages got through to Vic, wherever he was.

Answer me, goddammit! he snarled silently at the laptop. Come on, Vic, I'm not going to tell your wife where you are.

He had said as much in his e-mails, and pointed out that this was a matter of life and death, maybe Vic's own life or death.

Around nine P.M. Saturday night his cell phone had rung. It was Vic, looking more than a little annoyed.

"What the hell's going on?" he demanded, with no preamble.

"Vic! Where are you?"

"Never mind that. What's this shit about my life being in danger?"

Cochrane spilled the whole story to him, talking so fast at one point that Cardoza had to tell him to take a breath and slow down.

"That e-mail you sent me last week? With the attachment? I never even downloaded it."

"Good. Fine," Cochrane said. "Now you've got to give me your computer."

"Give you—Are you nuts?"

"I'll buy you a new one. But I need to have the one you're using now."

"Fuck you, Paulie. I'm not giving you my notebook."

Cochrane held on to his temper. "Vic, I sent the same material to Don and Sol. Somebody broke into their homes and stole their computers. They want yours, too."

"That's crazy."

"But it's true. They killed Mike, for chrissake! And at least one other guy I know of. They'll kill you if they have to."

Cardoza's face, on Cochrane's laptop screen, went crafty. "Shit, they don't know where I am. Nobody knows. Especially Lillian."

"They could trace this call."

"I'm calling from an Internet café."

"I need your computer, Vic. There are lives at stake. Including yours."

"You're not bullshitting me?"

"No bullshit."

Cardoza looked suspicious, then thoughtful.

"Vic, you know I wouldn't rat you out to your wife," Cochrane pleaded.

"I'm in Mexico," Cardoza said grudgingly.

"Mexico?"

"Cabo San Lucas, down at the end of the Baja."

One good thing about Washington, D.C., Cochrane thought now as the airliner roared down the runway, is that you can get a direct flight to almost anywhere. In five hours I'll be in Cabo San Lucas. I'll get Vic's notebook computer and bring it back to Gould. Then Elena will be off the hook and this whole business will be finished.

He closed his eyes and tried to sleep. And saw his brother's battered face.

Jason Tulius was in his office at the Calvin Research Center when the phone call from Zelinkshah Shamil came through. As soon as he saw Shamil's dark face on his wall screen, Tulius got up from his swivel chair and swiftly closed his door, then returned to his desk and pressed the "no disturbances" button on his phone console.

"You shouldn't call me here," he said to Shamil. "I've told you that before."

"This is an emergency."

"What do you mean?"

"This Dr. Cochrane, the brother of your murdered employee, he's left the country."

Startled, Tulius asked, "How do you know that?"

"I'm not without resources," Shamil replied, his face still deadly grim.

Thinking about it for a moment, Tulius said, "So what of it?"

"He has his brother's work, does he not?"

"Perhaps."

"Then why is he fleeing the country?"

Tulius tugged at his beard. "Perhaps to get away from Gould."

Shamil considered that briefly. "If so, Gould will send operatives after him."

"Probably."

"How is your staff's work proceeding? Have you duplicated the slain man's breakthrough yet?"

"It's only been two weeks, for god's sake," Tulius snapped. "These things take time."

"Dr. Cochrane has the information with him."

"Probably so."

"So we should get to him," Shamil said. "If he is willing to cooperate with us, fine. If not, we take the information from him. Either way, we get what we want."

"I don't want any violence."

Shamil smiled humorlessly. "Violence is a last resort."

"No," Tulius protested. "You can't go that route. This isn't Chechnya, for god's sake."

"He'll be in Mexico, at a resort by the sea. Tourists often get robbed in such places. Even murdered."

Tulius started to object more strenuously, but Shamil simply cut the phone link.

CABO SAN LUCAS:
HOTEL DE LAS FLORES

Flowers everywhere. Thick blooms of color cascaded down the tiled stairway that led from the lobby down and down and down five levels to the thatch-covered bar on the beach.

A stiff breeze was gusting in off the sea, cool and moist despite the blazing sun. The surf looked rough, thundering. Cochrane smelled the tang of salt in the air mixed with the perfume of the luxuriant flowers.

"But where's my room?" he asked the lithe young bellman who was carrying his single wheeled travel bag.

"*Qué?*" asked the bellman, smiling brightly.

"My room," Cochrane repeated, louder. Then, falling back on the primitive Spanish he'd picked up in Tucson, he added, "*Mi sala.*"

"Oh, *sí*," said the bellman, his smile widening. He pointed back up the wide, winding staircase. "Up there, señor. But is not *la playa muy bonita?* Beautiful?"

Cochrane nodded. "Yes, very beautiful. But I'm tired and I'd like to get to my room."

The bellman started up the stairs.

It didn't take long for Cochrane to unpack. He called for the house-keeper to take more than half his clothes to be laundered. Thank god for American Express, he said to himself. By the time I get home I'll owe them a year's salary.

His room was small and surprisingly dark. Its one window looked out on the staircase, shadowed by thick flowering vines. He could hear the pounding surf but couldn't see anything more than the tangled vines and the stuccoed wall on the other side of the stairs.

Tired yet keyed up, he stretched out on the bed to wait for Vic's phone call. If he calls, Cochrane thought. He might get cold feet and duck out on me. But he's got to call! He's got to! Elena's life could depend on it.

He hadn't realized he'd fallen asleep until he opened his eyes and saw that it was pitch-black in his room. Focusing on the green glowing digits of his wristwatch, he saw that it was 9:19 P.M. local time. He remembered he'd adjusted the watch on the plane from Washington.

No call from Vic. Cochrane sat up and fumbled for the lamp on his night table. He clicked the switch once, twice—nothing. In the darkness he groped for the telephone. No dial tone. "Power outage," he mumbled, swinging his legs off the bed and getting to his feet.

It was *dark*. Not a glimmer. Cautiously he felt his way along the wall to where he remembered the bathroom to be. And barked his shin on a wooden upright chair. Cursing, he found the bathroom door, banged his hip on the sink, and managed to find the toilet. Afterward, when he turned on the tap, barely a trickle of water gurgled out. Cochrane splashed his face, rubbed his eyes, slicked down his hair. Then he groped back across the room and reached the front door.

The broad stairway outside was lit by candles every few steps. The flickering light was almost beautiful, he thought, romantic. He heard voices and laughter from farther down the stairs, and a guitar strumming softly.

The bar on the beach was lit by dozens of candles. And packed with people. The blackout had driven everyone in the hotel to the bar, it looked to Cochrane.

If the phones aren't working, Vic can't call me, he told himself. I might as well get myself a drink and something to eat.

People were jammed three and four deep at the bar, kids mostly. They looked like American students, laughing, flirting, guzzling beer and margaritas, wearing jeans or cutoffs, the girls mostly in tank tops or halters. Brown bodies and bright teeth. Not a care in the world, Cochrane thought. They've got more money than they know what to do with. They ought to be home studying for their finals or looking for jobs but they're here having fun, getting drunk, getting laid, no worries about gasoline prices or wars in the Middle East. No worries about a woman being held in New York until I can find Vic and wrestle his goddamned notebook off him.

Pushing through the laughing, shouting, singing throng, Cochrane at last forced his way to the bar.

And saw Vic Cardoza working on the other side of it, pulling down the lever to fill a glass with Corona, his face set in the old crafty smile that Cochrane remembered so well.

He's working here as a bartender! Sonofabitch, Cochrane said to himself.

The sight of Vic's sly, shrewd, cunning face unleashed a flood of memories. Cochrane remembered that Vic had been their ringleader, head honcho of the Four Musketeers, the guy who thought up the tricks that they still laughed about decades afterward. The three of us got blamed for the mischief while Vic smiled and shook his head and thought up still more shenanigans. And there he was, working behind the bar in a Mexican tourist hotel down at the ass end of the Baja Peninsula.

Cardoza slid a foaming glass of beer to a flat-chested blond student in a tank top that barely covered her, then turned to Cochrane.

"'Bout time you got here, Paulie," he said, loud enough for Cochrane to hear him over the noise of the crowd. "Whatcha do, walk in from Washington?"

"No, Vic, I flew."

Cardoza looked Cochrane over, sizing him up. "So is all this shit you told me really true?"

"It's real, Vic."

"You're in deep shit, huh?"

"They killed Mike," Cochrane said tightly. "They're going to kill a woman if I don't deliver your computer to them."

With a shake of his head, Cardoza said, "Have a drink. On the house."

"I need your computer, Vic."

"Yeah, sure." He slid a brandy glass half filled with golden tequila across the wooden bar to Cochrane. "After this dump closes."

Cochrane sipped at the tequila. It tasted smoky, warming. I'd better go easy on the booze, he told himself. Still, he knocked back the rest of his drink gladly.

Cardoza worked his way along the bar, taking orders and filling glasses. When he finally got back to Cochrane he said, "Next one you pay for."

"Make it club soda."

The expression on Cardoza's face turned pitying. "You're still the pussy, ain'tcha?"

"With all the trouble I'm in, I need to stay sober."

"Whatsamatter, don'tcha trust me?"

"Sure I trust you, Vic. But I trust you better sober."

Cardoza laughed and said, "The soda spritzer won't work without electricity, and—"

At that instant the lights flared on. The crowd gasped, then roared its approval. The big stereo speakers on either end of the bar started blaring mariachi music. Couples paired off and began dancing.

The noise from the amplifiers was overpowering. Cochrane reached across the bar to grab Cardoza's arm. "I'm going back to my room. Meet me there when your shift's finished."

"What number?" Cardoza hollered over the noise.

Cochrane fished the hotel key from his pocket. "Three-fifteen."

"Gotcha."

"And bring your computer!"

Cardoza grinned his old, sly, scheming grin.

Cochrane made his way back up the curving staircase to his room, never noticing the tall, dark figure of Kensington standing at the other end of the bar, watching him.

CABO SAN LUCAS: HOTEL DE LAS FLORES

The pounding bass beat from the bar made Cochrane's room shudder. The room's door was thick enough to blot out most of the laughter and the higher-pitched tones of the overloud music, but the bass rumbled through.

No way I can sleep through this, he thought. So he opened his laptop and checked his e-mail. Three messages from Grace Johanson, back at the university, and one from the dean. He didn't bother to open them. The rest were notices, junk mail. Cochrane yawned and glanced at his mussed bed. It looked awfully good to him. Vic probably won't be finished until the bar closes down; god knows what time that'll be.

As he started to shut down the computer, a new message appeared on the list. From *E.Sandoval444@yahoo.com*.

Suddenly wide awake, he opened Elena's message.

PAUL: I'M FINE. PLEASE DON'T WORRY ABOUT ME. BUT IT'S IMPORTANT THAT YOU BRING THE THIRD COMPUTER TO MR. GOULD.

HE'S WILLING TO LET US GO ONCE HE GETS THAT THIRD COM-
PUTER. PLEASE DO IT, PAUL. I'M WAITING TO SEE YOU AGAIN. LOVE,
ELENA

His fingers shaking so badly he mistyped several words, Cochrane
replied:

DEAR ELENA: I'LL OBTAIN THE THRD COMPUTER TONIGHT, OR
RATHER TMORROW MORNING, BEFORE DAWN. IM IN MEXICO. SHOULD
BE BACK TOMORROW OR NEXT DAY, DEPEDING ON FLIGHT SCHED-
ULES. I LOVE YOU TOO. PAUL.

He sent his message, then stared at the laptop screen for the better
part of an hour, waiting for a reply. Nothing.

The music from the bar was still pounding away. Cochrane stretched
out on the bed, closed his eyes, tried to close out his mind. But he saw
Elena. With Gould. And Kensington. She said she's okay, he told himself.
She said he hasn't harmed her. But is it true? Or is he making her say that?

Unable to sleep, he went back down to the bar. The crowd was noticeably thinner, but Vic was nowhere in sight.

Don't panic! Cochrane commanded himself. He's probably gone back
to wherever he's living to get his computer.

He ran back up the steps and unlocked his door, half expecting to see
Cardoza already in the room. He wasn't.

The bedside clock said 12:18. Cochrane paced for an hour before it
clicked to 12:19.

A rap on his door, impatient, urgent.

Cochrane yanked the door open and there stood Vic Cardoza, a black
computer satchel hanging from his shoulder.

"So, you gonna let me in?"

"Yes, sure, come on in," said Cochrane, backing away from the door.

Cardoza stepped in, looked around as if inspecting for roaches, then
kicked the door shut. He did not take the computer bag off his shoulder.

"Lemme get this straight," he said, his eyes shifting from Cochrane to
the laptop still open on the desk and back again. "You sent me this message with Mike's science stuff in it."

Nodding, Cochrane explained, "And the people who are after me
want that information."

"They killed Mike?"

"Somebody did. Most likely them."

"And they're holding your girlfriend until you give 'em what they want."

"That's right. They want your computer, the hard drive. They want to make sure—"

"How they know I haven't already copied the material?"

Cochrane wanted to yank the computer off Cardoza's shoulder and push him out of his room. Instead he answered, "They don't. I guess they assume that since you don't know what this is all about you haven't sent copies to anybody."

Looking craftier than ever, Cardoza went to the only chair in the room and sat down, clutching the computer in his lap with both hands.

"So, Paulie, what's this all about?"

"You don't want to know."

"Sure I do."

"You don't want to get involved, Vic. They could kill you, too, just like they killed Mike."

Cardoza's brows rose slightly. "It's that important to them?"

"Yes."

He drummed his fingers on the computer bag for an agonizing moment. Then, "So how much is this worth to you?"

Cochrane blinked with surprise.

"How much...?"

"Money. *Dinero*. Yankee dollars. How much're you willing to pay for my computer?"

Holding back a sudden urge to spit, Cochrane said, "Christ, Vic, I'll buy you a new computer."

Cardoza laughed scornfully.

"For god's sake, Vic, there are lives at stake!"

"I gotta think of my life, pal. You think I *like* hidin' out down here? Tending a friggin' bar?"

"But Vic—"

"How much is my computer worth to you, Paulie? Ten thousand? A hundred thousand? What?"

Cochrane stared at the man. "You always were a prick, you know that?"

"I'd say a hundred thousand," Cardoza said, unruffled. "Your girlfriend worth a hundred thou to you, Paulie?"

"You sonofabitch."

"Make it two hundred thousand."

"Vic, I don't have that kind of money!"

"But the people who want my computer do, don't they? They must be loaded. Who are they, Arab oil sheikhs? Texas billionaires?"

Without consciously deciding, Cochrane swung his right fist into Cardoza's face, knocking him out of the chair and sprawling on the tiled floor. He grabbed at the computer case; its strap was still twisted around Cardoza's shoulder. The two men grappled on the floor, gasping, throwing punches.

Cochrane felt a strong hand clutch the back of his neck, squeezing so hard the pain almost made him black out. Then he was lifted to his knees and tossed aside like a crumpled wad of paper. He banged painfully against the bed and saw Kensington lifting Cardoza to his knees with one hand under his jaw as he slipped the computer case's strap off Cardoza's shoulder.

Letting Cardoza drop to all fours, Kensington hefted the computer in one massive paw.

"You boys shouldn't be fighting over this," he said, grinning viciously. "I thought you guys were old buddies, high school sweethearts, huh?"

Cochrane rubbed the back of his neck. He could barely move his head. Still on all fours, Cardoza scuttled away backward until he bumped against the wall.

"Now, you be good little boys," Kensington said, still grinning. "Don't fight."

Tucking the computer case under his arm, he left the hotel room, shutting the door softly behind him.

Cardoza sat with his back to the wall, legs bent beneath him, his eyes wide with fear and pain. He rubbed his left side, wincing.

"Who the hell was that?" he asked, his voice hollow.

Cochrane tried to move his head from side to side. It hurt ferociously, and his neck was stiff as concrete.

"He works for the people who want your computer," he replied.

"Jesus Christ."

"Sorry I got you involved in this, Vic."

"I'm not involved anymore," Cardoza said. "I'm out of it!"

"Wish I could say the same," Cochrane said.

Novel Reaction Produces Hydrogen

Hydrogen production remains a major stumbling block on the road to the hydrogen economy, a much-touted successor to the current oil-based economy. Today, hydrogen supplies are derived largely from fossil fuels, such as oil, via processes that produce carbon dioxide. Yet it's this global-warming gas that a switch to hydrogen is supposed to curtail. Hydrogen can be split from the oxygen in water using electricity, but that process requires a great deal of energy.

Mahdi Abu-Omar of Purdue University in West Lafayette, Indiana, says that he and his team weren't looking to produce hydrogen in their fundamental studies of a catalyst made of the metal rhenium. In one set of experiments with a solution of water and an organic liquid called organosilane, however, hydrogen started to bubble up from the fluid soon after the researchers added a small piece of rhenium to the mixture. The solution was at room temperature and of neutral pH, conditions that normally wouldn't have produced hydrogen.

"It was truly a serendipitous discovery," says Abu-Omar.

After performing the reaction, the researchers studied how the reaction works. They found that the water's oxygen atom bonds to the silicon atom of an organosilane molecule, leaving behind a hydrogen molecule composed of one hydrogen atom from water and another from the organosilane. The hydrogen yield is proportional to the water used. In essence,

Abu-Omar's group has found a new means of splitting water.

There are many hurdles on the way to making this hydrogen-production process practical, Abu-Omar stresses. For one thing, researchers will have to determine whether the reaction works on a large scale. And organosilane is expensive enough that the economics of the process would be prohibitive.

—Aimee Cunningham
SCIENCE NEWS
September 17, 2005

MANHATTAN:
GOULD TRUST HEADQUARTERS

Wo hat do you mean, you don't have it?" Cochrane shouted.

Lionel Gould looked like a fat Buddha, sitting in his high-backed desk chair, arms folded over his belly. Except that he was wearing an open vest and a wrinkled shirt rather than saffron robes. And he was frowning unhappily, not smiling.

"Just what I said," Gould replied, his voice a low growl. "Which is not good."

Cochrane had flown to New York on the first available plane and gone straight from JFK to the Gould Trust headquarters. Rain clouds were building up in the twilight sky as he was ushered into Gould's office. Sandoval was nowhere in sight and Gould angrily demanded that he turn over the computer hard drives.

"Kensington took the third computer from me last night," Cochrane explained. "You mean he's not here yet?"

"I mean," Gould rumbled, "that I have seen neither Mr. Kensington nor any of the three computer drives. Nothing."

"He's got them," Cochrane insisted. "All three of them."

"Then where is he? Where are those hard drives?"

Cochrane sank into one of the chairs in front of Gould's desk. "I don't know," he said weakly.

Gould glared at him, beads of perspiration dotting his upper lip, his forehead. Through the window behind him Cochrane caught a flash of lightning that backlit the towers lining Central Park.

"He broke into Don's house and Sol's, up in Massachusetts," Cochrane muttered, as much to himself as to the angry man behind the desk. "It must have been him. He took their computers. Then he showed up last night in Cabo and took Vic's notebook. That was the third and last of them."

"You saw him in Cabo San Lucas?"

Rubbing his stiff neck, Cochrane replied, "Saw him and got roughed up by him. He grabbed the third computer and left us both on the floor. I thought he'd be here by now."

Gould slowly shook his head. "I haven't seen him for several days. He was supposed to be following you and making certain that those computers were brought to me."

"He was in Cabo last night," Cochrane repeated.

"And he acquired the third machine there." Gould pursed his lips in thought. At last he said, "If Mr. Kensington has all three machines, and he is not here to give them to me, something must have happened to him. Unless he's offering them to someone else."

"Someone else?"

"A competitor. A rival. Tricontinental, perhaps. That oaf Garrison in Texas. Perhaps even an OPEC minister."

"But I thought you were all in this together."

Gould huffed. "The great international conspiracy, is that it? Well, yes, we do cooperate in many ways, at many levels. But what your brother has discovered is so big that, well...boys will be boys."

Cochrane stared at him.

"The possession of a cheap and efficient method of producing and distributing hydrogen fuel is so immense, so powerful, that it would give its possessor a huge advantage over all his competitors."

"But I thought you wanted to suppress it."

"Of course! It must be suppressed, for the good of the industry. But eventually the time will come to bring it out into the open, to swing the industry away from oil and into hydrogen. Whoever possesses your brother's process will be the king of the energy industry."

"But the others—your competitors—they'll know about the process. The can develop it for themselves."

"Not when I have the patents," Gould said, practically purring. "They can develop their own version of the process if they wish, but they'll have to pay royalties to me. I will have a corner on the market, as my esteemed predecessors would have said."

"But none of that will happen if somebody else gets my brother's data from one of the missing computers."

Gould's face instantly darkened into a thundercloud. "Exactly so, Dr. Cochrane. Exactly so. If someone else reduces your brother's work to practice before my legal staff obtains a patent on it...if someone else merely publishes your brother's papers, it could ruin my chances for patenting the process."

"Senator Bardarson," Cochrane remembered. "He knows—"

Gould waved an impatient hand. "The good senator won't rock the boat. He needs me too much to interfere."

"The National Science Foundation..." Cochrane's voice trailed off into an awed silence.

"If our current president were able to run for reelection, he'd be on my side, too. This is an immense business, sir. Truly immense. We're talking about a transformation as vast as the original move from horses to the internal combustion engine more than a century ago."

Cochrane nodded, accepting the reality of it. Then he spread his hands. "Well, I did what you wanted. Now it's between you and Kensington. Where's Elena? It's time we should be—"

"Ms. Sandoval is quite comfortable, I assure you. The real question of the moment, however, is: where is Mr. Kensington?"

"That's your problem."

"No, it's yours. How do I know you haven't done away with him and have the computers in your own hands?"

Cochrane felt truly surprised. "Done away with Kensington? Me?"

"The man has always been loyal to me. Why should he turn traitor now?"

"I can think of ten million reasons. Maybe more."

"I refuse to believe that Mr. Kensington would turn on me," Gould said stubbornly. "For any amount of money."

"Then where is he?"

"I'll have to put some people to work on that," Gould said. "In the meantime, you will be my guest. Here. In this building."

"You mean prisoner."

"Dr. Cochrane, this matter is much too important to allow you to wander freely. Guest, prisoner, whatever you wish to call it, you will remain here for the time being."

"Where's Elena?"

"As I said, she's quite comfortable."

"Where is she?" Cochrane demanded, his voice rising.

Gould made a strange smile as he pressed a key on his desktop phone console. "She's here in this building. I'll have her join us for dinner."

Cochrane followed Gould out of his office and down a flight of wide stairs to the living quarters on the floor below. A butler offered Gould a burgundy jacket, which he waved away. In his unbuttoned vest and rumpled shirt Gould led Cochrane through a richly appointed living room and into a small but very luxurious dining room: a solid teak table large enough to seat eight comfortably, thick Oriental carpeting, paintings on the walls that Cochrane would have expected to see in a museum.

The table was set for three. Damask tablecloth and napkins, solid silver tableware. A young woman in a maid's black outfit was pouring water into crystal glasses.

"Where—"

"Hello, Paul."

He spun around and there was Elena, beautiful as ever in a gold-trimmed black floor-length gown, cut quite low. Cochrane rushed to her, put his arms around her.

"You're all right?" he asked.

"I'm fine, Paul. Now that you're here, I'm fine."

He kissed her, then took a close look at her face. She wasn't smiling. Her eyes looked haunted.

Gould cleared his throat noisily. "You two will want some privacy. I'll go change my shirt."

Once Gould had left the dining room Cochrane clasped Sandoval by her bare shoulders. "Are you really okay? Did—"

"I'm perfectly all right," she said. "Really." But her voice was low, listless.

"Kensington's disappeared with all three of the computers," Cochrane told her. "Gould intends to hold us both here until he finds out what's going on."

"And once he does, he'll kill us."

Cochrane realized that she was right. It makes sense, he said to himself. We're loose ends. He'll want to wind us up.

"Then we've got to get out of here, away from him."

"Where?" she said, her tone hopeless. "How?"

Before Cochrane could answer, Gould came back into the dining room wearing a loose flowered Hawaiian shirt that hung on him like a ridiculous gaudy tent. His face was set in a jowly grimace.

"Mr. Kensington has been found," he said grimly. "Dead."

"Dead?" Sandoval gasped.

"In a rented car at a JFK parking lot. No sign of the computers, however."

"Whoever killed him took the computers," Cochrane said.

"Yes," said Gould. "Which is bad. Very bad."

A crack of thunder punctuated his words.

MANHATTAN:
GOULD TRUST HEADQUARTERS

It was a desultory dinner. Cochrane ate without tasting the mint-garnished New Zealand lamb chops on his plate, watching Sandoval picking listlessly at her food while Gould alternately stuffed his mouth and talked—sometimes shouted—into a cell phone. They paid scant attention to the lightning strobing outside, or the rumbles of accompanying thunder.

Courses were served, wines poured. No conversation among the three of them. Only Gould's increasingly irritated yammering into the phone, his face growing redder by the moment, perspiration trickling down his face, wilting the collar of his colorful shirt.

At last, as multihued sherbets were being placed before them, Gould carefully folded the phone and then threw it against the wall, narrowly missing a Velasquez oil.

"Apparently Mr. Kensington was ambushed as he picked up his rental car at the airport," he said, jabbing his spoon into the sherbet. "The police say there must have been several assailants. He was beaten to death. His luggage was in the car's trunk, but there is no sign of the confounded computers!"

"Where does that leave us?" Cochrane asked.

"In the same place I am myself," replied Gould. "Way up in the middle of the air."

Cochrane looked across the table at Elena. She caught his glance, then looked away.

Gould hefted a golden spoonful of sherbet, but plopped it back into its gold-rimmed glass. "Bah! The police are treating this as a mugging."

"They don't know about the computers?" Cochrane asked.

"I certainly haven't told them!"

Gould pushed his chair away from the table and got to his feet. He extended a hand toward Sandoval. "Come, Elena."

Cochrane jumped up from his chair. "What do you mean?"

Sandoval remained seated, her eyes shifting from Cochrane to Gould and back again.

"I said come, Elena," Gould repeated, more demandingly.

She stayed in her chair, frozen, unmoving. Cochrane saw that her eyes looked frightened.

Gould reached for her, saying, "Don't be bashful because your former lover is here. You're mine now. To the victor go the spoils."

Without thinking, without even realizing he was doing it, Cochrane swung a left that connected solidly with Gould's fleshy jaw. He fell back into his chair, arms flailing, blood spurting from his mouth. The chair tumbled over, spilling Gould into a fleshy heap on the carpeting.

"Paul!" Sandoval screamed.

Cochrane stepped over and hauled Gould to his knees by the scruff of his neck.

"You're a dead man, Cochrane," Gould snarled through bloody teeth.

"Am I?" Cochrane reached with his free hand and yanked a steak knife off the table.

"Paul, we can't get out of the building!" Sandoval was saying, pleading almost. "We're trapped in here!"

Hauling Gould to his feet, Cochrane jabbed the point of the knife at Gould's throat hard enough to make the man flinch.

"He's got us buttoned up in here," Cochrane muttered, "but we've got him."

"What good—"

"Move, you sonofabitch," Cochrane commanded, pushing Gould roughly. "If you want to live, you walk us out of here."

Gould's face was white, Sandoval's almost the same.

"I said *move!*"

Haltingly, Gould shuffled through the dining room and out into the foyer. Cochrane saw the elevator door and a small keypad mounted on the wall beside it.

"Get the elevator here."

Wordlessly Gould reached for the keypad.

"And if any of your goons arrive on the elevator, I'm going to stick this knife through your fucking neck," Cochrane said. "You'll spatter blood all over them. You'll bleed out before they can get a medic here."

His hand trembling, Gould tapped out a code on the keypad. The elevator doors opened instantly. No one was in the elevator.

With Cochrane grasping Gould's arm and walking just behind him, concealing the knife that he pointed at Gould's kidney, they went down to the street floor and walked slowly past the two uniformed security guards in the lobby. Out on the street it was raining softly, the last remnants of the thunderstorm that had passed by.

"There are cars down in the garage level," Gould said as Cochrane pushed him into the drizzling rain.

"And have you tell the cops we stole one of your cars?" Cochrane snapped. "Forget it."

Cochrane led them across the avenue, past six lanes of taxis and limousines waiting for the stoplight to turn green, and onto the sidewalk beyond, shining in the street lamps reflected by the puddles of rain. The rain felt cold. Cochrane could see that Sandoval was shivering in her bareshouldered gown; the dress was getting soaked and her hair was unraveling. Gould looked like a soggy mess.

"What now?" Gould asked.

"We get a taxi and you can walk back home."

Recovering some of his composure, Gould said, "Do you think there's anyplace on earth that you can hide from me?"

Cochrane felt like slugging him again. Instead he simply replied tightly, "We'll see."

MANHATTAN:
GRAMERCY PARK HOTEL

You were sleeping with him," Cochrane said.

"I didn't have much choice in the matter," Sandoval replied, her face a tight, hard mask.

They hadn't spoken more than a few words to each other since leaving Gould in the drizzle by Central Park. Cochrane had watched the pudgy, squelching, completely disheveled industrialist shamble back across the avenue toward his building. Only when Gould had entered its lobby did he hail a taxi and bundle Sandoval into it.

"We need a hotel," Cochrane said to the driver as he climbed in behind her and slammed the cab's door shut.

"You sure as hell look it," the driver called back over his shoulder, "if you don't mind my sayin' so."

"Someplace not too expensive," Cochrane added.

"Downtown," said Sandoval.

Grateful that they'd found a driver whose native tongue was English,

Cochrane sank back onto the leather seat, cold and dripping wet. He had the driver stop at half a dozen ATMs on their way downtown. He used every credit card he had to draw a total of four thousand dollars in cash. Gould might be able to trace the card transactions, he told himself, but we'll use cash from now on.

The taxi driver took them to the Gramercy Park Hotel, at the foot of Lexington Avenue. "Ain't the cheapest place in town, but you won't have any roaches, at least."

The hotel clerk looked at them with a mixture of disdain and disbelief: a bedraggled couple with no luggage.

"We got caught in the rain," Cochrane muttered, tugging the wad of fifties he'd accumulated. Whether it was the cash or the excuse, the clerk found them a small room with twin beds.

"That's all that's available at present," he said.

"We'll take it," Cochrane agreed gratefully.

As he locked the door and slipped on the security chain, Sandoval went straight to the bathroom. He heard the shower turn on, fidgeted for a moment, wondering whether he should go in and join her. He decided not to. Instead he stripped off his wet clothes and wrapped himself in a blanket from the closet.

Sandoval came out at last, a bath towel tucked around her like a sarong. He brushed past her and entered the steamy bathroom. When he came out she was sitting up in one of the beds, the sheet and blanket pulled up to her armpits.

"Yes, I was sleeping with Gould," she said, her voice flat, unapologetic, almost defiant. "As I said, I didn't have much choice."

Cochrane sat on the edge of the other bed. "You were trying to protect me, is that it?"

"Whether you believe it or not."

"I want to believe it."

"But you don't. Not completely."

"No," he admitted. "I can't."

"I decided that Gould was a better choice than Kensington," she said.

"Kensington was in Boston, burglarizing my friends' houses."

"I didn't know that."

"I guess you didn't," Cochrane said. He looked into her sea-green eyes and saw no trace of sorrow, no hint of regret or remorse. Nothing but a cold, hard anger.

"Let's forget about it," he said, sliding into his bed.

"Can you?" she asked.

"I don't know. Maybe. I can try."

"Kensington found me in Washington and told me either I went with him to Gould or he'd kill you."

"You believed that?"

Ignoring his question, "Once I was in Gould's place I had to go along with him. It was the only defense I had. Either I told them who your three friends were or Gould would send Kensington to beat it out of you."

Lying on his back, staring up at the faintly cracked ceiling, Cochrane muttered, "So that's how he got to Don's house. And Sol's. And then he just followed me and let me lead him to Vic."

From the other bed, Sandoval said, "I suppose so."

Turning to face her, he said, "But what about Senator Bardarson? I thought he wanted to help us."

"Gould got to him," she replied. "Bardarson will talk about moving from oil to hydrogen, he'll make that a central part of his election platform. But Gould will control your brother's hydrogen process. He'll decide when the switchover comes about. If ever."

Cochrane closed his eyes briefly. It's like swimming against the tide, he thought. He remembered building fortresses in the sand at Lynn Beach when he was a child. And watching tearfully as the tide inexorably wiped them away.

"It's hopeless, isn't it?" he murmured.

Sandoval reached up and switched off the lamp on the night table between their beds.

"I mean," Cochrane said into the darkness, "what I really want is to find out who killed my brother. Who murdered Mike?"

"Kensington," Sandoval answered firmly. "It had to be Kensington."

Then he recalled, "But Kensington's dead. Somebody killed him. Who the hell was that?"

Her voice came through the shadows. "There's somebody else in the picture, Paul. Somebody we don't know about."

"And whoever it is, he's got those three hard drives."

PALO ALTO:
CALVIN RESEARCH CENTER

Dr. Jason Tulius hunched forward in his swivel chair and stared at the three small oblongs of brushed aluminum that rested upon his desk. About the size of cigarette packs, but half the thickness. How many men have been killed for them? he wondered.

He looked up from the three hard drives at the quartet of dark-suited men who had brought them into his office. The four Chechens looked like thugs: squat, thick-bodied, hard-faced. The receptionist out in the lobby had been decidedly nervous when she'd called Tulius to announce their unexpected appearance. Their message had been simple:

"We have something for Dr. Tulius, from Mr. Shamil."

Shamil had already phoned Tulius, so he knew what their "something" was. Tulius told the receptionist to have a security guard escort the four men to his office. Both the guard and Tulius's secretary were obviously rattled by the four visitors, but he waved them out of his office and told them to shut the door behind them.

The four strangers had stood mute before his desk. Their leader—indistinguishable physically from the other three—had pulled the hard drives out of his baggy jacket and laid them carefully, almost tenderly, on Tulius' desk.

Now Tulius looked up from his desk at the four men. Their faces were swarthy, two of them were mustached, all of their jaws were dark with stubble. Their eyes were hard as chips of flint.

"Shamil says you need these," said their leader.

"Yes," Tulius replied, a little shakily. "Thank you. And thank Mr. Shamil for me."

"You are to telephone Shamil at once," he said.

"I will. Immediately."

None of them moved.

His hand trembling slightly, Tulius lifted his telephone from its cradle and tapped out Shamil's private number.

"I am Shamil," came the rough voice. No picture. Tulius kept his wall screen blank.

"Tulius here," he said, trying to sound unperturbed. "Your friends just arrived. With three gifts."

"Ah, good. The gifts we discussed."

"Yes."

"Put them to good use." And Tulius heard the click of Shamil's hanging up.

He replaced the phone and said to the quartet's leader, "Thank you. The guard outside will show you the way back to the lobby."

"We will be nearby if you need us," said their leader.

"I understand," Tulius replied, "but I'm certain that won't be necessary."

Without a further word or gesture, they turned and left. Tulius felt a wave of relief once they were out of his office. Then he looked down at the three hard drives again. Those Chechen toughs had somehow taken them away from Gould's people. Inside these three little packages was the data from Michael Cochrane's work. The key to producing hydrogen from water. The key to billions of dollars. Trillions.

Tulius thought of his grandfather and all the tales he'd told of Russian oppression. Of the Latvians' plea to Molotov when it became clear that Stalin was going to march into the Baltic republics. Molotov's blunt, cold reply: "It would be inexcusable for us not to take advantage of this opportunity." Tulius's grandfather had been a judge on Latvia's supreme court. He spent the years of World War II living in huts in the forest, freezing in the snows of winter, hunted by the Nazis and the Soviets both.

And then, after the war, half a century of living under the Russians' heavy hand. Tulius's father had been smuggled out of Latvia and came to America, content to work as a stock boy, a clerk, a salesman in a shoe store so that his son could go to a university and make a better life for himself. When the Communist rule in Russia finally collapsed, his father had joyfully returned to Latvia, to work for his nation's independence from the Russians. His reward had been arrest, imprisonment, and death from brutality at the hands of the still-despotic KGB.

Latvia and the other Baltic republics finally attained their freedom from Russia, but too late for Algis Tulius.

His son stared at the three small packets of brushed aluminum on his desk. The information in these hard drives could cripple Russia's oil exports, he told himself. I could send the Russian economy into a black pit of misery.

And what would I gain by that? he asked himself. Would it bring back my father? Would it please my grandfather? They're in their graves, beyond all pain and pleasure.

But I am alive. I could gain international fame by giving the world this means of producing hydrogen fuel. Tulius pictured himself at the Nobel ceremony in Stockholm, accepting the plaudits of the world.

But then he shook his head. No, it's Cochrane's work. Too many people here in my own lab know that Michael did the work, not me. I haven't done any real research work in more than ten years. I'm an administrator, not a working scientist any longer.

No one knows what's in these hard drives, he realized. No one knows who those four thugs were and why they came here. If I called Gould, how much would he pay me to deliver these hard drives into his own hands? I could retire, live like a king anywhere on earth I chose to.

Shamil would be furious, of course. But Gould would protect me from him and his Chechen animals. The FBI might be interested to know that four Chechen terrorists are in the country. The local police are still trying to find Michael's murderer. And if Shamil's been funneling UN money to me, he's probably been playing fast and loose with others, as well. He's vulnerable.

With these thoughts swirling through his mind, Tulius carefully placed the three hard drives in the top drawer of his desk. Then he picked up his phone once again and placed a call to Lionel Gould.

SAN FRANCISCO:
RUSSIAN HILL

I t was early afternoon when the airport taxi pulled up in front of the address Sandoval had given the driver. Cochrane paid the bill and the two
of them stepped out onto the sidewalk. They had hardly spoken a word to
each other in nearly forty-eight hours.

The morning before, Elena had gone off from the Gramercy Park Hotel on a brief shopping spree among the street stalls that lined Fourteenth
Street, using some of Cochrane's cash. He stayed in their room, staring
mindlessly at the TV news. Once she'd returned and changed, they
checked out and went to Kennedy Airport for a flight to San Francisco.

"Why San Francisco?" Cochrane had asked her.

Sandoval replied, "It's where I live."

They had to wait overnight at the airport before a pair of standby
seats became available for them, sitting up in one terminal gate after another. Fearful of being spotted by Gould's people, they had sat as far away
from one another as they could while enduring the agonizing wait. The

crowds thinned out during the night as flight departures and arrivals came further and further apart. Cochrane hardly slept, feeling more and more vulnerable as the terminal became emptier and emptier.

He was afraid of more than being discovered by Gould's hired thugs. He worried that if he stayed close to Elena he'd start arguing with her again. The thought of her with Gould tormented him. No matter why she slept with the sweaty fat bastard, he couldn't stand the knowledge that she'd gone to bed with him.

Macho bullshit, he told himself as he sat through the endless hours at the airport. She did it to protect me. Yeah. Right. And for the ten million Gould promised her. I can protect myself; I didn't ask her to jump into bed with him.

And how many others? he asked himself. How many? I'm just another john as far as she's concerned. Her ticket to the money. She said she loves me. Sure she does. Just as much as I love her.

And that's where it really hurt. He did love Elena, he realized. He wanted her to be with him always. But he knew that could never happen. Not now. It would never work. How could it?

Painfully stiff and puffy-eyed after a night of sitting up in the airport, he had walked down the aisle of the airliner, then watched Sandoval sit several rows ahead of him, her shoulders slumped tiredly. He had slept most of the way to San Francisco.

Standing now on the sidewalk in the early afternoon sunshine as the taxi pulled away, Cochrane felt weary, irritable, grimy in the clothes he'd been wearing since their dinner at Gould's residence. Squinting up in the bright sunlight, he saw an unpretentious row of three-story houses, each painted a different pastel shade, that marched down the slope of the street. The neighborhood seemed quiet; cars lined the curbs, but hardly any pedestrians were walking past. A cable car clanged faintly several blocks away. Looking farther down the street, he could see a glimmer of bright blue water in the distance, between rows of high-rise towers.

"This is my home," Elena said, her tone flat. She looked as tired as Cochrane felt.

"The whole house?"

She nodded as she went up the steps to the front door and tapped out the security code on the electronic lock. The door popped open; Cochrane followed her into the cool shadows of the entryway.

"You're my first houseguest," she said as she led him up the narrow stairway to the second floor. "No one's ever been here except me, until now."

"How come?"

"Safe house," she replied matter-of-factly. "The kind of work I do, I don't want anyone to know my home base."

They were in a spacious living room. Bay window fronting on the street. A fireplace, cold and dark. Big sofa, several comfortable-looking armchairs. Paintings on the walls. Impressionists, he saw. Reproductions. They reminded him of the museum in Boston.

She walked him back to the kitchen, opened the refrigerator, and pulled out a bottle of Corona Light.

"Would you like a beer?" she asked, rummaging in a drawer until she found a bottle opener.

Cochrane shook his head. The place looked spic-and-span. "You have a housekeeper?" he asked.

"An old Hispanic woman. She does several houses on this block. Once a week, whether I'm here or not."

"How long have you had this place?"

"Couple years," Sandoval said, after a long pull on the beer.

Nobody's ever been here before? Cochrane wondered how true that was. Maybe—

"I'm going to take a shower," she said, putting the bottle down on the counter. "What about you?"

"I—I'll wait until you're finished."

She stared at him.

He stared back.

"Paul, I'm not a whore."

"I never said you were, did I?"

"The thing with Gould—"

"You did it to protect me, I know."

"I did it to protect myself, too. I was in a tough situation, with Kensington there and all."

"Kensington's dead."

"And we're alive."

"So?" He knew what he wanted her to say. She wasn't saying it.

"So where do we go from here, Paul?"

"I wish I knew."

"It's up to you," she said, without moving a millimeter closer to him.

He looked into her unfathomable green eyes, his mind spinning. Then he heard himself say, "Elena... I don't want to lose you."

"I know," she answered softly.

"I don't have anybody else! There's no one else in my life, nobody at all!"

And it was the truth. He didn't want to lose her. Without her he was alone. Utterly alone. He loved her. Despite everything, he loved her.

She reached out and touched his cheek. He realized that tears were leaking from his eyes.

"I don't want to lose you," he repeated, sliding both hands around her waist, pulling her to him.

"You won't," she whispered to him. "I'm here, Paul. I'm with you. Always."

He held her and she rested her head on his shoulder and they were both sobbing softly.

After a long while she lifted her head slightly and suggested, "How about that shower?"

"Yeah," he answered. "Right."

That night, long afterward, they lay in bed together, warm and musky from lovemaking. Sandoval's bedroom was dark, although a faint misty light came from the curtained window. Cochrane could make out the plastered ceiling overhead.

"You ought to have a mirror up there," he murmured. "It'd be fun."

"Can't," she replied drowsily. "Earthquakes."

"Oh."

A silence. Then, "Paul, where do we go from here?"

"Gould wants those hard drives."

"I don't care what Gould wants," she said. "He's never going to pay us, no matter what we do."

"You think not?"

"Paul, you hit him. You threatened his life."

"I had to."

"I know. But you *humiliated* him. He's never going to forget that."

"So now he's out to get me?"

"You've made it a personal thing. He won't rest until you're dead."

Cochrane lay there in the queen-sized bed next to her, the reality of it sinking into his mind. "Christ," he whispered, "where the hell can we go?"

MANHATTAN:
GOULD TRUST HEADQUARTERS

Freshly dressed in a pale blue silk sports shirt and darker slacks, Lionel Gould sat down in the comfortable upholstered armchair by the window of his bedroom. Morning sunshine streamed through the opened curtains as he tapped out a number on the keyboard of his computer phone.

The phone rang once, twice. On the third ring a muffled voice muttered, "Hello?" The little screen stayed blank; apparently Dr. Tulius did not have a vidcam link on his bedroom telephone.

"Dr. Tulius," Gould said grandly, "this is Lionel Gould. Am I calling too early in the day?"

He heard some fumbling as he glanced at the ornate diamond-circled French Imperial clock on his night table. It would be 5:45 A.M. in California. Gould smiled to himself.

"Mr. Gould?" Tulius half whispered.

"I apologize for calling so early," Gould said, running a finger around the collar of his shirt. "I realize there's a three-hour difference out where you are."

"My wife's asleep," Tulius said softly. "Let me get to my desk. Just a moment...."

The line went dead. Gould figured that Tulius had put him on hold. He counted mentally, one–one thousand, two–one thousand, three...

Suddenly his phone screen came to life and he saw a pouchy-eyed Jason Tulius blinking sleepily at him, wearing blue-and-white-striped pajamas. He was evidently in a different room, an office adjoining his bedroom, Gould presumed.

"Again," said Gould, "I'm sorry if this is an inconvenient time for you, but my assistant told me you've been trying to reach me since Tuesday."

"That's all right," Tulius said, rubbing at his eyes with the heel of one hand. "I'm glad you called."

"Indeed."

Tulius looked disheveled, his beard uncombed, his pajamas wrinkled. But he said, "I have the, uh... packages you're interested in."

"The computers?" Gould blurted.

"I don't think we should talk about this over an unsecured line, Mr. Gould."

"All three of them?" Gould asked anyway.

"Their hard drives."

"That is good! Very good!"

"But there's a complication," said Tulius.

Gould made a little grunt. "Isn't there always?"

"It's very serious."

"What's the problem?"

"We shouldn't discuss this over the phone."

"Don't be melodramatic," Gould snapped. "No one's tapping your phone and certainly no one is tapping mine."

"But..."

Gould sucked in a deep breath. "My dear Dr. Tulius, how much do you want for those three hard drives?"

"It...there's more than money involved. I need protection."

"Protection from whom?"

Tulius replied, "Would it be possible for me to call you from my office at the center? I have a secure line there."

Gould saw that the scientist looked frightened. "How long will it take you to get there?"

"I can be there in an hour. Less, at this time of the morning."

Gould sank back in the yielding chair, thinking hard. *Tulius has the computer drives. Whoever took them from Kensington has brought them to him. Why him? Who else is involved in this? Whoever it is, they killed Kensington and they've got Dr. Tulius thoroughly scared.*

"Perhaps you'd better bring the, uh, packages to me here in New York. I can send a plane—"

"No!" Tulius snapped. "That would tip them off that I'm working with you."

"Them? Who?"

"Let me call you from my office," Tulius pleaded. "We can talk much more freely then."

Gould felt a gnawing anger rising in him. But he said mildly, "Very well, Dr. Tulius. In one hour."

"Right."

Gould's computer screen went dark. Reaching for a tissue from the box on the table beside him, he dabbed at his chin and his beaded upper lip as he thought hard. *Someone took those hard drives from Kensington and delivered them to Tulius. Someone who has frightened the bejeesus out of him. He wants to sell the drives to me, but more than that he needs my protection.*

Nodding to himself, Gould relaxed in the upholstered chair. Then he phoned his assistant and told him to get his private jet ready for a flight to California.

In San Francisco, Cochrane and Sandoval were already at breakfast in the spacious kitchen of her home on Russian Hill.

"Do you really think that Gould wants to kill me?" he asked, a spoonful of Rice Krispies halfway to his mouth.

She nodded solemnly from across the white-painted table. "It's a personal vendetta with him now. His ego is at stake."

"Then what are we going to do?" Before she could reply, Cochrane corrected himself. "No, not us. It's me he's sore at, not you."

"Us," Sandoval said firmly. "We're in this together."

"But—"

"What happens to you happens to me, Paul."

He shook his head, but said nothing. After a few more crunching mouthfuls of the cereal, he asked, "Does Gould know about this house?"

"Nobody knows about it," Sandoval replied. "You're the first person ever to be here, besides me."

"I guess we can lay low here for a couple of days."

Nodding, she said, "I have credit cards we can use, a California driver's license. The house is listed under a false name, too."

"Good enough, I guess."

"For a few days."

"Then what?" he asked.

"I don't know. Not yet."

Cochrane took a deep, sighing breath. He stared at her lovely face, so dead serious. Her sea-green eyes, so somber.

An idea struck him. "Listen," he said, "can you call Fiona, back in Boston?"

"We shouldn't go back there, Paul. Fiona's—"

"No, no. I don't want to go back there. But she's got my laptop. I left it with her. I gave Mike's CDs to Gould, but his data is still on my laptop's hard drive."

She looked horrified. "If Gould knew..."

"Call Fiona. Ask her to FedEx my laptop to my apartment in Tucson. It'll be there by tomorrow morning!"

Sandoval started for the phone, but hesitated. "Then what, Paul? Once you have the laptop, then what?"

"I don't know," he admitted. "Not yet. But at least we'll have a bargaining chip to deal with Gould."

She looked doubtful, but went to the telephone.

I'll leave Elena here and zip back to Tucson to pick up the laptop, Cochrane said to himself, the plan forming in his mind. Gould's people will be looking for the two of us together. It'll be easier for me to get in and out without her. And then I'll slip out of Tucson, by myself. I'll get out and go away somewhere. Elena will be safe as long as she's not with me. Gould's after me, not her.

But then he remembered that Gould wanted Elena. For himself.

Gould was in his limousine, on his way to La Guardia Airport, when Tulius phoned him back. The image on the little screen built into the limo's side panel was a trifle grainy, but Gould could see clearly the worry—the fright—on the scientist's face. He's scared, almost in a panic, Gould thought. And he's looking to me for help. That puts me in a strong position, Gould told himself. Which is good.

He could see that Tulius was in a spacious, well-appointed office. The Calvin Research Center, he thought. It was not yet seven A.M. in California, so the man must be alone in the building, except for whatever security guards he might have there. At any rate, Tulius was talking much more freely now.

"And this man you've been dealing with," Gould asked, "is an official at the United Nations?"

"UNESCO," Tulius replied.

"He's a Chechen?"

"From Chechnya, yes, that's right. He hates the Russians, wants to do whatever he can to hurt them."

"He's a terrorist, then?"

"No, no, no," Tulius corrected. "He's not the type to throw bombs. He's not suicidal. He wants to cripple Russia's oil industry."

"And how does he plan to accomplish that, may I ask?"

"With Cochrane's hydrogen process! Shifting from petroleum to hydrogen will knock the bottom out of oil prices. Just an announcement that the process works will send oil prices spiraling downward."

Gould nodded at the grainy image in the small screen. He's perfectly right about that, he said to himself. That's why there must be no announcement, no shift to hydrogen. Not until the time is exactly right.

"If I turn these hard drives over to you, Shamil's people will be furious. I'll need protection from them."

"These are the men who killed Kensington?"

"Of course! You told me that Kensington had the hard drives in his possession. Then these four thugs show up in my office and hand them to me. And your man Kensington was found dead."

"Without the hard drives," Gould muttered.

"I have them here. Locked in my desk."

The limo was pulling off the main road and onto the ramp that led to the private aviation sector of La Guardia, where Gould's Cessna jet was waiting for him.

"Very well," Gould said. "I shall fly to your center this morning. Expect me there by"—he calculated mentally—"eleven o'clock your time."

"No!" Tulius yelped. "If they see you here they'll know I've crossed them! They'll know I'm working for you!"

Gould held back a snappish reply. Instead he answered patiently, "My dear Dr. Tulius, it's common knowledge that the Gould Trust has made an offer to buy your Calvin laboratories. It would be quite natural for me to make an impromptu visit to your labs, unannounced, to see what I'm paying for. Nothing to alarm anyone."

"They're very touchy, suspicious—"

"Yes, I understand. While I'm in flight I will make arrangements to have a security team provide protection for you and your wife," Gould said. "You have children?"

"A son. He's at Berkeley."

"Then we'll provide protection for him, too. I'll also have my publicity people leak a story about this man Shamir in the UN—"

"Shamil," Tulius corrected.

"Shamil," said Gould. "And the FBI should be interested in the ruffians who murdered Kensington, I should think. They probably also killed your Dr. Cochrane in the first place."

Tulius looked shocked. "I never thought of that."

"We'll have them all rounded up pretty quickly, never fear," said Gould.

"That would be wonderful."

The limousine pulled up before a large hangar. Gould saw that his Cessna was on the apron, apparently ready to go.

"I'll see you in about four hours," he said to Tulius, then leaned forward in the limo's rear seat to turn off the phone connection before Tulius could reply.

Yes, he said to himself as the chauffeur opened the limo door for him, the FBI can take care of the Chechen gorillas; it will be good publicity for the Bureau to round up a gang of Muslim terrorists. And they'll lead straight to this Shamil character at the UN. Wonderful headlines: *Chechen terrorist cell headed by corrupt United Nations official.* My publicity people can use their contacts to make certain the story receives attention on all the networks. Meanwhile, I will acquire the Calvin lab and Tulius along with it.

That takes care of everything, Gould thought as he walked to his plane. Everything and everyone. Except for that man Cochrane. He laid hands on me. He threatened me at knifepoint. In front of the Sandoval woman, he made me look like a humiliated fool.

I'll find him. Wherever he's hiding, I'll find him and kill him.

And her, too. She betrayed me. She played up to me only to protect him. I'll find them both. They'll be together, without doubt. He sighed deeply, remembering. It will be a shame to get rid of her, but what else can I do? They'll both have to go.

PALO ALTO:
CALVIN RESEARCH CENTER

It was a busy morning for Jason Tulius. Promptly at nine A.M. his assistant tapped gently on his office door and informed him that a team of security specialists employed by the Gould Trust had arrived in the lobby. Tulius wasted no time having all six of them brought to his office. After more than an hour's conversation with them, he felt grateful and relieved.

"We already have a team watching your house," said their leader as he rose to leave. He was a tall, lanky, silver-haired man with a hawk's beak for a nose and piercing dark eyes. "We'll do a sweep of your building here and the grounds beyond. If they've got the place staked out, we'll nab them."

"And my son?"

"In Berkeley. We're on it."

The other five men, standing behind their leader, nodded somberly.

Getting to his feet, Tulius said, "Mr. Gould said something about the FBI."

"We often work with the Bureau. I have a meeting scheduled for this afternoon with the chief of the San Francisco office."

"That's fine," said Tulius. "Fine." He went around his desk and shook hands with each of the six men. They certainly seemed professional and utterly competent.

Once they left his office, Tulius went back to his desk and sat down, feeling that his situation had improved enormously. He was in good hands. Shamil and his thugs would be taken care of, as they deserved.

He unlocked the top right drawer of his desk, pulled it open, and gazed at the three small cases of brushed aluminum. They're worth a considerable fortune, Tulius said to himself. I wonder how much Gould will be willing to pay me for them.

Glancing at his desktop clock, he saw that Gould would arrive within a couple of hours. He'll pay handsomely to acquire this center, Tulius thought, but he ought to pay me a special bonus for delivering these hard drives to him. Enough to allow me to retire. Enough to set me up for life.

His intercom buzzed.

Slightly annoyed at the interruption, Tulius poked the keyboard. "Yes?"

"Dr. Cochrane is in the lobby, sir, asking to see you."

"Cochrane?"

"Mike's brother," his assistant's voice said. "You remember, he was here right after Mike was murdered."

All of Tulius's pleasant feelings of safety and a comfortable future drained out of him.

"Shall I tell the receptionist to send him up here?" his assistant asked.

Tugging at his beard, Tulius answered unhappily, "Yes, yes, send him in."

"There's a woman with him. Elena Sandoval."

"Of course," Tulius croaked. "Of course."

Cochrane had made up his mind by the time they'd finished breakfast.

As he carried their cereal bowls to the kitchen sink, he said, to himself as much as to Sandoval, "The Calvin Center. We've got to see Dr. Tulius."

Still sitting at the kitchen table, Sandoval asked, "Tulius? Why him?"

"Who else is there? Senator Bardarson's sold out to Gould. Nobody in the government is going to lift a finger for us, Gould's got them all under his control."

"But why Tulius?" she repeated.

"He's a scientist. He understands what's at stake." He turned from the sink to face her. "He's the only guy I can think of who might be able to help us."

"What about the scientist you were working with from the National Science Foundation?"

"Esterbrook?" Cochrane thought it over briefly. "Yeah, maybe. But he's in Washington and Tulius is just a car ride away, in Palo Alto."

Sandoval got up from the table and carried her juice glass to the sink.

"Paul," she asked softly, "just what is it that you think Tulius can do for us?"

"Get Mike's work published," he replied. "Get it out into the open so Gould can't keep it to himself."

"What good would that do?"

He stared at her. "Don't you get it? Don't you understand? Gould wants to keep Mike's work secret, you told me so yourself. He wants to hold it in his own hands while oil prices keep heading for the stars and he makes all those profits. He wants to be the one who decides when and how the hydrogen process is brought out into the open. He wants to be the one who controls the shift from oil to hydrogen."

"So?"

"So publishing Mike's work will make it public," Cochrane said, with growing fervor. "It'll make his process common knowledge. Nobody will be able to monopolize it. Nobody will be able to take out a patent on it. Ten thousand little guys will start tinkering with the idea, start producing hydrogen cars that really *work*! They'll start a new industry, hydrogen fuels. Cheap, easy hydrogen-fueled cars. Trucks. Planes. Nobody'll need oil anymore!"

"That's what you want to do?"

"That's it. Mike's work can be the basis for a whole new industry. Getting the whole friggin' world off the oil teat and into clean, cheap hydrogen."

Sandoval shook her head sorrowfully. "Paul, all you'd be doing is giving Gould another reason to have you murdered."

"So what?" he snapped, full of his own vision. "He already wants to kill me. This'll make it worth the risk."

She started to reply, but saw that it would be useless. With a heavy sigh, she said, "All right. Let's drive out to the Calvin Center."

• • •

Dr. Tulius did his best to appear calm and welcoming as Sandoval and Cochrane were ushered into his office. He got up from his desk, shook hands with them both, and guided them to the round conference table in the far corner of the room.

But only after he had closed the desk drawer containing the three hard drives. And locked it again.

"Now, then," he said once they were all seated around the table, "what brings you here this morning? Have you learned anything about Michael's murder? I must confess the police haven't spoken a word to me since the funeral. I was beginning to think they'd just dropped the case altogether."

Cochrane could see that Tulius was edgy. The man was tugging unconsciously at his beard, glancing nervously all around his office as he chattered, looking back at his desk and the digital clock that sat next to his computer keyboard. He wouldn't meet Cochrane's eyes.

Deciding to cut directly to the heart of the matter, Cochrane said, "Dr. Tulius, I have Mike's data."

"You do?" Tulius's white eyebrows rose so high his forehead wrinkled.

"All of it."

"But I thought—" Tulius stopped himself.

"You thought what?" Sandoval asked.

Before Tulius could think of a reply, Cochrane leaned forward intently and said, "Mike's work shows how to bioengineer a strain of cyanobacteria so they'll produce gaseous hydrogen. Lots of hydrogen. Put a sheet of those bugs in your car and they'll make hydrogen fuel for you. All you need to do is fill your tank with water and let the bugs split the water into hydrogen and oxygen. Cheap and easy."

"That's..." Tulius groped for a word. "Interesting."

"It's more than interesting," Cochrane snapped. "It can move the world off oil, off fossil fuels altogether."

"If it works in the real world, Dr. Cochrane. After all, laboratory data is one thing, but that doesn't mean—"

Sandoval interrupted, "Michael Cochrane was killed over this. You know that as well as we do."

"Still..."

Earnestly, Cochrane explained, "We've got to publish this work, Dr. Tulius. We've got to get it out into the open scientific literature so that no one can claim possession of it, no one can bottle it up, suppress it."

"We?"

"I'm not a biologist," Cochrane said. "You are. You can get this work published by the top journal in your field. You can call an international news conference, even."

Tulius licked his lips. "I ... I suppose I could."

"This could make you famous," Cochrane urged. "Calvin Research Center would become a world-class organization."

"I would like to think that we already are."

"You know what I mean. Your lab would be the center of world attention. You could write your own ticket."

"The oil industry would not be pleased," Tulius muttered.

Sandoval replied, "The oil industry would have to get on the bandwagon. They'd have to! And the auto industry, too."

"Perhaps."

"No 'perhaps' about it," Cochrane insisted. "This will be the biggest thing to hit the energy industry since they sank the first oil wells in Pennsylvania."

Tulius turned from Cochrane to Sandoval, all the while tugging nervously at his beard. Then he pushed his chair away and rose to his feet. Walking slowly back to his desk, he glanced again at the clock.

"You're right, of course," he said, turning back toward his seated visitors. "Look. It's half-past ten. Let's have some coffee and begin to write the opening paragraphs of the paper."

Cochrane glanced at Sandoval, grinning. "Okay. Great."

Tulius called his assistant and ordered coffee. "Bring some sweets, too. Sticky buns, if they have any in the cafeteria," he said into his phone.

When he returned to the table, Cochrane said, "Mike's data will make up the heart of the paper. All we have to do is write an explanation of what it's about."

"Yes," Tulius said agreeably. "And Michael's name should be on the paper."

"He ought to be the first name. Then yours."

Nodding, Tulius said, "And your own."

"Mine? I didn't do any of the work. I don't belong on the paper."

Tulius said, "My boy, you have no idea of how many times a person's name is added to a paper even though that person didn't contribute directly to the research."

"Department heads," Cochrane said. "I know."

Tulius's phone buzzed. He hurried to his desk and picked it up.

"Yes," he said. "Come right in."

The office door opened, but instead of the assistant bringing in coffee, Lionel Gould stepped in.

Cochrane felt his jaw drop open. Gould looked equally surprised. But he recovered quickly.

"Dr. Cochrane," he said, with a broad, toothy smile. "What a pleasant surprise."

PALO ALTO:
CALVIN RESEARCH CENTER
PARKING LOT

To his shame, Akhmad Kadryov was asleep, snoring gently as he sat slumped behind the wheel of his rented Toyota Corolla.

He was rudely awakened by a hard tapping on the door window beside him. Startled, he saw a stern-faced young man wearing a dark suit staring at him. Kadryov saw the reflection of his own stubble-jawed sleepy face in the man's rimless mirror glasses.

"Roll it down," the man demanded, through the closed window. His blond hair was cut so short he looked almost shaved bald.

Blinking sleep from his eyes, Kadryov rolled down the window.

"You work here?"

Without thinking, Kadryov nodded.

"Lemme see your ID."

Kadryov fumbled through his pockets, stammering, "I . . . I must have left it home."

"Better go home and get it, then."

The blond didn't look like the type who brooked arguments. Kadryov touched the butt of the pistol tucked into his waistband, hidden beneath his windbreaker. He thought briefly about toughing it out with this security type, but remembered that his assignment was to watch, not fight. He was supposed to be keeping Tulius under surveillance; he'd been watching the scientist's house since midnight. When Tulius had left early that morning, Kadryov had followed him to the Calvin Research Center and parked in the employees' lot. Then he'd drifted to sleep.

Nodding wordlessly at the blond, Kadryov started his rental car with a roar and drove slowly off the parking lot. As he passed the building's front entrance he noticed a long black limousine parked in front of the main entrance. There were three bulky black SUVs parked in visitors' slots, as well, with several other men in dark suits and sunglasses standing by them. The blond who had accosted him was walking toward them.

Kadryov pulled out onto the access road, but drove less than a block before parking next to a high hedge that screened another office building. He got out of the Toyota and walked back to the end of the hedge, where he had a distant but clear view of the Calvin Center and its parking lot. He thought about phoning his cell leader, whom he knew only as Aslan, but decided against it. Wait and watch, he told himself.

He went back to the car and pulled his binoculars from the glove box, then returned to survey the parking lot again. Tulius's silver Lexus was still in its slot. Good. And the limousine and those SUVs hadn't moved. I wonder who is the VIP of the limousine? Kadryov asked himself. Whoever he is, he's brought a considerable amount of security along with him.

The late morning sunshine felt warm on his shoulders, although a cooling breeze was coming in off the hills that edged the seaside. He put the binoculars down. It wouldn't do to have someone driving by wondering why a short, stocky, swarthy man with a thick dark mustache was spying on the Calvin Research Center. Instead he returned to the car and zipped up his windbreaker.

Wait and watch, he told himself. Wait and watch.

This is an unexpected pleasure," Gould said as he sat himself beside Sandoval at Tulius's round conference table. With a smirk, he added, "Ah, there are no steak knives in sight. I suppose I'm safe, then."

Cochrane, too stunned to get up from his chair, asked, "What the hell are you doing here?"

Gould laughed. "I've come to check out my latest acquisition."

"Acquisition?" Sandoval asked.

"Didn't Dr. Tulius tell you? The Gould Trust is buying the Calvin Research Center. Lock, stock, and barrel, as they say."

"I'll be damned," Cochrane muttered.

"Probably so," said Gould cheerfully. "Probably so."

Tulius hadn't moved from his chair, either. "The deal isn't finalized," he said weakly.

"Oh, it will be, I assure you," Gould said. "This research institution will make a fine addition to the Gould Trust. The jewel in our crown, so to speak."

Tulius said nothing.

"You've sold out to him," Cochrane said. "You've let him buy you out."

"More than that," said Gould, his voice hardening. "Dr. Tulius is holding certain properties of mine. Properties that were stolen from me. I want them. Now."

His eyes widening, Tulius sprang up from his chair and hurried to his desk. He unlocked the drawer and took out three brushed aluminum oblongs.

"The hard drives," Cochrane murmured.

Laying the drives on the conference table in front of Gould, Tulius said, "Dr. Cochrane also has the data in his own laptop."

Gould looked at Cochrane, his eyes hard as ice. "Is that so, Dr. Cochrane?"

Before Cochrane could answer, Sandoval said, "Yes, it's true."

"I should have thought of that," Gould muttered, half to himself. "With all this shuffling back and forth, I forgot."

Cochrane asked Tulius, "How'd you get the hard drives? I thought—"

"What you think is of no consequence," Gould snapped. "Where is your laptop? I want it."

Bargaining chip, Cochrane thought. If I can keep him from getting my laptop, we've got something to bargain with.

Gould frowned at his silence. "Dr. Cochrane, I have a dozen security agents here. We can bring you to a nice, quiet place and extract the information from you in any of several ways. All of them rather unpleasant—for you."

"The laptop's being delivered to his apartment in Tucson," Sandoval said, her voice flat, emotionless.

Cochrane glared at her. She looked back at him, helpless, defeated.

Gould pulled a tissue from his pocket and mopped at his face. Pushing himself up from the table, he said, "It seems we must journey to Tucson, then."

"Me, too?" Tulius asked.

Thinking it over for a moment, Gould replied, "No, that's not necessary. This is between Dr. Cochrane and myself. And the lovely Elena, of course."

From his spot by the hedge, Kadryov saw three people emerge from the Calvin Center's front entrance, two men and a woman. Quickly he yanked a digital camera from his pocket and snapped as many images as he could before they all got into the waiting limousine. Most of the dark-suited security people piled into two of the SUVs, leaving four of them standing by the third one.

Frantically, Kadryov pawed at his cell phone.

"Well?" Aslan's voice.

"There's something going on," Kadryov said. "Important people have visited Tulius and now they are leaving."

"Important people? Who?"

"I don't know! But they are in a limousine and there's a squad of guards in SUVs going along with them."

He could hear Aslan's heavy breathing. Then, "Follow them. See where they are going."

"And Tulius?"

"I'll have someone else take up the watch on him."

Kadryov nodded, clicked the phone shut, and sprinted to his Toyota, hoping that the limousine hadn't gotten too far away for him to pick it up.

TUCSON:
SUNRISE APARTMENTS

A Federal Express truck was standing by the front entrance of the Sunrise Apartments building when Gould's limousine pulled up behind it.

Gould, Sandoval, and Cochrane had flown in Gould's twin-jet Cessna from the Palo Alto airport to Tucson International, where a fresh limo was waiting for them in the bright, hot sunshine of early afternoon. Only one of the security men had accompanied them; he sat up front in the limo with the driver.

Cringing in the blazing sunlight, Cochrane held out a hand to help Sandoval exit the limousine. The driver hurried around the long black car to offer help to Gould as he struggled his bulk through the open rear door. The security guy stood by the front door of the limo, staring squarely at Cochrane through his dark glasses.

They started for the front door of the apartment building, Cochrane in the lead.

"Say, you wouldn't be Paul Cochrane, would you?"

Cochrane turned to see the FedEx driver standing a few feet away.

His heart sinking, Cochrane admitted, "Yeah, that's me."

"Good. Thought I'd missed you." The driver sprinted to his truck, disappeared inside, then came out bearing a square FedEx packing box in his hands.

"I need a signature," he said, pushing the box at Cochrane.

My laptop, Cochrane knew as he scrawled his name on the printed form on the deliveryman's clipboard.

Gould beamed at him. "It seems we arrived just in the nick of time."

Cochrane tucked the package under his arm and led them into the air-conditioned lobby. The driver and security man trailed behind him, Sandoval, and Gould.

Once inside the apartment, Cochrane put the package on his kitchen table and ripped it open, then slid his computer out of it.

Worldlessly, Sandoval took the empty box and stuffed it into the wastebasket beneath the sink. Smart, Cochrane thought: she doesn't want Gould to see who sent it here. She's protecting Fiona. And her own safe haven.

The driver and the security man had helped themselves to chairs in the living room, stationing themselves between Cochrane and the front door.

Gould said impatiently, "Well, start it up."

"The battery's dead," Cochrane said, opening the laptop. "I'll have to plug it into the wall."

Fiona had included the AC power pack and its cords. Reluctantly, Cochrane unwound the black lines and plugged one end into the computer, the other into a wall socket beside the sink. The computer stirred to life when he pushed the "on" button, quickly flicked through its self-analysis, then played its usual little tune to announce it was ready to work.

Gould edged up beside him, his eyes on the screen, his forehead beaded with perspiration. Cochrane thought about turning his air-conditioning cooler, but decided, To hell with it; let the bastard sweat.

But Sandoval went to the thermostat on the wall and clicked the temperature lower. Cochrane heard the air conditioner grumble and then hum into action.

"Well?" Gould said, as Sandoval returned to the table.

Cochrane thought about picking up the laptop and heaving it through the kitchen window. But that would accomplish the same result Gould wants, he told himself. He *wants* to destroy Mike's work.

Instead, he leaned over the table and tapped on the keyboard until Mike's data began to scroll across the display screen.

Gould huffed at the equations rolling past. "That's it?" he asked.

"That's it," Cochrane said tightly.

Dabbing at his sweaty face, Gould said, "Very well. Erase it."

Cochrane hesitated, then hit the "select all" key. Mike's words and equations immediately were highlighted in yellow. "Erase," Cochrane tapped.

ARE YOU SURE YOU WANT TO ERASE THE ENTIRE DOCUMENT? Y/N.

Before Cochrane could react, Gould leaned over his shoulder and pressed the Y key with a heavy thumb.

Mike's document disappeared.

Cochrane straightened up, looked at Sandoval. Her face was expressionless.

"Now erase it from the recycle bin," Gould said.

Cochrane's eyes widened.

"Oh, yes," said Gould. "I know something about computers. I know that they hold a copy of everything you erase in their recycle file. Erase it, please. And then I'll have to take the hard drive. I want your brother's work completely gone, once and for all."

Tulius had watched Gould and his people escort Cochrane and the Sandoval woman from his office. Feeling that he was in much deeper water than he wanted to be, he sat at his desk for several minutes, then went to the window and saw Gould's limousine pull out of the center's driveway and onto the access road leading to the freeway.

His phone rang. The private, secure line.

He went back to the desk and pressed the console's "on" button. Zelinkshah Shamil's face appeared on the wall screen. His dark face looked suspicious, almost angry.

Without preliminaries, Shamil said, "I've been informed that Lionel Gould has visited your laboratory."

Tulius sank into his swivel chair, heart pounding.

"Gould?"

"One of my men photographed him leaving your building and e-mailed the picture to me. I recognized him immediately."

Feeling thoroughly frightened, Tulius temporized, "Yes, Mr. Gould was here. He's made an offer to buy Calvin Research. He dropped in— completely unexpected—to inspect the labs."

"He didn't stay long."

"No, he didn't."

"Who were the people with him?"

"Security."

"There was a man and a woman who didn't look like security types to me."

"The woman was Elena Sandoval."

"Who is she?"

Tulius could feel sweat popping out on his brow. "She was with the other fellow."

"And who is he?" Shamil demanded impatiently.

"A scientist."

"What's his *name?*"

Tulius thought about lying, but he couldn't think of what to say on the spur of the moment. So he confessed, "Cochrane."

"Cochrane?" Shamil snapped. "Isn't that the name of your employee, the one who was killed?"

"Yes," Tulius admitted. "That was his brother."

"Why is he going with Gould?"

"He...he's trying to find out who murdered his brother."

"And Gould's helping him?"

"I suppose so."

Shamil's face radiated distrust. "Where did they go?"

"I don't know. They didn't say."

"Cochrane," Shamil muttered. "With Gould."

"I...I think Cochrane lives in Tucson," Tulius blurted. "He works at the university there."

"Dr. Tulius," said Shamil, his tone lower, darker. "I don't like the idea that you are friendly with Gould. He's the enemy."

"He's made an offer to buy Calvin Research!" Tulius bleated. "He popped in here unexpected, unannounced. There was nothing I could do about it."

"Truly?"

"I got rid of him as quickly as I could."

"And this man Cochrane just happened to be in your labs at the same time."

"He's investigating his brother's murder. I told you. The woman with him is a private detective, I think."

Shamil seemed to think that over for a few moments, while Tulius's pulse thundered in his ears.

"And the data from those hard drives that my men gave you?"

"My people are working on that," Tulius lied. "It should take several days, maybe a week."

"Very well," said Shamil, looking completely unconvinced. "Perhaps I should visit your laboratory myself."

Tulius felt his insides go hollow. But he took a deep breath and then replied, "In a few days. Once we have the data from the hard drives. Then you can fly out here."

Shamil nodded warily. "Until then."

The wall screen went dark and Tulius sagged in his chair. Gould said he'd get the FBI to round up Shamil's people, he told himself. The sooner the better. The sooner the better.

Shamil stared at the darkened wall screen in his New York office. He turned to his computer and looked up the University of Arizona faculty. A Dr. Paul Cochrane was listed in the astronomy department. From a white pages directory he obtained Dr. Paul Cochrane's street address and telephone number.

Then he phoned Aslan, in California. Their conversation was brief, guarded.

"Get to Dr. Paul Cochrane in Tucson." Shamil gave the Chechen cell leader Cochrane's address and phone number. "Immediately," he added.

"And?" Aslan asked.

"Phone me once you have him."

No reply except the click of the phone.

TUCSON INTERNATIONAL
AIRPORT

Aslan Denikin felt distinctly uncomfortable as he and two of his cell members walked hurriedly along the airport terminal toward the baggage claim area. They could not bring guns into the plane with them, of course, so they had disassembled all three of their pistols and then packed the pieces into a scuffed old duffel bag, which Aslan checked at the Palo Alto airport when they boarded the flight to Tucson. *The X-ray screening is only as good as the people watching the screens,* he told himself. *They won't recognize the disassembled pieces of the pistols,* he hoped.

While one of his team went to rent a car for them, Aslan hung back from the crowd at the baggage carousel, watching for security agents as the duffel went around the slowly moving conveyor twice. By the time his man returned from the rental counter, he decided it was probably safe to pick up the duffel.

He nodded to the third man of his team, who went quickly through the thinning crowd of arriving passengers and scooped up the duffel the next time it passed. Aslan had made certain that all three of them had shaved. Profiling or not, he did not want any of them to look like a skulking, stubble-jawed alien.

The three men found their rental car, a white Ford sedan, in the airport parking garage. Despite its being under a roof, the car was baking hot inside. Aslan took the wheel, started up the car with a roar, turned the air-conditioning up full blast, and headed out toward the address of Dr. Paul Cochrane.

In the back seat, his two cell members were busily assembling the pistols and loading them.

Now, then," said Gould as he sat in his shirtsleeves on the sofa of Cochrane's living room, "we have some final arrangements to make."

"You've got what you came for," Cochrane said tightly, standing in the middle of the room. "You've won."

Sandoval was still in the kitchen, standing tensely beside the refrigerator, her eyes shifting from Gould to Cochrane and back again. Gould's driver and security goon were sitting in the armchairs closest to the front door.

"Yes, I've won," Gould agreed, smiling. "You gave me a few bad moments, I'll admit, but that's all over now, isn't it?"

"So what happens now?" Cochrane asked.

With a massive shrug, Gould said, "I leave with the spoils of victory."

Cochrane glanced at Sandoval.

Gould laughed. "Oh, no, not her. She's all yours. I was referring to your brother's data."

"It's erased. Gone."

"Still, I'd prefer to bring your laptop along with me. Experts have been known to retrieve data that's supposedly been erased."

Cochrane made a gesture of concession. "Take it."

"I'll write you a check for it." Gould looked around for his jacket.

"It's here," Sandoval said, lifting the shapeless garment from one of the kitchen chairs.

She carried it to him, and Gould extracted his checkbook from an inside pocket. Wordlessly, Sandoval brought the jacket into the kitchen and draped it back on the chair.

"Three thousand dollars should cover it," Gould muttered. "More than cover it, I should think."

He scribbled his signature, tore the check out of its book, and handed it to Cochrane.

Cochrane didn't move. "What happens next?" he asked.

"Next?"

"You just hand me a check and then leave?"

"Yes," said Gould. "What else would you expect?"

"What if I go to the police?"

"With what?"

"You stole my computer."

"I'm paying you for it," said Gould. He laid the check on the little table at the end of the sofa. "There. Paid in full."

"So now you leave?"

"Now we leave," Gould echoed. He pushed himself up from the sofa with a grunting effort.

"Who killed my brother?"

Gould shrugged again. "Let's blame it on Kensington. He won't mind."

"But you said he didn't do it."

"That was then, this is now. You can tell the police that Mr. Kensington murdered your brother." He turned toward Sandoval. "You can make up the details, can't you, Elena? You have a vivid imagination."

Cochrane took a step toward Gould. Gould's two men shot up from their chairs.

"Now, now, Dr. Cochrane," Gould said, wagging a stubby finger, "you mustn't let your temper get the better of you, the way you did in my home. That will be the death of you."

"Is that a threat?" Cochrane growled.

"A threat? Would I make a threat in front of witnesses? Do you take me for a fool?"

Cochrane's jaw was clenching so tightly it hurt.

Laying a fatherly hand on Cochrane's shoulder, Gould said, "My dear Dr. Cochrane, I never make threats. I take actions. And remember, revenge is a dish best taken cold."

He turned toward Sandoval again. "My jacket, please, Elena."

The intercom from the building's lobby buzzed harshly, once, twice, three times.

Aslan and his two cell members had parked in a visitor's slot, close to the Sunshine Apartments' front entrance. No one was in sight; the parking lot was baking hot in the blazing sunshine.

As the three men went to the double glass doors, they pulled their pistols out and fitted silencers to them. Aslan scanned the list of residents, found P. COCHRANE.

Turning to the youngest of them, he said, "Once we get into the lobby, you stay inside. Let no one in. Keep the elevators clear. Keep the gun out of sight." The youngster nodded.

Then Aslan pressed the buzzer under Cochrane's name.

The intercom buzzed again impatiently.

Cochrane glanced at Gould, then pushed between the two men standing by the door and pressed the button on the intercom wall panel. "Yes?"

"Delivery for Dr. Cochrane," came a guttural voice.

Gould said to Cochrane, "Tell him to leave it in the lobby."

"I can't come down right now. Leave it there, please."

"Needs signature."

Without waiting for orders from Gould, Cochrane said, "Okay, bring it up."

Frowning, Gould waved his two men to either side of the door. "Were you expecting a package?" he asked Cochrane.

"I get books and things all the time."

Sandoval came around the counter that served as a partition between the kitchen and living room.

Gould said to his driver, "You open the door and take the package. Dr. Cochrane, best you stay back here with me."

Cochrane stepped away from the door and went to one end of the coffee table, between Gould and Sandoval.

A gentle rap on the door. "Delivery for Dr. Cochrane."

The driver opened the door a crack and it was suddenly slammed back, staggering the driver backward. Two burly men pushed in. Gould's security man reached inside his jacket and one of the intruders shot him, his gun silenced to a barely audible *pfft*. The other shot the driver before he could recover his balance, twice in the chest.

Sandoval stifled a scream as the driver crashed to the floor at her feet, his chest soaked with blood, his eyes staring blankly. The security man slid to the floor, leaving a smear of blood on the wall by the door.

"Quiet!" Aslan commanded. "Not a sound!"

Cochrane goggled at the two dead bodies, the two swarthy men in windbreakers waving their automatics at them. He reached for Sandoval, standing there horrified, her hands on her face.

Gould stared, too, as he touched the stem of his heavy gold wrist-watch. Perspiration streamed down his fleshy face.

"Who are you?" he asked, his voice shaky.

"That's of no matter," said Aslan. Pointing his pistol at the laptop still on the kitchen table, he demanded, "Give me that computer."

"You're too late," Cochrane said. "It's been erased."

Aslan glanced furiously from Cochrane to Gould and back again. "Which of you is Cochrane?"

"I am," Cochrane said.

"Then you must be Lionel Gould."

"That I am," Gould replied, his voice steadier. "What do you want? Why are you here?"

"I'll ask the questions," Aslan replied. Turning to Cochrane, he said, "Dr. Cochrane, you will take your laptop and show me how to access your brother's work."

"I told you, it's been erased." Pointing to Gould, Cochrane added, "He made me wipe it out."

"You expect me to believe that?"

"It's the truth."

Pointing with his pistol at the driver, dead on the floor, Aslan said, "Dr. Cochrane, you have ten seconds to bring up your brother's work on that computer. Otherwise you will join these two on their way to hell."

"And what good would that do you?" Cochrane snapped.

Aslan nodded knowingly. "Yes, of course. Killing you would not be wise." He turned toward Sandoval. "But shooting this woman—that's a different matter, isn't it? You wouldn't want to see her shot, would you?"

Suddenly desperate, Cochrane insisted, "I'm telling you, the data you want has been erased from the laptop!"

"My first shot would not kill her, of course. Perhaps I'll merely put a bullet through one of her lovely legs."

Cochrane's hands balled into fists.

"Or perhaps her belly," Aslan continued, looking Sandoval over. "Gut wounds are very painful. A slow death."

Gould raised a hand, like a traffic cop signaling to stop. "You ought to know that a team of my security people is on its way here at this very moment."

Aslan's expression hardened. "Don't try to bluff me, Mr. Billionaire."

"I summoned them the moment you broke in." Raising his left arm, Gould went on, "With this. It's a communications device in addition to being a timepiece."

"I don't believe you."

Gould shrugged.

Suspiciously, Aslan asked, "Where would this security team be coming from?"

"The campus," Gould replied. "I had a team deploy with the university's security director as soon as I decided to bring Dr. Cochrane home from Palo Alto this morning."

"You're bluffing," Aslan repeated, less firmly than before.

"It should only take them a few minutes to get from the campus to here. They should be arriving at any moment."

For several heartbeats Aslan stood silent, his mind racing. Then he decided. "Very well. Dr. Cochrane, pick up your computer and come with us."

"Paul," Sandoval said, reaching a hand toward him.

"It's all right," he said, heading back to the kitchen. "I'll go with them."

"Quickly!" Aslan commanded.

Cochrane disconnected the power cable, shut down the laptop, and closed its lid. All the time he watched Sandoval, standing in the living room looking frightened, uncertain. Gould, a few paces away from her, looked somehow sure of himself despite the sweat streaming down his face, staining his collar.

"Come on," Aslan prodded. "Come on."

Cochrane tucked the laptop under his arm and came around the kitchen counter.

"I don't know who's paying you or how much," said Gould, "but I can easily double it."

"Yes," Aslan replied, with a malicious grin. "You could fill our hands with gold, couldn't you?"

"Of course."

Waving the automatic in Gould's face, the Chechen snarled, "I should shoot you. Here and now. Kill you and rid the world of a parasite."

"Parasite? Me?" Gould frowned with loathing. "Let me tell you—"

Shots! Muffled, but clearly gunshots. Several of them.

The man still standing by the door turned and started to open it a crack, but before he could, Sandoval covered the distance between them in two lightning-fast strides, jabbed stiff fingers into the man's windpipe, then slammed the heel of her hand into his nose. Cochrane could hear cartilage crunching from all the way across the room and the man's face spurted blood as he slammed against the wall.

Aslan turned toward her, slack-jawed with surprise. Cochrane threw the laptop at his gun hand, then leaped at him with a flying tackle that sent them both sprawling to the floor. He grabbed for Aslan's gun arm with both his hands. The Chechen pounded his ribs with his free hand as they rolled across the carpeting.

Gould waddled around the coffee table and dropped to his knees on Aslan's outstretched gun arm. As Gould twisted the pistol from the Chechen's hand, Cochrane punched Aslan's face with both his fists.

The front door burst open and four dark-suited men boiled in, guns in their hands.

"Hold it!" their leader shouted.

Cochrane looked up. Sandoval was standing over the Chechen gunman, who was slumped on the floor by the door, his face a bloody mess. Aslan was grimacing with pain—whether from Cochrane's punches or the weight of Gould kneeling on his arm, Cochrane could neither tell nor care.

Gould heaved himself to his feet, then looked at his wristwatch.

"Eleven minutes," he murmured. "Not as good as it should have been."

"There's a lot of traffic out there, Mr. Gould," the security man apologized.

Cochrane went to Sandoval. She was trembling visibly, but the gunman at her feet wasn't moving at all.

"My god," he said to her, "he looks dead."

She nodded, then leaned against him.

"Are you all right?" he asked, folding his arms around her.

"I am now," she said.

They heard sirens wailing.

"Someone's summoned the police," Gould said. "Best we make our exit."

"And leave us with this mess?" Cochrane grumbled.

"I'll have my lawyers contact the local police," Gould said. "They'll explain everything."

Cochrane realized that Gould held the pistol he'd taken from the intruder, who still lay on the carpet of the living room, unmoving except for his eyes, which flicked from Gould to Cochrane and back again. Gould's four security men were standing by the door. He's got all the cards in his hands, Cochrane said to himself. As usual.

"Pick up that laptop," Gould said to one of his men. Then, turning to Sandoval, he asked, "Would you care to come with me, Elena?"

She shook her head and clung to Cochrane.

Gould shrugged. "Adieu, then, Dr. Cochrane. Until we meet again. And trust me, we will meet again."

They left as the sirens grew louder.

TUCSON:
POLICE HEADQUARTERS

Cochrane's knuckles were skinned and sore. His glasses had been bent askew in the brawl. Sandoval, sitting beside him, seemed totally untouched by the violence they had gone through.

After spending most of the afternoon talking with Lieutenant Danvers and other Tucson detectives, they had been walked down a corridor and ushered into a stuffy, windowless conference room.

"An FBI agent is driving over from Phoenix," Lieutenant Danvers had told them. "He should be here shortly."

Then she left them alone to sit at the oblong conference table, waiting for the FBI agent to show up.

Fiddling with his bent glasses, Cochrane said to Sandoval, "You were incredible back there. Where'd you learn that martial arts stuff?"

She made a tight smile. "I told you, Paul, in my business a girl has to be able to defend herself."

"Defend yourself? You beat the crap out of that guy. He's dead, for chrissakes."

"I didn't mean to kill him. That shot to his throat . . . it must have ruptured the blood vessels in his windpipe and he bled into his lungs."

"He drowned on his own blood?"

She nodded, then looked down, as if ashamed.

"But what if—"

The door to the corridor opened and three men entered the conference room.

"I'm Special Agent Ignacio Yañez," said a sturdy-looking man in a tight-fitting tan sports jacket and darker slacks. "These two gentlemen are lawyers from the Gould Energy Corporation."

Yañez took the chair at the head of the table; the lawyers sat opposite Sandoval and Cochrane. Yañez had burly weight-lifter's shoulders that strained his jacket when he moved his arms. His face was not much darker than Cochrane's, but his hair was midnight-black, as was his bushy mustache. The two lawyers both wore impeccable three-piece gray suits: Brooks Brothers, Cochrane guessed. They each placed compact notebook computers on the table and opened them. Yañez put down a pad of paper and a ballpoint pen.

Yañez cleared his throat noisily, then said, "I know you've told your story to the Tucson detectives all day, but I'm afraid I'm going to need to hear it from you again."

Cochrane glanced at Sandoval. The two lawyers tapped on their computer keyboards.

More than an hour later, Special Agent Yañez looked as if he didn't believe a word that any of them had told him. "And you're saying that this was a terrorist attempt to kidnap Lionel Gould?"

"That is correct," answered one of the lawyers.

Turning to Cochrane, Yañez said, "Tell me again what Gould was doing at your apartment."

"He was looking for information on the work my brother was doing at the time of his murder."

"And?"

"He took my computer, my laptop."

"Which he paid for," the other lawyer jumped in.

"All nice and legal, huh?"

Both lawyers nodded in unison.

"And the two other guys were terrorists."

"Apparently so," said the first lawyer.

"Muslims," said the second. "From Chechnya."

"The one live suspect admits to being a Chechen. He's here illegally."

"They are part of a conspiracy that reaches into the United Nations bureaucracy in New York," the first lawyer said.

"So you told me."

Cochrane said, "Look, we've been here all damned day, just about. We haven't even had lunch. Can't we go now? You've got our statements."

Yañez looked distinctly unhappy. But he admitted, "Washington says they're taking jurisdiction. I'm just supposed to hand everything over to them."

"Well, then," said the second lawyer, shutting his notebook with an audible click.

"Unless you are charging Dr. Cochrane or Ms. Sandoval," the first lawyer said.

"There's an open murder investigation in Palo Alto that seems to be connected with all this," Yañez said.

Cochrane said, "That was my brother."

"I checked with the Palo Alto police," said the FBI agent. "They don't consider you a suspect."

"That's good to know," Cochrane said.

"So we're free to go?" Sandoval asked.

With a shrug of his big shoulders, Yañez pushed his pad of lined paper toward her. "Write down an address and phone number where I can reach you. E-mail address, too, if you have one. Same for you, Dr. Cochrane."

"We'll both be at this address," Sandoval said. And she wrote down a totally fictitious address in Denver, Colorado.

LAS VEGAS: McCARRAN INTERNATIONAL AIRPORT

They had more than an hour to kill before their flight continued on its way to San Francisco, so Cochrane and Sandoval left their Southwest Airlines plane to stretch their legs in the terminal.

After leaving the police headquarters building in Tucson, they had gone straight to Cochrane's apartment. They had to step over the yellow crime scene tapes across his front door. There was still blood smeared on the wall and staining the living room carpet. Cochrane quickly packed his roll-on suitcase and they left for the airport. He picked up his accumulated mail as they were leaving the apartment building and stuffed the envelopes into his suitcase.

The first available flight had a layover in Las Vegas. Sandoval bought two first-class tickets and they left Tucson just before sunset.

Cochrane spent the first leg of the flight opening his mail. Junk, most of it. A letter from his sister-in-law Irene, asking him where he'd gotten to;

she'd phoned him half a dozen times and gotten nothing but his answering machine.

And a notice from the university, suspending him without pay until he could attend a formal meeting to decide the future of his employment at Steward Observatory.

"Looks like I'm out of a job," he muttered, handing the stiff sheet of stationery to Sandoval, sitting beside him.

She scanned it, handed it back to him. "Doesn't matter," she said, leaning close to him. "You wouldn't want to stay there anyway: too easy for Gould to find you."

He looked at her. She was completely serious. "You really think Gould's after me?"

With a solemn nod, Sandoval replied, "Absolutely."

Cochrane was feeling depressed when they walked off the plane. A stroll through the terminal only worsened his dark outlook. Slot machines lined the terminal's corridors. People were eagerly jamming coins into them.

"Christ Almighty," he complained. "If gamblers could win, the casinos would've gone out of business in the fifth dynasty of ancient Egypt."

Sandoval smiled minimally. "Hope springs eternal, Paul."

"A fool and his money," he growled.

"Come on." She tugged at his arm. "Let's get back to the plane."

Once aloft and heading for San Francisco, Sandoval tried to cheer him up. "It'll be all right, Paul. I can sell the house; it ought to bring in a million-two, maybe more. And I've got nearly another mil in stocks and CDs."

"You'd sell your house?"

"I've already put it on the market."

"But where can we go? If Gould's really after my butt, where in the world can we hide?"

She made a bigger smile for him. "Australia, maybe. Tahiti. Singapore. There are places."

"How'll I make a living?"

"You won't have to. You've got a woman of property mad about you."

She leaned closer to him and he kissed her. But he was thinking, What kind of a life can we have together? Am I putting her in danger?

Gould Trust to Acquire Calvin Research Center

NEW YORK, NY—The Gould Trust announced that it plans to acquire Calvin Research Center, of Palo Alto, California. The Calvin laboratories, named after the late Nobel Prize–winning chemist Melvin Calvin, are dedicated to studies of photosynthesis and its possible applications in agribusiness and the energy industry.

A Gould spokeperson said that Gould Trust will fully fund Calvin's existing research programs and plans to expand into new areas of investigation. The financial terms of the acquisition were not released to the public.

—*WALL STREET JOURNAL*

SAN FRANCISCO:
RUSSIAN HILL

You've been moping for two days now," Sandoval said.

"I know," Cochrane replied. "Guess I haven't been much fun to be with."

It was morning, bright and breezy outside as the two of them sat at the breakfast table in the kitchen of Sandoval's house. She had made scrambled eggs for them; Cochrane had brewed the coffee from freshly ground beans. The kitchen walls were painted a cheerful yellow, Sandoval was smiling brightly at him, yet Cochrane felt down, dull, depressed.

"It's chilly in here, isn't it?" She got up and went to the thermostat on the wall. Cochrane heard the rumble of the heater down in the basement.

Returning to the chair beside him, Sandoval said, "It can get uncomfortable this time of year. Mark Twain said the coldest winter he ever spent was a summer in San Francisco."

Cochrane tried to make a smile for her. He almost succeeded.

"What is it, Paul?" she asked, her face going serious. "You worried about Gould?"

He looked down at the remains of his eggs on his plate. "I'm not charmed with the idea of looking over my shoulder for the rest of my life, no."

"We'll get away from him. The real estate agent has several leads for the house. If you want, we can fly out of here and let her sell the house while we're in Tahiti or Tasmania or wherever we decide to go."

"It's more than that." As he spoke the words, he realized it was true. "More than that," he repeated.

She grasped his hand in hers. "What, Paul? What's eating at you?"

"Gould," he answered. "He's won. The sonofabitch has won."

Sandoval blinked at him. "Of course he's won. What did you expect?"

"He's got Mike's data and he's going to sit on it until hell freezes over."

"No," she said, smiling slightly. "Only until he's made as much profit from oil prices as he can. Then he'll step in and be the big savior with your brother's hydrogen process."

Nodding, Cochrane said, "He'll get credit for moving the world off petroleum and on to hydrogen fuel."

"Maybe the Pope will make him a saint."

Cochrane laughed bitterly. "Yeah. Maybe he will."

"There's nothing we can do about that, Paul. We've got to think of our own safety, our own survival. You can't solve the problems of the world."

"I could...if..."

"If?"

He sucked in a deep breath, then exhaled wearily. "If I had a copy of Mike's work, I could change things."

"Change how? What good would it do? Sell it to the highest bidder? They're all in this together, Paul. Tricontinental, Garrison, OPEC: whoever you sold the data to would suppress it, just like Gould."

"I wouldn't sell it," Cochrane said, looking away from her. "I'd publish it."

"Like you wanted Tulius to do."

"That's right. Let the whole fucking world know about it. Tell them all how to make hydrogen fuel from Mike's process."

"But what good would that do? You wouldn't make a cent out of it!"

He turned back toward her, looked steadily into her almond-shaped eyes.

"I'm a scientist, Elena. That means I try to learn about the ways the universe works, and when I've learned something I tell the world about it.

Can you understand that? It's not about money, god knows. If I'd wanted to make money I'd've become a banker or a lawyer or something like that. Maybe a plumber."

She was staring back at him.

"But I chose to be a scientist. Because I want to understand things. And I want to share what I learn with the rest of the human race. That's what I do. That's what I am."

"And if you had your hands on your brother's work you'd share it with everybody?"

"I'd put it out on the Internet. Send it to every Web site I could think of. All the universities. All the news networks. All the chat rooms and bloggers. Fuck Gould and the rest of them! I'd spread it around so that *nobody* could keep it a secret, nobody could suppress it."

She pulled away from him slightly, edged back in her chair. "Gould's right to be afraid of you," Elena murmured.

Cochrane made a self-deprecating smile. "Big talk. I don't have Mike's data. Nobody does except Gould and people Gould controls. So I guess I won't save the world, after all."

Sandoval did not reply to him.

Terrorist Scandal Hits UNESCO Official

NEW YORK, NY—Already plagued by scandals such as the Iraq oil-for-food debacle, the United Nations Educational, Scientific, and Cultural Office (UNESCO) was rocked by the arrest yesterday of one of its minor officials, charged with heading a terrorist cell.

Zelinkshah Shamil, a Chechen national, was arrested by the FBI in his office at the UN Secretariat building. An FBI spokeman said Shamil was head of a terrorist cell that murdered several people in New York, Palo Alto, California, and Tucson, Arizona.

Shamil claimed diplomatic immunity, but the U.S. attorney general for New York said that under the provisions of the Homeland Security Act, a foreign national can be considered an enemy combatant even if he has diplomatic status.

—*INTERNATIONAL NEWS SERVICE*

SAN FRANCISCO:
RUSSIAN HILL

They were sitting on the sofa in front of the gas-fed fireplace, watching the silent blue flames as the darkness deepened outside the big bay window of the living room. Cochrane heard the distant clang of a cable car trolley; otherwise the night was blessedly quiet.

"I closed on the house this afternoon," Sandoval said, staring into the fire. "We can leave whenever you want to."

They had planned to drive to Vancouver, then fly to Sydney.

"You think Gould will try to track me down in Australia?" he asked her.

She shook her head. "I don't know."

He reached out to slide an arm around her shoulders, but Elena pulled away slightly.

"What's the matter?" he asked.

"I can't," she said, still not looking at him.

"Your period?"

"No, it's not that."

"Then what?"

Elena turned toward him at last. "It's what you said a few days ago, about being a scientist and all that."

He felt his brows knit. "What's that got to do with—"

"It made me realize what a gulf there is between us, Paul."

"What gulf?"

"More than you realize," she said. "More than you realize."

"I don't understand."

She didn't reply. Instead, she got up from the sofa and headed for the stairs. He followed her.

Once in bed, he reached for her again.

"Please, Paul. Don't."

Puzzled, nettled, feeling frustrated, he lay in the darkness staring at the ceiling. She turned her back to him. He suppressed an angry complaint, turned on his side, and closed his eyes.

When he awoke, she wasn't in the bed with him. He sat up, reached for his glasses, saw that the digital clock on the night table read 3:47 A.M. The bedroom was dark. And cold.

He tossed the bedcovers aside and stood up. There was enough light seeping through the window curtains for him to find the jeans he had thrown over the back of the chair in the corner. He pulled them on, then wormed his arms into the shirt he'd left there. Barefoot, he went to the bedroom door. Where the hell is she? he wondered.

Light was coming up the staircase from the floor below. Cochrane padded down the carpeted steps and saw Elena sitting on the fragile little chair at the ornate inlaid desk in the corner of the living room. A laptop computer rested on the desk, but it was closed and she was writing on a sheet of paper in longhand. He saw that she was fully dressed in a dove-gray pantsuit.

"What's going on?" he demanded, striding across the living room toward her.

She jerked visibly with surprise.

"Paul!"

"What are you doing? What's going on?"

There were tears in her eyes, he saw. Streaks runneling down her face.

"Elena, what's the matter?"

"I didn't want to wake you up," she said in a choked whisper.

"What are you doing?" he repeated.

"I'm . . . leaving."

"Leaving?"

"It won't work, Paul. Us. It just won't work. It can't."

"What do you mean?"

She looked utterly miserable. "What you said about being a scientist. It made me realize, understand. You'd find out, sooner or later. And then you'd hate me."

"I don't know what you're talking about!"

She got up from the delicate antique chair, crumpling the note she'd been writing. Pointing to the laptop, she said, "This is my farewell gift to you, Paul."

He stared at her.

"It's got your brother's data in it. Everything. You can broadcast it wherever you want to. You can stop Gould from suppressing your brother's work."

"But why do you have to leave?" he asked.

And suddenly his legs went weak. He staggered toward her, but she backed away from him. He grabbed for the back of the spindly little chair, sat on it heavily, felt it groan beneath his weight.

"My god almighty," he whispered. "This is Mike's laptop."

Sandoval stood there, tears running down her cheeks, hands clenched together.

"The one the cops couldn't find. You've had it all along."

She nodded.

He stared at her. "*You* killed Mike. You killed my brother."

"I didn't mean to, Paul. I didn't mean to."

"You were the woman Mike was fooling around with. You were sleeping with him. To get your hands on his discovery."

"I didn't mean to kill him," she repeated, sobbing.

"Mike brought you into his lab through the building's back door and you murdered him."

"He got abusive, Paul. He hit me. He wanted to make out right there in his lab and when I wouldn't he punched me. He was drunk; we'd had too much wine at lunch. He was violent!"

"And you killed him."

"I was trying to defend myself."

"Yeah, I've seen how you can defend yourself."

"I didn't mean it!" she pleaded. "He hit his head on the corner of the lab bench. It was an accident!"

"You were screwing my brother. And then you killed him."

"An accident. Honestly, Paul...."

"You took his laptop. You've had it all along. All this time."

"I knew if I told you I had it, you'd figure it all out. I didn't want to lose you, Paul. I love you!"

"Yeah. And how many others?"

"Paul! Please!"

"So you were going to leave me."

"Because I love you," she said, barely able to get the words out. "Because I couldn't stay with you with this between us."

He felt as though all the strength had drained out of his body. He wanted to get down on the floor and lie there till hell froze over.

"So you're leaving," he heard himself say. "Where're you going? Back to Gould?"

"Paul! No!"

"Go on and go, Elena," he croaked. "I won't stop you. I can't. Go ahead, get out. Leave me alone."

"What about you? Where will you go?"

"What difference does it make?"

"I can give you some money...."

"My brother's blood money? Fuck it! I'll go back to Tucson and wait for Gould to catch up with me."

"Paul, please...."

"Go!" he roared. "Get the hell out of here!"

She turned and ran out of the living room. Cochrane sat on the silly little chair, bleeding from every pore. He closed his eyes but the pain wouldn't go away. He heard the garage door rattle open, then a car start up. Mike's red convertible, he knew without looking.

Long after she had driven away he still sat there. The sun came up and the morning brightened and Cochrane still sat on the little chair, his whole body numb except for the throbbing of his bad leg.

At last he turned to his brother's laptop, opened it, booted it up. The data was all there, every bit of it. Blindly, automatically, Cochrane pulled up his Internet address book and began e-mailing Mike's work to everyone he could think of.

Hours later he struggled to his feet, alone. He limped upstairs and began to pack his clothes.

PALO ALTO:
CALVIN RESEARCH CENTER

Jason Tulius fumbled in his desk drawer for a tranquilizer. The pair of FBI agents had just left his office, apparently content with his claim that he had no idea that Shamil was connected with Chechen terrorists.

"I admit that I had some qualms about accepting funding from UN-ESCO," he'd told the agents. "But, after all, the agency does fund some scientific work. I didn't think there was anything actually illegal in what Mr. Shamil was doing."

The agents had nodded and tapped on the keyboards of their pocket-sized computers. Then they had accepted coffee and doughnuts from Tulius's executive assistant. And then, finally, they had left.

It's over, Tulius told himself once they'd left his office. It's over and I'm all right. Gould will buy the lab and I can look forward to a comfortable retirement in a few years.

After we've duplicated Michael's work, he added silently.

He reached for the brushed chrome coffee jug, still on the metal tray resting on his desk, and poured a trickle of coffee into his empty mug. Caffeine and tranquilizers, he thought, popping a pair of pills into his mouth. Two of the major food groups.

Leaning back in his swivel chair, Tulius waited for the pills to soothe his lingering anxiety.

But Ray Kurtzman barged through his office door, a quizzical grin on his bearded face.

"Looked at your e-mail this morning?" Kurtzman asked before Tulius could complain about his sudden interruption.

His brows knitting, Tulius replied, "My e-mail? Why?"

Sitting in front of the desk, Kurtzman said, "There's a message waiting for you. From Mike's brother, I think."

Tulius reached for the keyboard on his desk. "What does he want?"

"He's giving us a gift," said Kurtzman. "All Mike's data. The stuff Mike wouldn't show you."

"The hydrogen process?"

Kurtzman nodded as Tulius tapped away at the keys with trembling fingers. Michael Cochrane's data began to scroll slowly down his display screen.

"It's all there," Kurtzman said. "I spent an hour looking it over."

"Cochrane sent it to you?"

"Must've been him. Who else?"

"And he sent a copy to me," Tulius said.

Kurtzman replied, "And to a Dr. Esterbrook at Georgetown University with a 'cc' to the National Academy of Sciences. And to *Science* magazine. And *Nature*, over in England. And everybody else he could think of, it looks like."

Tulius scrolled up to the address list. It more than filled the screen.

"Oh, my god," he moaned.

Kurtzman nodded. "Yeah. There goes any chance of keeping Mike's work proprietary. Cochrane's blabbed it to the whole friggin' world. It's public information now. No patents, not even proprietary rights, I guess."

"This is a disaster!"

Strangely, Kurtzman smiled. "For the Calvin Research Center, maybe. But for the human race, it's a gift. Now anybody who wants to can figure out how to produce hydrogen. If he has the brains for it, and there's plenty of people who do."

"It's the end of the petroleum industry."

"I guess it is. Not overnight, but the end is in sight." Kurtzman seemed happy about the prospect.

But Tulius wondered how Gould would react.

MANHATTAN:
GOULD TRUST HEADQUARTERS

Lionel Gould scowled at the display screen on the wall of his private office. Page after page of chemical formulas and mathematical gobbledygook scrolling past: all of Michael Cochrane's work, apparently.

Standing before his desk in a nervous knot were two of Gould's corporate lawyers and the chief scientist of the Gould Trust.

Wiping at the perspiration beading his forehead, Gould looked up at them, his face a thundercloud.

"Is this what I think it is?" he growled.

"It's Michael Cochrane's work," said the scientist, in a voice that quavered slightly. "His hydrogen process."

"You've checked its authenticity?"

"As far as I was able to, sir. I have a team looking it over now."

"But as far as you can see, it's authentic?"

The scientist swallowed visibly before replying, "Yes, sir, I believe it is."

Gould turned to the attorney who specialized in patents and intellectual properties.

"What does this do to our chances for obtaining a patent on this hydrogen process?"

The attorney hid his tension better than the scientist, but still he licked his lips before replying in a subdued voice, "I'm afraid it throws the information into the public domain. It will be impossible to claim patent protection for it."

"Paul Cochrane," Gould muttered.

"Sir?" asked all three men in unison.

"Nothing," Gould answered. He took a deep breath, then slapped both hands on his desktop hard enough to make the three men flinch.

"Very well, then! We can't claim exclusive rights to this process, but by god we'll be the first ones to offer it to the public!"

Banging on his intercom keyboard, he boomed, "Get Zelinski and Adamson in here! At once! We have a lot of work to do!"

The scientist and the two lawyers scuttled out of his office. Gould leaned back in his padded chair and mopped his face again. Cochrane's won, he told himself. The idealistic young twit has made it impossible to keep his brother's hydrogen process safely locked up. So we go in the opposite direction: Gould Energy Corporation will be the first to offer hydrogen power to the world. We will lead the way to a new era.

He spent the rest of the day rattling off orders to his department heads and corporate executives. He told his secretary to set up an emergency meeting of the corporation's board of directors.

To his public relations director, he blustered, "This is not a crisis, it's an opportunity. I want this breakthrough announced as good news, wonderful news for the entire world. Never mind what happens to the corporation's stock. Never mind what the oil industry's prices do. In fact, we should be prepared to buy when those shares come tumbling down!"

His aides and department heads from Dallas to Dubai nodded their heads in agreement, no matter what their inner feelings.

"We'll make this look like you're giving a Christmas present to the world," said the sharp-featured woman who ran his public relations department.

"That is good," said Gould, thinking: When they hand you a lemon, make lemonade.

It wasn't until the long, tension-charged day was over and he had taken his private elevator up to his penthouse quarters that Gould allowed the fury to overtake him.

Cochrane! he fumed silently. He thinks he's won.

Gould stalked through his sumptuous living room, his fingers curled into claws, perspiration dripping from his face. He snatched at the graceful Athenian vase on the end table and hurled it into the Gainsborough portrait above the fireplace. Its shattered pieces slashed the canvas. Then the table lamp. Gould yanked it out of its socket, power cord dangling, and banged it to the floor. The carpeting was too thick, the lamp bounced instead of breaking, so he kicked it across the room. Then he knocked over the delicate little table itself, stamped on its slim legs, crushing them into kindling.

Smashing, tearing, throwing, Gould rampaged through the room and on into the dining room, where he knocked over chairs, hurled delicate china platters and exquisite stemmed glassware against the walls. He gasped and grunted with a furious need to destroy, to demolish, to work out the frenzy that boiled in his blood.

His butler and one of the housemaids cracked open the pantry door, eyes goggling wide as their master stormed through the dining room trashing everything he could get his hands on.

"Shouldn't we do something?" the maid whispered. "Call his doctor?"

The butler shook his gray head. "No. For heaven's sake, don't let him know we're watching this!"

"But all those beautiful things! He'll hurt himself."

"Leave him alone. I've seen him like this before."

"You have?"

"When his second wife left him. He went wild, just like this."

"His second wife? The one who died in the auto accident?"

The butler nodded.

At last Gould ran out of things to smash. He sank heavily on the only chair still upright in the dining room, his shirt drenched with sweat, his arms hanging limply at his sides, his chest heaving painfully.

"Cochrane," he muttered again, his voice murderously low. "Cochrane."

Gould Energy Corp. Confirms Hydrogen Fuel Breakthrough

HOUSTON, TX—In what he playfully described as "an early Christmas present to the world," Lionel Gould, president and board chairman of Gould Energy Corp., personally confirmed rumors that a new breakthrough will make it possible to produce hydrogen fuel efficiently and economically.

"This is the beginning of a new era," Gould announced at a news conference in Houston. "The age of petroleum is about to end. The age of hydrogen is beginning. And we at Gould Energy intend to lead the way."

The scientific breakthrough was made at the Calvin Research Center of Palo Alto, California, recently acquired by the Gould Trust, a not-for-profit philanthropic organization based in New York. The process involves using primitive bacteria to produce pure hydrogen, which can be used directly as fuel in cars, trucks, planes and other transportation systems. Gould added that hydrogen could be used for heating fuel, as well.

"Within a few years the United States will no longer be dependent on oil imported from overseas," Gould stressed.

Gould's announcement confirmed rumors that had been blazing through the Internet for several months. Bloggers and scientific Web sites alike were buzzing with the anonymous revelation of the Calvin Research Center's work.

Oil stocks plummeted on the world's stock exchanges, but Gould said he expected energy stocks to recover, since most of the energy corporations around the world were also moving to develop hydrogen fuels.

"We intend to be at the forefront of the shift from petroleum to hydrogen," Gould said. "But we welcome competition from others in the industry. Competition is the heart of the free enterprise system."

—*Houston Chronicle*

UA Professor Killed In Hit-and-Run Accident

TUCSON—A University of Arizona faculty member was killed in a hit-and-run accident yesterday afternoon.

Dr. Paul Cochrane was struck by an unidentified sedan as he crossed the intersection of Campbell Street and Speedway. According to witnesses, the dark-colored sedan sped through the intersection against the traffic signal and struck Cochrane in the pedestrian walkway, then raced away without stopping.

Cochrane was pronounced dead on arrival at the nearby UA Hospital's accident ward.

"It's almost like the car was trying to hit him," said one witness. "It just bore down straight at him."

"He was limping," another witness told police. "He never had a chance to get out of the car's way."

According to police, Cochrane was on his way to a meeting at the Steward Observatory to discuss his reinstatement on the UA faculty, after an absence of several months.

—ARIZONA DAILY STAR